The Cottage
at Firefly Lake

The Cottage
at Firefly Lake

JEN GILROY

FOREVER

NEW YORK BOSTON

This book is a work of fiction. Names, characters, places, and incidents are the product of the author's imagination or are used fictitiously. Any resemblance to actual events, locales, or persons, living or dead, is coincidental.

Copyright © 2017 by Jen Gilroy
Teaser excerpt from *Summer on Firefly Lake* copyright © 2017 by Jen Gilroy

Cover design by Elizabeth Turner
Cover copyright © 2017 by Hachette Book Group, Inc.

Hachette Book Group supports the right to free expression and the value of copyright. The purpose of copyright is to encourage writers and artists to produce the creative works that enrich our culture.

The scanning, uploading, and distribution of this book without permission is a theft of the author's intellectual property. If you would like permission to use material from the book (other than for review purposes), please contact permissions@hbgusa.com. Thank you for your support of the author's rights.

Forever
Hachette Book Group
1290 Avenue of the Americas
New York, NY 10104
forever-romance.com
twitter.com/foreverromance

First Mass Market Edition: January 2017

Forever is an imprint of Grand Central Publishing.
The Forever name and logo are trademarks of Hachette Book Group, Inc.

The publisher is not responsible for websites (or their content) that are not owned by the publisher.

The Hachette Speakers Bureau provides a wide range of authors for speaking events. To find out more, go to www.hachettespeakersbureau.com or call (866) 376-6591.

Library of Congress Cataloging-in-Publication Data has been applied for.

ISBNs: 978-1-4555-6959-5 (mass market); 978-1-4555-4033-4 (ebook); 978-1-478-96946-4 (downloadable audio)

Printed in the United States of America

10 9 8 7 6 5 4 3 2 1

ATTENTION CORPORATIONS AND ORGANIZATIONS:

Most Hachette Book Group books are available at quantity discounts with bulk purchase for educational, business, or sales promotional use. For information, please call or write:

Special Markets Department, Hachette Book Group
1290 Avenue of the Americas, New York, NY 10104
Telephone: 1-800-222-6747 Fax: 1-800-477-5925

For my dear mom, in loving memory

Acknowledgments

Although my name is on the cover, many people contributed to making the dream of my first published book a reality.

I'm indebted to my literary agent, Dawn Dowdle, for her support and wise counsel. She took a chance on me and was tireless in her efforts to find this manuscript a home.

My editor, Michele Bidelspach, has helped me grow exponentially as a writer, and thanks to her insightful comments, my characters and the world of Firefly Lake took on new depth, emotion, and life. I'm blessed with the care and attention Michele gives to me and my writing.

Elizabeth Turner, art director at Forever, designed the cover, which captures the feel of my book so beautifully. Thanks to her, as well as Jessie Pierce, editorial assistant, Laura Jorstad, copy editor, and the entire Grand Central, Forever team for supporting my debut release with enthusiasm and professionalism.

I'm also grateful to the Romantic Novelists' Association (RNA) and the anonymous reviewers who critiqued this manuscript and others through the RNA New Writers' Scheme. Their supportive critiques not only shaped this story, but also helped me see myself as a "real writer." Among many RNA friends, special thanks are due to Julie Cohen. Her faith in this story, guidance, and cheerleading have been invaluable.

Thank you as well to the Romance Writers of America (RWA) contest judges who saw early parts of this manuscript via chapter contests and gave helpful and encouraging feedback.

To my 2015 RWA class of Golden Heart finalists, the Dragonflies: I'm happy to be on this journey with you. Thanks for the friendship, laughter, and support. The dragonfly reference is for you.

Writing friends to whom I owe special gratitude for being there for me are Susanna Bavin, Jennifer Brodie, Tracy Brody, and Arlene McFarlane. You ladies are fab!

My husband, Tech Guy, our daughter, English Rose, and Heidi, the sister of my heart, have been a constant source of love and support. Thank you for always believing in me.

I've dedicated *The Cottage at Firefly Lake* to my mother. Mom was a small-town girl whose dad had her in a boat before she could walk. She shared her love of reading with me and, no matter what life brought, always encouraged me never to give up. Mom was killed in a road accident when I'd just started this book. In the months that followed, writing gave me brief respite from all-consuming grief.

This one's for you, Mom. Love you lots. Bye for now.

The Cottage
at Firefly Lake

Chapter One

Sean Carmichael balanced the canoe paddle on his knees, scanned the lake and sandy shoreline, and lingered on the cottage hugged by tall pine trees.

"Dad?" Ty brought the rental canoe alongside his. The white Carmichael's logo gleamed with fresh paint. "You want to deliver this canoe to the Gibbs place or sit in the middle of the lake all afternoon?" His fifteen-year-old son flashed a teasing grin.

"Just waiting for you to catch up," Sean teased back.

"Race you?" Ty's blue eyes twinkled.

"Sure."

Shadow, their black Lab wedged into the hull, thumped her tail as Sean dipped the paddle and the canoe shot forward through the pristine water of the Vermont lake. Twenty feet from shore, Sean slowed to let Ty cruise past him.

Ty scrambled out of the canoe and waited for him in knee-deep water. He pinned Sean with an accusing look. "You gotta stop doing that."

"What?" Sean jumped out of his canoe and dragged it to the sandy beach. Shadow loped by and splashed Sean's board shorts and T-shirt.

"Letting me win." Ty pulled the other canoe onto the beach, then fisted his hands in his T-shirt. Big broad hands like Sean's that could already do a man's work. "I'm almost sixteen. I'm not a kid anymore."

"I know." Sean swallowed a sigh.

"Some car." Ty pointed to a black BMW parked by the cottage under the pines. "New people renting the Gibbs place this summer?"

"Not that I heard." Sean tugged on his baseball cap to shield his face from the July sun. Not much ever changed in this little corner of Vermont's Northeast Kingdom.

Ty tossed a stick for Shadow to chase. "Why's it called the Gibbs place anyway? There've never been any Gibbses around Firefly Lake."

"Not since you'd remember." No Gibbs had been back here in years. Eighteen years, if anybody was counting. Which Sean wasn't. "We better get a move on. After we deliver this rental, we have to paddle back and do some more work on the racing canoe before your mom picks you up."

"I've got other stuff I want to do. Can't the work wait till tomorrow? Or I could call Mom and ask her to pick me up later." Ty's voice was hopeful.

"Sorry, but no. Your mom likes to keep to a schedule." And his ex-wife's schedule was the kind Sean had never managed to live up to. "Besides, the work can't wait until tomorrow. We made a commitment to the customer."

Ty's mouth flattened into a stubborn line. "*You* made a commitment to the customer, not me."

Sean grabbed one end of the rental canoe and Ty the other, lifting it above their heads. "You're as much a part of this business as me."

"What if I want something else?" Ty's voice was sharp.

Sean's chest got heavy as worry for his son sparked memories of what—and who—he'd once wanted. "I have a good life here. All I want is for you to have a good life too. This business is part of our family. I wanted to take on Carmichael's when I was your age."

"I'm not you."

"I know you're not, but unless you talk to me, how will I know who you are or what you want?" Sean stopped by the patch of grass in front of the cottage, and he and Ty eased the canoe to the ground.

"Whatever." Ty clumped up the steps to the wide porch. White clapboard walls rose behind to a second story.

Sean bit back the frustrated words he might have said before he pushed his son away. He couldn't lose Ty. His father and grandfather were the past, but his son was the future. The future of the business they'd built together. A legacy.

Following Ty, he rapped on the screen door. A radio inside was tuned to a news station, and light footsteps tapped down the hall. "Son, I want the best for you—"

"Uh, Dad." Ty's voice cracked.

Sean's head jerked up and the world fell away.

A girl in her early teens stood on the other side of the half-open door. She wore an aqua bikini top with a white sarong tied around her hips. And she had long brown hair and big brown eyes like melted chocolate drops.

Sean took a step back and bumped into Ty. No, it couldn't be Charlie Gibbs because Charlie was seven months younger than Sean. But she had Charlie's face and hair and those eyes that had always seen straight through him.

Forgetting the past was up there with all the other things Sean was good at. Except, sometimes, that past caught him when he least expected.

"Can I help you?" The girl had a slow drawl, Southern definitely, Texas maybe.

Ty edged forward, and there was a smile of pure masculine appreciation on his son's face. "I'm Ty Carmichael, and this is my dad. Somebody here rented a canoe from us." He pulled off his fishing hat and stuck it into the back pocket of his shorts. "We own Carmichael's, the marina and boatyard next door."

"I'm Naomi Connell." The girl smiled back and showed a mouthful of braces. "I don't know anything about a canoe rental."

"Maybe your dad booked it?" Sean's voice was higher, like it belonged to some other guy.

Naomi studied him. "My dad's not here, but I can ask my—"

"No!" Sean broke in. "If there's been a mistake, my brother will pick the canoe up later." Sweat trickled down his back, beneath his shirt.

Naomi quirked an eyebrow, and what was left of Sean's heart, the heart Charlie had ripped out of his chest and shredded, thudded against his ribs.

Inside the cottage the radio stopped. "Who's at the door?" It was a woman's voice, and her words were clipped. An accent Sean couldn't place. His stomach churned.

Naomi, the girl who was and wasn't Charlie, spoke back into the shadowy hall where beach bags and summer shoes were piled in an untidy heap. "Some guys are here about a canoe rental."

She turned again to Sean and Ty and opened the door wider. "You want to come inside? We made iced tea." A smile flowered across Naomi's face. A smile that was sweet, innocent, and so much like Charlie's it made Sean's heart ache.

"Sure." Ty's smile broadened. "Iced tea sounds great." He shook sand off his feet and moved toward Naomi as if pulled by a magnetic force.

"We have to get going." Sean grabbed Shadow's collar as the dog nosed her way into the cottage.

"Sean?"

He froze, and the past he'd spent eighteen years forgetting slammed into him.

Charlie's brown eyes met his, surrounded by the thick, dark lashes that had always reminded him of two little fans spread across her face when her eyes were closed. Instead of being laughter-filled like he remembered, though, her eyes were wary, framed by brown hair cut into an angular bob, which sharpened her heart-shaped face.

"Charlie." He forced her name out through numb lips. Above loose white pants, her lemon tank top molded to her lush curves like a second skin. His body stirred, and awareness of her, and everything they'd once meant to each other, crashed through him.

She gave him a bland, untouchable smile. The kind her mom and sister had perfected. Not a smile he'd ever expected to see on Charlie's face. "It's good to see you again."

"Really?" Sean drew in a breath.

Charlie's smile slipped. "We were friends."

"Friends?" Sean caught her dark gaze and held it. Her jaw was tight, but her skin was burnished like a ripe peach.

Shadow strained forward, tail wagging a greeting.

"It's been a long time." Her voice was cool, but when she bent to pat the dog her hand shook.

Sean opened his dry-as-tinder mouth and closed it again before he said something stupid. Something he'd regret. In that time, he'd built a life. And the girl who'd been his best friend, his first love, and his whole world wasn't part of it.

He glanced at his son and Naomi where he and Charlie had once stood, Charlie tilting her face up to his for a good-night kiss. His stomach knotted at the look on Ty's face. Long ago, he'd looked at Charlie that way. Like she was the prettiest girl in the world. The only girl in the world for him.

"Let us know what you want to do about the canoe." Even though his pulse sped up, his voice was as cool as Charlie's as he pulled the rental agreement from the pocket of his shorts and held it out. He was thirty-six, not eighteen, and he'd made sure he never thought about those good-night kisses or any other memories he'd buried deep.

Charlie took the paper at arm's length. "I'm sure there's an explanation for the order."

"Ty?" He inclined his head toward his son.

"But, Dad—"

"No."

With a last look at Naomi, Ty vaulted over the porch railing and landed on the ground below.

Sean turned, his steps deliberate. This time he planned on being the one who walked away.

* * *

Sean Carmichael looked good, too good, and he was as self-contained as always. Unlike her. Charlie sucked in a deep breath against the volcano of emotion that threatened to erupt from her chest.

"Auntie Charlotte?" Naomi whispered. "Are you okay?"

"Fine, honey." The comforting lie she'd make herself believe. She forced her feet to walk across the porch and stop by the railing. "Sean?" Firefly Lake was a small town. She'd have to face him sooner or later and tell him a truth she'd rather avoid. At least one of them.

He paused at the bottom of the steps, and his big body stiffened. "What?" Voice tight, he half turned, his dark-blue eyes fixed on her in the way that had always unnerved her because she was sure he could tell what she was thinking.

"Wait." She scanned the piece of paper he'd given her.

"Why?" The black dog by his side looked at her and then back at Sean, eyes wise.

"The rental's fine." She wouldn't fall apart. Even though the sight of him almost brought her to her knees. "Can your son leave the canoe in the boathouse? Naomi will get the key and help him."

He glanced at Ty. The boy had Sean's sandy-blond hair, thick, rumpled like he'd just rolled out of bed. He had Sean's height, but his eyes were a lighter blue, his face thinner. The memory of what might have been squeezed her heart.

In profile, Sean's nose still had the bump from where he'd broken it playing hockey the winter he'd turned sixteen, but his sensuous mouth was bracketed by fine lines, no longer the face of the boy she'd known.

"Of course." Sean's eyes were shuttered. Like Charlie was any other customer.

Naomi darted into the cottage and reappeared seconds later holding the boathouse key by its red cord. "Auntie Charlotte?" She looked at Ty and tossed her hair over her shoulders.

"Please unlock the boathouse and then wait on the beach." The past reared up and choked Charlie and made it hard to breathe. It reminded her of when she'd been a girl like Naomi and head over heels in love with Sean. Her whole life ahead of her, no mistakes yet. No regrets either.

"Sure." Naomi skipped down the steps.

"Auntie Charlotte?" Sean rested one bare foot against the bottom step, his legs muscular and dusted with dark-blond hair. At eighteen, he'd still been lanky, but now he was a man, all lean, long-limbed magnetic strength.

"Naomi is Mia's daughter. You remember my sister?" Charlie's legs trembled, and she wrapped a hand around the porch railing to steady herself.

"Yes." Sean's voice was deeper than she remembered, rougher, with an edge to it that set her nerve ends tingling. "But Charlotte? You hated that name."

"People change." When she'd left Firefly Lake, she'd left Charlie behind and turned herself into Charlotte. A person who wasn't the scared girl she'd been, who'd convinced herself she'd made the only choice she could.

Sean tapped one foot on the step. "If you say so."

"Ty, your son?" Her tongue tripped over the words. "You and your wife must be proud of him." She pushed away the stab of pain sparked by the thought of Sean's wife. Pain as sharp as it was unexpected.

"He's a good kid." Sean's expression softened to give her a glimpse of the boy he'd been. "He's working with me for the summer."

"You've done some building." Charlie gestured toward the beach that narrowed at the point, still framed by the trees and rolling hills she remembered from childhood summers. Carmichael's was on the other side, and an unfamiliar tin roof glinted in the sun.

"We put in a new workshop last year. I built a house there a while ago too. Moved out from town." Sean smoothed the bill of his ball cap, and Charlie couldn't help but notice there wasn't a wedding ring on his fourth finger.

Sean must be married. He had a son and he'd always been a conventional guy. Loyal and true. Her heart twisted tighter and there was a sour taste in her mouth. "So you stayed here."

"I always wanted to take on Carmichael's." Sean paused. "But since we're taking this trip down memory lane, what about you? Did you get what you wanted?"

When you ran out on me and on us. The words he didn't say hung heavy between them.

"I'm a foreign correspondent for the Associated Press, based in London, but I travel all over. Wherever the next story is, I go." It was the life she wanted and had worked hard to get. And she loved it. At least until four months ago.

"You always wanted to see the world." Sean's voice was flat.

"Yeah, I did." She looked at the beach where Ty and Naomi tossed a Frisbee. The dog darted between them. Naomi laughed at something Ty said and he laughed too, Sean's laugh.

Charlie's stomach rolled. She had to get a grip. Focus on who she was now, not who she'd been. She wasn't looking at herself and Sean on that beach.

"Must be an exciting life." Sean's voice had an edge of steel.

Excitement wasn't all it was cracked up to be. Charlie's hands were clammy. She sat on one of the Adirondack chairs Mia had found in the shed and crossed her right leg over her left. Her pants covered the scar tissue that stretched from her left knee to her ankle. "It pays the bills." But there wasn't much left over to save for the future and she wasn't getting any younger.

"Charlotte..." He hesitated, and the name he'd never called her rang in her ears. "Why are you here?" His eyes narrowed into blue slits, framed by spiky lashes several shades darker than his hair. "You could have put that canoe in the boathouse as easy as Ty."

Her heart thudded, a dull throb that hurt more than the ache in her leg. "I didn't expect you to turn up on the doorstep, but since you did, I don't want you to hear this in town."

"Hear what?" He tugged on his T-shirt and smoothed it over a still-taut stomach, although his shoulders were bigger, the muscles more defined.

"Mia and I and her two girls, we're here for a month to sell the cottage." She swallowed the lump in her throat. Selling was the right choice, the only choice.

"Your folks, they..." Sean yanked off his hat and sat sideways to face her on the middle step, the weathered boards creaking under his weight.

She nodded. The only sounds were the buzz of the cicadas and the whisper of the wind in the pines.

"I'm sorry." His voice was gruff.

"We lost Mom last Christmas. Cancer." Charlie blinked as tears pricked the backs of her eyes.

"That's rough." He paused for a heartbeat. "My condolences. My mom will be sad to hear about your mother."

And the cottage was her last tangible link with her mom, and the place Charlie had always thought of as home. It was the only constant in her life after the summer she'd turned ten and they'd left Montreal for her dad's new job in Boston. But she had to be practical. The money from the cottage sale would secure that future she worried about.

Sean put his hat back on and looked out at the lake. "What about your dad?"

"He died five years ago." Charlie shivered. "He had a heart attack on the golf course."

"My dad went like that a little over a year ago. Over in the marina." Sean's voice caught and he tented his hands on his knees, the strong, capable hands that had taught her how to paddle a canoe and build a campfire. Hands that had comforted her when she'd been scared of the bear with the sharp yellow teeth Mia told her lived in the boathouse. And hands that had loved her and taught her how to love back.

"He was a good man, your dad." Honest, upright, and devoted to his family. Everything Charlie's dad wasn't.

"He had a good life." Sean gave her a brief smile. "Even though he went too soon, he went doing what he loved, with the family he loved around him. A man couldn't ask for more." His face changed, tenderness wiped away, and a muscle worked in his jaw. "You're here to sell the cottage."

"Yes." She'd made her decision and wouldn't go back on it now that she was here. "It's the last piece of Mom's estate." All the beauty, vibrancy, and love that had been her mom reduced to a dry sheaf of papers.

"You could have sold the cottage from anywhere." Sean's voice rasped.

Charlie hugged herself. "This place was special to
Mom. I owe it to her to come back one last time." Maybe
she owed it to herself too.

"There should be a lot of interest." Sean got up from
the step. "It's the biggest cottage on Firefly Lake. Since it's
only a few hours from Burlington and Montreal, it's easy
to get here on weekends. Even from Boston like you did.
It'll be sold before you know it, and you'll be back on a
plane."

Charlie pushed herself out of the chair and stood. "We
might not sell it in the way you think. You see, there's a developer interested."

"A developer?" Sean moved toward her so fast Charlie
rocked against the porch railing. Pain radiated up her leg.

"They haven't made us an offer yet, but they're talking
about a tasteful little resort." Pinned between Sean and the
railing, the top of her head level with his broad chest, Charlie reminded herself to breathe. She'd forgotten how big
Sean was, how male. "They'd give us a good price."

"What do you mean a good price?" Sean's expression
hardened. "Firefly Lake hasn't changed in generations.
People come here because it hasn't changed."

"A resort development won't change things much."
Charlie avoided his gaze.

Sean's laugh was harsh. "You really believe that? Everywhere else, life has sped up, everybody rushing without
knowing what they're rushing to or why. Here things stay
pretty much the same. At least the same in the ways that
matter. Don't you care about keeping it that way?"

"Yes, but in this economy not as many people are buying summer cottages." Her heart raced, and she pressed
a hand to her chest. "Besides, Vermont has legislation to

protect the landscape, and developers have to meet certain criteria before they can get a building permit."

"Keep renting the cottage out until the economy gets better." His blue eyes blazed with the anger she'd only seen once before. "That seemed to work fine for the last eighteen years. Don't talk to me about some law. You can't sell all this to a developer." He raised an arm to take in the cottage, the forest behind it, the beach and the lake, hazy blue in the afternoon sun.

"That's not your decision to make. I need to let the cottage go." And she needed to forget about sentiment and think with her head, not her heart. Let the past go and use the money she'd get for the cottage to live the rest of her life, a life she'd almost lost.

"You were good at that weren't you?" His face reddened. "Letting go of things you no longer wanted."

"That's not how I remember it." She forced a calmness she didn't feel. "But if you mean what was between us, that was a lifetime ago, like the cottage is a lifetime ago."

"You really think so, Sunshine?"

Charlie flinched as Sean's old nickname for her drove a spike through her battered heart.

"In all your talk about this place being special to your mom, it sounds like you've forgotten how special it was to you too."

He whistled for his dog, the shrill sound slicing through the air. And when he walked away, this time Charlie didn't try to stop him.

Chapter Two

Sean pushed open the workshop door and sent it crashing back on its hinges. "Trevor?" The familiar smells of wood, canvas, paint, and varnish enveloped him. Three half-built canoes rested on struts, and a row of handcrafted paddles lined one wall, supported by rough pine pegs.

"What's up, bro?" His twin's hands stilled on the paddle he was carving and his mild blue eyes met Sean's gaze, his square face placid as always. A pair of safety glasses dangled from a strap around his neck and bumped against the denim work shirt he'd paired with his usual faded jeans. "Was your ex bent out of shape because you and Ty were late getting back? She should be used to you by now."

"Not so you'd notice."

His ex-wife was always calm, always in control. The only unexpected thing she'd ever done was leave him, seven years into their marriage. She wanted someone different, something different. A life Sean couldn't give her.

Trevor ran a hand through his blond hair, several shades

darker than Sean's. "Well, you're sure pissed about something, the way you barged in here like a bear with a sore paw, banging the door."

Shadow shot by them in a blur of black fur and disappeared into the office tucked at the back of the workshop.

Sean drew in slow, steady breaths. He hated it when Sarah picked up Ty and took him back to her new life in Kincaid, leaving him alone out here. It always reminded him that his son had a whole other family that didn't include him. As if he needed the reminder.

But it was more than the ache of missing Ty. Seeing Charlie again had stirred up emotions he'd thought he was long over. One look in her eyes and the love, the loss, and the regrets bubbled to the surface.

"It's nothing." He shrugged.

Trevor's eyes narrowed, and he studied Sean the way he had since they were kids. "This doesn't have anything to do with Charlie Gibbs, does it?"

"You knew she was back in town?" Sean resisted the urge to grab his twin by the shirt collar and shake him. "And you didn't tell me? You let me take that canoe over there."

"I didn't know before you went." Trevor's voice was calm. "The name on the order's Connell, not Gibbs."

Sean ground his teeth. "How did you find out Charlie's back?"

"When I was in town picking up lumber, I heard talk at the diner that the Gibbs girls were nosing around. That's gotta be a big deal for you." Trevor ran a hand across the paddle and fingered the half-completed design of maple leaves.

Sean forced a laugh. "Seeing Charlie again was a surprise, that's all."

"The kind of surprise you wouldn't want." Trevor stared at Sean several seconds too long before he pulled the safety glasses over his head and set them on the workbench. "Linnie has this friend, Marcie, who's single again. She's a real nice woman. Linnie could set you up."

"Have you forgotten what happened the last time you two set me up?" Sean gave his brother an amused look.

"How were we supposed to know when she found out your son was a teenager, she'd make up some emergency and get a friend to crash the date?" Trevor raised his hands in mock surrender. "Linnie was so mad she hasn't spoken to her since."

Sean gave a wry laugh, then sobered. "You and Linnie have been married forever, but I'm fine on my own. Between Ty and Carmichael's, I haven't got time for a woman."

"You would if you found the right one. Why can't you at least have a drink with a woman who's not only nice but seriously hot?" Trevor's face was unusually somber. "A girl like Charlie wouldn't have been happy here. Sure, she ran out on you, but if you'd been thinking straight, you'd have broken up with her first. I don't want you getting hurt again."

"Not going to happen, little brother." Trevor was the younger twin by ten minutes, and Sean never let him forget it. "Charlie Gibbs is ancient history."

"You're getting that look again." Trevor slid a hammer into an open toolbox.

"I don't have a look." Sean scowled. "Anything between Charlie and me was over years ago. I haven't thought of her in . . . I don't know how long."

But after seeing her today, he hadn't been able to stop

thinking about her. Thinking about the two of them together.

How they'd raced their bikes along the dirt paths that
edged Firefly Lake. Fished for brook trout in the beaver
pond in the woods behind the marina and had bubble-blow-
ing contests with the gum they'd bought for pennies from
the jar in the bait store.

And how when they were older, Charlie's mouth had
curved into a special smile for him, her cherry-red lips
swollen by his kisses. How her luscious body had fit with
his like the two were made for each other.

She was part of almost every memory Sean had of summers in Firefly Lake. He'd told her his hopes, his dreams,
and his fears, and before she'd betrayed him, he thought
they'd known each other mind, body, and soul.

"The word in town is Charlie and Mia plan to sell the
cottage to some developer for one of those hotel com-
plexes." Trevor's worried voice yanked Sean back to the
present. "Do you think they'll do that?"

"Charlie said they're thinking about it." Sean grabbed
the broom propped against the wall near the woodstove and
swept scattered wood chips into a pile. The Charlie he'd
known would never have sold out, but that Charlie was long
gone, if she'd ever even existed. The girl he'd called Sunshine because she'd been his sunshine, coming back to Firefly Lake each year as spring slid into summer, lighting up his
life like a birthday sparkler.

"Folks in town said that kind of development could ruin
us." Trevor ran a hand over the paddle again, burnished
gold in the late-afternoon sun that flooded through the windows overlooking the lake. "Especially if they put in a
marina."

"Where did you hear that?" Sean gripped the broom tighter.

"It's only talk, but lots of hotels rent boats, or people might bring a boat with them to explore the lakes and rivers around here." Trevor looked at Sean with a trusting expression. "I told everyone you'd fix it."

Sean dredged up a smile. "Carmichael's has been in Firefly Lake for almost seventy years, ever since Grandpa started making boats for summer tourists. It would take a lot more than some resort to put us out of business." He swept the last wood scraps in jerky motions.

"What about the boatyard?" Trevor rubbed at the paddle with sandpaper. "People who come here to get away from it all won't want that on their doorstep, us hammering and sawing all day long."

"Any resort won't be on our doorstep. The woodlot's between the Gibbs place and ours, and that's state land."

"I guess folks in town don't know what they're talking about."

And his laid-back brother would put the worries out of his mind as easily as he'd change from his work clothes at the end of the day.

"I intend on keeping this business going for Ty." Sean had promised his grandfather and then his father he would. "Maybe those girls of yours will take an interest someday or have kids who do."

"Crystal's the only one who might be interested, but she's always had her heart set on working with animals." Trevor put the sandpaper away. "You coming to the softball game? It's Friday night. Everyone will be there."

Everyone meaning Sean's mom, his three older sisters and their families, and Trevor, Linnie, and their four girls.

His family, his friends, and his neighbors, people he counted on and who counted on him. "With Ty at his mom and stepdad's this weekend, I want to put some quotes together."

"You need to get a life." Trevor grabbed his lunch box and tucked it under one arm. "If you change your mind, come by anyway. Linnie's made those oatmeal raisin cookies you like."

"Save a couple for me." Sean grinned. "Put them in one of those pink baskets Linnie gives Mom. Bring it to work tomorrow."

"Like hell I will." Trevor grinned back. "You want those cookies, get them yourself. I'm not your cookie gofer."

"Smartass." Sean tossed Trevor the sweatshirt he'd left on the workbench.

When the door shut behind his twin, Sean moved into the office. The oak desk that had belonged to his grandfather, then his father, spanned one wall. It was bare of papers, apart from a tidy stack in the in-tray his sister, who helped out three mornings a week, had left for him earlier. He sat in the swivel chair, flipped open his laptop, and powered it up. A bank of filing cabinets covered the wall across from the desk. Shadow snored in her dog bed at one end, two brown leather armchairs in front.

With its wood floor, white walls, and high ceiling, the office was one of Sean's favorite places. Uncluttered, spare even, the only ornament a painting of Firefly Lake his grandmother had done in the 1950s. Sean always found solace here. Order. A sense of permanence and of belonging.

He took a folder from the top of the tray, then set it aside and scrubbed a hand across his face. There were half a dozen quotes he could work on, should work on.

Instead, he pulled the chair closer to the desk, slid his reading glasses on, and typed Charlie's name into the Internet search engine.

Over the years, Sean had told himself he wouldn't look for her. What they'd shared was over. But now it was different. Charlie was a threat to his business.

Who was he kidding? It was more than business. He wanted to know about Charlie's life and who she was now. Even if it was like ripping skin off his hand with a table saw, it was time to face truths he'd avoided for years.

An hour later, when the brightness of the day had softened into a purple twilight and loons called on the lake, their haunting cries echoing, Sean clicked the last file closed and slipped off his glasses. He propped his elbows on the desk and rested his chin in his hands.

She'd kept it from him. Yet what had happened to Charlie was bad. So bad she'd been lucky to come through it alive.

Except she was now Charlotte, a stranger. She lived in London, a place he'd never been, and seen and done things he couldn't imagine. Charlie Gibbs had disappeared without a trace, but Charlotte Gibbs was everywhere.

Her face, familiar yet unknown, stared out at him accompanying articles with sharp, insightful writing that cut to the heart of a story, dug deep and exposed its human face. From Middle Eastern riots to the plight of small African farmers, Charlotte Gibbs gave ordinary people a voice.

And her voice rang out as well. A voice that demanded justice, fairness, and, most of all, compassion.

He'd known she'd become the journalist she'd aimed to be. News had trickled back to Firefly Lake over the years, but the gossip died down and folks had moved on. Everyone except him apparently.

The truth hit him with the unexpectedness of a sucker punch.

Sean's stomach quivered as he turned in the chair. Through the half-open window behind the desk, pine trees bracketed the point and framed the view he'd looked at his whole life. A crescent moon hung low and etched a silver trail across the water. After almost half a lifetime of his missing her, being angry with her, loving her, and hating her, Charlie was back on the other side of that narrow spit of land.

And although she'd tried to hide it, she was hurt...but he'd said she could put that canoe in the boathouse as easy as Ty. His heart clenched. He'd said worse, too. Spoken to her like he never spoke to any woman, let alone someone who'd once been so much a part of his heart.

Guilt stabbed at him like the red-hot poker in the old woodstove come winter. If he'd known what she'd gone through, he'd have handled things differently. If the sight of her on the porch of that cottage hadn't shaken him to the core, he'd have been civil. The gentleman his folks had raised him to be.

Sean stood, slammed the window closed, and pulled at the blinds to shut out the night. Charlie fought for everybody else, everywhere else, but it didn't change the fact she'd given up on him, given up on them, and run out of his life without a backward glance.

Trevor's words rang in his ears. He'd given his life to this business. He'd nurtured it, grown it, and protected it. He checked the time on his laptop. If he hurried, he could get into town before the softball game ended.

It was too late to fix what had gone wrong between him and Charlie, but Carmichael's was different. He wouldn't let the business or his family be hurt.

Tendrils of mist clung to the surface of the lake when Charlie came out of the woods on Monday morning, her sandals noiseless on the carpet of pine needles. The water was as smooth as glass, the air still, washed clean with dew. At the edge of the beach, she toed off her sneakers and left them beside the granite boulder eighteen more years of winter storms hadn't budged. She set her camera on its flat top and rolled up the legs of her sweats. When she waded into the water, its coldness numbed her toes.

Behind her, a branch snapped. She tensed with the alertness years of reporting from war zones had made second nature. Creeping out of the lake, she curled her fingers around a rock. Its edges dug into her palm. A crow swooped out of a tall pine, its cry shattering the silence.

As Charlie turned, a big black dog loped out of the forest. When it spotted her, it bounded across the sand, barking, and skidded to a stop inches from her feet.

Sean's dog.

She relaxed her grip on the rock and shoved her sweats down her legs one-handed to hide her scar. Since the dog was here, Sean or his son wouldn't be far behind. Or Sean's wife. Charlie's stomach rolled. "You're a good dog, aren't you?"

The dog barked louder.

Sean jogged out of the woods, and a jolt of desire zinged through her. A white T-shirt molded to his chest, and black running shorts hugged his thighs. His athletic shoes hit the ground in a steady rhythm, and an iPod was clipped to his waist. He was all sexy ridges and big, powerful male. A little bit sweaty and way too tempting.

He stopped beside the dog, grabbed its collar with one hand, and yanked the earbuds out of his ears with the other. "Shadow won't hurt you." His gaze zeroed in on the rock. "You weren't going to throw that at her, were you?"

"Of course not." Charlie dropped the rock on the sand, and her eyes landed on his lean, muscular legs. Sensual awareness hit her with the force of a tsunami.

"Then why were you holding on to that rock like you were going to aim it at someone?" Damp from his run, the hair at his temples curled in soft tendrils.

Her fingers tingled. "You never know who might be in those woods." If they were watching her and waiting to strike when she least expected it.

Sean gave her a half smile, a quick tilt of his lips gone almost before she registered it. "You don't remember much about Firefly Lake. All you're going to find in those woods is folks looking for some privacy."

Charlie remembered all right. From the time they'd hit fifteen, she and Sean had also been looking for privacy in these same woods. "It's six in the morning." Heat crept up her cheeks.

He smiled again, teasing with a familiar sexy edge, and the quivery feeling in her stomach intensified. "You were never a morning person, but here you are, up with the dawn." He moved toward the tree line and stretched one long leg over a fallen log. "You still like taking pictures?" He inclined his head to her camera.

"I do." Charlie pushed away the memory of his legs wrapped around hers, his face inches away, flushed and intent on pleasuring her, like she was pleasuring him. She sat on the log with a *thump* as Shadow darted toward her and flopped at Charlie's feet.

"Get any good shots?" Sean finished stretching and sat beside her, arranging his big body with a lean grace no other man she'd known had ever matched.

"The light isn't right." Heat sizzled along her nerve ends.

"You didn't come out here to take photos, did you?" On Friday he'd been clean-shaven, but today dark-blond stubble shadowed his jaw, giving him a rolled-out-of-bed look, which turned her insides to mush.

"I'm still jet-lagged." She settled for a half-truth. "Since I couldn't sleep, I thought a walk would help." And distract her from the pain in her leg, which, despite the little white pills, had kept her awake, things she didn't want to think about going around in her head.

And distract her from the dream she'd had in a fitful moment of sleep just before dawn. Sean braced on his forearms above her and his body deep inside hers. The love on his face, which had morphed into distrust.

"So did the walk help?" Compassion and understanding, acceptance too, flickered in the depths of his blue eyes. The real Sean, not the dream phantom.

"You know, don't you? About what happened to me?" She waited and bit her lower lip. She could handle his teasing, handle his anger even. What she couldn't handle was his compassion, the way he always understood her.

"Type *Charlotte Gibbs* into any Internet search engine. A lot comes up."

A lot she probably wished hadn't. "You shouldn't believe everything you read online."

"Some of those newspapers are reliable enough." He sounded neutral, not questioning, but not judging either.

She dug her feet into the sand, cool and damp, not yet warmed by the heat of the day. "I was only doing my job." But she'd always done more than her job and volunteered for the toughest assignments because she was a solo act.

"A roadside bomb went off twenty feet in front of you. You were lucky." His gaze pinned hers. "Despite everything."

And because of that luck, she'd vowed to make some changes in her life, to start over and use the second chance she'd been given. "I'm glad my mom...she didn't live to see what happened." She blinked, and the sudden dampness behind her eyes caught her unaware.

"You want to talk about it?" His voice was gentle.

Charlie shook her head, tried to smile and failed. Once, Sean had been not only her lover but her best friend as well. The one she'd gone running with, pounding along the trails on this side of the lake. The one she could talk to about anything.

"I can't." Not to Mia, not to Max, her editor, and not to the counselor the AP made her see for what the doctors said was post-traumatic stress disorder. A neat label for the messy tangle that had become her life. Whenever she tried to talk about her feelings, the words stuck in her throat and choked her.

She reached for Shadow and stroked the dog's silky ears. Sean wasn't the boy he'd once been. He was a man, with a wife and family. "Won't someone—your wife— wonder where you are?"

Sean looked out at the lake. The sun had burned away the last of the mist, and a pair of ducks swam in a neat line toward the reeds. "No." He turned back to her, fine lines around his eyes and outlining his nose and mouth showing her the man, not the boy. "I'm divorced. Sarah's my ex-wife. We have joint custody and this was her weekend with Ty. She'll drop him off in a few hours for work."

"I see." Charlie didn't see. The Sean she'd known had been a forever kind of guy. "I'm sorry."

"Don't be." He shrugged. "Sarah and I are happier apart than we ever were together. She's got a new life and two more kids. Her husband's an accountant in Kincaid. Ty has two families." He brushed sand off his shorts. "She wanted someone different, that's all."

Charlie's breath hitched. Had Sean wanted someone different too? She picked up a stone from the beach, jet black and worn smooth, and turned it over in her hand. Standing, she moved to the water's edge and tossed the stone, the splash sending ripples pooling across the surface of the lake.

"You've lost your touch." A pebble ricocheted past her, skimming the surface five times before sliding under the water. "It's in the wrist, remember?" Sean found another stone and handed it to her. The brief touch of his fingers against hers made her skin burn.

Charlie tried again, flicking her wrist in the long-forgotten childhood movement. "One, two."

"Better." Sean scooped up a handful of small stones from the water's edge and gave her half. "What about you? Did you ever marry?"

"No husband. No kids either." She pasted on a smile and stared at the lake. It still had the same reedy smell, and little foam-topped waves tumbled onto the shore with a soft hiss.

"Why not?" He sent another stone skipping across the sapphire-blue water. "You must have had opportunities."

"It's hard to have a relationship when you're only in the same city with someone three months out of twelve." She tossed one of her stones, and it sank near the shore with a dull *plop*. "The men I meet, we're both always on the road. A few weeks here and there between assignments. That kind of life's no basis for a real relationship."

Maybe if she'd loved someone enough to want to build a life together, she'd have found a way to work it out. Or found a man who was willing to work it out with her. Instead, she always broke things off before they got serious.

The sun glinted off Sean's hair, still the color of ripe wheat. "You just never met the right guy."

She shrugged. "Maybe." Or maybe she had, and nobody else had ever come close. The handful of pebbles slipped out of her grasp and landed on the wet sand with a thud.

"What's with you, Gibbs? You always were a pro at skipping stones."

"I'm out of practice." Nowadays she was more used to people who threw rocks. Or worse.

Sean picked up one of the stones she'd dropped. "I don't recall you being a quitter." He reached for her hand and tucked the stone into her palm.

"It's only a game." She tried to pull her hand away, but he held it fast, tracing his thumb around the faint ridge of scar tissue that bisected her left index finger and stretched from her knuckle to the fleshy part where it joined her thumb.

"I remember when you got this." His voice roughened, and Charlie's heart kicked into her throat.

"I caught it in that fishhook." She swallowed. "You drove me to the hospital to get it stitched since Mom and Dad and Mia were at the Inn on the Lake for the end-of-summer dance." And Sean had soothed her with gentle words and an even gentler touch.

"You could have gone to the dance, but you stayed with me to close the boathouse. You didn't even cry when the hook went in." His voice low, intimate, he moved and closed the space between them. "You were the bravest girl I ever knew."

"I'm not that girl anymore." Her voice caught and she focused on the churned-up sand at her feet.

Maybe she'd never been that girl. Mia claimed the pretty-daughter crown, the perfect daughter who always did what their parents expected. But Charlie was the family disappointment, the one who chafed against authority and who embraced the role of the feisty, take-charge, always-in-control girl so nobody would guess how much she hurt inside. How she'd felt she never belonged.

"I know you aren't." Sean stood so close his musky, male scent tickled her nose. He dropped her hand and cupped her jaw, his breath feathering the hair that grazed her chin. "I think you're still pretty brave. After that bomb went off, you risked your life to try to save your colleague, even though you were hurt too."

Charlie's breath hitched. "Like I said, it was my job. When you're on assignment, your colleagues are like your family. You look out for each other."

He moved even closer until the blue of the sky and the lake mingled with the deeper blue of his eyes. "Why, Charlie?"

"Why what?" The tendrils of hair at his temple were so close, she could reach up and touch them. Trail her fingers down past his ear to the sensitive spot on his neck.

"You and I always looked out for each other." His

voice hardened, and he dipped his head, his lips inches from hers.

Mesmerized by the desire in his gaze, she lifted her hand to touch one blond curl. "I couldn't—"

"Couldn't or wouldn't." He closed the remaining space between them and tunneled his hands in her hair.

"I..." Her legs trembled and she swayed into his body.

"Aw hell, Sunshine." He ground out the words through his teeth before he covered her mouth in a kiss that was both heartbreaking and punishing. Sweetness, lust, and anger mixed in one.

In spite of herself, Charlie let her mouth open under his. She grabbed at his forearms to keep her balance as almost-forgotten sensations churned through her. He deepened the kiss and she moaned. Even when they were kids, learning about love together, Sean had always known how to make her respond, his touch and his mouth sure. With a gasp she tore her mouth away from his and let go of his arms.

"This is a mistake." She stepped back, light-headed, her legs shaky.

"A big mistake." Sean's voice rasped and his breathing was unsteady.

Charlie wiped a hand across her mouth, the imprint of his lips still there, his taste still strong, reeling from how fast the old heat between them had sparked and flared into life. "I shouldn't have..."

"I shouldn't have either." He glanced at Shadow digging a hole farther down the beach. "There's something about you, Charlie. There always has been."

"There's something about you too, Sean, but I can't, we can't..."

"I know." His eyes were bleak, two blue flints when he turned back to her. "When are you selling?"

"After the land survey is done. The developer is keen, and when they make an offer there'll be no reason to wait."

"You think people who come here to stay in some fancy hotel will want to skip stones on a beach?" Sean untangled his iPod earbuds. "Or go skinny-dipping in the moonlight because there's nobody else around and they can?"

Charlie gasped as he leaned in and touched her cheek, a faint grazing of his fingers against her skin. "Don't."

"Or have you forgotten about that too?" He took his hand away, but his eyes raked her from head to toe and lingered on the curve of her breasts.

"That's the past. What would Mia and I do with a cottage here? With Mom gone, there's no reason to hang on to the place."

"People in Firefly Lake don't want some developer coming in." Sean's jaw was tight, his face all hard planes and angles. "Businesses around here are family-owned, but you think you can come back, after all these years, and sell out without considering everybody who lives here year-round? People who'll still live here after you're long gone again?"

"I don't. Mia and I—"

"I'm not going to make this easy for you." A pulse in Sean's jaw twitched, the only indication he held on to his control by a thread. "None of us are. You should think again before you make that deal. Think about what you're signing away."

"That's a low blow." Charlie took a step back. "The guy I knew always played fair. He'd never stoop to emotional manipulation."

"The girl I knew was my best friend. The one I trusted more than anyone. But you broke that trust, didn't you?"

His words ricocheted into the sudden chasm between them to lodge in Charlie's heart. "That girl's gone." The words came out in a croak through her stiff lips.

His voice was bitter. "That guy is too."

Chapter Three

Ty's dad, who'd just kissed Auntie Charlotte, was less than fifteen feet away. Naomi ducked behind a tree and held her breath as he and Shadow disappeared along a narrow trail, no more than a green outline hacked out of the bushes.

So much for thinking she could bump into Ty by accident. Instead, she'd gotten herself trapped in the woods between the cottage and the beach. Even though when she'd seen him on the path behind the marina yesterday, Ty hadn't said he was going fishing *this* morning.

Naomi wasn't spying exactly. The marina was right next door, and her mom kept nagging her to get off the couch and get some exercise. It wasn't as if there was much else to do around here.

She lifted her hair off her neck and waved away a cloud of mosquitoes. Auntie Charlotte was still on the beach. She shifted from one foot to the other and touched a hand to her cheek and her hair. Like Ty's dad had done.

Naomi fingered the phone in her skirt pocket, wishing she could text Alyssa, her best friend back home in Dallas. Although she was too far away to hear what they'd said, what she'd seen Auntie Charlotte and Ty's dad doing was big. Too big to share with Alyssa, or anyone.

Naomi stuck her head around the gnarled tree trunk. The coast was clear. She eased through the undergrowth and rejoined the sandy path, forcing her legs into an easy stroll.

"Honey?" Rounding a curve in the trail, she jumped at the sound of Auntie Charlotte's voice. "What are you doing here?"

Naomi's face heated. Seeing her aunt kissing Ty's dad was even more embarrassing than the time back in seventh grade when she'd gotten toilet paper stuck in her skirt and the boy she'd had a crush on had been behind her in the lunch line. Her thoughts whirled and she pointed to a patch of greenery. "Studying nature."

Her heart thudded. Auntie Charlotte couldn't have seen her snooping around. She must have taken a shortcut. There was no other way she could have gotten to this part of the trail this soon. "My science teacher says plants are the lungs of our planet."

Auntie Charlotte grinned. "That's poison ivy."

Naomi scooted backward and caught her sandal on a tree root, staggering to keep her balance. "I couldn't sleep. I'm not used to sharing a room with Emma."

Which was true. Her seven-year-old sister had to be the noisiest roommate ever. She tossed and turned like her bed was a trampoline. She talked in her sleep. Then Emma would wake up and want the bathroom, a drink of water, then the bathroom again. And since she was scared of the dark, she refused to go on her own.

"It's different for you here, huh?" Auntie Charlotte's brown eyes were warm and loving, like she remembered being Naomi's age. Almost fifteen and not sure who you were or who you wanted to be.

"It's like some museum." Naomi wrinkled her nose. "The cottage doesn't have a television or air-conditioning, and the water smells weird." She checked the ends of her hair, surprised the strands were still dark and as glossy as ever. "I'll have to get Alyssa to FedEx me more conditioner. There's no way that store we stopped at in town has any brand I'd use."

Auntie Charlotte laughed. "You're a lot like your mom."

Naomi linked an arm with Auntie Charlotte's. "Maybe, except Mom doesn't like being here, but I think you do, so I'm cool with that. Really." Also, Ty was the cutest boy she'd ever met, which counted for a lot.

"I may not see you very often, but you're an excellent niece." Auntie Charlotte tucked her camera into her hoodie pocket.

"Really?" Naomi gave a little skip and smiled. Auntie Charlotte flew in and out of Naomi's life once or twice a year bringing presents, like dolls in national costumes and wooden boxes that smelled of spices and that Naomi kept on a special shelf in her bedroom. She might not know Auntie Charlotte well, but she still told all her friends how fabulous she was. And although she'd never tell Alyssa or anyone, she wanted to be as fearless and independent as Auntie Charlotte when she grew up. Those sexy curves wouldn't hurt either.

"Absolutely." Auntie Charlotte gave her a thumbs-up.

Naomi moved closer. "Mom never talks about Firefly Lake. What was it like coming here when you were my age?"

"A lot like it is now." Auntie Charlotte's eyes got a far-away look, like she remembered something happy but sad too. "This place hasn't changed much."

"There isn't anything to do. No mall. No Starbucks." Naomi slowed her pace because Auntie Charlotte's left leg dragged.

"When we go into town, I'll take you to a diner where I used to go. There's probably still a movie theater and a bowling alley." Auntie Charlotte gave her a half smile. "I was never bored. I canoed, played tennis, rode my bike, and swam in the lake. Hung out with some of the local kids too."

None of which, apart from maybe the tennis, sounded exciting. "Any cute boys?" Naomi made her voice light, like she didn't have a special reason for asking.

"Sure there were." Auntie Charlotte's eyes narrowed. "You and Ty Carmichael seemed to hit it off."

Naomi gave an elaborate shrug like it wasn't important. Nothing much got by Auntie Charlotte, which was probably why she'd won all those awards for her job. "He's okay." She made her tone casual.

"Okay?" Auntie Charlotte stopped, and although it sounded for a second like she was trying not to laugh, she cupped Naomi's chin in a gentle hand. "You be careful, honey. With a boy like Ty, before you know it, you could be in over your head." She dropped her hand and started walking again, faster this time. "Besides, your mom doesn't want you dating until you're sixteen." Her voice was serious, amusement stripped away.

A stupid rule and one more example of how her mom didn't understand her. Naomi lengthened her stride to keep up. "Who said I wanted to date him?"

"Even though you may find it hard to believe, I was a teenage girl once. Your mom was too."

Naomi could picture Auntie Charlotte being her age, but her mom? Never in a million years. Naomi made herself laugh, like it was all a joke. "Forget about Ty. Let's talk about Ty's dad. When he and Ty brought that canoe around, it looked like the two of you knew each other pretty well."

"The Carmichaels' cottage was next door and my dad kept a boat at their marina. Ty's dad and I knew each other as kids. We were friends. A very long time ago," she added in a lower voice.

To Naomi it looked like they'd been a lot more than friends. Still were, if how the two of them locked lips on the beach was anything to go by. But that was the thing with grown-ups. Even as nice a one as Auntie Charlotte never told you the whole truth.

"Why don't we make some breakfast?" Auntie Charlotte's voice turned bright and breezy. "Surprise your mom and Emma with pancakes."

"You can make pancakes?" Naomi choked back a laugh. "Mom says you can barely boil an egg."

"She's right." Auntie Charlotte grinned, like she was Naomi's age and they were friends, getting away with something. "But when your mom wasn't looking, I picked up a pancake mix at the grocery store. The instructions on the box say all you have to do is add water."

"Mom doesn't like us eating processed food." Naomi stopped where the path opened out of the forest at the back of the cottage, the shadows cast by the towering trees giving way to a cloudless blue sky. Although she loved Auntie Charlotte, she loved her mom too, and her mom was the best cook ever.

"One pancake mix won't kill us, and I won't tell if you don't." Auntie Charlotte wrapped Naomi in a hug. It was the kind of hug Naomi remembered Auntie Charlotte giving her when she was little. "Besides, we're on vacation."

"I guess." It didn't seem much like a vacation. Not with her dad back home working and her mom and Auntie Charlotte talking about lawyers and Realtors and other boring stuff.

"That's my girl." Auntie Charlotte flashed Naomi another conspiratorial smile and went into the cottage.

Naomi lingered behind and scanned the line of trees that curved into the hazy blue of the point where Ty told her the Carmichael's workshop was. Auntie Charlotte was right. She was on vacation and deserved to have some fun. Hanging out with Ty could be a lot of fun.

She found her phone again. This time she could text Alyssa. She'd been fifteen for a whole four months, and she knew lots about boys. She was also an expert in those flirting tips they'd pored over in *Seventeen* magazine.

Ty was the hottest guy Naomi had ever met. And meeting him was more exciting than Christmas, the last day of school, and Fourth of July fireworks rolled into one. She couldn't stop thinking about him. How he'd looked at her with those dreamy blue eyes. How he'd tossed her the Frisbee, then leaned in so close his warm breath brushed her cheek.

Alyssa would help Naomi figure out this thing with Ty. Figure it out so her mom and Auntie Charlotte wouldn't suspect a thing.

"Of course I'm listening to you." Two days later Charlie twirled the straw in her chocolate milk shake, as thick and creamy as the ones she remembered from when she and Sean used to stop by the North Woods Diner on Saturday night after a movie.

"No, you weren't." Mia's breath caught, and she glanced toward the diner exit. "I said there's no reason for us to stay here a whole month. Once the land survey's done, the Realtor says Tat Chee Properties will make us an offer. After we do some token negotiating, we sign the papers and the cottage is sold. Then we can be out of here."

"Just like that?"

Mia's chin jerked. "Mom's estate settled. For a small-town lawyer, Nick McGuire seems to know what he's doing."

Charlie picked up her vegetarian burger, then set it down again. Tucked into one of the diner's high, red-padded booths, the scarred wooden sides bearing the initials of several generations of Firefly Lake teenagers, she was co-cooned from the rest of the world. "I want to be out of here as much as you do, but let's not rush into anything."

"Why not?" Mia nibbled a piece of lettuce like an elegant rabbit. Immaculate in a white shift dress, her long dark hair caught in a twist at the back of her head, she still looked every inch the beauty queen she'd once been.

"Mom never wanted to let the cottage go." And although they were very different women, Charlie had loved her mom with all her heart. She pushed her plate away, half the burger and most of the fries untouched. "I think we should take our time and make sure it's the right decision."

"What other decision is there?" Mia's voice was flat. "The cottage is a shack, a waterfront shack, but still a shack. If I were that developer, I'd bulldoze it." She raised one groomed eyebrow. "Give me a place in Florida any day."

"You have a place in Florida." Charlie rolled the paper place mat between her fingers. If she and her sister were closer, they could talk openly instead of in this stilted way like polite strangers. But they hadn't been close in years.

"True." Mia gave a high-pitched laugh, and her perfect features were strained. "You're not worried about that petition, are you?" She picked up the yellow sheet Charlie had plucked from the stack on the diner's front counter. SAY NO TO RESORT DEVELOPMENT was splashed in thick black letters across the top. "People in small towns like this don't want change. Once they see the resort and the jobs it'll create, they'll support it fast enough."

"I'm not sure." Charlie read the sheet again. "Grassroots protests can be pretty powerful." Especially with someone like Sean behind it, someone who loved this place with every fiber of his being.

"Which you'd know all about." Mia dabbed at her mouth with a napkin. "You've been protesting things since the day you started to talk." Her voice softened. "I know the cottage always meant more to you than me, but you have to be sensible."

"Why? Did you ever think being sensible is overrated?" The one time she'd been sensible, she'd paid for it with a lifetime of heartbreak. Charlie finished her milk shake and shook her head at a petite waitress bearing down on her with a wedge of apple pie as big as a doorstop.

"Charlotte..." Mia paused as the waitress removed her plate and replaced it with a bowl of fruit salad. "You've been through a lot and maybe you're not thinking clearly. Selling the cottage is the best thing. There's nothing for either of us here."

Except memories. And regrets. Charlie bit back a sigh. Why had she let Sean kiss her the other day? If she'd stopped him, she could have kept on pretending her feelings for him were over years ago.

The instant his warm lips hovered over hers, she yielded, sucked in by a surge of desire so strong she hadn't been able to resist one sweet taste of him, then another. Before she knew it—and despite all her good intentions—she was sucked into the past again, the girl she'd once been, the choices she'd made. Choices she never thought of. Until now.

"Do you really think Mom would have wanted us to sell to Tat Chee?"

Mia wrinkled her perfect nose. "Mom would have done what Dad wanted. And Dad would have sold the place, no question." She levered a watermelon cube onto her fork. "Besides, where else are we going to get that kind of money?"

"I need money, sure, but it's not everything," Charlie said. At least it never had been here.

She looked out the diner window. Dusty pickup trucks with canoes on top were parked next to shiny city cars that belonged to the summer people and the New Vermonters—people from Boston and New York who came to the Northeast Kingdom for the natural scenery and slower pace of life.

People who didn't see her Vermont. The Vermont that was picking blueberries in the patch of tangled bushes behind the cottage. Catching fireflies in a cracked mason jar on summer nights when the moon bathed the dark hills in white light. And the sense of belonging and being at home in her skin Charlie had never found anywhere else.

"This isn't about Sean Carmichael, is it?" Mia's caramel eyes narrowed. "Why did my husband have to rent that canoe in the first place, let alone from Carmichael's?" She reached for Charlie's hand, her fingers cool. "Having Sean turn up on the doorstep our first day, it's no wonder you're all churned up."

"Of course it's not about Sean." Charlie pulled her hand away and bit the inside of her lip. "And I'm not all churned up. Jay wouldn't remember about Sean and me."

"I suppose not." Mia's expression was doubtful. "Besides, there probably isn't anywhere else to rent a canoe around here."

"It'll be fun for the girls." Charlie peeked around the corner of the booth. Her nieces leaned against the battered jukebox at the front of the diner. Naomi wore cute denim shorts and a teal halter top. Emma, a blond pixie in a pink sundress, tapped her feet to the beat of a country song about big-city blues.

"Charlotte?" She swiveled her head at Mia's voice. "Maybe coming back here was a mistake. Sometimes it's better not to go digging up the past." Mia raised a hand to signal the waitress for the check, and her diamond tennis bracelet slid up her slender forearm.

Letting Sean kiss her and kissing him back, that was a mistake that she regretted as soon as it happened. But coming back to the cottage? No. That wasn't a mistake. The cottage was where she felt closest to her mom, where she needed to come to truly say good-bye to her.

"Who said I was digging up the past?" Charlie got out her wallet from the buttermilk leather bag she'd tossed on the seat beside her and pulled out some bills.

"I didn't. I only meant..." Mia paused, and for an

instant the sister Charlie barely knew looked younger, vulnerable even, like the sister who'd bandaged Charlie's skinned knees when she'd fallen out of the tree behind the cottage and soothed away the pain with a story, cookies, and cuddles. "You're my little sister. When you got hurt, I wanted to come to you, but Jay had a big deal going on at work. He was in California and I couldn't leave the girls alone."

"I understand." Charlie pushed the bills across the table to her sister, then fumbled with her bag.

"Do you?" Mia looked at her empty water glass. "I was so scared I might lose you. As for you and Sean, the two of you were intense. Sometimes I worry you never really got over him and then Dad, after he loaned that money to Sean's dad, what he made you do—"

"Stop." Charlie glanced around. "That loan's always been a secret. As for Sean and me, it's over, done." In spite of, or maybe because of, that toe-curling kiss. "I'm not digging up anything. I'm letting go of the past. I need the money—that's what selling the cottage is about." She grabbed her bag and slid toward the end of the booth. "And you didn't lose me."

"I know." Mia fingered the clasp on her bracelet. "We're back here together, one last time. And we're doing the right thing. I'm sure of it. No matter what anybody around here thinks."

Halfway out of the booth, Charlie stopped, catching something in Mia's eyes. "Is everything okay with you and Jay?"

"Of course." Mia's laugh tinkled out. "He works a lot. You don't get to be vice president of sales for a Fortune Global five hundred without working pretty much twenty-four/seven." She dug into her clutch purse, not meeting Charlie's eyes.

"You'd tell me if you ever needed help with the girls or anything, right?" Charlie searched Mia's face. Something about her sister's expression troubled her and made her wonder what Mia wasn't telling her. "I…" She stopped. She couldn't ask her sister outright because she didn't see Mia often enough to talk about anything beyond the superficial.

"The girls and I are fine." Mia's phone rang. "Wait a second. It's Jay." She plucked the phone out of her purse and waved Charlie into her seat. "Don't go."

Charlie slid back into the booth as her sister greeted her husband.

"What?" Mia's voice sharpened. "You promised Naomi. And me."

Charlie studied her sister's oval face. Her bow-shaped mouth pursed as she frowned.

"No, I'm not telling Naomi. You have to tell her yourself." Mia glanced at Charlie, her brown eyes like flints. "Not tomorrow, today. Call back in ten minutes and I'll make sure Naomi can talk to you. In the meantime, think about how you'll tell her." She clicked off without saying good-bye.

"What is it?" Charlie gulped at the pain on her sister's face.

"Jay has to go to Dubai for work. He's not coming here for Naomi's birthday." Mia swallowed hard.

"No." Charlie put a hand to her mouth. "I'm so sorry."

"Life happens." Mia's face was wan. "But Naomi…I'm not telling her. Jay has to do it."

Charlie reached across the table and patted Mia's hand,

still clenched tight around the phone. "We'll make it up to Naomi. I'll help you."

"Thank you." Mia's voice cracked. "Jay's calling back in ten minutes, and I already promised Emma she could buy candy at that store across the street. Can you meet us at the car in half an hour?" The black BMW Mia had rented in Burlington was sleek and elegant. Just like her.

"Are you okay?" Charlie took a deep breath.

"Fine. It's not the first time..." Mia stopped and again dug in her purse. "I must have left it at the law office."

Charlie slung her bag over one shoulder. "Left what?"

"The pen Jay gave me for Christmas. Gold, engraved with my initials." Mia's expression turned hopeful. "If it's not too far for you to walk, could you go back for it?"

"Of course." Today was one of Charlie's good days. A pain-free day when she could almost pretend the accident hadn't happened. "But you—"

"I said I'm fine." Mia bit her bottom lip.

With one last look at her sister, Charlie made her way out of the diner, its air-conditioned coolness giving way to the heat of the day.

The squat, white clapboard diner anchored one end of Main Street, a tidy thoroughfare lined with old brick buildings and bisected by a pocket-sized village green. Pots of summer flowers brightened the sidewalk in front of each business. Mom-and-Pop businesses, which sons and daughters took over from their parents, generation after generation. Charlie turned right and headed up Main toward the park, the lake sparkling blue in the distance.

Mia hadn't lost her, at least not in the way she'd meant. But after seeing Sean again, Charlie understood with frightening clarity that somewhere along the way she'd lost herself. Lost the girl she'd once been.

The girl who couldn't wait to come here every summer and who'd ticked off the months on the calendar until it was June again. The girl who'd bounced on the backseat of the car in excitement and counted the familiar landmarks, each one bringing her closer to the lake, closer to Sean.

The girl who stood up for what she believed in no matter what.

And the girl who'd loved Sean Carmichael with all her heart and couldn't imagine a future without him in it.

Sean had driven the curving highway that edged Firefly Lake hundreds, maybe even thousands of times. But each time he hit the flat stretch where it narrowed into Lake Road, the town of Firefly Lake sheltered in the scoop of the lake the first settlers had called a harbor, his grip on the wheel relaxed and warmth flooded his chest. This was home. The place he was meant to be.

The place where four generations of his family slept in the graveyard nestled at the foot of the hill. Where he'd gone in and out of friends' houses like they were his own. And where people still looked out for each other, and a man's word was his bond.

He eased his foot off the accelerator and the green, vintage MG convertible he'd spent two years restoring slowed. Cruising by the sign that said WELCOME TO FIRE-FLY LAKE, POPULATION 2500, HOMETOWN OF NHL ALL-STAR LUC SIMARD, he turned right into Main Street. It divided the town in half and ran in a straight line from the lakeshore and Old Harbor Park at one end to the railroad tracks at the other.

Idling behind an SUV with a Quebec license plate, towing a sailboat, Sean tapped his fingers to a Lady Antebellum song on the radio and glanced at the park. A white-painted bandstand sat in the middle, and at the far end, beyond the tennis courts, playground, and kiddie pool, sat the Firefly Lake Marina, a clutch of buildings that hugged the lakeshore.

As far back as he could remember, his dad had owned the small marina outside town, which handled canoe and motorboat rentals. Buying the business in town six months earlier had given Carmichael's access to sailboat and cabin-cruiser people who had serious money to spend.

After the SUV turned off to the marina, Sean continued along Main Street, past Mario's Pizza, Tremblay & Sons Plumbing and Heating, the Firefly Lake Craft Gallery, the Daily Bread Bakery, and Len's Hardware. He slid the MG into an empty parking space between the Cozy Corner Craft Shoppe and McGuire and Pelletier's law office and cut the engine.

Halfway out of the car, a prickle of awareness slid through him. The door of the law office swung open and Charlie came out. In a blue T-shirt and white pants, she was all lush curves and sweet femininity. And she tempted him in a way he hadn't been tempted in a very long time.

"Charlotte." His voice was tight as he forced himself to use her new name. The name that felt wrong on his lips for the woman who, despite all logic, still tugged at the deepest part of him and chipped at the barriers he'd put up around his heart.

"Sean." She pulled the sunglasses on top of her head onto the bridge of her nose, hiding her eyes.

She looked cool and fresh, but with a sexy twist that

made Sean remember how her mouth had opened under his and she'd melted into him, the heat in the kiss they'd shared and how, with only a single honeyed taste of her mouth, the same almost-out-of-control desire had sparked between them.

Which meant he'd wanted to go farther, to slide a hand beneath her shirt and touch her soft skin. Swing her into his arms and take her back into the woods like he had so many times before.

No, he was an adult. He wanted to take her back to his big, empty bed and make love to her until he got the wanting her out of his system once and for all. But she'd pulled away and stopped him from making an even bigger fool of himself.

He slammed the car door. "What are you up to?"

She gave him a tentative smile. "Running some errands."

"McGuire and Pelletier are handling the legal side of the cottage sale?"

"They're still the only attorneys in town." She shifted, and rested her weight on her right side. "I see somebody started a petition." She pulled Trevor's flyer off one of the wrought-iron lampposts the town had installed at intervals along Main Street, a nod to Firefly Lake's nineteenth-century heritage.

"So?" He eyeballed her. "You always talked about power to the people."

Charlie tilted her head to one side, the way she used to when she was getting ready to argue with him. "There's the Inn on the Lake, lots of bed-and-breakfasts, the motel out by the highway. What difference does one more place make?" She pushed her hair away from her face, distracting Sean with the sweet curve of her jaw and luscious outline of her lips. "It's the summer people who keep a town like Firefly Lake alive."

Sean clenched his jaw and forced himself to ignore the kissable dent in her chin. "That *one more place*, as you put it, is one too many. It's the people who live here all year, the true Vermonters, who give Firefly Lake its heart and soul."

"The fact that this resort would be next to Carmichael's doesn't have anything to do with it?" Charlie pulled off her sunglasses. "That's the real reason you don't want the development, isn't it? If the resort was going to be built somewhere else, you wouldn't bother with petitions." She crumpled the flyer and tossed it into a nearby trash can.

"That developer isn't putting in a marina?" Sean stared her down.

"They're still working on the plans." Charlie stared back, unflinching. She'd never been a girl who backed away.

"I have a business to run and I can't..." The hairs on the back of Sean's neck raised and he turned. His mom and Trevor's wife hovered in front of the Cozy Corner Craft Shoppe, next door to the law office. His sister-in-law gave him a slow smile, and his mom pushed her glasses up her nose.

"Sean?" His mom reached his side in three brisk strides. "With Charlie?" His mom was seventy-two, her once-blond hair silver, her gait slower, but she still didn't miss much. For an instant, Sean was a kid again, caught sneaking a cookie before dinner.

"Mrs. Carmichael." Charlie pasted a bright smile on her face. The smile she'd always used to hide what she thought and felt. She clasped his mom's hand and leaned in to kiss her.

His mom kissed Charlie back, a stiff grazing of cheeks. "You remember Linnie?" She turned to the redhead at her side.

"Sure I do." Charlie's expression softened, and there was a warmth in her voice that hadn't been there before. "Linnie and I were partners in crime way back."

"Holy terrors is more like it. Your mothers used to despair over what the two of you got up to." His mom darted another glance at Linnie. "Linnie settled right down, though, and she and Trevor have been married going on nineteen years."

"It's great to see you again." Charlie hugged Linnie.

"You too." Linnie returned the hug. "It's been a real long time. Too long."

"Yeah." Charlie stepped away. "I'm sorry—I meant to keep in touch, but..." She stopped and fingered the tiny gold heart on the chain around her neck.

"Well, you're here now. Maybe we should ring a few doorbells and run for old times' sake." Linnie's voice was amused.

"What are you two doing here?" Although Sean loved Firefly Lake, at times like this he wished it were a bit bigger and a lot more anonymous.

"It's Wednesday," his mom said. "You know I have craft and chat on Wednesdays." She pointed to the craft shop, where colorful balls of yarn were piled high in the front window. "Linnie led a quilting demonstration this week." She turned to Charlie. "She made two quilts last winter. Even though she has four girls to look after and a part-time job."

"Linnie, you always were good at crafts." Charlie chuckled. "Remember when I tore my jeans climbing out the window of the shed behind your folks' place? You sewed them up so neatly, my mom never noticed."

Linnie's smile was crooked. "If I wasn't getting into trouble with you, I was getting you out of it."

"Now you're a quilter. That must be relaxing."

To Sean's surprise, Charlie sounded like she meant it.

"It is." Linnie's hazel eyes glowed. "I'm working on a double wedding ring pattern. That one's complicated, but if you're here for a while, I could get you started on a pillow cover or a small wall picture. It'd be fun and we…"

Sean shot her a warning glance and Linnie stopped. Her face reddened, and she looked at her sandals.

"I was sorry to hear about your mother," his mom said. "I never see that cottage without thinking of her sitting on the porch or playing her piano, you and your sister singing along. Beatrice sure loved it here."

"Yeah, she did." Charlie's eyes were two dark pools of pain, and her jaw twitched, the nervous tic Sean remembered from when she was a kid.

"Your grandfather McKellar built that place. He was a banker in Montreal and he had money enough. He could have hired somebody, but no, he wanted to do it for his family. Every board, every nail that went into it was put there by Andrew McKellar's hands." His mom's lips tightened. "I hope you and Mia know what you're doing, all those big plans I hear the two of you have."

"Mom." Sean flicked a glance at Charlie, who'd grabbed the lamppost and held on like her life depended on it.

"I'm not saying anything different from what other folks are saying. People around here respect tradition, community, and family." In her pink blouse and white skirt, his mom looked as fragile as one of the china figurines she'd collected since she was a girl. But the set to her jaw and edge in her voice belied that fragility. "Neighborliness is a way of life in the Kingdom, and for all he wasn't born and raised here, Charlie's grandfather knew that."

And his descendants didn't. Or they'd forgotten and it was his mom's duty to remind them.

Sean glanced at Charlie again. Her face grew whiter by the second, her dark eyelashes and brows standing out in stark contrast. An old, almost-forgotten urge to protect her, to help her, vied with the need to keep his distance. "Everyone's wondering what will happen with the Gibbs cottage, Mom, but there's no need to get personal."

His mom's shoulders slumped, hurt flashed in her blue eyes, and the lines between her nose and mouth deepened. "No offense intended."

Charlie wet her lips with her tongue, the sensual gesture sending heat straight to Sean's groin. "None taken."

"Ready to go, Ellen?" Linnie's eyes met Sean's gaze in wordless sympathy before she took his mom's arm in a firm grip. "See you around, Charlie." She shepherded his mom along Main Street toward the bakery, since his mom always stopped at the Daily Bread for cinnamon buns after craft and chat.

Sean let out the breath he hadn't realized he'd been holding. Charlie had destroyed his trust and turned his world upside down. Now she could change the place he loved and his family's livelihood.

Change him too, because painful as it was to admit, she'd already gotten under his skin.

So he'd stood up for her against his mom, caved as soon as Charlie got that vulnerable look on her face, the look he could never resist.

Chapter Four

"Y our mom hasn't changed much," Charlie said in that clipped voice Sean couldn't connect with her. The Charlotte voice spoke of the person she'd become, all the places she'd seen. How far away from Firefly Lake she'd gone. She shoved her sunglasses back onto the bridge of her nose.

"She loved your mom. They were friends, way back." Until their friendship had ended without him ever knowing why. No more phone calls or visits on the front porch, no more Christmas cards even. Beatrice Gibbs had disappeared from his mom's life like Charlie had disappeared from his.

He exhaled, anger with his mother coupled with anger at himself. The Gibbs cottage was personal. What had possessed him to go out on a limb for Charlie?

She gave him a sad smile. "Talking about Mom gets to me. I still...I can't believe she's gone."

Despite his anger, Sean's heart clenched at the pain in

her face. "I feel the same way about my dad." The loss that caught him when he least expected and tore his guts out. Which meant he still hadn't gone through all his dad's files or old handwritten invoices.

"It's tough." Her voice was soft.

"I liked your mom. For all she was quiet, she was smart and funny and she sure loved her music. And she was real stylish. Mom and my sisters always talked about her clothes. She looked like she stepped out of some fashion magazine, that's what they said."

"Mom liked you too." Charlie surprised him. She gestured to his tennis whites. "I better get going and leave you to your game."

"Going where?"

"I'm meeting Mia and her girls at the car over by the park." She tugged on her shoulder bag and pulled out a key ring, which drew Sean's attention to the enticing swell of her breasts. Breasts that had fit into his hands like they belonged there. "Playing tennis with anybody I might know?"

"Nick McGuire."

"The lawyer?" She swiveled to the law office, gold letters across the front window.

"The same. He came back from New York City last winter."

"The two of you are friends?"

"Sure. We play hockey in the winter and tennis in the summer." He grinned. "I kick his ass most of the time."

"You and Nick were never friends before. He—"

"Lived in one of the big houses on the hill. Graduated from Yale Law School and one of his sisters went to Harvard." Sean's phone vibrated and he dug in the pocket of his shorts, pulling it out.

"I'm not judging you. It never mattered to me where you lived or what your dad did for a living."

"It mattered to your dad, though, didn't it? It mattered I lived on the mill side of town, my family built boats, and none of us were headed for college, let alone the Ivy League." His tone was harsher than he'd intended. Dr. Gibbs was dead. He couldn't look down on Sean ever again. And Sean wasn't still the boat guy and golf caddie Dr. Gibbs had ordered around.

Charlie stood there and fiddled with her keys as he read the text from Nick apologizing for having to bail on their tennis match.

"I'm proud of Carmichael's, I always was, and I wanted to make a success of it. But your dad would have been thrilled if you'd hung around with a guy like Nick instead of me."

"I doubt it." Her smile teased him. "Nick's two years older than us. If he'd been hanging around anyone, it would have been Mia. His family had money, sure, but whether he deserved it or not, he had that bad-boy reputation. You remember that motorcycle of his? Mia says she doesn't, but I do."

Despite himself, Sean laughed. "You said my mom hasn't changed, but from the sounds of it, Mia hasn't changed much either."

Charlie laughed too, throaty, sexy, and endearing. "She hasn't." Her gaze locked with his and, despite her dark glasses, something sparked between them. Something hot and elemental that stripped away the years, the hurt, and the betrayal to leave Sean's heart raw and exposed.

"Listen." He hesitated, his usual cool logic battling with something else, that reckless something Charlie had always stirred in him. "Nick is standing me up. Some crisis with a client." His blood pounded in his ears. "I've booked a court and it would be a shame to let it go to waste. You want to play some tennis?"

"Tennis?" She jerked back.

He stepped forward and narrowed the space between them again. "You were an ace tennis player. Since you seem set on forgetting everything about this place, I think it's time you remembered. Don't you?" He paused, quirked an eyebrow, and tried to hide a grin before he went for the kill. "Unless you're afraid of a little competition."

"Competition?" Charlie's voice hummed along Sean's nerve ends, and the wind caught her hair and whipped it across her face. With the chocolate-brown tendrils brushing her jaw, she looked more like the girl he remembered. The one who'd starred in all his teenage fantasies; the one he was still aware of in a way he'd never been aware of any other woman.

"Only for fun." Sean damped down the tug of desire. "Seeing as you're not dressed for tennis."

"These are yoga pants. They're fine for tennis." A smile tugged at the corners of her mouth. "My shoes are tennis shoes." She paused. "But like I told you, I'm meeting Mia and the girls."

"The courts are still over by the parking lot in Old Harbor Park. Besides, your sister was never on time for anything." He waited, his heart pounding. In business he'd learned it didn't pay to rush, not if you wanted to close the deal.

Sure, they weren't on the same side about the cottage, but he felt bad about what had happened to her. There was also that connection between them. It defied logic but made him want to spend time with her, maybe have some fun.

"I can't run around a tennis court. Not yet." Her smile disappeared. "At least not like I used to."

"Aw, Charlie." He winced with what the admission cost her. "Are you up to volleying, then? Best of five." He looked at her sideways. "I'll do most of the work. You used to like that fine."

She flushed pink, as sweet and innocent as the seventeen-year-old he'd known. Back when it had been her first time and his too. "No need to go easy on me." She gave him the cocky grin that always hid the vulnerable girl beneath. "You have a spare racket?"

"Sure do." He moved to the MG and grabbed his tennis bag from the back. "A sun visor as well." He tossed it to her and she caught it one-handed.

"You want to take the shortcut?" Charlie fell into step beside him.

They rounded the corner beside the craft shop and followed the narrow path behind Main Street to cut across lots toward the park.

He remembered all the times he and Charlie walked this way together. Times when there weren't memories and mistakes and hurting piled between them. The times he'd held her hand and snuck a kiss when they got to the alley between the movie theater and Simard Creamery.

He glanced her way, her head level with his shoulder, face shadowed by the brim of his visor. And for a crazy moment, Sean wondered what might have been. What if they'd stuck it out? What if she'd settled down here and they'd made a family together?

He tightened his grip on the tennis bag, glad Charlie

didn't seem any more inclined to talk than him. They came out of the alley and crossed the street to the courts on the edge of the park. Red, white, and blue petunias out front banked three rows deep.

"You can still change your mind." He pushed open the gate to the court he'd reserved and let her go ahead of him. He wouldn't think about kisses past or present, quick or hot. Or the way those pants outlined her curvy butt. Who'd have thought yoga pants could be both functional and sexy?

She slid her sunglasses into her purse and left it by the gate. "Not a chance. I'll even let you serve first."

Sean took his racket, handed her the spare one, and grabbed a tennis ball, then jogged to the other side of the net. Guilt clashed with desire. Maybe Charlie wasn't up to this. Maybe he'd pushed her too hard.

Then she swung the racket and eyed him like she used to, looking for his weak spots. She was up for this all right. "What are we playing for?"

Sean gulped. When he and Charlie had played tennis, they always played for stakes, and he'd usually get her naked. "You choose first."

She balanced the edge of the racket on the sunbaked court. "If I win, you get whoever started that petition to back off."

"You, of all people, should know I can't do that."

"You didn't start it?" She raised the racket and eased her legs apart. When she leaned forward, he caught a tantalizing glimpse of the sweet slope of her cleavage.

"No." Sean bounced the ball once, twice.

"You know who did." She bent her knees, those pants hugging the mouthwatering curve of her hips.

He looked into the endless blue of the sky where an aircraft had left a thin white trail.

"Okay." She jogged on the spot, her pert breasts bouncing like twin flags waving him over. "If I win, you'll back off about us selling the cottage. Maybe you can't do anything about certain members of your family." She gave him a stern look over the net. "But you personally will back off."

"If I win, you'll tell me the truth about why you're so keen to sell the cottage to a developer." He flexed his arm, ready to serve. "From what I hear, not a local outfit either."

She hesitated. "Deal." She moved into position. "Whenever you're ready."

Sean sent the ball over the net in a slow, gentle arc. It bounced once before Charlie returned the serve, nice and easy.

Sean hit the ball back to her, still keeping the pace slow. Again she returned it, just as slow. Sean's racket connected with the ball as he put some weight into it. Charlie whacked it back with a cute little hip wiggle that cranked his lust up another notch. The ball skimmed the top of the net.

"You okay?" He dragged his gaze away from her hips and then her breasts and, with a wiggle of his own, sent the ball back to her.

"Why wouldn't I be?" Again she returned it. "I was the Inn on the Lake girls' tennis champion six years in a row. Remember?" She eyed him over the racket, and then her tongue darted between her teeth to moisten her lips.

"Old news, Gibbs." Sean copied her sensual gesture and her eyes widened. Then he gave her a bland smile and got into the rhythm of the volley.

He reached over his head to hit the ball, sending it high.

He clocked Charlie tracking the distance. He had her. The ball was going wide.

Before Sean registered how she'd done it, the ball shot back toward him. A yellow missile headed straight for his crotch. He jumped to one side and the ball bounced out of bounds.

"One nothing, my serve." Charlie's voice had a throaty, teasing note, but despite her naughty grin, her eyes had a steely glint. Perhaps the old Charlie was still there beneath the veneer of Charlotte. "Unless you've had enough? Maybe my last shot was too much for you? You're older than me."

She stopped, her racket raised in midair, the ball in her right hand. She was left-handed and always used it to her advantage.

"Older and better, Gibbs." Sean flexed his shoulder muscles and waited for the serve.

Charlie had a strong serve, but she had a weak backhand. Which he'd always used to his advantage.

By the time the score was tied at four, Sean's shirt was soaked, his hair plastered to his head, the tendons in his right arm on fire. Charlie's white pants were streaked with dirt and her top clung to her breasts, her bra outlined beneath. It was a sight he'd have appreciated more if his lungs weren't about to burst from his chest.

"Ready to call it?" Poised to serve, Charlie spoke in a breathy whoosh. And it was Charlie's voice, low and as sexy as whipped cream on hot cocoa, not the voice of the unknown Charlotte.

"Did I ever call a game?" Sean crouched, ready to hit the ball back.

She shook her head and served another blistering shot

across to him. The kind of shot the kids she'd played against in tournaments used to dread. But Sean was ready, and he grunted as his racket connected with the ball.

"Charlotte, what are you doing?"

Charlie swiveled and the ball bounced past her.

Mia Gibbs stood on the other side of the chain-link fence. A couple of inches taller than Charlie, her white dress unwrinkled, her dark hair covered by a wide-brimmed straw hat, Mia looked a lot like she had eighteen years ago. Still a mirror image of Beatrice Gibbs. Beside her, Naomi held the hand of a cute little blond girl.

"Playing tennis." Charlie dropped the racket. "And you made me lose."

As Sean walked around the net, Mia shot him a wary glance. "Sean?"

"Mia." He inclined his head. He'd never had much to do with Charlie's big sister. She'd kept herself apart from the locals and stuck close to the cottage and her mom.

Mia turned back to Charlie, and her expression softened into one that was almost pleading. "You should be taking things easy, honey."

"Who said?" Charlie stuck her chin out, pulled at her shirt, and peeled it away from her skin. "My doctor said I could do what I want, within reason."

Mia put an arm around Charlie and Sean caught his breath. Mia's brown eyes were warm and loving, and her beautiful face wore an uncertain expression. Had he been wrong about her years ago? His sisters had called Mia stuck up, but maybe she was shy and, in her own way, as vulnerable as Charlie.

"Tennis, your leg, and you and Sean were…" Mia stopped and pressed her lips together.

"I'm tired of sitting around like some invalid." Charlie handed Sean the sun visor. "I wanted to play tennis, and I'm fine. Besides, it wasn't even a real game."

"Hi, Mr. Carmichael," Naomi said in that sweet Texas drawl. Her brown eyes shone like a hopeful puppy.

"Hi." He swallowed a sigh. She'd come by the marina a couple of times in the last few days looking for Ty. Although Sean couldn't prove it, he suspected his son had been dropping by the Gibbs cottage.

"This is my little sister, Emma." She patted the girl's shoulder.

He crouched to the smaller girl's level to say hi and Emma grinned. Freckles dusted her button nose.

"You won, Sean, fair and square. I'll keep my part of the bet." Her voice got tight.

He looked up, but the expression in Charlie's eyes was unreadable.

"What bet?" Mia shepherded her daughters toward the black BMW. The kind of car that stood out in Firefly Lake, even in summer.

"Nothing. I'll be with you in a minute." Charlie pushed her hair back behind her ears; sweat-dampened strands clung to her neck. "Thanks for the game. It reminded me..." Her breath hitched.

"Of what?"

"Forget it." Her expression turned wistful and her eyes grew sad.

"Honey?" Mia said. "We should get back to the cottage. The Realtor and land surveyor are coming by again this afternoon."

"I have to go." Charlie handed Sean his racket.

Of course she did. In the end, Charlie always did what

her family wanted. Why did one game of tennis, that wasn't even a game of tennis, make him think this time could be any different?

Over by the park, Charlie got into the car beside Mia, while Naomi and Emma scrambled into the back. She turned and, for a brief instant, her gaze caught his before she looked away.

Sean rubbed his chest. He should have left well enough alone. In making Charlie remember how she used to be, how they used to be together, he'd made himself remember everything he'd once felt for her. If he wasn't careful, what he could feel for her again.

He grabbed his tennis bag and left the court, slamming the gate so hard behind him the fence rattled.

Despite everything, spending time with Charlie still made his heart beat faster. One look from her chocolate-brown eyes still had him thinking about wanting her, having her.

He pulled a water bottle from his bag and drained it as he followed the path back to the car. He was older, smarter, and his priorities were different. Stopping the cottage redevelopment for a start. That was business.

And when it came to business, Sean prided himself on always knowing what and who he was dealing with.

Her aching muscles would heal. If only Charlie were as sure about her aching heart. She shifted on the couch and rested her head against the cottage's mellow pine wall. Twenty-four hours after that tennis game with Sean, she'd rediscovered muscles she'd forgotten existed. Feelings she'd gotten good at forgetting existed too.

"You said we own the wooded lot?" In her black

trousers, red silk top, and kitten heels, Mia looked like an exotic bird that had flown off course and ended up beside Charlie by accident.

Charlie jackknifed upright, and her leg and every other part of her body protested.

"Yes. You also own the wooded lot." In front of the fireplace, Nick McGuire sat in the oak armchair that had belonged to Charlie's dad. Nick's blue shirt, the same color as his eyes, was open at the neck, and he wore a pair of sand chinos. "You own an extra hundred feet of lakeshore too, because the woodlot borders the lake."

The woodlot between the Gibbs cottage and Carmichael's place. Memories Charlie had made herself forget reared up to choke her. She and Sean had built forts there and used fallen branches to make secret hideouts. They'd pretended they were explorers in search of buried treasure. When they were older, they made love under the big maple tree, and sunlight had filtered through its canopy of leaves, dappling Sean's strong body, slick against hers.

"That can't be right." Charlie picked up her glass and sipped iced tea. "The woodlot is state forest land."

"We checked the records. Twice." Nick cleared his throat. "The new survey is correct. The state land is on the other side of the road."

"If we've got more land, we should get more money for the cottage." Mia waved her hand, and her diamond engagement ring sparkled in the light that streamed through the living room windows, open to catch the afternoon breeze off the lake. The ring that symbolized the gaping void between her sister's life and hers. The husband, family, and home Charlie didn't have. "If Tat Chee Properties still wants to buy the cottage," Mia added.

"They still want to buy it all right. I've already had Brent Michaud, your Realtor, in my office." Nick drummed his fingers on the file folder on his knees. "The Tat Chee team's coming up from Boston tomorrow, and Brent said he'd bring them over around noon. Tat Chee wants more land here. Now they've got the option to get some."

"Mom and Dad never told us." Charlie pinned Nick with the look she used sometimes in interviews. The look that most of the time got even reluctant people to talk. "All the years we came here, everybody said the woodlot was state forest land and couldn't be developed."

"Your father might not have known." Nick's gaze slid to her mom's piano, which hugged the wall opposite the couch. "This property was always solely in your mother's name. Your grandfather left it to her. I've seen a copy of his will."

"You can't be serious." Mia's laugh was brittle, and Charlie's head snapped around. She sucked in a breath at the fear and hurt on her sister's face, wan despite the skill-ful makeup. "Mom never said a word and she, we . . . were close."

"I am serious," Nick said.

"And?" Charlie searched Nick's face, strong features framed by short, dark hair.

Nick looked from Charlie to Mia and then back to Char-lie. "There by the lake, the property line between your place and Carmichael's runs within ten feet of Carmichael's workshop."

Mia shrugged, elegant as always, but her shoulders were tight and her mouth was pinched. "It's only a lot of forest."

Charlie fisted her hands to stop them trembling.

"Brent didn't know the details, but if they can get ahold

of more land, Tat Chee's considering a much bigger operation. Maybe even a full-service marina." Nick looked down at his empty tea glass. "It's only a guess, but Tat Chee might want to develop right to Carmichael's. Maybe make an offer to buy Carmichael's place, at least the workshop and marina portion along the lake. That lot's an odd shape. By Sean's house the property line's farther away."

"Does Sean know?" Charlie forced the words out.

"Not yet." Nick shifted in the chair and didn't meet Charlie's gaze. "You're my clients. It's your property. I had an obligation to tell you first."

Mia refilled Nick's glass from the pitcher on the coffee table, her hand shaking. "You've told us, so we can all move on." She set the pitcher down with a *thud*. "In the long run, Sean and his family might even benefit." Her voice hitched.

Charlie turned to her sister. Mia's face wasn't only pale. It was as blank as a doll's and her eyes were empty. "You know how much Carmichael's means to Sean. His grandfather and his dad built that business. He'd never sell it."

"If Dad were still alive, he wouldn't worry about sentiment." Mia twirled her engagement ring, which was loose on her finger.

"Mom would have worried because Mrs. Carmichael was her friend." Charlie's chest got tight.

"Mom's gone, and she and Mrs. Carmichael fell out years ago." Mia's voice was devoid of emotion. "It's up to you and me to do what's best for our futures."

She *was* thinking about her future. Except, in only a few days, the future had gotten tangled in her past. Charlie glanced at Nick. "Can you wait until after Tat Chee visits before you tell Sean? So we have a better idea of what they intend, if the marina story is true."

"I'll try, but you must remember what Firefly Lake's like. News gets around fast." Nick studied his shoes. "Sean's a buddy of mine. I'm close to a conflict of interest here."

"As you said, we're your clients." Mia's smile was as sweet as honey, and her eyes were bright. Too bright. "Charlotte and I are sisters. We'll work this out."

"Absolutely." Charlie flashed Mia a smile almost as sweet and twice as fake. "Mom left this property to both of us, which means one of us can't sell unless the other agrees."

"But we're on the same side, aren't we?" Mia reached for Charlie's hand and squeezed it.

Charlie squeezed Mia's hand back, hard. "Family is family." Although she and Mia might disagree in private, her loyalty would always be to her sister, not Sean.

Chapter Five

Charlie shook a blanket across a smooth patch of sand in front of the cottage and weighted the corners with stones. She knelt beside the fire pit and stacked the kindling and wood she'd gathered from the pile out back. The sun nudged the hills on the other side of the lake and stained the western sky pink.

"Charlie?"

Sean's voice was deep and comforting, like a fleece blanket on a winter night. "Hi." She rocked back on her heels, conscious of her windblown hair and the JOURNAL-ISTS FOR HUMAN RIGHTS sweatshirt she'd paired with the sweats that didn't rub against her scar. "Come to collect on our bet?" She kept her voice light.

"I wanted to make sure you were okay. We gave each other quite a workout yesterday." Sean crouched beside her. He wore a pair of faded Levi's with a blue T-shirt the same color as his eyes, CANOE WHITE WATER in black let-ters across his broad chest.

Her throat got tight. He'd thought about her, worried about her even. "Apart from some sore muscles, I'm fine."

She'd never admit how the pain in her leg had kept her awake most of the previous night. She'd sat at the window of her old room as the sky changed from dark to light, thinking about Sean, about what it would mean to sell the cottage to Tat Chee. Thinking about Mia, and how she could bridge the distance between her and her sister to ask Mia what was wrong. Thinking about her mom and how she'd never really known the woman who'd given her life. And thinking about her job. She'd always loved her work, so why did it seem like it no longer fit? But if she told anyone about her doubts, she wouldn't fit in the one place she'd always truly belonged.

Her thoughts had dipped and whirled like a flock of sparrows, the pain in her heart worse than the pain in her leg.

"Ty said Mia and the girls went to the band concert in town." Sean pulled a handful of kindling into a small ball.

"They needed time on their own." She'd needed time away from them too; she'd never been good at family togetherness.

"You're still some tennis player." Sean's teeth flashed white in the growing darkness.

"So are you." She used a handful of sticks to make a tepee around the kindling. The kiss and then the tennis game had changed things between them. As much as she wanted to pretend Sean meant nothing to her, she couldn't ignore the truth. She was still as attracted to him as ever, but that didn't mean she'd act on it.

"Here, let me." Sean arranged larger pieces of wood around the sticks, building the campfire the way he'd taught her long ago.

Charlie fumbled for the box of matches, lit one, and touched it to the kindling, sparks shooting into the summer night. "About that bet, like I said, you won fair and square."

"I did." Sean sat beside her on the blanket and stretched his long legs in front of him. "So are you going to tell me why you're really selling to that Tat Chee Group?"

"Tat Chee Properties."

"Tat Chee Group's the parent company. Headquarters are in Hong Kong with offices in London, San Francisco, and Vancouver." Sean was dispassionate. "As well as a small office in Boston."

"You've done your homework." Charlie shifted her legs away from his and drew in a shaky breath. "I know you don't want us to sell to them, but with the economy the way it is, even if we found another buyer, they wouldn't offer us what Tat Chee will."

Sean was silent for a long moment. "I can't believe it's only about the money. The girl I remember loved this place more than anywhere else. She'd never have sold her birthright to the highest bidder."

"That girl's gone." She crossed her arms over her chest. "The accident changed me. It could have been me who died by the side of that road. But it wasn't, and I've got a second chance. As for the money, I have medical bills. Insurance didn't cover some of the extras."

And you're responsible for yourself, said her inner voice. *You don't have anyone else you can count on. And your career is all you have, so what will you do if you can't go back into the field like you did before?*

Or ever. She pushed that thought away. She was going back to work in just over three weeks. As Max, her editor, kept reminding her on his weekly calls.

Max said the calls were because they were friends. However, Charlie suspected they were really because Max wanted reassurance she was the same journalist she'd always been, willing to risk everything to get a story.

"Apart from the medical costs, the money will give me options to move on, start over." Even though the cottage was the closest she'd ever had to a home, it kept her stuck in the past. Kept her wanting things she had to let go—the things Mia had. A real home with a husband and family.

"That's what you said when you broke up with me." Sean's voice was harsh. "You needed to start over, move on."

His words ripped through her, the pain as fresh as on that cool August night she'd told him she was leaving. When, with each word that had come out of her mouth, she'd known she was hurting him, believing whichever choice she made she'd lose him anyway.

"Don't. We were kids. Your life was here. It's still here. My life wasn't." Her heart swelled even as her stomach churned.

"That had never been an issue before. It's not like you ever lived in Firefly Lake year-round. Why then? Why did you say you needed to move on? Less than twenty-four hours earlier you said you loved me. You kissed me good night, the same as always." The pain he'd buried still lurked in the blue depths of Sean's eyes. Pain she'd put there.

"I did love you." Her voice rasped and her chest heaved. Between that last good-night kiss and the next day when her dad had ordered her to find Sean and tell him it was over, her whole world had changed.

"Why should I believe you?"

"I'm telling you the truth." Despite the warmth of the fire, she shivered and her body crumpled inward. "But I'd just turned eighteen. We were headed in different directions. I was going to college. You were never going to leave here and I...I couldn't stay."

"Okay." He let out a breath. "I accept we were young. Maybe we'd have broken up anyway, but the way you handled it. That's what I don't get, and I can't forgive or forget. I trusted you."

And she'd betrayed him. Charlie's head spun and spots flashed behind her eyes. "I did what I had to do." For him, even more than for her.

"Was there someone else?" Sean's voice was rough.

"No." Her eyes watered, and she blinked away hot tears. The irony wasn't lost on her. She'd never had kids or fallen in love again after she left Sean. She'd never let any other man see into her heart or touch her soul. She'd never let herself trust.

"Then why?"

Charlie's heart pounded. There it was. The opening she needed. Part of moving on, part of her second chance at life, was putting right the past, and she owed Sean the truth. She pressed a hand to her throat to hold back a whimper. Her stomach hardened, and time slowed so it almost seemed to stop.

Beyond the circle of firelight, water lapped against the dock, and still Sean studied her. In his expression, there was hurt, anger, and, most of all, distrust.

Her lungs constricted until it was hard to breathe. "When I left, I was eight weeks' pregnant. With your baby."

* * *

Charlie's words hit Sean like a kick to his solar plexus, winding him. He tried to work moisture into his dry mouth. "Why didn't you tell me?" Fury rolled over him in a wave. She'd broken his trust, but he'd never imagined deception of this magnitude.

"I was scared." Her voice was small and she scrubbed a hand across her face. "Then in a few weeks, it didn't matter."

"You lost the baby?" Sadness mixed with his anger, the same gut-wrenching sadness reflected in her eyes.

"Not lost." She wheezed as she sucked in air. "When you lose something, you can try to find it again. I couldn't because I miscarried. At eleven weeks and three days, when I was at school in Montreal."

"God." Nausea churned through him. "I'm sorry—"

"My roommate helped." She broke in as if he hadn't spoken. "She went with me to the ER when the bleeding wouldn't stop." Her voice was a flat monotone.

He reached for her hand, cold and unresponsive in his.

"The doctor said I was young. I'd have other kids." She pulled her hand away and curled her knees up to her chest. "But I never did."

Sean's throat was sore. "Charlie—"

"The doctor even said it was a blessing, as miscarrying meant there was something wrong with the baby." She made a low moaning sound, like an animal in pain. "Miscarriages are common, no big deal, he said, but it didn't happen to him, did it? How could he know? I wanted to tell you, but I couldn't and . . ." She dropped her head onto her knees.

His anger receded to leave a leaden ache in his heart. "I can't imagine what you went through, but you still could have called me." He touched her rigid shoulder. "I'd have gone wherever you were, anytime, day or night."

Charlie raised her head, moisture shimmering in her eyes. He'd only seen her cry once. Back when she'd told him it was over between them she'd turned away, but not before he'd glimpsed a trickle of silent tears on her face.

"I couldn't make you feel responsible. Your grandfather was sick and your dad was having problems keeping the business going. You and Trevor were working nights at the creamery to earn extra money."

All that summer his grandfather's life had ebbed away until he was a shallow husk of the man Sean had looked up to all his life. His dad's blond hair had turned silver almost overnight, and still the bills piled up in the marina office. And all summer Sean had known he was the one his family counted on.

But none of that mattered, then or now. "You were having our baby. Don't you think you should have given me the chance to take responsibility?"

"Maybe I was wrong." Her eyes pleaded with him to believe her, to understand. "But I didn't want to trap you. Trap either of us. Even if you didn't want to admit it, we were growing apart. We hardly saw each other. When we did, we didn't talk a lot."

"I thought we wanted to do other things than talk." He gave her a knowing look. "All those times out on the lake in Dad's old cabin cruiser, in the woods or in my truck parked on the dirt road behind the arena in town. You wanted me as much as I wanted you. Or was it all a lie?"

Her face went white. "That was sex."

It was great sex, but he'd been young, stupid, and crazy in love, so he hadn't always worn a condom. "I guess your safe times weren't safe."

"I guess they weren't." Her expression would've broken his heart, except he'd never let her or anyone get close enough to break his heart again.

"Wasn't a baby a reason to start talking to me instead of breaking up with me?"

"I was young. I wasn't thinking straight. And my dad—"

"He knew?" His breath caught in his throat.

She hugged herself like a little girl, lost inside the baggy sweatshirt. "I didn't tell him, but my mom found the pregnancy test. She wanted to help me, but she couldn't stand up to Dad. She said she had to tell him. Mia tried to help—she was always the peacemaker—but Dad was so angry none of us could reason with him...He...he...hit me." She put a hand to her cheek.

The sweet smell of the wood smoke choked Sean. If Dr. Gibbs hadn't already been dead, he'd have killed him. With his bare hands. "He had no right to do that."

"The names he called me were worse. He said I was a disgrace to the family. A disappointment. And he told me I couldn't see you, talk to you, or write you ever again." She opened her mouth, then closed it again like she couldn't find the right words.

"You were an adult. You could have done what you wanted."

"He said he'd take away my college money if I didn't do what he said." Her jaw clenched. "I never told you much about what it was like growing up because I was ashamed. I was never good enough for Dad. Mom loved me, sure, but Dad controlled her, controlled all of us. And Mia was so perfect. In Dad's eyes, she never did anything wrong. I didn't belong. I had to get away from home, and college was the only way out. I needed that degree to go to journalism school. Being a journalist is what I'd wanted my whole life."

"I thought you wanted me too, and a life here. I thought you belonged with me." Sean tasted bitterness. Although he hadn't truly grasped what was wrong in her family, he'd wanted to give her the family she didn't have. The sense of belonging and security he'd dimly recognized she craved. But she'd turned her back on him.

"I did want you." Her brown eyes were bleak. "But Firefly Lake was my summer life. I had this whole other life too. I ran track at school, I was on the debate team, and I wrote for the paper. I went to Bermuda every spring break because Dad golfed there. We skied at Aspen after Christmas. It's not that I didn't want you to be part of that life." Charlie bit her bottom lip. "But my dad...he...kept Firefly Lake separate, like that life wasn't real or important. We were summer people, you were town, so I didn't really belong here either."

Sean's stomach dropped. "Our baby was sure real and important."

"Yes, it was." Her voice cracked. "But what if I'd told you I was pregnant? You'd have done the right thing. You'd have stood by me, maybe even offered to marry me. How could you have supported a wife and child?"

"I'd have tried." Because back then he'd wanted to give her the world and everything in it.

"I know you would." Her voice softened. "But what would that have done to us? My dad would have cut me off, and Mom and Mia would have had to go along with him. As for your family, your mom never understood what you saw in me, and your parents had such high hopes for you."

"None of that would have mattered to me," Sean said.

"It would have and you know it." She gave him a sad smile. "Besides, I'd have always wanted something else, somewhere else. I'm not domestic, settled. Not like Linnie."

"I never thought you were. I loved you for who you were. Or who I thought you were." An owl hooted, a gentle nighttime sound at odds with the feelings that churned inside Sean. Anger, disappointment, and betrayal. Maybe the two of them wouldn't have made a go of it, but she'd lied to him about a child that was as much his as hers.

"I don't think you knew who I was." Her gaze pinned his. "You didn't ask about the classes I planned to take at McGill or my writing."

"I was working all the time to keep Carmichael's from going under." Sean rubbed his taut neck muscles.

"See? Everything with you was always about Carmichael's, what the business needed, what your family needed, but I was changing." She drew in a breath. "You weren't changing, didn't even see any reason to change. Remember when I wanted you to go to that concert in Burlington with me? I won free tickets, but you had to work on some big order."

"One time." Mixed with his anger was guilt. He'd known the concert was important to her and he'd wanted to go, but his dad couldn't manage without him.

"What about when I wanted us to go camping for a weekend?"

He poked at the fire with a stick. "This isn't about some trips we didn't take. It's about you having so little belief in me, so little trust, you didn't talk to me and you destroyed us. It must have taken you all of five minutes. Hi, bye, it's over. Then you ran up the path behind the marina and I never heard from you again."

Her chest heaved. "I panicked. Maybe I didn't handle things right, but back then I didn't see any other way. Carmichael's was always more important to you than me, so I'd have lost you in the end anyway."

"That's not true." A steel band tightened around Sean's chest. When Charlie left him, she'd left behind an emptiness that, despite making a success of Carmichael's, making a success of himself, and becoming a father, he'd never managed to fill. "I loved you and—"

"You loved the business too. I wanted to be a journalist like you always wanted to take on Carmichael's." She glanced around as if she'd find answers in the woods or on the beach. "Besides, I thought you'd forget me."

"Never." Sean gave a harsh laugh. "Even though I wanted to."

"You didn't get in touch or come after me."

"You told me we were finished." His stomach knotted. "Even so, I did come after you."

"When?" She stiffened.

"Six months later I went to Montreal."

"You didn't call. I didn't see you." Her shoulders sagged.

"I saw you." He looked at the inky sky carpeted with stars. "You were coming out of some class in one of those old buildings at McGill, laughing and talking with your college friends. Your arms were full of books and there was a light in your eyes I'd never seen before. A light that told me you were going after all those big dreams you had."

"I—"

He held up a hand. "I didn't want to stop you from going after those dreams, so I got back in my truck and came home. You wanted to do important things, and you have. I couldn't have lived with myself if I'd gotten in the way of everything you wanted to achieve."

"I never knew." Her voice was a whisper in the night. "But you went on with your life. You got married, and you had Ty. You've made a big success of Carmichael's."

"You went on with your life too. After McGill, you went to Columbia Journalism School. You've achieved a lot. You should be proud. I am."

"You are?" Her eyes widened.

"Sure I am." Although it didn't change the fact he couldn't trust Charlie, he respected how she'd set her sights on a goal and worked for it. It wasn't surprising that goal had taken her beyond Firefly Lake. Ty might not want to talk about it, but Sean suspected his son struggled with that same push and pull.

The firelight cast shadows across her face. "Despite everything, you were my best friend and I missed you. Every so often I'd check to see if Carmichael's was still here. It was and I knew you'd be here too. And I hoped you were doing okay."

Charlie had been his best friend too, almost since the day she'd turned up at the marina with her mom and Mia and he'd pulled her in his red wagon up and down the boat ramp to the lake.

"Faster," she'd said, and her brown eyes framed by thick lashes melted his six-year-old heart. "I want to go faster."

That long, lazy summer afternoon while Mia cut out clothes for her paper doll family and his mom and Charlie's mom sat on the shaded porch, drinking lemonade and talking, he and Charlie had built sand castles on the beach.

He'd shown her the frog that lived under the porch and the fossils his grandfather had given him. He'd let her ride his new bike, running alongside, holding the handlebars so she wouldn't fall.

And every time she'd smiled, an endearing, gap-toothed grin that made him smile back, he'd known she wasn't like other girls. Not like his big sisters. Not like the girls at Firefly Lake Elementary School either.

Charlie Gibbs was special, and she'd kept on being special right until she'd run out of his life.

"You were my best friend too." Sean's voice was low and hoarse. "What if the baby had been born? Would you have told me then?" His words dropped into the thick silence between them, and his throat closed.

"I don't know. My dad was already talking about adoption, but I hadn't thought that far ahead." Her chin trembled and she stared at the moon that hung low and dipped into the dark treetops.

Sean exhaled. "It's been a lot of years, and we're different people than we were back then." And maybe their relationship then was flawed, but why had she lied to him about something as important as a child? Why hadn't she let him be there for her?

"In some ways maybe, but you're settled here like you always were, and I'm still a free spirit. I have an apartment in London, but that's it."

Whereas he had a son, a dog, and a family business to run. All of which usually made him feel good, but tonight all he felt was numb and curiously empty.

"You're heading back to London soon?"

"In three weeks unless we wrap things up sooner." The breeze brushed tendrils of her hair along the smooth line of her throat he'd loved to kiss, the spot that always made her quiver when he touched it.

He rubbed a hand across his face, then caught her looking at him. Caught the sadness in her eyes and the uncertainty. And something else. Something primal that caught him deep in his soul. She was the only woman who'd ever touched the essence of who he was.

But he wouldn't act on it. Not this time. Not like when he kissed her. An impulsive, illogical kiss he couldn't get out of his head.

He got to his feet. "I trusted you, but you destroyed that trust." His eyes met hers, and all of a sudden he wanted to hurt her like she'd hurt him. "By not telling me about the baby, you betrayed me, betrayed us. But you're right about one thing. My life's here and I like it the way it is."

It was a life with loyalties and responsibilities, which kept him rooted and safe. Whereas Charlie was his past and, in a few weeks, that past would be gone again. He swallowed the lump in his throat. Gone like their baby.

In the woods, bats swooped, their wings a soft whir, and Sean breathed in the familiar scents of crisp pine, clean water, and cool night air. Illuminated by firelight, the years slipped away and Charlie looked a lot like she had back when she first captured his heart.

Mustering all the willpower he had, Sean turned away. He wasn't the guy he'd been back then. And the girl he thought he'd loved wasn't that girl at all.

Chapter Six

Charlie didn't want to think about what Sean would say when he found out about what Tat Chee planned. Or what she'd say if he asked what she was going to do about it. Or if she could live with herself if she ignored her principles and everything she held dear, and let the sale go ahead.

She stretched and set aside the book she hadn't been reading. The lake was sapphire blue, dotted with sailboats, green, red, and white striped sails taut in the wind. Puffy white clouds scudded across the sky, and sunlight flickered through the branches of the pine trees that surrounded three sides of the cottage, dappling the shaded porch.

From her seat on the top porch step she looked down the rutted driveway where their Realtor Brent's SUV had disappeared an hour before, taking Mr. Cheung and Mr. Lee from Tat Chee Properties back to town. She didn't speak Cantonese, but the middle-aged men's smiles and gestures when they spoke quietly to each other didn't need any translation. They wanted the extra land and lake frontage.

She didn't want to keep picturing Sean's face when she told him about the baby last night either. She hadn't planned on telling him, but the words had spilled out and now she couldn't take them back.

"Hey, Auntie Charlotte." Naomi sat beside her, sweet in a yellow sun top, legs long and lean like a colt's below white shorts. "What are you up to?"

"Nothing much." Apart from avoiding Mia, pretending she could handle her feelings for Sean, and telling herself Tat Chee would have a change of heart about the cottage property. Charlie tried to smile at her niece. "You look pretty. Are you ready for the party?"

"As if. I still have to wash my hair, fix my makeup, and decide what to wear." She fanned herself with Charlie's discarded book. "It's lucky our birthdays are on the same day, isn't it?"

"Absolutely." Although turning fifteen was a lot more exciting than thirty-six. She rested her elbows on the yoga pants that hid her scarred leg. At least it was only her leg and she was still here to celebrate another birthday.

"Are you wearing your green dress?" Naomi set the book on the step.

"What green dress?" Charlie stiffened.

"The one hanging in your bedroom closet." Naomi's expression was earnest. "I didn't snoop, but when you asked me to get your sweatshirt this morning, I saw it."

That green dress. The dress Charlie had to have from the moment she spotted the column of shimmering fabric in the window of the little boutique in Milan, the beaded bodice winking at her in the burnished glow of the Italian sun. The instant she'd tried it on it made her feel sexy and feminine. In a foolish moment she'd once imagined wearing it for Sean if she ever saw him again. Imagined the blue heat in his eyes as he took the dress off her with exquisite slowness and then pulled her against his hard body.

The dress didn't belong in the backwoods of Vermont but, at the last minute, she'd folded it into her suitcase, which went to show her imagination was way too vivid. She should've used the space for a few extra sweatshirts.

"The party's at Mario's Pizza in town," Charlie said.

"It's your birthday. You can wear whatever you want. Do you have shoes to go with the dress?"

"I do." Black stilettos with diamante straps, which made her feel sexy and feminine, too.

"I bet Mr. Carmichael would like to see you in that dress." Naomi gave her a knowing smile.

"I'm sure he wouldn't be the least bit interested." Not if the expression on Sean's face before he'd turned and stalked into the blackness of the forest the night before was anything to go by. It was full of sadness and anger mixed with disappointment—in her and what she'd hidden from him.

"Sure he would. I saw how he looked at you when you were playing tennis. Even though you were all messy, he couldn't keep his eyes off you." Naomi's smile widened. "My friend Alyssa says it's one of the ways you know a guy likes you."

"Sean had his eyes on the tennis ball, pumpkin. Not me." Charlie tried to keep her voice light.

"I still think you should wear the dress to the party," Naomi said.

"It's a small party, only you, me, your mom, and Emma."

Naomi twirled the ribbon tie on her top. "I invited Ty

and he said he'd come. I said he could bring his dad if he wanted."

"You what?" Charlie stopped. "Honey, I..." Words were her business. Why was it sometimes so hard to find the right ones? "This is a family birthday meal."

"Since Dad canceled, it doesn't seem special. It's my birthday. I don't know anybody else around my age here but Ty. He friended me on Facebook and he's taking me canoeing on Monday."

Charlie sucked in a deep breath. If she'd been a mom, she'd have known how to handle stuff like this. "It's great you've made a friend here, but remember what I said about Ty. I don't want you getting in over your head."

"He's fun and super cute. Besides, I can talk to him." Naomi stared at her turquoise-painted toenails decorated with a daisy motif. "Mom's always on her phone. Emma's a little kid. I'm bored out of my mind stuck here in the middle of nowhere."

Charlie covered one of Naomi's hands with hers. "I hope you can talk to me if you need to. Your mom must miss your dad. It's bad luck he couldn't fly here for the weekend, but he's got an important job. Lots of people depend on him."

That's what Charlie's mom said all those times her dad stayed behind in Montreal and then Boston, and Charlie and her mom and Mia had come to the cottage on their own.

"Sure I can talk to you." Naomi's smile was too quick. "But Ty's near my age. I really, really like him, and I think he likes me."

"Did you tell your mom about this canoe trip?"

"Not exactly." Naomi crossed her legs at the ankles.

"Well, she knows I'm going canoeing, but I said someone who worked at the marina was giving me a lesson. I didn't tell her it was Ty."

A red squirrel ran along the porch railing, took a flying leap to the trunk of a pine, and then disappeared into the branches. "Honey," Charlie began.

"Emma's coming," Naomi added. "I told Mom since Dad rented a canoe for us, we need to learn about water safety."

All of which sounded to Charlie like a remarkable combination of the truth and an outright lie. Just what she would've said at Naomi's age.

"I'm sure Ty's nice, but you know how your mom feels about you seeing boys." Although she'd avoided Mia for years, not wanting to be confronted with her sister's perfect life, the old loyalty was still there, buried deep.

"I'm not dating him. It's only a canoeing lesson." Naomi's brown eyes, the chocolate-brown eyes Charlie saw in the mirror every day, were pleading. "You won't tell her, will you?"

"I guess not. As long as you're telling me the truth."

"Of course." Naomi's expression was innocent, maybe too innocent.

"Your mom loves you and she wants what's best for you. I do too." Charlie pushed away her doubts. She couldn't prove Naomi was lying to her. "We don't want you to make a mistake, that's all."

Like the kind of mistake she'd made with Sean. A mistake that had shaped her whole life and still had her churned up like the scared eighteen-year-old she'd once been. "You have to tell her you invited Ty to the party."

"Relax. I'll take care of it," Naomi said, a heartbreaking mix of child and adult. "I know what I'm doing."

"I hope so." Charlie had thought she'd known what she was doing. Thought she'd made the right choice. Except she'd never been sure, and coming back here had made her even less sure. "While you're at it, you'd better tell Ty you didn't mean to invite his dad along. Promise me?"

"Absolutely." Naomi tightened the strap on one of her sandals.

"Want to play with my Barbies?" Emma came out of the cottage, lugging a pink bag.

"You two go ahead," Charlie said. "I need to talk to your mom for a minute."

"Not about, you know?" Naomi put a finger to her lips.

"No." Charlie shook her head.

"I knew I could count on you." Naomi gave her a thumbs-up.

"I hope I can count on you too." Charlie got to her feet and patted the top of Emma's head. The little girl rewarded her with a giggle.

A giggle that made Charlie's heart beat faster even as she tried to ignore the sweet image of another little blond head, the one that might have belonged to her daughter. The child she'd loved and wanted more than anything. That child would've been seventeen now with their adult life ahead of them. A precious gift from the man she'd loved and wanted more than anything. The man she'd have done anything to protect.

Following the clatter of pans, Charlie made her way into the cottage. She was done avoiding. It was time for her to really talk to Mia.

Bypassing the living room, she found Mia in the kitchen. Her hair was secured with a clip on top of her head, and she'd covered her shorts and top with a blue floral apron. A slab cake sat on a rack on the counter, golden brown and perfect.

"You didn't have to make a cake," Charlie said. "It must be ninety degrees in here."

"I wanted to. It wouldn't be a birthday without cake." Mia retrieved a bowl of creamy white frosting from the table.

"We could have ordered one from the bakery in town." Charlie lolled against the counter and turned her face toward the fan whirring on the windowsill.

"A store-bought cake wouldn't be the same." Mia slid a butter knife from a drawer and swirled it through the frosting. "I always make Naomi a birthday cake, and Emma too. Like Mom always made our birthday cakes, remember?"

"We used to help her, but you were better at it than me."

"Only because you couldn't be bothered." Mia's eyes twinkled as she dug in the drawer for another knife. "Here, wash your hands and help me."

"Really?" Charlie ran cold water and squirted liquid soap onto her palms.

"I asked you, didn't I?" Mia's teasing smile blotted out any sting in her words. She slathered frosting along one edge of the cake. "I've got decorations. I brought them from home."

"You like all this, don't you? Baking and cooking? Homemaking?" Charlie took the knife and tried to copy Mia's practiced motions, which weren't as easy as they looked. They were the same motions she'd watched her mom and Mia make countless times when they baked together all through her growing-up years, while Charlie sat at the kitchen table and pretended to read, the odd one out.

She clenched her fingers around the knife handle, the buttercream frosting as slippery as a ski slope.

"All I ever wanted was to be a mom, to make a home for my family. I didn't want what Mom had with Dad. I set out to make sure my life was different." Mia's voice was tight. "It *is* different."

"I didn't want what Mom had either. I heard the arguments." She'd also lived with the cold silences, somehow worse than the angry words. Charlie stared at her sister's beautiful face, trying to see the girl she remembered, not the woman she'd become—a woman whose life was the polar opposite of Charlie's. It was the kind Charlie might have had if it hadn't been taken away from her. Or if she'd made different choices. Her eyes smarted. "You did well at college. Didn't you want anything more?"

"I was never ambitious, not like you. I got what I wanted. I have a good life and a lovely home." Mia opened one of the white-painted cupboards Charlie remembered from childhood. "I volunteer at Emma's school. I play golf."

"Mom volunteered and she played golf." Charlie brushed a hand across her eyes. "But did you ever think she stayed with Dad because she didn't have any other options?"

Mia shut the cupboard without taking anything out. "Dad wasn't the easiest man to live with, but Mom took her marriage vows seriously." Mia's voice was low. "I do too."

Charlie dug her knife into the bowl again and snuck a taste of icing when Mia wasn't looking. "If she was so serious about her marriage vows, why do you think Mom didn't tell Dad she owned the woodlot?"

"We don't know that for sure." Mia gave Charlie a hard

stare. "But whatever she did or didn't do doesn't matter anymore. The land is ours. We can sell it. I'll go home to Dallas, you'll go back to England or wherever you're sent, and everything will be like it was before." She tapped Charlie's fingers away from the bowl.

"No, it won't." Charlie leveled more frosting onto her knife and started on the corner of the cake farthest away from Mia. "Mom's gone. The cottage will be too if Tat Chee gets ahold of it."

Mia pushed back the curtain and looked out the kitchen window, where smoke from a campfire drifted across the tree line. "Mom's at peace. You know what she was like at the end. The cancer went right through her and she wasn't Mom anymore." Her voice wobbled, and she dropped the curtain to tuck her hands into her apron pockets. "As for the cottage, what does it matter what Tat Chee does with it?"

The knife slipped from Charlie's grasp and scored a corner of the cake. Crumbs showered across the counter. "A small, tasteful resort is one thing, but now they're talking about a big hotel and marina complex. I'm not sure I can go along with that idea."

"Why not?" Mia grabbed a paper towel and wiped away the crumbs without looking at Charlie. "An easy sale to get us out of here fast. What's to disagree with?"

Charlie's stomach roiled, and she forced herself to breathe. "It's all so much bigger than we first thought. That water feature Mr. Cheung mentioned, there's a whole lake out there. He also talked about a casino, remember? How can you think Mom would have approved of something like that here?"

"Maybe the new plan isn't what we expected, but I thought you wanted to sell the cottage and leave. There's no point in keeping it. That's what you said." Mia balled up the paper towel and tossed it in the trash with a jerky motion.

"After hearing them today, I don't think Tat Chee is the right buyer. Not for Firefly Lake and the Northeast Kingdom, and not for Mom either."

Mia's shoulders slumped and her mouth got a tired, pinched look. "Maybe not, but would anybody ever be the right buyer for you?"

Charlie opened her mouth and closed it again. Maybe if they found a nice family, a happy family, she could let the cottage go. "Don't you remember coming here every summer? Don't those memories mean anything to you?"

"They mean something all right." A single tear slid down Mia's face and she brushed it away, leaving a streak of icing sugar across the high cheekbones Charlie had always envied. "I remember Dad complaining about the traffic and going on about bass fishing and golf, me trying to keep you quiet because he didn't like anybody talking while he drove."

"You..." Charlie stopped. There was a coiled tension in her sister, and her dark eyes were bleak.

"I also remember how I was trapped here all those summers. You were always off with Sean or Linnie, but Mom depended on me and I couldn't...I couldn't make things better between her and Dad, no matter how hard I tried." She rubbed her face again.

"I never knew." Guilt stabbed Charlie. "I thought you wanted to be at the cottage with Mom. You two were so close. You liked all the same things, and you always knew exactly what to wear and say like she did. And you're so beautiful, like she was. I never belonged."

So she'd left and she'd kept on leaving. Sean, her family; even in her job she never stayed long in one place or with the same team.

"Oh, honey." Mia's voice caught, and she reached for Charlie's hand. "How could you think you didn't belong? Mom loved you and she worried about you because she didn't know what you needed or how to help you. I love you and worry about you too."

Charlie squeezed Mia's hand, then fumbled for the cake knife. She loved and worried about Mia, but the two of them had lost their way. And a lot of it was her fault. She'd shut Mia out because the contrast between her life and her sister's hurt too much.

"I know we haven't seen each other much lately because it's hard for you to visit with your job, but you're my sister and we're in this together." Mia's expression was cautious.

"Of course we are." Charlie took a steadying breath. "I still think we should sell the cottage. I need the money, but imagine what a marina on the doorstep would do to Carmichael's. Not to mention casino traffic. Maybe we could break the lot up and give Carmichael's right of first refusal on part of the wooded lot."

"As if Tat Chee would go for that." Mia ran the knife across the top of the cake and smoothed wayward buttercream peaks and troughs. "You saw their faces. They want all the land, maybe more."

Charlie gripped the edge of the countertop. "I'm only suggesting—"

"Don't." Mia waved away Charlie's protest. "I won't sell one inch of our land to Carmichael's. We already saved their business once."

"Apart from Mom and Mrs. Carmichael, we're the only

ones who ever knew Dad loaned Sean's dad money to keep Carmichael's going. I'm sure Mrs. Carmichael wouldn't have said anything. She was so embarrassed." Charlie swallowed hard as pain ripped through her.

"And Mrs. Carmichael doesn't know the terms of that deal either, does she?" Mia dropped the knife into the bowl with a *clang*. "What you did for Sean. And then the miscarriage. You'd never talk about it, but it must have almost destroyed you."

It had, so she couldn't talk about it. Until last night. Hot tears burned at the back of Charlie's eyes. "Sean idolized his dad. Mom and Mr. Carmichael and Dad are gone. We've kept the secret all these years. Can't you let it go?"

"No." Mia's voice was raw. "Even though she didn't know the whole story, I bet Mrs. Carmichael can't let things go either. That loan destroyed her friendship with Mom. Mom grieved over that until the day she died."

"Maybe this is a chance to put things right, to heal. Mom couldn't stand up to Dad, but she was the most forgiving person I've ever known." Charlie ran a spatula around the inside of the bowl like she'd seen her mom do, to scrape up the last bits of frosting. "Holding on to some old grudge doesn't do any of us any good."

"Mom was the best." Mia's voice wobbled. "But we need to sell, and if we break up the lot, we won't get nearly as much money."

"Okay, so let's try to find another option." Charlie fought to steady her breathing. "Please?"

"Have you talked to Sean? Are you hooking up with him again?" Mia tightened her apron ties. "From what I saw the other day, he still has a thing for you."

"I'm not hooking up with him." The desire that churned

through Charlie was about the past, not the present. "I haven't talked to him about the cottage either. I wouldn't, not without talking to you first." Instead, she'd talked to him about their baby. Her stomach heaved. "As for him having a thing for me, that's in your imagination."

"I know what I saw. Unlike Dad, I never had anything against Sean or his family. He's a decent guy and decent guys are hard to find, but you're moving on. You always do." Her voice was suddenly flat.

"If you can find another buyer who can offer us what Tat Chee will, go ahead, even talk to Sean if you think it might help. Without Dad's money, Carmichael's would have gone under and, good man or not, do you think Sean would have stayed with you back then? The business always came first for him."

Charlie swallowed around the lump in her throat. She'd wanted to come first in Sean's life, but she'd never been sure she had.

From her apron pocket, Mia's phone rang, and she pulled it out. "It's Jay. You carry on."

Charlie dumped the last of the frosting on the cake and pushed down with the knife until the smooth surface cracked. Why had she told Sean about the baby? All she'd done was dig up feelings she thought she'd buried years ago. At least she hadn't told him about the loan. That was one secret he didn't need to know.

Mia disconnected the call without saying good-bye and put the phone on the counter with a *thud*, startling Charlie.

"Everything okay?"

"Of course. Jay says hi." Mia inspected the cake, her eyes too shiny. "What are you doing? Here, like this." She picked up her knife and filled in the hole Charlie had made.

"It's only a cake. It doesn't have to be perfect." Charlie laced her fingers together.

"I'm sorry." Her breath stuttered. "You're right."

"I'm sorry too." She reached for Mia like she had when they were kids and their mom insisted they make up after an argument. She hugged her sister close, breathing in the sweet freesia fragrance Mia always wore. "What's wrong?" she whispered.

"Nothing." Mia's voice was muffled against Charlie's shoulder.

"Please talk to me. I know something's wrong. I knew it from the moment you picked me up at the airport in Montreal. You're like Mom, sweet, never a bad word for anybody, but something's changed. You're my sister and—"

"We hardly know each other." Mia's voice was small, and it cracked on the last two words.

"We can fix that." Charlie patted her sister's tense back. How long had it been since she'd touched Mia like this? Years. Her sister had never needed this kind of comfort before. Or if she had, Charlie had never noticed. "Tell me. I want to help."

"The girls might hear." Mia sniffed.

Charlie moved away and peeked out the kitchen door before closing it. "They're on the beach. Nowhere near the water," she added, catching the anxious look on her sister's face. "Is this about you and Jay?"

Mia sank to the floor and covered her face with her hands, shoulders shaking. Charlie sat beside her and pulled Mia into the shelter of her arms. She'd never seen Mia lose control, and it scared her.

"I thought he'd change. I kept telling myself if I loved him enough, if I was the best wife, the best mother, I could change him." Mia's hands dropped away, and Charlie caught her breath at the dullness in her eyes.

"I've got you, honey. You can tell me." Charlie smoothed Mia's hair, dark and glossy like their mom's before she got sick.

"I stayed the same size I was when I got married. I dressed right, or at least how Jay wanted me to dress. I've tried so hard to be the perfect executive's wife." Mia's face twisted in anguish. "I think he's having an affair. Another one."

"Mia, honey." Charlie's voice cracked. She'd never liked her brother-in-law, but she'd never pegged him for a cheater either.

"I'm ashamed. If I was good enough, he wouldn't cheat." Her voice broke.

"You're more than good enough. You shouldn't stay with him, not like this." Charlie tried to work moisture into her dry mouth.

"What choice do I have?" Mia pulled away. "I'm not like you. I don't have a job. I have a degree in music and a teaching credential I never used. All I ever wanted was a family, and look at me. I may not have anything."

"Of course you have something. You have two beautiful daughters and you have me. I'll help you. I'm on your side and I always will be." Even if it meant selling the cottage to Tat Chee. Charlie's stomach lurched, and she tasted bile.

"I've been a terrible sister." Mia lifted her puffy, tearstained face, and Charlie reached to the counter and grabbed some tissues from the box.

"I haven't been such a great sister either." A piece of Charlie's heart melted. "But we're stuck with each other." She tried to smile. "You're right, we don't know each other, but maybe we can start over."

"I'd like that." Mia used a tissue to blow her nose and managed a shy smile. "I was always jealous of you."

"Of me?" Charlie's mouth dropped open. "You're so beautiful and you always did everything right. You were Mom and Dad's favorite. I could never measure up. I was jealous of you."

"No." Mia shook her head. "I did what I was told, but right from when you were little, you had the courage to live your life and make your choices. Do you think I would have married Jay if he hadn't come from what Dad thought was the right kind of family, if he hadn't gone to the right schools, belonged to the right clubs?"

Charlie flinched. Making her own choices meant she'd gotten pregnant by a boy who didn't come from what her dad considered the right kind of family. And she'd ended things with Sean because she was scared of her dad and thought Sean would dump her anyway. "You want to sell the cottage to Tat Chee because you need the money?" Charlie's voice was high and reedy.

Mia's face went red, and she dipped her head. "I don't know what to do about Jay and me. Maybe he's not having an affair, or if he is, maybe it's just physical. When I caught him before, he said it didn't mean anything. And I believed him. I'm a fool."

Didn't an affair always mean something? Charlie's breath left her lungs in a whoosh. What had happened to her sister? The Mia she remembered wouldn't have put up with a husband who cheated on her, not for a moment. She'd been prom queen, head cheerleader, and the perfect, popular girl Charlie wanted to be. But this new Mia was a woman with blank eyes, forlorn and somehow broken.

"At least if I had money that was mine, I'd have something to fall back on for me and the girls," Mia said. "Everybody will think I'm a failure." She winced and buried her head on her knees.

"You're not a failure, so who cares what anyone else thinks. You could live to eighty or more. That's a lot of years. Do you really want to spend them with Jay?" Somehow Charlie had to get through to her sister, help her realize that no matter how bad things seemed, she still had choices.

"Mom didn't have those years." Mia looked up, her face blotchy.

Grief flooded Charlie. Why had her mom died when she'd still needed her? When Mia did too.

"The girls need their dad, and I can't walk away from Jay. I've been with him since I was nineteen and . . ." Mia's voice was thick with tears.

"You don't have to decide anything today." Charlie twisted her hands together to stop them from shaking. "Why don't you go upstairs and get changed. I can finish here."

"No, I'll do it." Mia squared her shoulders. "You're the birthday girl. What kind of sister am I, getting both of us all upset today, of all days?"

"A real sister." Charlie tried to smile.

Mia's lips trembled. "Maybe I've never said it before, but I'm glad you're my sister. I may have been jealous of you, Charlie, but I've always been proud of you too."

"You called me Charlie." She looked at Mia in wonder. "You haven't called me Charlie in, I don't know, years, I guess."

"Charlotte was never my sister, but Charlie is, if she'll have me. If she'll give me another chance."

"I'll have you, Mimi." The old name for the big sister she'd once looked up to. Charlie's throat clogged.

"Nobody but you and Mom ever called me Mimi, but I like it." Mia's eyes lost their horrible blankness and turned soft and gentle.

"I like it too." Charlie nestled into the curve of Mia's shoulder. The world telescoped to the two of them, and a sense of security and belonging Charlie had never felt before. She'd run from her family as far and as fast as she could, never realizing her sister hurt as much as she did. Never realizing her perfect sister was as flawed, and as human, as she was.

"I'll finish decorating the cake," Mia said, practical again. "I can imagine what would happen if I let you at it."

Charlie laughed. A real laugh that bubbled up from deep inside and healed some of the hurt she'd carried for years. "I'd ask Naomi to help me."

"She's a good girl." With one last hug, Mia got to her feet. "I know she thinks I'm strict, not letting her date, but I can't risk her getting hurt. Some boy could break her heart. I'm her mom. It's my job to keep her safe."

"Nobody's going to break her heart." Charlie hoped she was right.

Mia snapped the lid off a plastic box and shook out pink and purple birthday candles with matching holders. "I'm being silly. What kind of trouble could she get into here? In Dallas I worry about her friends and what she's doing at the mall. In Firefly Lake she doesn't have any friends. There's no mall, and she can't get into town unless we drive her."

Guilt sliced through Charlie, razor-sharp. "There's something I have to—"

"Look at the time." Mia made an apologetic face. "I made

an early reservation at Mario's. If Emma eats late, she gets cranky. You go get changed. I'll bring you a glass of milk and some of those oatmeal cookies I made yesterday."

And milk and cookies had been their mother's remedy for everything from a skinned knee to a broken heart.

Leaving Mia in the kitchen, Charlie climbed the stairs, her feet following the wooden grooves worn by several generations of her family. She stopped on the landing halfway up and looked out the window at the forested island in the middle of the lake. When she was small, she pretended a mermaid lived on that island. A mermaid who wore a shimmering green dress and granted wishes with a flick of her sparkly tail.

She and Mia had to sell the cottage. But not like this. Not if the price of leaving the past behind to secure her future meant everything good about that past would be destroyed.

She pressed her forehead against the windowpane, squeezed her eyes shut, and saw her mom's face. Gentle and loving but always with an undercurrent of sadness and heartbreak. The same kind of heartbreak Mia's face now wore.

Charlie flipped her eyes open and continued up the stairs. She had to talk to Sean. No matter what he thought of her. If today had shown her anything, it had shown her she didn't want to sell to Tat Chee.

And Sean was the only one who might be able to help her and Mia find another solution.

Chapter Seven

Sean hesitated beneath the striped awning outside Mario's pizza restaurant in town. His thoughts were still as jumbled as they'd been twenty-four hours earlier when Charlie dropped the bombshell on him that Ty wasn't his first child.

But Sean had missed the excited anticipation of that first baby and the grief of losing it. By not telling him, Charlie had taken those feelings from him, as good as stolen them.

While a night out with his son wouldn't make the pain go away, maybe it would distract him. He followed Ty into the cozy, wood-beamed restaurant and greeted his sixteen-year-old niece stacking menus behind the front counter. "Hey, Crystal." He kissed her on the cheek. "You didn't say you had to work here tonight. If I'd known, I wouldn't have asked you to help at the marina this afternoon."

"You know I always like helping you." Crystal hugged

him, then pulled two menus from the lopsided pile. "I wasn't supposed to be here, but we got some parties booked and Mario needed extra staff last minute." She led Sean and Ty to a small table in an alcove at the back of the restaurant where tall windows overlooked the lake. "This one okay for you?"

"You don't want to sit on the deck?" Sean glanced at his son.

"Nope." Ty grinned at Crystal.

Sean pulled out a chair on the side of the table that faced the lake. "It's a nice night. It'll be winter before you know it, and we can't sit out then."

Ty shook his head and mumbled something indistinguishable before opening his menu.

Sean studied his son's bent head and the thick shock of blond hair that stuck up at an unfamiliar angle. He took a closer look. His son had used styling gel on his hair, and he caught a whiff of his own aftershave. Both of which would explain why Ty, who was usually in and out of the shower and dressed in five minutes, had spent half an hour after work locked in Sean's bathroom, leaving Sean to shower in the main bath. "Want to share a Vermonter?" He set his unopened menu aside.

"What?" Ty tugged on his shirt. A blue one Sean hadn't seen before. Ty also wore an unfamiliar pair of tan cargo shorts and new sneakers.

"Mario's Vermonter pizza. I asked if you wanted to share one. Like we usually do." His son was fixed on a point behind Sean's head.

"I don't want pizza." Ty didn't look at him.

"Why did you insist on coming here, then?" Sean tried to keep the frustration out of his voice. "I'd have barbecued and we could be home watching the game. You were the one who wanted to go out."

Ty snapped his menu shut. "I'll have spaghetti and meatballs. We don't always have to have the same thing. It gets boring, you know?"

"I like pizza." Although Sean guessed he could order an individual Vermonter instead. "Ty, is something bothering you?"

"No." His son grabbed a breadstick from the glass in the center of the table.

"Your mom wasn't happy you wanted to stay with me this weekend. I know it's hard for you, but we've got a joint custody agreement." Sean grabbed a breadstick too. "We each have the same amount of time with you. You need to stick to the schedule we worked out."

"That agreement sucks." Ty crumbled the breadstick. "Mom lives twenty miles away. In summer, when I'm working here, I spend half the time in the car. You're driving me or she's driving me. I hate it."

Regret punched Sean's chest. "I know you do, and it isn't the greatest with your mom in Kincaid and me here, but that's where she lives. We all have to do the best we can to make things work."

"I don't see why she can't live here." Ty stuck out his lower lip, reminding Sean his son was still a boy with a lot of growing up to do.

"Your mom was never happy in Firefly Lake." Sean kept his voice neutral so he didn't sound like he was judging his ex-wife. "In three years you'll be eighteen. Old enough to make independent choices." He pressed his lips together. No matter how much he wanted to hold back time, Ty would be grown in the blink of an eye.

"Yeah, but then I'll have to build boats like you and Uncle Trevor, so even if I can finally live in one place, I'll still be stuck here." Ty looked toward the door and a slow smile spread across his face.

Sean's heart pounded. He'd lost Charlie, his grandfather, his dad, his marriage, and now a baby. He couldn't lose Ty too. "Hang on. You need to tell me if you don't want..." Sean paused, because Ty had stopped listening. If he'd even been listening in the first place. "Ty?" His son was halfway out of the chair and his blue eyes had a light in them Sean had never seen there before.

"I saved you a special table right by the window." Sean turned toward Crystal's voice. "You can see the lake and watch the sun set over the mountains."

"Hey, Naomi." Ty pushed back the chair with a scraping sound. "Happy birthday."

"Naomi." Charlie's voice this time. "You promised me you—"

"Chill, Auntie Charlotte." Naomi's cheeks were rosy and her eyes sparkled.

Sean looked at Charlie. Her emerald halter top had a plunging neckline, and a gold heart necklace dipped into the lush slope between her breasts. Her cream pants hugged the curve of her hips and flared at the knee, stopping at a pair of green-jeweled sandals. Her eyes narrowed and she flicked a glance at Naomi.

Sean dragged his eyes away from Charlie with an effort. She was even sexier than she'd been at eighteen and, despite everything, still sent the same liquid heat searing through him.

"Ty? Is there something you want to tell me?" At least his son had the grace to flush, red spreading up his neck to the tips of his ears.

"Naomi?" Mia stepped between her daughter and Ty. "What's going on?"

"It's my birthday." Naomi gave her mother an innocent butter-wouldn't-melt-in-her-mouth smile. "I invited a friend. We'll push some tables together. No problem."

"Sean." Mia was elegant in a black-and-white-patterned dress that showed her tanned legs, but her voice was tight. "I guess you didn't know anything about this either."

"No, I didn't." And when he got Ty alone, he'd ground him for a week. Keep him so busy at the marina he wouldn't have time to wander over to the Gibbs cottage.

"Charlie?" Mia turned to Charlie, whose expression held the same mixture of innocence and guilt it had when she was ten and his dad caught her about to take a speed-boat for a spin. "You knew something, didn't you?"

Charlie sat in the nearest chair, which happened to be the one beside Sean's. "I didn't expect to see Sean here." The sisters exchanged a look that was warmer and more loving than he expected. "It's my birthday too."

"Of course it is," Mia said. "Naomi should have been more sensitive."

"Mom, don't get weird." Naomi crossed her arms. Adorable in a white vest and denim miniskirt, she could have been Charlie at fifteen. "None of this is Auntie Charlotte's fault. Or Ty's either. He didn't know I didn't tell you I invited him and his dad."

"I don't mind you inviting friends, but you lied to me and maybe your aunt." Mia glanced at Charlie again.

Naomi gave Ty the kind of smile designed to send a teenage boy to his knees. The kind of smile Charlie had once given Sean. "I'm sorry, okay? Mr. Carmichael didn't know either, but it's great he and Ty are here." She grabbed a chair and dragged it over to sit beside Ty.

"We'll talk about this later." Mia rearranged her face into a polite, social smile. "Forgive me. You're Naomi's guests." A pulse worked in her jaw and she clasped her hands together. "There's more than enough birthday cake to go around."

"Thank you," Sean said. Naomi was only here for a few weeks. Not long enough for Ty to get serious about her. Or get his heart broken.

Beside him, Charlie sucked in a breath.

"Uh, Dad." Ty's voice cracked. "You didn't tell me you invited Uncle Trevor's family and Grandma tonight."

"What?" Sean spun around.

Crystal returned, this time with Linnie, Trevor, two of her sisters, and his mom.

"I didn't invite them. All I said was we planned to drop by Mario's for pizza. How was I to know they'd show up?" Sean suppressed a groan.

"Dad." Ty went red again. "You know how they are."

Yeah, he did. His family liked to spend time together.

"Sean?" Linnie glanced at Charlie and then Crystal, and her eyes narrowed as they landed on her daughter. "Trevor didn't tell me we were getting together with Charlie and her family."

"Trevor didn't know. I didn't either." The start of a headache pounded behind Sean's temples, together with a sense of foreboding.

"How nice to see you all again." Mia gave a tense smile as Crystal, helped by Ty and Naomi, slid two more tables into place. "Mrs. Carmichael, why don't you sit here by me? I'm sure my mom would have loved for you to join us."

"Thank you." His mom sat in the chair Mia held out for her. She arranged her purse on her lap and eyed Sean. She was not happy about this, her expression said, but she'd put up with it. At least for now. "Since you and Charlie are all grown up," she added, "you must call me Ellen."

Mia squeezed in next to Naomi and gestured to her younger daughter. "Emma, you sit beside your auntie Charlotte on the end."

Under the cover of his family settling themselves, Sean touched Charlie's arm, her skin soft and warm under his fingers. "I swear to you, I didn't know about this. There's no way I'd have come here tonight and intruded on your family party if I'd known you'd be here."

She looked at him sideways. "We were set up."

Sean glanced at Ty, his blond head nestled close to Naomi's dark one, the two of them intent on the menu they shared. "They were both part of that setup. Crystal too." Things had gone further between his son and Charlie's niece than he'd thought. He clenched his hands under the table as his mouth went dry.

"Here we are." Charlie shifted on her chair and tried but failed to laugh. "This is sure a birthday to remember."

"Yeah." Sean forced his gaze back to hers only to imagine Charlie pregnant with his child, her stomach rounded, her breasts fuller, and her skin luminous. Then Charlie losing that child alone, without him even knowing it had existed—a child that had been conceived around this time of year. A lifetime ago.

His vision blurred and the headache slammed into him.

"You're still as pretty as a picture, Mia." His mom's clear tones carried above the restaurant din and stopped

Sean's wayward thoughts. "You're the image of your mother as I remember her."

Charlie flinched.

"I hear your husband's a big executive with one of those, what do you call them, multinational companies. I'm sure your dad couldn't have been more proud you made such a good marriage." His mom's voice was brittle.

"You want to color the place mat, Emma?" Voice tight, Charlie opened a box of crayons, and her hand shook.

"Your dad was proud of you, Charlie," he murmured.

"How could he be?" Her voice was lifeless. "I wasn't perfect enough for him."

"There's no fun in perfection." Sean's heart won out over his head, shocking himself and wanting to shock her. Wanting her to know what she'd meant to him. And what she'd thrown away. "I never wanted to be with someone who was perfect. I only ever wanted to be with you."

Charlie found an empty picnic bench on Mario's deck and shivered in the cool night air. The lake was misty purple in the twilight, with salmon clouds streaking across the western sky. Naomi and Ty were shadowy figures on the town dock. Would her child have looked like one of them? Not knowing was a wound that would never heal.

She inhaled a deep breath of the clean, crisp air. She'd made it through the meal. Blown out the candles on the birthday cake and pretended to make a wish, so Naomi wouldn't guess anything was wrong. Pasted on a smile for the photos and made silly faces because Naomi and Emma asked her to. All the while, she'd been conscious of Sean beside her, how his big body bumped against hers, how his deep laugh rumbled out, how his forearms were tanned below the rolled-up sleeves of his white shirt, and how his faded Levi's hugged his thighs.

And the words he'd said still rang in her ears. Charlie had only ever wanted to be with him. Despite everything, a part of her still wanted that.

"What are you doing out here by yourself?" The bench creaked as Sean's mom sat across the table from Charlie. The breeze lifted her white hair, which was still thick and glossy.

Charlie's heart sank. A cozy chat with Ellen Carmichael was the last thing she wanted. "Getting some air. Mia and Linnie are talking about baking."

"Oh, honey, you tried to please your mom, but you were never a baking-and-sewing kind of girl, were you?" Her Vermont accent was as thick as the sap that flowed from the sugar maple trees in syrup season. Then Ellen chuckled, a feminine version of Sean's laugh.

"No." In spite of herself, Charlie laughed too.

Behind her glasses, Ellen's sharp blue eyes searched Charlie's face. "Sean still talking to Trevor?"

"There's some problem with a boat." Before she left the table, Sean had half risen as if to follow her, before Trevor grabbed his arm and pulled him back.

"You weren't like Mia or my girls or Linnie. You weren't like any girl I'd ever met." Ellen gave Charlie a wry smile. "You still aren't."

Charlie eyed the older woman across the picnic table. "You always had a problem with that."

Ellen shook her head. "No, I didn't. What I have a problem with is how you broke Sean's heart."

In Mario's parking lot, a car horn blared and Charlie

jumped. The hurt hadn't all been on Sean's side: Breaking up with him had broken her heart too. "Did he tell you that?"

"Of course not, but a mother knows these things." She slid her arms into the sleeves of a pale-blue sweater and covered her light summer dress. "He's a grown man, but I don't want to see him hurt again. Or see him unsettled again, either."

"There isn't anything going on between Sean and me that would hurt him or unsettle him. We're not even friends anymore." Charlie traced a pattern on the table, following the grain of the wood with her fingertips.

"Don't pretend with me." Ellen was firm. "Sean has always known where his responsibilities lie, but right from when you were a little girl, you stirred up everyone and everything around you, him most of all. You're still doing it." Ellen's eyes narrowed. "What you and Mia are planning to do with that cottage, you've got the whole town up in arms."

"I can assure you we—"

"I've said my piece to your sister." Ellen pinned Charlie with what as kids she and Sean had called "the look." The one that meant his mom wouldn't stand for any back talk. "As I told her, your grandfather must be spinning in his grave with what's going on. A foreign company coming in that, from the sound of things, doesn't have any respect for the place or the people who live here."

"We want to sell the cottage, but I—"

Ellen raised a hand. "The cottage sale is between you and your conscience. As is what you're doing to Sean."

"I'm not doing anything to him." If anything, Sean was doing things to her. Reminding her how she used to want him. How easy it would be to want him again.

"There's still plenty of sizzle in those sparks that were flying between the two of you tonight. I know my son." Ellen leaned closer to Charlie. "He's never looked at anyone, the woman he married included, the way he still looks at you."

"I'm sure that's not true." Charlie avoided Ellen's eyes, afraid the older woman would read the truth in her face.

Sean had tracked the neckline of her top and lingered on her bare shoulders before his gaze dropped to her breasts. His big hands had brushed hers, slow and deliberate, when she handed him the water jug. Time after time he'd watched her, his eyes dark blue with an unmistakable glint, and she couldn't deny she'd savored every moment of it.

"I know what I saw." Ellen's shoulders drooped and she looked older, frail even. "I've never shied away from calling a spade a spade. Young Ty, the way he and Naomi looked at each other, is a different matter, which I'm sure your sister will put a stop to. You and Sean are both adults and whatever's between you is your affair, but don't you go leading him on if you plan to run out again."

"I'm not leading him on. After we sell the cottage, I won't be back here ever again."

"From the time you were little I always knew you'd make a big success of your life and you sure have. You've done your mother and all of us proud." Ellen's chin trembled. "Your mother was like a sister to me and you were like another daughter, but you left Firefly Lake and you never came back, which tells me you didn't belong here, not really. If you truly did belong here, if your heart was here with us, you couldn't sell that cottage. And Sean doesn't belong anywhere else."

"I know." Charlie's throat was scratchy. Maybe she belonged here more than Ellen thought. Maybe that was why, deep down and against all logic, she didn't want to let the cottage go.

Ellen patted Charlie's shoulder. "Sean needs a woman who will work together with him in the business, like his dad and I did, like his grandparents did."

Charlie's stomach flipped. She wasn't that kind of woman. She'd never wanted to be that kind of woman either. A woman like her mom who'd lost herself in someone else, sucked away until there was nothing left of the person she used to be.

Ellen's expression softened and Charlie glimpsed unexpected affection behind the gruffness. "I always did speak plain, but I've known you your whole life and I loved your mother." She pulled off her glasses, fumbled for a tissue in the pocket of her sweater, and dabbed at her eyes. "Beatrice McKellar was my best friend the whole time I was growing up. She'd come to the cottage with your grandparents every June, and for the next three months we spent most of our free time together."

"Mom told me." Charlie's chest ached.

"When Beatrice married your dad, she changed, but she was still my friend until your dad, he ... I didn't mean the things I said to her back then." Ellen's voice cracked. "I never had a chance to tell her I was wrong. I blamed her for what your dad did, and I shouldn't have. She was a good woman and she didn't have an easy life."

Charlie gripped the edge of the table, the wood sticky beneath her fingers. "Sean still doesn't know about the loan?"

Ellen stared at her hands. "Rob made me promise I'd never tell the kids, and I've kept my promise. My husband was a proud man, and it about killed him to take money from your dad. He worked himself into an early grave. He was set on paying the money back and wouldn't be beholden any longer than he could help it, he said."

"I'm sorry," Charlie whispered.

Ellen shredded the tissue, her fingers twisted with age and a lifetime of hard work, the knuckles red and swollen. "We needed the money, but your dad took advantage of us, and I can't forget that. It's best for everybody if our families stay apart. You and Sean, Ty and Naomi, so nobody else gets hurt, no more lives are destroyed. I didn't sleep right for years. I worried I'd lose my home because it was security for the loan. I worried about Sean, and I worried about your mother and how I'd lost her friendship."

"I'm sorry," Charlie said again around the lump of regret lodged in her chest.

"If you're truly sorry, you won't sell the cottage to that developer." Ellen's blue eyes, the same color as Sean's, searched Charlie's face. "And unless you plan to stick around for longer than five minutes, you'll stay away from Sean and help keep Naomi away from Ty."

"How can you ask me to do that?" Charlie's breath caught.

"I could say it was for my son, my family, and the place I've lived in all my life." The skin bunched around Ellen's eyes, and her expression was pained. "But that wouldn't be the whole story. Your mom loved you and Mia more than anything, but after you two, she loved that cottage and this town."

"I loved her too." Charlie's heart thumped, quick and painful.

"I know you did." Ellen reached across the table and clasped Charlie's hand. "Your mom knew it, even though you were never one to wear your heart on your sleeve." She paused and licked her lips. "In your mother's memory, for her, you think about what I've said."

"Of course." Charlie dredged up a smile.

Ellen cleared her throat. "Your mom wouldn't want you to make a mistake or do anything you'd regret."

She got up, her sensible rubber-soled shoes soundless on the wooden deck.

Charlie pressed a hand to her mouth and stumbled down the steps to the beach. Ellen had only pointed out the obvious. So why did it hurt so much?

She slipped off her sandals and dug her feet into the soft sand. Avoiding Naomi and Ty, who sat side by side, almost but not quite touching, Charlie walked along the water's edge. She rummaged in her purse for her phone and scrolled through emails, texts, and news headlines.

She was a foreign correspondent, a respected award-winning journalist. She covered serious stories and she had a serious life—the life she'd single-mindedly focused on getting for the last eighteen years. A life a world away from Firefly Lake.

Charlie rubbed her hands along her arms to warm them. Away from the restaurant; it was quieter. The faint twang of country music from a pickup parked in Mario's lot was a counterpoint to the lap of the lake against the shore. A damp weedy smell tickled her nose, and around the curving lakeshore, lights twinkled like pinpricks in the gentle darkness.

She sat on the sand, tapped on her phone, and checked news sites and her Facebook and Twitter accounts, the familiar work tasks steadying her as they always did. They were a reminder of the world she'd go back to in a few weeks, one where there was no place for Sean, no matter how much she might want there to be.

Her phone shrilled and shattered the silence of the night. "Max." That world crashed into her.

"Charlotte." Her editor's clipped British voice echoed across the thousands of miles that separated them. "I have a story for you when you're back."

"Great." She tried to inject enthusiasm into her voice. "Where are you?"

"Indonesia." A tapping noise meant he was typing as he talked. "I want you to cover a women's cooperative in Ladakh. Ease you back in. Hello?"

"I'm still here." She drew a map in the sand and marked Firefly Lake with a white pebble.

"Thought I'd lost you." More tapping. "Sorry. Ladakh. You hear me?"

"Yes, Northern India." Charlie sketched Asia.

"From there you can go on to China." She'd met Max in China ten years earlier, the veteran reporter who'd shown her the ropes. "I want a human rights piece, the impact of media censorship."

"Okay." She clutched her phone in one hand and with the other held her stomach. Cell phone coverage could be spotty here, but Max's voice was as clear as if he were at Mario's.

"You get people to trust you and they talk. I want your grassroots angle, raw, hard-hitting journalism but with empathy. You know what I mean?"

Yeah, she knew what he meant. Except maybe she wasn't that person anymore, but she couldn't tell Max that, couldn't disappoint her mentor and friend. "I'll get onto some background."

"I knew I could count on you. I miss you." His gravelly voice softened. "It's not the same without you."

"I miss you too." In a lot of ways, Max was the dad she'd never had. He had a heart of gold beneath his crusty exterior, and was a man she admired and respected. "I have to go."

Sean stood five feet away, a navy hoodie tied around his shoulders, and the wind off the lake ruffled his thick hair. He was as ruggedly handsome as the Vermont landscape he was so much a part of. Charlie's breathing sped up and desire coursed through her.

"Are you keeping busy over there in the wilderness?" Max teased. "Any power-hungry deer?"

"You wish. Bye, Max." Charlie made herself laugh before disconnecting. Max's banter was as much a part of him as his iron-gray hair, the phone wedged to his ear, the mug of black coffee cooling on his desk, his well-worn sweaters, and the fierce intellect she'd first feared and then learned from.

"I didn't mean to interrupt." Before she could scramble to her feet, Sean dropped to the sand beside her.

"I was done." She gestured to her phone. "That was my editor, Max. He's in Indonesia."

"Archipelago, colonized by the Dutch." Sean's lips twitched.

"How...?"

"Come winter, Friday's quiz night at the Moose and Squirrel." His smile broadened. "You think because I play pool in a bar I don't know anything about the world?"

"Of course not." Charlie scratched at her sand map and blotted out India, China, and Indonesia.

"I wouldn't want to think you'd gotten all stuck up." He waited for a beat. "What did my mom say to you?"

"Nothing much." Charlie managed a no-big-deal kind of shrug. "She talked about when I was a kid and my job mostly."

"Why don't I believe you?" Low and rough, Sean's voice sent tingles along her nerve ends. "By the time I spotted her with you, Trevor had the customer on the phone."

"Your mom's looking out for her family."

"Interfering with her family's more like it." Sean's expression was pained. "What did she say?"

"You should talk to her." Charlie shivered.

"I will." Sean shrugged out of his hoodie and handed it to her, his mouth tight. "I'd like to hear your version first."

"She's worried about Ty and Naomi." Charlie pulled Sean's jacket over her arms, and the lingering warmth of his body heated her skin.

"After what happened tonight, I'm worried about them too. What are they thinking of, sneaking around?"

"We snuck around when we were their age." Charlie hugged herself.

"That's why I don't want them doing it, but if any of us try to stop them seeing each other, they'll only be more set on it." He exhaled and looked at the night sky.

"Mia's scared." Charlie hesitated, torn between her loyalty to her sister and her need to make him understand. "Naomi's only fifteen, a young fifteen. Mia doesn't want her dating until she's at least sixteen. I respect that."

"I know. I already talked to Naomi. She's invited Ty back to the cottage to play Monopoly." He chuckled, deep, warm, and inviting. "The junior version so Emma can play."

"How clever of Naomi." She grinned. "Mia thinks it was her idea, doesn't she?"

"You bet. You always knew my secrets, Gibbs." He stopped, the playfulness gone as if it had been snuffed out.

"I'm sorry." Charlie's throat got tight. "About everything."

"Me too." The serious expression on his face, and in his eyes, told her he meant it. "You were right. That last summer I wasn't paying enough attention to you."

"It's the past." She shrugged so he wouldn't guess how his admission sparked feelings she'd buried deep.

How abandoned she'd felt when Sean had been caught up in Carmichael's. How hurt and alone. The fear when she found out when she was pregnant, and the miscarriage pain that seared her soul. Abandonment, hurt, fear, and pain she'd carried for years until they became part of her, and meant she could never let herself get close to anyone or trust again.

With an effort, she pushed those feelings back where they belonged. "Your mom loves you and she wants the best for you."

"She needs to let me decide that. Back then we were kids who got caught in what our families wanted. Maybe in some twisted way, you were even trying to protect me."

Charlie froze, her muscles tight. Sean didn't know about the loan. Ellen said so. And nobody beyond her parents and Mia had ever known the terrible choice her dad had forced her to make.

"I've read some of your stories. I know what you did for work, how you stayed behind to try to help your colleague even though you were injured too." He slid an arm around her shoulders. His touch was warm and comforting, and he smelled of cedar mixed with sandalwood soap.

"Anybody would have done what I did." She licked her lips.

"No they wouldn't. When that bomb went off, everybody else got out of there fast, but not you." Sean's breath ruffled her hair.

"It didn't make any difference." Charlie stopped as the memory blindsided her. "Ethan died in my arms. I felt the life go out of his body. The doctor was too late and all the blood...I didn't know what to do, how to help." Her body shook and Sean hugged her tight. "I still...I think about what I could have done, how I might have saved him..." She buried her face in his wide shoulder.

"From what I read, you did the best you could." Sean rested his chin on her head. "You were hurt and in shock. Nobody in that situation could have done anything more."

"He was only thirty-three. He had a wife and two young kids he adored. He was a great photographer. He had everything to live for." She stumbled to her feet.

Sean got to his feet too and pulled her in to his muscled chest. Beneath her ear, the rhythmic beat of his heart slowed her frantic breathing. "You also have a lot to live for."

"I can't stop thinking about it." The words burst out of her like tearing a dressing off a wound.

"You need to let it go." His voice was husky.

"I can't. I try but..." She clenched her teeth and held back a moan. "It's there, every day, even here."

"It must be sucking the life out of you."

Her eyes widened. Sean had always known her better than anyone, but it rattled her he still did.

"You ever try writing about what happened?"

"I can't write about it. Writing would make it..." She burrowed into the clean cotton of his shirt and breathed in his crisp aftershave.

"Real?" Sean tipped her chin up with a gentle finger, and his steady blue gaze pinned hers. He dropped a tender kiss on her forehead before he stepped back and took the warmth and comfort she'd missed all these years with him.

She fumbled for her sandals and jammed her feet into them. "I should get back. Mia will wonder where I've gotten to."

"Always running, aren't you?" Sean's voice had a hint of steel.

"Of course not." She brushed sand from her clothes to hide the tremors that shook her from head to toe.

"You can't deny there's still something between us." Moonlight gilded the strong planes of his face. "I think that's what my mom talked to you about too."

"She...I...no." He couldn't have guessed, could he? Guessed she'd never really let go of her feelings for him. If coming back here had shown her anything, it had shown her that.

He reached out and traced the inside of her wrist. "We've got a lot of history between us, and we need to deal with it, once and for all."

Charlie's spine tingled. "I left and we both got over it. End of story."

"Not buying it." Sean dropped her wrist and fished his car keys out of the pocket of his jeans. "But since you're the one talking about a story, maybe you can tell me what the real story is here." His eyes flashed blue fire.

Charlie shrugged out of his jacket and handed it to him.

"I don't know what you mean." She hated the wobble in her voice.

She'd run for too many years to stop now. She hadn't let herself trust anyone, not even Max. In fact, where trust was concerned, she'd pretty much convinced herself she'd forgotten how.

Chapter Eight

Naomi slid her sunglasses on and turned to look at Ty in the back of the canoe.

She'd really and truly gotten away with it. She'd strolled out of the cottage with her little sister, headed for the canoeing lesson. Then she'd ducked into the woods where Ty and Crystal waited, and bribed Emma with the promise of a new Barbie outfit to stay at the marina with Crystal. She hadn't done anything wrong exactly. Emma would be safe with Crystal, and Naomi was still learning about canoeing. It wasn't like this was a date or anything.

"You okay?" Ty gave her a slow smile, which made her stomach lurch like on a roller coaster, half scared and half excited.

"Great." She tugged on the orange life jacket. She could swim, but Ty had insisted she wear this dumb thing. Even said he wouldn't take her out until she put it on. It covered up the outfit she'd worn specially, her favorite short white shorts and turquoise crop top, which would have looked even better if her mom had let her get her belly button pierced.

"You're sure Emma won't tell your mom?" Beneath his life jacket, Ty wore a pair of blue swim shorts and a white T-shirt, and each time he raised the paddle, the muscles in his forearms rippled.

"Absolutely." Naomi wished she could take a picture to prove to Alyssa she was actually alone with a hot guy. A guy who was almost sixteen and so high on the scale of hotness, Alyssa would never believe it. "Emma will have way more fun with Crystal than she would with us."

"Emma's pretty little." Ty dipped the paddle in the water again, a smooth rhythmic motion Naomi could have watched all day.

"She keeps secrets all the time." But Naomi had never trusted Emma with a secret this big, a secret that could get Naomi in more trouble than she'd ever been in before if her mom found out.

"You sure Crystal won't tell either?" Naomi flicked her hair over her shoulders, like Alyssa did.

Ty laughed. "No, 'cause I've got lots of stuff on her. Besides, she likes working at the marina more than I do." He glanced at the black sports watch on his wrist. "I thought we'd head over to . . . " He stopped and scanned the forested shoreline. "Lie down."

"What?" Naomi leaned forward.

"Lie down," Ty said again. "In the bottom of the canoe."

"My clothes, my hair." The hair she'd spent a whole hour straightening and then curling again into smooth bouncy waves.

"You want my dad and your aunt to see us?"

Naomi slithered down, squeezed under a crosswise

piece of wood, and stretched out her legs until the top of her head almost touched Ty's bare feet. The bottom of the canoe smelled like fish. "You said your dad went into town."

"He did, but he must have come back." Ty jerked the paddle, and spray hit Naomi in the face.

She spluttered and spit out lake water. She pulled her sunglasses off, peered over the side of the canoe, and blinked as the sun dazzled her eyes. "That lawyer guy's there too." He and Auntie Charlotte and Sean's dad were in a huddle outside the Carmichael's workshop.

"Nick McGuire's a friend of Dad's."

The canoe rocked, and the fish smell got stronger. Naomi lay flat again and pressed a hand over her mouth and nose, the taste of the tuna sandwich she'd had for lunch at the back of her throat.

"You notice whenever he's around your aunt, my dad gets real weird?" Ty paddled fast and the sky became a blue blur streaked with white. "You see him at dinner at Mario's?"

"You mean how he kept touching her like it was all accidental?" Naomi took her hand away from her face, pressed it on her stomach, and willed herself to not throw up. She wiggled away from a shiny black bug, inches from her face on the side of the canoe.

"Yeah. How they kept looking at each other."

"It was pretty weird." It had also been kind of exciting, like one of those romance novels her mom read that Naomi sometimes snuck a peek at.

The canoe slowed, and the rocking motion lessened. "We're around the point. You can sit up." Ty reached out a hand to her. "You okay? You look kind of funny."

"I'm fine." She slipped her hand into his, wishing her palm wasn't sweaty. She eased back up and rubbed her other hand across her forehead, half turning to face Ty. "Your dad doesn't have a girlfriend?"

"Nope." Ty steered the canoe farther out into the lake. "If you want a drink, I put waters and sodas in the cooler."

Naomi grabbed the bag he indicated. She pulled out a can of soda and popped the metal tab.

"Since he and my mom split up, he's dated a couple of women, but nothing serious." Ty looked at her instead of the lake. "You sure you're okay?"

Naomi hugged her knees. "The fish smell made me feel sick." And she was scared. Scared she'd be found out, scared of what she was doing and where it might lead. Maybe her mom was right. Maybe she was too young to handle boys.

"I fish all the time. I guess I never notice any smell." Ty trailed the paddle in the water. "See the island over there?" He pointed to a wooded outcrop in the middle of the lake. "We can go ashore. Sit a while until you feel better."

"Okay." Naomi swallowed soda from the can and savored the sweet liquid as it trickled down her throat. "Thanks."

"Sure." Ty turned the canoe again and paddled toward the island.

"How old were you when your parents broke up?" She swallowed more soda, the drink settling the sick feeling in her stomach.

"Really little, about six. My mom remarried ages ago. My stepdad, Matt, he's okay. I've got two half sisters, Emily and Olivia." Ty steered through some rocks, smooth and gleaming black beneath the water's surface.

"What was it like, before they split?" Naomi's heart hammered, and she tried to make her expression casual. Her mom pretended everything was fine, but Naomi knew better. Something was going on. Something bad, and she was scared, more scared than she'd ever been. Other families broke up, but never in a million years had she thought hers might.

"I don't remember much, but mostly they stopped spending time together. Dad was always at work. Even when he was home, they didn't talk a lot." Ty jumped out of the canoe into waist-high water and grabbed the front. "Sit tight. I'll have you on shore in a second."

The canoe slid onto the sand. Naomi half stood, then sat again as the world spun around her. "I, uh..."

"Here, I've got you." Ty lifted her out of the canoe like she was Emma's age and set her on a patch of dry sand farther up the beach.

She stuck her head between her knees, and hot tears pricked behind her eyelids. She was an idiot. A dumb crybaby. If she could have, she'd have walked right across the lake, back to the cottage, to her bedroom under the eaves. Where she'd stay, hidden beneath the quilt, until it was time to go back to Dallas and she'd never have to face Ty again.

"Naomi?" Ty's voice was anxious. Not like she was an idiot at all.

"I'm sorry." What was she was sorry about?

"Your mom and your dad, are you worried about something, like they could split up?"

"Yeah." She raised her head, not caring if he saw her tears or that her mascara must be streaked across her red cheeks. "My dad was supposed to come here for my birthday and he didn't, and my mom, she pretends nothing's wrong. When I know it is. Auntie Charlotte said I could talk to her, but I can't, not about this."

"That sucks." Ty touched her arm. "But my dad says he and Mom are happier apart than they ever were together. It might be like that for your parents. Whatever happens, it has nothing to do with you and me."

Naomi sniffed. Ty didn't look like he thought she was a freak. His blue eyes were warm and caring. He looked at her like she was pretty, and special.

Ty unzipped his life jacket. "You're different from the girls around here." He gave her the slow smile again, which made her happy and excited and scared, all at the same time. "I'd like to hang out with you."

"I'd like that too." Instead of sexy and confident, her voice came out in a squeak. She tugged on her life jacket.

"You need help getting that off?" Ty's hands covered hers, tanned and lean, the knuckles dusted with light blond hairs.

"I'm okay." Naomi stared at his hands, mesmerized, then at his face. His lips were firm and his jaw had a hint of blond stubble. Blood thundered in her ears. She'd practiced kissing a pillow, but there'd never been a guy she wanted to kiss for real. Until now.

His eyes were the same blue as the lake, and in the sunshine his hair was like spun gold. He leaned in close and his lips brushed her cheek. They were soft and gentle, a faint caress promising more. If she wanted it. His hand grazed her bare shoulder and she got goose bumps. "Are you feeling better?"

"Yeah." She reared away from him. All of a sudden, she didn't know what she wanted.

Ty sat back on his heels. "I won't push you to do anything you aren't ready for."

"Okay." Her voice squeaked again. She coughed. "Maybe we should uh..." She gestured to the canoe. "You're supposed to teach me about safe boating."

"I am." Ty laughed, deep and sexy. "You don't know much about boats, do you?"

"Before today, I was never in a canoe. Or any boat. I'm pretty much a city girl." She laughed too, but hers was high-pitched, nervous.

"You'll get the hang of it in no time." Ty picked up a paddle. "My dad said he taught your mom and your aunt how to handle a canoe. Your aunt always liked it more than your mom did."

"I'm a lot like my auntie Charlotte." Naomi tried to ignore the green slime streaked across her shorts.

"My dad said you sure look like her." Ty showed Naomi where to put her hands on the paddle. "But when I asked him about her, he said there wasn't anything to tell."

"There wasn't?" Naomi tried to copy the motions Ty made look easy.

"Nope." Ty moved her hands and curled his fingers around hers.

Naomi stared at his hands on top of hers and her skin tingled. "Like this?"

"You've got it." His voice was rough, and electricity crackled between them.

Naomi's stomach somersaulted. This time it had nothing to do with a fish smell and everything to do with Ty. She tilted her chin and looked at him from under her lashes like she'd seen Alyssa do.

* * *

"When did you plan on telling me?" Sean slammed his fist on the desk. Papers scattered, and the door that separated his office from the workshop rattled in its frame.

On the other side of the desk, Nick sat in one armchair while Charlie perched in the other. Cool and fresh, her white pants and top set off her dark hair and eyes.

"I asked Nick to wait before telling you." Charlie clasped her hands. "Until we found out more about Tat Chee's plans and what we have to deal with."

"Instead, I get a call from some San Francisco attorney. A Tat Chee attorney who asks if I want to sell my property and do a deal that would cut out the Firefly Lake Realtor." Sean's voice vibrated with anger, and he crumpled the survey Nick had given him. "Why didn't you tell me about this earlier?" He swore under his breath.

"I couldn't." Nick was cool and lawyer-like. Not like the guy Sean shot the breeze with over a beer and pool at the Moose and Squirrel. The bastard looked like a lawyer, too, in his white shirt and navy dress pants.

"I thought we were friends, but you…you…" He'd trusted him. Sean fought to steady his breathing. "Carmichael's isn't for sale. Not for any money."

"I'm sorry." Nick grimaced. "If my law partner wasn't on vacation I'd have handed this case over as soon as I found out about the survey."

"You have to believe this was a big surprise to Mia and me. We never knew Mom owned the woodlot." Charlie leaned forward, her luscious breasts held in check by the four white buttons on her blouse.

"You won't give me a chance to buy part of it?" Sean

rolled his chair back, away from Charlie's tempting breasts, and gripped his closed laptop.

"No."

"Why not?" Sean rolled his tight shoulders.

"I can't... you know." Something that looked like regret flickered in her eyes.

"From what I've heard about Mia's husband, it doesn't sound like she needs the money." His voice was harsher than he'd intended. "This doesn't have anything to do with Ty and Naomi, does it?"

"No." Charlie avoided his gaze. "Naomi apologized about inviting you both to dinner without telling her, and Mia's okay with Ty coming by the cottage when we're all there."

Sean turned back to Nick. "Tell me about the marina and Tat Chee's plans. Give it to me straight. You owe me that."

Nick shifted on the chair. "Tat Chee acquired a controlling interest in Mackenzie Marine last year. Mackenzie's a big player. Not only boats, but full-service marinas with winter storage. They operate all across North America."

"Carmichael's wouldn't stand a chance." Sean slammed his hand against his chair. "Then there's the casino, fronted by some damn water feature. Anything else you've kept from me? A theme park? A zoo with exotic animals?"

Nick shook his head, his expression strained. "I feel bad, buddy. The cottage sale was supposed to be straightforward. I'd never have taken it on if I'd known it'd get complicated. You may want to get independent legal advice. I can recommend someone." He glanced at Charlie. "Mia and Charlotte are my clients."

"The fact McGuire and Pelletier has handled Carmichael's business for almost fifty years doesn't mean anything?" Sean's pulse sped up and he glared at Nick across the desk. One night last winter after a few beers, he'd told the guy about Charlie and him and now Nick was siding with her?

"Of course it does." Nick eyeballed Sean. "But I've never been your lawyer. We both know that would be a conflict of interest. All I meant—"

"I know what you meant." Nick might not have intended to, but by siding with Charlie and Mia, he'd as good as betrayed him. "I'll contact someone in Kincaid." He'd call the firm that had handled his divorce. Although he'd made Sarah a fair settlement, Carmichael's hadn't been part of it.

"Let me talk to Mia and see if we can work something out." Nick turned to Charlie. "Is she at the cottage?"

Charlie nodded. "Baking probably, or playing Mom's piano." She gave Sean a half smile. "Someone from the marina took Naomi and Emma canoeing."

"Someone..." Sean's stomach knotted. Only Ty was at the marina this afternoon.

"They booked a lesson. Since Jay rented that canoe, they need to know how to handle it. It's not like I can take them out." Charlie looked at her leg but not before Sean glimpsed the pain in her eyes.

"We do orientation sessions all the time." He hoped his gut was wrong. Hoped Ty hadn't lied to him. A memory of the little boy who used to follow him around everywhere washed over him. The boy who'd turned into a teenager Sean didn't understand and, most of the time, had no idea how to parent.

"I'm confident we can work something out." Nick's voice rumbled, lawyer-like again.

"Confident?" Sean fisted his hands. The guy must have

taken a special class in law school, Keeping Clients Calm 101. But he wasn't the client and Nick was supposed to be his friend.

"I get you're upset," Nick began.

"Upset?" Sean's voice rose. "Why wouldn't I be upset about having Mackenzie Marine in my backyard?"

Nick made an apologetic face and got to his feet. "Give me some time to see if we've got any options. You still up for tennis this week?"

"Sure." Sean itched to get the racket in his hand and kick the guy's ass on the court. Which wasn't fair, but it wasn't like he could kick Mia's ass. Or Charlie's. No, he wanted to do something entirely different with Charlie.

The office door closed behind Nick with a soft *click*.

Charlie leaned forward in her chair. "We need to work together on this. I've already talked to Mia, and if we can find another buyer who can match Tat Chee's offer, she'd be okay with that. She said I could talk to you."

"Why?" His heart gave a painful thump.

"Even though it wouldn't be in my backyard, I have concerns about this development too." In just over a week, Charlie's hair had grown a bit, a tousled look that suited her more than the short, business-like bob. Her lips were glossy pink, still with that delectable curve Sean had licked until she'd moan in his arms.

"Why should I believe you?" She'd already shattered his trust beyond repair. And he couldn't stop thinking about the baby and what he'd missed.

"A casino isn't right for Firefly Lake. Neither is the kind of marina Tat Chee would put in." Her smile was half serious, half teasing. "Don't get me started on that fountain with dragons spewing out water."

"Why do you think I can help you?" Anger was pitted against loss and thwarted desire, and he felt light-headed.

"You're a big part of this community, and people like and respect you. Last time I checked, the petition had almost fifteen hundred signatures, and in a town this size that tells me something." Her tone cajoled him.

"Do you still want to sell the cottage?" He took a shallow breath and leaned forward. Which was a mistake because now he was in touching and tasting distance of her.

"Of course." Charlie looked down, but not before Sean caught the flicker of uncertainty in her eyes. "But my mom loved Firefly Lake. Maybe we can come up with a better option, one that won't change everything she loved. What do you think?"

Sean's breathing sped up. By working with her and Mia, he might be able to protect Carmichael's. Protect his family, his community, and his way of life. But he'd also have to spend more time with Charlie. "I guess I could talk to the chamber of commerce and the Rotary Club."

"You're president of the Firefly Lake Rotary Club." Charlie's eyes twinkled. "I saw a picture in Nick's office of the two of you at some Rotary dinner. You have influence."

"Maybe I do, but why should I use it to help you and your sister?"

"This isn't about helping us. It's about Carmichael's and Firefly Lake, and this whole special area." Her eyes were wise, seeing through him like always. Seeing what mattered to him.

"I'll think about it." His gaze locked with hers and something sizzled between them. The heat that had always been there—but had deepened because they weren't the kids they'd been.

"We don't have anything against you." She took a business card from the holder on the desk and traced the letters of his name. "But Mia...she's dealing with...some stuff...She's the only family I've got."

Sean knew all about family loyalty. How it could suffocate you and force you into choices you didn't want to make. "What kind of stuff?"

"I can't..." She swallowed, and a pulse worked in her jaw. "A Tat Chee development would hurt a lot of people. Mom wouldn't have wanted something that hurt people who were her friends. Hurt the place she never forgot. Mia and I don't want that either."

"It has nothing to do with you and me?" Sean looked into her face, the girl he'd loved still there beneath the woman she'd become.

"Of course not." Charlie's voice trembled.

"Deny it all you want, but we're still hooked together." He gave a harsh laugh. "Beyond trying to get it out of our systems, I don't know what the hell we can do about it."

Charlie came around the desk. She licked her lips and his body leaped. "Even if there is still something between us, we can't do anything about it."

"Starting something again would be a bad idea." Sean pushed the words out, over the tightness in his chest.

"A very bad idea." Her voice was a sensual caress.

"What if we can't help it?" He stood and shoved the chair away, sending it crashing into the wall to overturn. He reached for her, and the shock of her warm, bare skin jolted through him.

"I shouldn't..." But even as she spoke, she leaned into him, soft, like the Charlie he remembered. Her head fit into the curve of his shoulder like it belonged there.

"Me neither." He dipped his head and brushed his mouth against her neck, peaches and her scent greeting him. The one he could have picked out blindfolded even after all these years.

"Your mom told me to stay away from you." She angled her neck toward his mouth.

"I told her to butt out." He licked the sensitive cord in her neck, and she gasped.

"You did?" She whimpered as he intensified the caress.

He drew back. "You and me, we're none of her business."

"There isn't a *you and me*. There can't be. I'm only here for just over two more weeks." Her words came out in a breathy moan. "Whatever this is, it can't go anywhere. I don't want anyone to get hurt." Her small hands were gentle on his forearms. That gentleness was a side of her she didn't let many people see.

"I know the rules." He pulled her close again to stroke his way up her sides, before he trailed his fingers across the tops of her breasts.

She twisted against his touch and made a sound deep in her throat. "Unlike me, you always played by the rules."

"Maybe it's time I broke a few of them." He covered her breasts with his hands and traced the outline of her bra beneath her blouse, the nub of the clasp at the front.

"I—"

He put a finger to her lips and stopped whatever she'd intended to say. For an instant she went stiff in his arms, as if to push him away. "We're not kids anymore. We're adults, unattached adults. Aren't we?" He slid one hand under her top, the softness of her skin shocking him with its familiarity.

"I'm not involved with anyone." She trembled at his touch.

"There isn't anybody in my bed either." He rocked his hips into hers to show her what she was doing to him. All the while, he continued his lazy exploration of the satin-covered cups of her bra, the two hard points of her nipples. "We both want this. Don't we?"

She hesitated for a long moment, and in her dark gaze, reluctance battled against desire. Then she tilted her head and covered his mouth in the kind of sweet kiss she'd given him long ago.

He opened his mouth and kissed her back. Heat roared through him as he undid the top two buttons on her blouse and teased his way down to the clasp of her bra. He opened it one-handed and bit back a groan at the heavy weight of her breasts.

"What?" Charlie wrenched her mouth away from his, her lips pink and glistening.

"I always had a thing for your breasts," he whispered, his breath feathering her hair.

"They're not the same as they were." She covered herself with her hands. "I'm older and—"

"Sexier than ever." He lifted her, set her on the edge of the desk, and eased her hands away. "You're beautiful."

Her flushed face and breasts spilling out of her top were an irresistible combination of sexy and sweet.

"I'm older too."

She brushed a hand against the front of his jeans and his body swelled. "And bigger." She traced the stubble on his jaw before kissing him again, harder this time and not as sweet, her fingers sliding beneath his T-shirt.

Chapter Nine

She'd missed this, missed him. Charlie lifted Sean's T-shirt and slid her palms across his bare chest to reacquaint herself with his body. This was bad, said the logical part of her. Except it was good. She moaned as Sean returned her kiss and deepened it, his tongue tangling with hers.

Nobody had ever kissed her like Sean. She traced the flat plane of his stomach, and his muscles bunched. She smoothed the fine trail of hair from his navel up his chest. No other man had ever made her feel this good.

And she wanted to fill the lonely places in her life. To forget the past and not think about the future. Be only in the present. To be wanted in the way Sean had always wanted her, and to want him too. She wrapped her uninjured leg around his waist and pulled him back onto the desk, her mouth still fused to his.

He pulled his mouth away, and his breath fanned her hot face. His eyes were dark blue, the pupils dilated, his cheeks flushed. "Charlie?"

"Don't stop." She arched against him as his hand covered her breast. She twisted, knocking the desk tray onto the floor. Metal clanged against wood, and papers flew.

Sean groaned as she trailed kisses across the contours of his chest. "Wait." His hoarse breath rasped against her ear. "Let me lock the door."

"No." She started to pull away, but then he chuckled, a low throaty sound that heightened the ache between her legs.

"Why not? You want this as much as me." He dipped his head, found her bare breast, and sucked it into his hot mouth.

Charlie cried out at the sweetness and pleasure of it, and she buried her face in his shoulder to hide the sudden rush of tears.

The office door banged open and Sean sprang upright, dragging her with him.

"I'm sorry. I knocked. When nobody answered, I came right in, like always." The female voice was laced with laughter.

"Linnie." Sean pulled Charlie's top together, his fingers fumbling with the buttons. "Trevor's in Kincaid with a delivery. What are you doing here?"

The woman who might have been her sister-in-law stood inside the door, a cardboard box under one arm, a travel mug in her other hand. She wore white capris, a yellow T-shirt, and a smile she couldn't hide. "Dropping off those bird carvings Trevor borrowed. He forgot them this morning. I told him I'd come by on my way back from the farm stand on the highway."

"This isn't what it looks like. I know what it must look like but..." Charlie pressed her palms against her burning face.

"Hey." Linnie's smile broadened as she moved farther into the office. "I thought Sean might want some coffee." She set the box on top of a filing cabinet and the mug on the desk. "It looks like I was wrong. You're already giving him everything he wants."

Sean's laugh rumbled. "Sorry. Next time we'll lock the door for sure."

"Next time?" Charlie tried to wriggle out of his arms, but he held her tight. "There won't be a—"

"Yes, there will," he said into her ear, his words for her alone. "We both know it." He ran a hand down the curve of her spine, his touch hot through her top.

Linnie cleared her throat. "Charlie, you and me always got on real well. I missed that when you left."

"I did too." They'd been friends. The kind of friend Charlie hadn't known she'd miss until it was too late.

"You should drop by." Linnie's hazel eyes twinkled. "Since you and Sean are so friendly again."

"I...we aren't...not like you might think." Charlie linked her arms in front of her chest and tried to squeeze her breasts back into her bra, all the while conscious of Sean righting the overturned chair, picking up the scattered papers, the desk tray. Her face flamed hotter.

"Whatever." Linnie grinned and a dimple appeared in her right cheek, like the teenager Charlie remembered. "Are you going to the fair?"

"The fair?" Charlie glanced at Sean.

"Blueberry Jam." His voice was rough.

"Friday through Sunday, the third weekend in August at the fairgrounds by the lake," Linnie added. "There's a music festival and local food show too. Remember?"

"Yeah, I do." Charlie gave up on her bra and hugged

herself. The first time Sean kissed her, the two of them had been sitting on top of the Ferris wheel at the fair, the night sky carpeted with stars.

"I'm sure Charlie has more important things to do than go to a small-town fair." Sean set the tray on the desk and shoved his hands into the pockets of his jeans.

"Mia's girls might like to go." Charlie glanced at Sean, remembering the light in his eyes that long-ago summer night. How he'd leaned in close and covered her mouth with his and she'd thought she'd love him forever.

Linnie curled a strand of red hair around one finger, and the tiny diamond in her engagement ring winked at Charlie. "I enter my crafts, baking too. Sean's sisters, my girls, the whole family gets involved." Linnie nudged the cardboard box. "Sean and Trevor enter wood carvings of birds and animals. Sean's birds are in here. You should see his work. The detail is incredible."

Sean took his hands out of his pockets and grabbed the box. "Leave it, okay?"

Linnie made a teasing face and turned back to Charlie. "I'll help you make something to enter if you want."

"Me? You can't be serious." Charlie swallowed a laugh.

"Why not?" Linnie gave Charlie a playful grin. "Sean likes these oatmeal raisin cookies, which are super easy to make."

"Linnie, I mean it." Sean turned her to face the door.

"You come by anytime," Linnie said over her shoulder. "We live across the street from Carmichael's place, forty-seven Spruce Cove Road." She moved away from Sean, found a pen and a scrap of paper, and scribbled on it. "Here's my number."

"I always liked you, Linnie. Right back to first grade

when you didn't tell on me for knocking poster paint over on your new sneakers...but you're pushing your luck. Out you go." Sean pointed to the open office door.

Linnie looked at Charlie, her mischievous expression wiped away. "I think you should know. My daughter Crystal is over at the marina." She hesitated for a fraction of a second. "With little Emma."

Sean stiffened. "Ty must have called Crystal to help out."

"Is Naomi at the marina?" Charlie studied Linnie's face.

"No." Linnie's voice was low. "Ty wasn't either."

"Ty wouldn't..." Sean rubbed a hand across his face. "You can't be sure."

"I'm a mom of four teenagers." Linnie patted his arm. "Not a lot kids do gets by me. Besides, I remember what Trevor and I used to get up to."

Like what Charlie and Sean used to get up to. "I'll talk to Mia. Thank you."

The warmth in Linnie's smile told Charlie they might find their way back to being friends again. "See you soon, Charlie. I meant what I said about dropping by."

After the door shut behind Linnie, Charlie came around the desk. "I should go too." She picked up her bag from under a chair. "I shouldn't have started something I can't finish."

Sean moved toward her and she scooted behind the chair. "I have to check on Ty first, but why can't you finish it?" His voice was low and sensual. "If Linnie hadn't walked in on us, I'd have locked the door and we'd have been doing what we both want."

"No, I wouldn't." She clenched her fingers around the chair back.

"You're lying." His voice turned harsh.

How, after all this time, did Sean still know her so well? "Okay, maybe I would have, but it wouldn't have solved anything."

He cupped her chin and then, almost as if he couldn't help himself, his index finger traced the outline of her lips. "I can think of a few things it may not have solved, but it would at least have taken the edge off."

Her face and mouth tingled with the imprint of his touch, and she twisted away. Linnie had interrupted them just in time. Sean tempted her, but she couldn't act on it. She had to get this conversation onto safer ground, fast. "Look at what you've achieved with this business. You always wanted to make it a success."

"I wanted you too. And I thought we wanted each other." Sean leaned against the desk. Sunlight streamed through the half-open window and turned his hair gold. "A few minutes ago, you still wanted it."

"We were always good at sex, but we have to control ourselves." Even though she wanted nothing more than to throw herself back into his arms, Charlie slung her bag over her shoulder, her legs shaking. She'd tried to change the subject to Carmichael's, the one thing Sean had always liked to talk about, but this wasn't safer ground. It was the exact same ground.

"You really think you can control yourself? Or I can?"

"We have to." Her mouth went dry at the thought of how things might have been different for her, for them. If she hadn't left. If she'd told him the truth about the baby and the loan. If she hadn't broken his trust and his heart. "We can try to be friends. Nothing more."

"Friends?" Sean snorted. "How you were wrapped

around me was a lot more than friends." He bunched his shirt into his jeans and covered the narrow strip of skin that had been firm and hot to her touch. "Unless you mean friends with benefits, but what's between us isn't casual."

She forced herself to keep breathing. "It isn't, but apart from you and me, there's Ty and Naomi to consider." And her sister didn't need any more worries. "They have feelings for each other, and I can't let Naomi get hurt." Hurt in the way she'd been hurt. Hurt so badly she'd been careful never to let herself get close to anyone or feel much of anything ever since.

"I know." Sean's voice was tired, older. "I can't let Ty get hurt either. He's a lot like me, and she's like you." He scrubbed a hand across his face.

She backed toward the door, her heart thumping. "I'm glad we understand each other."

"Understand each other?" His eyes narrowed as he followed her. "Is that a challenge?"

"No, it's—"

His mouth covered hers again. Then he drew back, ending the punishing kiss almost as soon as he'd started it. His gaze raked her face. "Before you leave again, whether you want to or not, we're going to have to deal with what's still between us."

Charlie pushed open the office door. Shadow shot through it, tail wagging and barking a greeting.

"Saved by the dog." Shadow skidded to a stop beside him and Sean smiled. The kind of smile Charlie had never been able to resist. A smile that touched all the places in her heart she'd locked away long ago.

Desire rocked through her, together with a sense of loss

and regret so strong it left her breathless. She reached for Shadow and crouched to the dog's level.

When she was eighteen, she'd convinced herself she'd done the right thing, the only thing she could do. She was sure that if Sean had to choose between Carmichael's and her, he'd choose the business. So she'd broken up with him before he could break up with her. And also because if she hadn't ended their relationship, her dad would have taken back the loan and Sean would have lost Carmichael's anyway.

But now she wasn't sure. Maybe the right thing had been the wrong thing.

And maybe she hadn't only lied to Sean. Maybe she'd lied to herself too.

Sean lifted the burger from the grill onto a plate. "You want to eat out here?"

Ty grunted. His back to Sean, he leaned against the rail of the deck toward the lake, where the sun nudged the hills amid a rosy curtain of cloud. "Whatever."

Sean set the plate on the patio table and went back for his burger. "Busy at the marina today?"

Ty turned. "Steady." He pulled out one of the patio chairs and folded his long body into it, bare apart from a pair of colorful board shorts.

"When I dropped by around three, Crystal was there. She said you took one of the canoes out." Sean sat across from Ty and helped himself to potato salad.

He needed to be subtle. He wouldn't accuse Ty. He'd keep things easy and relaxed. Like all those parent-your-teenager books he'd read, which said you had to keep the channels of communication open. Make sure your kid knew you trusted him, wouldn't judge him. While you set boundaries.

"You have a problem with that?" Ty ate some burger and washed it down with half a glass of milk.

"Is there any reason why I should have a problem?" Sean forced himself to sound calm and reasonable. His son was turning into a man and he could handle this man-to-man. Or man-to-almost-man.

"No." Ty bit into a cob of corn with the straight teeth that were the product of two years of orthodontia. "I took somebody out."

"Somebody?" Sean poured a glass of water from the jug. "Naomi's little sister, Emma, was with Crystal."

"Why don't you come right out and say it?" Ty dropped the corncob and wiped his mouth with a paper napkin. "You were checking up on me. You know who I took out."

So much for subtle. "I hoped you'd tell me." He curled a hand around his water glass.

"Why would I?" Ty gulped the last of his burger and shoved his chair away from the table.

"Naomi seems like a nice girl, real pretty too, but you know how her mom feels about her dating and..." Sean stopped. He was screwing this up big time.

"We're not dating. We're hanging out." Ty stared at the insect-repelling candle in its tin bucket on the far side of the deck and rolled his shoulders, well-defined abs that Sean hadn't noticed before bulging.

"It's good to make new friends." Sean sounded like one of those pastel greeting cards in the rack at the drugstore in town. The kind of cards his mom and sisters bought. "I never said you can't hang out with Naomi, but you shouldn't get serious about her. You're only fifteen." And he had to keep his son from making the same mistakes he had. From getting hurt like he had, this time by another Gibbs girl.

"I'll be sixteen in November." Ty tipped back in the chair and balanced it on two legs. "Besides, when you were my age, I hear you totally had the hots for Naomi's aunt." He shot forward and the chair hit the deck with a *thump*.

"Who said that?" Sean pushed away his half-eaten burger.

"Crystal heard her mom and dad talking." Ty scratched a mosquito bite on his forearm. "You done?"

"Help yourself." Sean slid his plate across the table. "Charlotte Gibbs and I were friends and yes, I cared about her." And when he and Charlie were Ty and Naomi's age, they'd made out every chance they got. Sean suppressed a groan.

"You cared about her?" Ty's tone was mocking. "Crystal heard Aunt Linnie say you had it for Charlie Gibbs bad." His blue eyes challenged Sean, daring him to deny it. "In fact"—he drew out the words—"Uncle Trevor said you were all over her like a bad case of poison ivy."

Yep, that was Trevor. His twin was quiet, but he sure had a way with words when he wanted to.

"Back then, Charlotte and I, we were..." They were what? Sean rubbed the tight muscles in his neck. "We'd grown up together, gotten to know each other every summer when she and her family came here to their cottage."

"And?" Ty tapped one foot against the deck.

"We thought we were in love. But we were kids. We didn't know what love was." Because real love was about honesty and trust. Everything Charlie hadn't shown to him.

"I saw how you looked at her at Mario's. You never

looked at Mom that way." Ty twirled the end of his corncob between his fingers.

"Your mom and I weren't right for each other. You know that." The night was drawing in, and although Ty's face was shadowed, the hurt little boy still lurked in the blurred outline of the young man.

"Did you love Mom?" His son's voice cracked.

"Of course I did."

Except not in the way he'd loved Charlie. Not with his whole heart and soul. Not to the fiber of his being. Even back then, Sean had known his love for Sarah was different, more superficial, and although they'd never talked about it, maybe Sarah had too. Shame scorched him.

Sean stretched out a hand to touch his son's wrist and Ty flinched. "She's your mother. I'll always love and respect her for that."

"You and Naomi's aunt, you weren't…you know… when you and Mom were together." Ty's face flushed red, and he looked at his bare feet.

"Absolutely not." Sean pulled his chair around to sit beside Ty. "I never cheated on your mother, not with Charlotte Gibbs or anybody else."

Thinking about someone other than your wife didn't count, did it? Not that he'd thought about Charlie a lot. Except, sometimes when he hadn't made Sarah happy, he wondered if he'd have made Charlie happy either.

But first Charlie and then Sarah had left him, so he'd thrown himself into Carmichael's, building the business to secure his family's future. To prove himself, even though somewhere along the line he'd lost sight of who, or what, he was proving himself for.

"Your mom's a good person and she deserved to find a

man like Matt. Someone who is right for her and can make her happy like she deserves." Sean lifted his hands up, then let them fall to his sides.

"I guess." Ty grabbed his T-shirt from a patio chair and shrugged into it. "I like spending time with Naomi. She's different from the girls around here. Why can't you understand?"

Because Sean understood all too well. "She's going back to Dallas in a few weeks. Her mom and Charlotte are selling the cottage. She won't ever come back here."

"She might." Ty finished the remains of Sean's meal and grabbed an apple from the fruit bowl. "Just 'cause her aunt dumped you doesn't mean Naomi would do the same to me."

"You're out of line."

"If you say so." Ty's voice got louder and more insolent.

"I do. No matter what Linnie and Trevor said, anything between Charlotte and me was over years ago. It's also none of your business." Sean's stomach rolled. He'd never lied to Ty. He'd always prided himself on his honesty. But the lie had come out and now he couldn't take it back. Couldn't explain either, at least not without making things even worse.

"Naomi and I are none of your business either." Ty whistled for Shadow and shoved his feet into a pair of flip-flops.

"It's my business as long as you live under my roof." Sean gripped the arms of the patio chair.

"Then I'll live with Mom all the time." Ty polished the apple on his shirt. "She wants me to be happy."

Sean's chest tingled. This couldn't be happening. What would he do if Ty chose to live with Sarah? If Ty walked out of his life without a backward glance? He didn't want to alienate his son, or stand in the way of his dreams, but he had to keep Ty safe. "Does your mom know about Naomi?"

"I told her there's this girl I've been hanging with." Ty stuck his bottom lip out like a rebellious toddler. "She said it was great."

Sean took a deep breath. "Naomi lives over a thousand miles away." And even though she looked like her younger, mirror image, Naomi wasn't Charlie.

"So?" Ty rolled his eyes and scraped his chair away from the table.

Sean forced a calmness he didn't feel. "If you truly care about Naomi, you'll respect what her mom wants. Her mom says Naomi's too young to date. Whatever you want to call it. If you meet Naomi without her mom knowing, it's wrong and not how you've been raised."

"I only took her canoeing, okay? It's not a big deal. Come on, Shadow." Ty grabbed the dog's collar and clumped down the deck steps.

"It *is* a big deal." Sean followed, taking the steps two at a time. "Besides, you've only known her, what, a week?"

"Eleven days." Ty flung the words over his shoulder.

"Where are you going?" Sean grabbed Ty's arm, but his son twisted away.

"The workshop." Ty kicked sand into a cloud and Shadow barked, eager to join in a game. "Happy? I'm going to do some work. Like you always do."

Sean pressed his hand to his stomach. "I always tried to be there for you. Stuff at school, sports, the camping trip we go on each summer."

Ty spun around and his expression was hard. "Maybe you were there for me, but you weren't there for Mom.

Sure, she's happy with Matt, but when the two of you were together, you worked all the time. Everything was always about Carmichael's."

"Your mother understood I had to build the business." Which wasn't another lie, but it wasn't exactly the truth either. After the first few years, neither he nor Sarah had wanted to spend time together, so he'd used work as an excuse, while she spent more and more time with friends and her family. "I'm glad your mom's happy. All she and I want is for you to be happy. For me, that means not rushing into anything. You have your whole life ahead of you."

Maybe if he'd waited, he'd have admitted Sarah wasn't right for him, and she'd have admitted it too. But she'd been pretty and fun and, by wanting to be with him, she'd helped dull the pain of Charlie's betrayal. When she wanted to get married and start a family, he decided he could settle. Turned out he'd been wrong, and Ty paid the price. More shame, this time mixed with guilt and regret, rolled over Sean.

"Hanging out with Naomi makes me happy," Ty said, his eyes cold. "Just because you screwed up your life doesn't mean I'll do the same with mine. You can stop with the advice."

Ty set off down the path at a jog, Shadow at his heels. Seconds later the workshop lights went on and country music blared out from the iPod dock Ty kept on his workbench.

Sean sat on the bottom step, his legs shaky. Purple mackerel clouds hugged the pine-fringed shore. At the end of the point, water splashed against the rocks. Lights twinkled out of the darkness, the chorus of crickets and tree frogs a counterpoint to the music.

Even before he'd had his face glued to her breasts earlier,

it hadn't been over between him and Charlie. There was unfinished business—feelings he didn't want to have and had no idea what he was going to do—or even if he should do anything—about. His responsibility was first to his son, and then to the rest of his family and the business.

When the last notes of a Dean Brody song about "Canadian Girls" that Ty had found on YouTube faded away and was replaced by Taylor Swift singing "Love Story," choices Sean guessed were deliberate and meant to torment him, he went back up the steps and into the dark house.

The house he'd built after he and Sarah split up. Where he rattled around on his own and Ty lived with him the weeks he wasn't with Sarah and Matt.

He flipped on the kitchen lights to reveal granite countertops, stainless-steel appliances, and the white, Shaker-style cabinets Linnie and his sisters helped him pick out. At one end, a farmhouse table and six chairs, a set meant for a family, not a divorced dad who struggled with his one kid—who was so afraid of losing that kid he sometimes came down too hard. Like his dad and grandfather had on him.

He pulled out a chair and sat, took the phone from its charger, and scrolled to Sarah's number. Marriage should be forever, but he'd failed his ex, or maybe they'd failed each other. But he wouldn't fail his son. He had to talk to Sarah and fix this mess. He counted to five and hit her number.

"Hey, Matt," he said when his ex-wife's husband answered. "It's Sean. Is Sarah around?"

"Sure. Hang on a second."

Twenty miles down the road in Kincaid, Sarah had made another life, another family. And until tonight, Sean would have said Ty was okay with how everything had turned out.

"Hi." Sarah came on the line. Her voice was still girlish, like it was the summer he met her when she waitressed at the Inn on the Lake. The same voice she'd probably have when she was a grandmother and they were still trying to make an effort for Ty's sake, splitting time with Ty's children. "Is Ty okay? He's not hurt, is he?"

"Ty's okay." At least okay in the way Sarah meant. "But we need to talk."

Chapter Ten

I don't like leaving you alone out here all afternoon." Mia patted Charlie's arm. "You're sure you won't come to the movie with the girls and me?"

"I'll be fine." Charlie closed her laptop on Max's latest email and got up from the couch. "You go have fun." The air was sticky with heat, and she lifted the hair off her neck. Firefly Lake was as still as glass. Dark clouds were banked at the town end, and heat lightning flashed over the hills.

"You promise you'll lie down?" Mia picked up her purse. "Rest your leg?"

"I promise." After she emailed Max and made yet another excuse about why she hadn't sent him the background research she'd promised. The research Max was pressuring her for, and she'd started half a dozen times and not finished. Research for the story that was waiting for her.

Mia cleared her throat. "It means a lot you're on my side. Jay, he...I still don't know what to do."

"Hey." Charlie hugged her sister. "We'll figure something out."

Mia's eyes glistened. "I know you don't want to sell to Tat Chee, but—"

"There's got to be another option," Charlie broke in. If she couldn't find one, she'd have to make a terrible choice. Another one.

"I miss Mom so much." Mia hesitated, halfway out the door. "But with you, us together here, it's like I've got a part of her back."

"Me too . . . with you." Charlie's throat got thick. "Go on. The girls are waiting in the car."

"Okay." Mia touched Charlie's cheek, like their mom used to do.

After the door closed behind her sister, Charlie moved to the piano and ran her fingers across the yellowed keys. "I love you, Mom," she whispered. "Maybe I was wrong about you. Maybe you didn't always do what Dad told you to. Maybe you didn't tell him about the woodlot because it was the only part of yourself you had left. Am I right?"

She played a chord and the notes echoed, high-pitched and musical like her mom's laugh. "We didn't always understand each other and a lot of that's my fault. I shut you out because I thought you loved Mia best. I was wrong and I need you. I need your help. What am I going to do? I have to help Mia, I want to help her, but I want to do the right thing too. For you. For all of us."

Dust motes danced in a shaft of sunlight, and Charlie closed the piano lid. Ghosts didn't answer, no matter how much you wanted them to. Thunder rumbled, and she wrapped her arms around her middle, hugging herself.

And then there was Sean, who was all too real, all

too present. The man she'd made out with like some sex-crazed teenager. The man she couldn't stop thinking about. Her sister needed her help, needed her as an ally. Sean was their adversary and she wasn't on his side, so why couldn't she stop thinking of him?

Her thoughts circled like a hamster on a wheel. She wandered into the hall and kept one eye on the sky. A cloud blotted out the sun, and she shivered.

"Charlie?" Sean's voice came from the other side of the screen door, deep and as smooth as dark chocolate and twice as tempting. "Can I talk to you?" He wore a white Carmichael's polo shirt and navy chinos, and his expression said he wasn't going to leave unless she agreed.

She opened the door, the hinge squeaking. "What is it?"

Thunder rumbled again, closer.

He came into the hall and stopped in front of her. The scent of wood and some spicy soap tickled her nose. "I drove by Mia and the girls heading into town, so I figured you'd be on your own."

Charlie's heart pounded. "This isn't a good time."

Lightning forked over the lake, where the water was gray and sullen.

"Charlie." Sean stopped her. "When you were in my arms, I haven't felt like that in a long time."

She curled her bare toes into the rag rug. "I haven't either." The heat in his gaze bored into her. "But we've gotten it out of our systems."

"Have we?" Sean's voice was gruff. His big body filled the small hall.

"I did." She linked her shaky fingers together. She couldn't let him guess how she felt, couldn't strip her emotions bare to leave her heart exposed and defenseless.

"You keep on lying and your nose is going to grow. Like Pinocchio." His gaze sharpened.

Charlie winced as new guilt piled on top of old to lodge in a hard lump at the base of her breastbone. "I . . ."

Sean's mouth twisted. "I don't trust you, but it doesn't mean we can't help each other out. I had another call from that San Francisco attorney today, and Tat Chee wants the marina, so they've upped their offer."

"You said no?" The lump moved to her throat; she forced the words out.

"Of course." Sean's face was dark. "Then I called a guy in the Rotary Club who works for the regional planning commission. He might be able to pull some strings and make it harder for this site to be used for anything commercial."

"Is that ethical?" Lightning lit the sky and she shivered.

"Maybe not, but you could argue what Tat Chee's doing isn't squeaky-clean either. They've cut out the local Realtor. They're pressuring a neighboring property owner." A gust of wind jangled the chimes on the porch, and Charlie jumped. "Besides, to build the complex they're talking about, they'd have to cut down a big chunk of old-growth forest, maybe even dredge part of the shoreline for the water feature."

"What are you suggesting?" Charlie crossed her arms.

"You have any contacts in the Burlington media?"

"No." She shifted from one foot to the other. "Mine are in New York and Boston."

"A story about a big developer coming into this special place with plans that could destroy the environment and change the way of life might help nudge a building permit hearing the right way, if you get my drift."

"That would be good for you, but Mia and I could lose a buyer." She hugged herself. "It sounds like Tat Chee will up their offer to us too. Despite what you think, Mia needs the money."

"Why?"

"I can't tell you." Although she got where Sean was coming from, she was on Mia's side. Her sister and nieces needed the fresh start and independence from Jay the money from a sale to Tat Chee would give them. She had to help them.

"Does it have anything to do with her husband?" Sean searched her face, his expression probing.

Charlie picked at a hangnail. "I didn't say that."

"You didn't have to." Sean let out a breath. "Okay, Mia needs money."

"I do too." The ever-present worries gnawed at her. Her investment portfolio had tanked along with the economy, and London was expensive. How would she save for her future? And what if the nightmares didn't go away and she couldn't work for months, years?

Lightning illuminated the hall, followed by a clap of thunder, which rattled the windows. Charlie squeezed her eyes shut as the familiar panic spiraled through her.

"What's wrong? You're shaking." Sean steered her toward the couch. "Sit."

"I'm not Shadow." She tried to laugh but failed, flinching as thunder boomed again.

"You never used to be scared of storms." He patted her back like he'd have patted his dog.

Charlie opened her eyes. "I'm not scared." Another crack of thunder hit, and she lurched to her feet. "I'm fine." She stumbled to the window and slammed it shut. Rain lashed the beach, and the trees in the woodlot were bent almost double in the wind.

"If you say so, Pinocchio." Sean dragged her against his chest. "I've got you. You're safe. Hold on to me."

Fear rose in her throat and choked her. Past and present blurred until Sean was the only solid point in a world that tilted and spun out of control. "Don't leave me."

"I won't." His voice was steady.

She curled her fingers tighter around his. "Loud noises, they, it's…" She was babbling. She couldn't stop. Nor could she stop her teeth from chattering, nor the tremors that cascaded through her body.

"It's only a summer storm." He pulled her onto the couch and grabbed the blanket from the back. "Breathe with me." He wrapped the blanket around her shoulders.

Charlie focused on Sean's regular breathing. Her breath came in short wheezes. "I'm trying."

"One, two," he said. "Easy does it."

"But—"

"If you're talking, you're not breathing."

Charlie breathed with him until she lost track of time and almost forgot the storm. Until the world narrowed to only her and Sean, the thump of his heart against her chest, the rhythm of his breath and his hands tracing slow circles on her back.

She opened her eyes and eased away from him. "The storm stopped?"

"Looks like it." Sean pointed out the window to where a watery sun poked out from behind a cloud and steam rose off the lake. "It's moved over the mountain to Kincaid."

"Thank you." Her voice shook as she grabbed her

phone. She'd hung on to him for twenty minutes. "I don't usually, you know…"

She winced as the reality of what had happened hit her. Not only had she had a panic attack, but she'd had one with Sean. She'd hidden the attacks from Mia, her friends, everyone, because she was afraid of being judged, afraid of that post-traumatic stress disorder label. Yet she'd had a crack-up in front of the one person she needed to be on her guard with. The one person she couldn't trust and who couldn't trust her either.

"It's okay." Sean rested his forearms on his thighs. She didn't see judgment in his face, only compassion, maybe even understanding.

She took a breath. Despite everything between them, she needed him to know this was part of who she was now. "The thunder was a trigger. It reminded me…"

"Reminded you of what?" His voice was gentle.

"All the time I've spent in war zones. Kids only a few years older than Ty, but with old men's eyes, killing like it was a sport. The heat, the noise, the dirt." She looked at her hands, at the faint white line on the left one that marked the fishhook scar. "Their stories haunt me, but they're stories I had to tell."

Sean's eyes darkened. "Tell me. Help me understand. It's a world away from what I know. I build boats."

"Which isn't likely to get you blown up." She let go of her phone and set it on the coffee table.

"True." He gave her a wry smile. "I want to know about your life. What you do. Why you do it."

"I chase stories like some people chase storms. I show how global political issues impact ordinary people and their families. I loved it until…" Her heart pounded. Until the earth had blown up in front of her. And people she'd talked to five minutes before had been blown up too.

He held her gaze. Waiting.

She gulped. "You asked if I'd written about what happened in Syria. Nobody ever asked me that before. Maybe if I write, I can start to let it go."

"And then?" Sean's gaze never left hers.

"I'll go where I'm sent, where the next story is. It's not always about people trying to kill each other for a cause most of them don't understand." She got to her feet and put distance between them. "I'm a foreign correspondent. It's my life. It's what I know, what I'm good at, who I am."

"Did you ever think it doesn't have to be that way?" His voice was quiet, and the words dropped between them like pebbles into the lake.

"I fought for years to do front-line reporting. To be accepted." She willed herself to keep talking, even if she didn't like his answer. "Are you saying I should give it up?"

"Of course not. All I'm saying is the job almost got you killed, so maybe you should think about that." He stood and rammed his hands into his pockets.

"Everybody, the guys in the newsroom, my dad, they all said I'd never make it. But I did. Even my mom wondered why I couldn't do something like travel writing or fashion journalism." Charlie backed toward the window. "Can you see me writing about beach resorts or hemlines? That's Mia's life, not mine."

"What I hear is you're still hung up on being good enough for your dad and competing with your sister." He followed her, and his gaze drilled into hers.

"That's a cheap shot." Charlie shrugged because she didn't want him to see he'd hit a nerve. "Especially coming from a guy like you whose future was mapped out for him from the day he was born. My dad's dead, and why would I compete with Mia?"

She hadn't competed, because her sister was so perfect she couldn't. She'd run away instead. Except Mia wasn't as perfect as Charlie assumed and had been fighting demons of her own.

"You're right. It was a cheap shot, but maybe I know where you're coming from. I don't have much of a life beyond work either."

"Oh." Her breath caught at his soft admission. For the Sean she'd known, work had always come first and he'd never complained, never questioned it.

"I care about you. Whether I like it or not, whether I want you to be or not, you're part of my life." He stared at his feet, his voice almost inaudible. "It matters to me what happens to you."

Emotion lodged at the back of Charlie's throat like the big green marble Sean had given her for her seventh birthday. The one he'd bought with his allowance after the two of them had spotted it at the hardware store in town and which she still had in her box of treasures.

"You're part of almost every memory I have of summers in Firefly Lake." His voice was unexpectedly intimate, and his eyes turned misty blue. "I want you to take care of yourself."

She shouldn't let herself get close to Sean again, but he looked good. He smelled good. And when she was around him, she felt like herself again. Like the girl she'd lost all those years ago. The one who thought she could take on the world as long as she had Sean by her side. She moved toward him.

"What the...?" He pushed by her. "The woodlot's on fire, a lightning strike."

She spun to face the window. An orange glow flickered over the trees. Sean spoke into his phone, sharp, urgent sentences, before he disconnected and ran into the hall.

She followed him and shoved her feet into the nearest pair of shoes, Naomi's sneakers.

"Get out to the road, away from the fire." He flung open the screen door and shaded his face with his hand. "Take my car into town." He tossed her the keys.

She let the keys fall on the mat. "No. I'm staying here to help you." She darted in front of him and blocked his way. On the porch, a smoke smell mingled with the fragrance of her mom's rosebushes.

His eyes narrowed. "What about your leg?"

"It's fine." Fanned by the wind, the flames crackled. Cold sweat beaded on the back of her neck.

"I don't believe you, but I don't have time to argue with you." Sean took the porch steps at a run and she followed him. "It'll be half an hour or more until the volunteer fire department gets here from town. We need to try to save the cottage." He turned toward the smoke, which curled over the trees, and checked the wind direction.

"What about Ty?" Charlie grabbed beach towels from the clothesline and slung them over her arm. "Shadow? And Carmichael's?" She covered her mouth with her free hand. On the other side of those trees, the flames inched closer to Sean's place.

"Ty left before the storm hit to deliver a boat to the Inn on the Lake. He texted me when he got there. Sarah was on her way to pick him up. I'll call him, but he's safe." His voice roughened and Charlie grabbed his arm. "I'll call

Trevor too. He's at the workshop with Shadow, and there are guys at the marina. They'll know what to do."

"You should go home. Trevor's a great guy, but—"

"I'm not leaving you." He squeezed her hand before scanning the woodlot again. "Get those towels wet." He pointed to the canoe on the beach, where Naomi had left it earlier. "Make sure the paddles are with the canoe."

Charlie touched his cheek with a gentle finger, light beard stubble rough beneath her palm. "Thank you," she whispered.

Because of what it might cost him to stay. What he might be giving up for her.

Charlie's touch burned Sean's face like a brand, hotter than any fire. He raced to the back of the cottage. If they were lucky, the wind wouldn't pick up any more. Or change direction.

He checked the tree line again as he fumbled with his phone. No signal. Ty had to be safe. And Trevor, Carmichael's. For an instant, he stood frozen to the dry grass. Tongues of flames arced skyward and cut a swathe between the lake and the road. Forcing his legs to move, he grabbed the hose from the reel by the kitchen door and soaked the ground between the cottage and the forest's edge.

Charlie stumbled out of the cottage and darted past him toward the canoe, her arms piled high with bags.

"Here." Seconds later she was back and threw a wet towel around his neck, another towel already in place to cover her nose and mouth. "The canoe's set if we need it, and I've closed the windows. I got a ladder from the shed and propped it against the porch in case the roof catches fire. And I took the chair cushions inside because they'd be flammable."

"You fix us a snack too?" Sean teased to try to get that look off her face. The look that told him she was more scared than she'd ever let on.

"You wish, Carmichael." Charlie grabbed the hose and trained it on what had once been her mom's garden. She stamped her feet and churned the sodden ground, turning Naomi's white sneakers black. Her wet jeans clung to her legs like a second skin, and her green WORLD WILDLIFE FUND T-shirt had a jagged tear at the hem.

"Watch your step." Sean started on the woodpile and tossed armfuls of wood away from the cottage.

"Oh, I'm watching." For a split second, she grinned, and it was like they were teenagers again. The teasing smile that said she was his girl and the one that made him happy he was her guy. Then the smile slid away and her face got tight, her eyes enormous in her white face.

Sean heaved wood onto the lawn until there was a bare space where the woodpile had been. "You got your wallet?"

"It's in my purse in the canoe. I've got my passport too."

Of course she'd have her passport. She'd be back on a plane and out of his life again before he knew it. He kicked at a pile of stray wood chips.

She tightened her grip on the hose and aimed it into the forest, as if she could single-handedly push back the fire. "It's bad, isn't it?" Her voice shook.

"Bad enough." He closed his hands over her icy fingers. "It's been a hot, dry summer here. The ground and those trees are like tinder."

"What about Carmichael's?" She searched his face, compelling him to tell her the truth. "And your house?"

"I don't know. I tried to call, but either the thunderstorm or the fire hit cell coverage." He coughed as acrid smoke burned into his lungs. "The house is farther back than Carmichael's, but with the way the wind's going…" The business he'd put his heart and soul into. The house where Ty had done most of his growing up and a dog he counted as family. "I'm sure Trevor has everything under control."

He rubbed a hand across his burning eyes. His twin would save the books with their grandfather's hand-drawn plans and their grandmother's painting. The things insurance money couldn't replace.

Charlie dropped the hose and touched his shoulder in wordless sympathy. That sixth sense she'd always had for what he felt and thought. "How much time have we got?" She took her hand away and picked up a rake.

"Five minutes, tops." He was grateful she'd never been the emotional type. Most women would have been crying and carrying on, hindering instead of helping. Not Charlie. She'd always been cool under pressure, and he'd loved how they'd been equal partners, a team.

"Okay." She dragged undergrowth away from the foundation with the rake,then pulled at vegetation with her bare hands to leave cleared soil behind.

"The wind…" He stopped, not wanting to frighten her even more.

"It's changed?"

"Looks like it."

A deer and a pair of foxes darted out of the woods and streaked past them, heading for safer ground.

"The animals know." She pointed to a flock of birds rising out of the trees. Their wings were a dark cloud against the livid red sky. "They do too."

Sean dragged the brush she'd cleared farther down the driveway. Maybe it was pointless. Maybe they should both have headed for town when they'd had the chance. Crouched on her hands and knees, Charlie tore at the rosebushes beside the porch.

"Charlie." Sean raised his voice above the roar of the fire.

"What?" She half turned. Her face was smeared with dirt, and her hands were spattered with blood from the thorns.

"We need to get out of here." He raised the hose high, one last time. Water arced in a big circle. "Now."

She clutched her throat. "My necklace. It's gone." She pawed in the dirt, her motions frantic.

"There's isn't enough time. You have to let it go."

"I can't. Mom gave it to me." Her voice was a high-pitched wail.

Sean crouched beside her in the carnage of the turned-up soil. Something glinted in the sunlight. Her gold heart necklace had snagged on a root, its chain broken. He tugged it free. "The lake." He thrust the pendant into her hand and urged her along beside him.

"What about your car?" She wheezed.

"Too late." He pointed to the flames that cut across the woodlot and devoured everything in their path, inching closer to the makeshift firebreak and the road. "Charlie?"

She stood motionless by the porch steps, and the wind whipped her hair around her face.

"Charlie?" He shouted louder and then, when she didn't respond, swung her into his arms and ran with her to the canoe. He slid it partway into the water and bundled her into the bow.

"Sorry." The word came out in a gasp. Her chest heaved and her eyes were blurry, unfocused. "For a second there, I..." She stuffed the necklace into the pocket of her jeans and dragged her hands through the water, washing away the blood. "Mom...I loved her so much, and she gave this little heart to me..."

"She loved you too. It'll be okay." He hoped like hell he was right. He pushed off and the canoe scraped the sandy lake bottom.

"I'm out of practice," she muttered as Sean stepped into the canoe and moved her purse, a backpack, a pink tote, and what looked like a dry-cleaning bag folded in two, clear plastic over shiny green fabric.

He knelt in the stern and picked up his paddle to push the canoe farther into the water. He couldn't let himself think about Ty. Or Shadow. Or Carmichael's. He couldn't think about anything but getting them to safety.

Sean jerked his head around as a boom sounded above the crackle of the fire. Ten feet away, the tree he and Charlie had built forts under as children teetered and crashed onto the boathouse. Flames licked into the roof, arced toward the dock.

He dipped the paddle into the water. "Teamwork."

"We're in this together. I've got your back." Her voice was muffled, like she was trying not to cry.

He steered the canoe toward the middle of the lake. The wind cut across his face, and a cloud of ash momentarily blinded him. "One, two," he counted, and on three, the canoe moved forward. Charlie matched him stroke for stroke as she paddled in the rhythm he'd taught her long ago.

About five hundred yards out, he stopped. His body was

drenched in sweat, and he shook from the exertion and the aftermath of the adrenaline rush.

"Sean?" Charlie's voice was high and raspy, and the canoe lurched as she paddled solo.

"We're far enough out. We can rest here." He tried his phone again. Nothing. She turned to face him and rummaged in the pink tote. Barbie dolls like his nieces used to play with tumbled out. "You saved Barbie?"

Her face flushed and she pulled a bottle of water from the bag. "Emma loves these dolls and she'd have been heartbroken if they'd burned up." She twisted the cap off the water and handed it to him.

He tipped the bottle into his mouth. Liquid trickled down his throat and soothed the rawness. "What else did you save?"

"The teddy bear Naomi's had since she was born. Mia's family photos, my camera and computer, some clothes." She pushed the dry-cleaning bag under her seat.

"What's in there?"

"A dress." She crossed her arms over her chest, and her breasts heaved beneath a picture of a panda. "And shoes."

Of all the things he'd have expected Charlie to save, a dress and shoes wouldn't be them. It was a fancy dress, by the look of it.

But there were a lot of things about this Charlie he hadn't expected.

Her vulnerability during the thunderstorm, which had shocked him and, in equal measure, made him want to protect her. Charlie Gibbs had never needed protection, by him or anybody else.

While he knew she loved her nieces, he guessed she didn't see them much, and he'd expected it would be more

of a hands-off kind of love. Instead, she was a real part of
their lives and knew what was important to them.

He swallowed, and fear cut off his windpipe. Fear that
had nothing to do with fear for his son at the inn, or
the fire that still raged on shore, the cloud of smoke and
ash drifting closer toward Carmichael's. Instead, it was an
even deeper, more primitive fear. He'd never imagined, despite everything, despite how she'd broken his trust and his
heart, and hadn't told him about their child, that Charlie
would still have this kind of hold over him.

A hold so strong it had driven him to keep her safe at
all costs and almost made him forget how things had ended
between them. The lies, the hurting, and the silence.

The canoe rocked in the wind and drifted out into the
lake as memories washed over him.

He and Charlie playing on that beach, building elaborate
castles with turrets and moats, eating peanut butter and
jelly sandwiches, which tasted of sunshine and sand.

Mrs. Gibbs, as beautiful as any movie star, reading on
the porch or dancing to pop music from a battery-powered
radio. Charlie and Mia dancing along with her.

Mia sunbathing on the dock in a tiny bikini and always
too grown-up to build a sand castle. Reading fashion magazines and flirting with city boys, the sons of doctors and
lawyers from nearby cottages.

Summer smells of barbecues and suntan lotion and the
sweet taste of strawberry Popsicles, which melted in his
mouth, the juice trickling down his chin.

Dr. Gibbs, arriving late on Friday nights in a dark suit, a
tie loose around his neck, sucking away the fun, the music,
and the laughter. A handsome man with dark hair threaded
with silver and blue eyes like flints, whose presence made

the air thick and heavy. Everyone, even though nobody ever said it aloud, counting the hours until it was time for him to go back to the city again.

And always, there was Charlie, his sunshine. The girl he'd fallen in love with more each summer. Their childhood friendship had deepened, matured, until the day she'd told him it was over.

In the distance, emergency sirens wailed. Sean reached for Charlie's hand. She met him halfway and linked her fingers with his.

"Ty's okay. There's no way the fire can jump across the water at the end of the point, and the inn's a couple of miles beyond there. But your house, Carmichael's..." She stopped.

He nodded, unable to speak. Even if the worst happened, a house and a business could be replaced.

He tightened his grip on Charlie's hand. Her knuckles were scraped and bloody, and she was covered in mud and soot, her hair a wild tangle around her face. In all the years he'd known her, she'd never looked more beautiful.

Or more lost and alone.

Chapter Eleven

Charlie couldn't stop shaking, and despite taking one of her little white pills, she found that her leg hurt more than it had in weeks. She sat on the only unscathed Adirondack chair, which had ended up at the edge of the lake, and pulled the blanket one of the paramedics had given her tighter around her shoulders.

The yard was a soggy mess of emergency vehicles, and tire tracks extended across the beach. The boathouse was gone and the charred remains of the dock floated in the water. But the cottage was safe. At least most of it.

She squeezed her eyes shut, still seeing the flames that had devoured the old wood of the porch. The firefighters had perched on ladders to beat back more flames that threatened the roof, before they smashed through Naomi and Emma's bedroom window. She fisted a hand to her mouth and opened her eyes again.

Beyond the ruined porch, Sean was in a huddle with the forest fire warden and crew from the fire station in Kincaid.

He had an arm around Ty, and behind him stood a woman who must be Sarah. Ty's mom. Sean's ex-wife.

A woman who was everything Charlie wasn't. She was tall, Nordic blond, and slender with pale blue eyes, wearing a pink vest and a short white skirt that showed off her long, smooth legs and toned figure. Throat dry, Charlie tried to untangle her snarled hair with her fingers.

"Gorgeous, isn't she?" Linnie knelt beside her.

Charlie didn't need to ask who Linnie meant. "Yeah." She gave up on her hair and looked at the cuts on her hands.

"Sarah's a preschool teacher, so she's great with kids." Linnie opened a first-aid kit and began to clean Charlie's right hand. The antiseptic stung and made her eyes water. "She sings in the church choir, makes jam, and sews most of her clothes."

"And?" Charlie caught the teasing glint in Linnie's eyes.

"Whenever I'm around her for more than half an hour, I want to throw stuff just to shake things up a bit." Linnie patted Charlie's good knee.

"What happened between her and Sean?" Although Sean had said Sarah wanted someone different, she wanted to know what Linnie thought.

Linnie finished cleaning Charlie's right hand and started on the left. "I don't know, not really. Sarah's nice enough and she's a good mom to Ty and little Emily and Olivia. A great cook too. She makes a banana cream pie to die for."

"When I knew him before, Sean didn't like banana cream pie."

"He still doesn't, which pretty much sums it up. Sarah and Sean, from what I saw, even when they stood to get married, never fit together." Linnie pulled out bandages and a roll of surgical tape from the first-aid kit.

"Why not?" Sarah sounded conventional and settled. The kind of woman who should have been exactly right for Sean.

Linnie leaned back on her heels and slid a bandage out of the package. "Sarah's allergic to dogs and she hates boats and most outdoor sports, although she's always in the gym. If she'd been caught in the fire, you can bet we'd have heard her screams from town. Not like you. Sean said you were real brave."

"He did?" Charlie looked back at the cottage and at Sean, who still had his arm around Ty like he couldn't bear to let his son go. All of a sudden, she found it hard to breathe.

"I heard him when he was on the phone to Trevor after cell coverage came back." Linnie wrapped the bandage around one of Charlie's palms and secured the ends with tape. "My husband surprised me. Since he's the younger twin, he's always looked up to Sean. But when Sean wasn't there, he coped fine."

She tapped Charlie's bandaged hand. "Apart from some water damage, Carmichael's is okay and Shadow is too. The wind changed direction, so the fire veered away from Sean's house."

"Straight for the cottage," Charlie said.

"You can rebuild the porch if you want and fix the roof. Replace the broken windows and repaint. It could have been a lot worse. You're both okay and so is Sean's car." Linnie finished wrapping Charlie's other hand and closed the first-aid kit. "Anyway, you're selling." She hesitated for a heartbeat. "Aren't you?"

"I don't have much choice."

Linnie's eyes narrowed. "You always have a choice."

And the choice was to support herself. She was on her own. The money from the cottage sale would give her stability and financial security. And Mia was even more desperate. If they couldn't find another buyer, they'd have to sell to Tat Chee. A pang of loss rippled through her.

Charlie looked at her bandaged hands. "Hey, you did a good job. Really professional."

Linnie flushed and smoothed her T-shirt over her shorts. "I wanted to be a nurse."

Charlie tilted her head. "We used to talk about everything. How could I have forgotten that?"

"I never told you. I never told anybody because I didn't think I was smart enough. I was always average at school." Linnie looked at her feet. "Not like you. You're smart. You always knew what you wanted and you went for it."

"Maybe it looks like that." Linnie couldn't see inside her, couldn't see the reasons why Charlie made the choices she did. Or feel the regrets.

"I married Trevor. I loved him. I still do." She looked at Charlie as if daring Charlie to contradict her. "Then before I knew what hit me, I had a husband and four kids under six."

"You're a great wife and mom." Charlie stopped at the pain in Linnie's eyes.

"I love my girls." Linnie twisted her hands together. "But I'm thirty-six, and I'm still working part-time at the Firefly Lake Market, same as I did in high school. Talking to the same customers about the price of eggs and the best way to cook pork chops."

"I never thought you wanted anything else." Charlie wiggled from under the blanket to put an awkward arm around Linnie's tight shoulders.

"I did, but my folks told me not to be silly." Linnie's shoulders slumped. "My brother's the smart one. He went to college, and he teaches math at the high school. End of story."

Charlie sucked in a breath. How could she not have guessed how Linnie felt? "I always thought you were smart. If you weren't, you wouldn't have gotten me out of trouble so many times when we were kids."

Linnie leaned into Charlie. "But now it's too late for me."

"Of course it isn't. I'll help you any way I can. What do you want to do?" Not that she was one to offer advice. Charlie toed off Naomi's ruined sneakers. Not when she'd made enough mistakes herself.

"I don't know. What I do know is in ten years I'll be nearing fifty. The girls will have left home and that pink polyester uniform Jerry makes us wear won't look any better on me than it does now." Linnie tried to smile, but tears shimmered deep in her eyes.

"You work for Jerry Roy? He's ancient. He's run that market since forever." Charlie's mouth dropped open in astonishment.

"Hardly. He's only in his early fifties, but the men in that family all went bald young." She grinned, a real smile this time. "Trevor and Sean have sure kept their looks. At least I had the good luck to marry a guy who was hot in high school and has stayed hot. Even after all these years, he's still fantastic in bed."

Charlie's face flamed. Sean had been fantastic in bed. How fantastic she hadn't realized until she'd been with guys who weren't. "I, uh..."

"Sorry." Linnie stood and brushed sand off her shorts. "I

forgot you never wanted to talk about stuff like that." She whistled, long and low.

"What?" Charlie flipped her head around as Mia's car pulled into the driveway. When the BMW bumped to a stop, Naomi got out and ran toward Ty. Mia followed, holding Emma's hand, and picked her way across the rough ground. Although she oozed effortless chic in white designer jeans and a simple black T-shirt, the sadness in her face tugged at Charlie's heart.

"Look at those sneakers. Jimmy Choo?" Linnie elbowed Charlie in the ribs.

"How would I know?" Charlie elbowed Linnie back. "And how would you know?"

"I read the celebrity magazines when it's slow at the market. I may not live in the bright lights, but it doesn't mean I don't follow what's going on in the world." She sobered and hooked Charlie into a one-armed hug. "Thank you. I'll think about what you said."

Returning Linnie's hug, an embrace both familiar and new, Charlie remembered something about having a friend she didn't work with. She could talk with a girlfriend in a way she couldn't with a work colleague. And if she was a true friend, if she was someone like Linnie who'd known her since childhood, she was the kind of friend you could count on.

Mia tapped a black sneaker on the sand, her phone wedged to one ear. "I need two rooms. For tonight and probably all next week." She glanced at Charlie. "You look pale. No wonder."

"I'm fine." Charlie tried to sound convincing to silence the doubts telling her maybe she'd never be as fit as she was before. If she wasn't, how could she go back into the field and be the kind of journalist that defined who and what she was?

"Lean on me." Mia wrapped an arm around Charlie's waist. "There's a golf tournament at the Inn on the Lake. They said they're all booked."

"They probably are." Charlie made herself stand straight. "I can stay here. It'll be like camping." She clasped Emma's hand and tried to make the little girl smile.

"You can't stay at the cottage. They won't even let us inside until the insurance company comes out and the building...you...what?" Mia spoke into the phone again.

Linnie linked an arm with Charlie. "You know I'd have you stay with us, but we have a small house and the girls have friends over this week."

"I understand." Charlie glanced toward the driveway where Sean walked Sarah and Ty to a blue Ford Taurus. Naomi tagged behind.

"I can't stay there, not with two young girls. My sister can't either." Mia put a hand over her phone. "They're calling Shady Sands, the motel with the bar out front, where the road crew—"

"Shady Sands would be fine for me." Charlie smothered a smile as she remembered some of the places she'd stayed. She'd have missed a lot of stories if she'd been holed up in some fancy hotel with the rest of the media pack.

"Shady Sands is full too." Mia tightened her grip on Charlie. "As is the Cozy Pines Bed and Breakfast and every other place between here and Kincaid." She swiveled to look at Linnie. "I managed to get one room at the Inn on the Lake. Over the kitchen with one bed for the girls and me to share."

"I'll call around," Linnie said, "but folks come from

all over for the golf tournament, and the fair's coming up. Most of us have people staying." She glanced at her watch. "I need to get home. I can drop stuff off later if you two need to borrow clothes or anything. If you're really stuck, I'll put a couple of the girls in a tent in the backyard so Charlie can at least have a bed."

"Thanks," Charlie said.

"Naomi?" Mia called to her daughter, who still stood in the driveway with Ty. "Come back here. I need you and Emma close."

Charlie squeezed Emma's hand again. "The inn will be fun. There's a swimming pool and maybe your mom will let you order room service. You can take your Barbie dolls with you too. It'll be an adventure." Over Emma's head, she glanced at Sean coming up the driveway, his stride purposeful.

"I guess." Emma's lower lip wobbled and she clutched her Barbie bag in one small fist. "But I like it here with you. I was scared when I saw the fire and the policeman wouldn't let us drive down the road. What if the fire comes back?"

"The fire's all out, honey. I like it with you too, but at the inn you won't be far away from me. Please don't cry." Panic curled in the pit of her stomach and Charlie looked for Mia, who was on the phone again. Crying children were her sister's department.

Linnie, who would have known what to do, was already halfway down the driveway, her SUV spraying gravel.

"Hey." Sean knelt beside Emma. "Those dolls are special to you, aren't they?"

"That's why Auntie Charlotte saved them. She's a heroine."

"Exactly." Sean looked Emma over. "She needs you to be a heroine and help your mom and your sister. Can you do that?"

"I'll try." Emma looked at Charlie and then back at Sean. "The fire's really out? You promise?"

"Pinkie swear." Sean linked his little finger with Emma's.

"But the fire could still come back, and if Auntie Charlotte can't stay at the inn with us she won't have anybody to look after her. She'll be all alone." Two tears spilled out of Emma's blue eyes and trickled down her face.

"Your auntie Charlotte won't be alone, sweetheart. She'll stay with me. I'll keep her safe." Over Emma's head, Sean's gaze met Charlie's and held.

Emma skipped. "You've got a real big house. Crystal showed me the day we..." She clapped a hand over her mouth.

"But—" Charlie began.

"Emma, please tell your sister to get off the phone and come back here." Mia had disconnected her call. "I know Sean wants to help, but you can't stay with him," she added when Emma was out of earshot.

"Why not?" Charlie glanced at Sean, but his expression didn't give anything away. Only his stance, watchful and wary, told her he held himself in check.

"People would talk." Mia's skin was stretched tight across her sculpted cheekbones.

"I'm a grown woman and—"

"Gossip still hurts no matter how old you are." Mia made a soft sound and stared at the lake. "Besides, I could've lost you today." She dropped her phone into her purse with a jerky motion.

"You didn't." Warmth bloomed in Charlie's heart. This was the Mia she remembered, a mother hen worried about her chicks.

"Sean saved you." Mia shot him a look of gratitude. "People will talk anyway, but if you stay at his house, they'll talk even more."

"Whether I stay with him or not isn't anything to do with anybody else." Charlie pressed her lips together.

"It's something to do with *me*, Sunshine." Sean moved in close, and his voice was a sexy whisper. "I want you to stay with me, and I won't take no for an answer. For once in your life don't argue." He grinned before he turned to Mia, his expression firm. "If any of the town gossips say one word, tell me and I'll deal with them."

"I..." Charlie's tongue got wedged to the roof of her mouth. She recognized Sean's teasing banter. That firmness too. Sean always took a stand for people he cared about.

"Thank you. I didn't mean..." Mia hugged her purse. "I don't want Charlie to get hurt. Or anybody to get hurt." She glanced at Sean and then Naomi, still watching the driveway where Ty and Sarah had disappeared. "If Charlie comes over to the inn with me, I'm sure we could borrow a folding bed for a few nights."

"No." Charlie's stomach knotted.

She didn't want to share a room with Mia and the girls. Not with the nightmares that still plagued her and woke her with a silent scream, disoriented and drenched in sweat.

Charlie looked at Sean for a long moment. She didn't want anybody to get hurt either. She'd broken her heart over Sean once, and she'd be foolish to let herself get drawn into his life again, or into Firefly Lake either. The close-knit web of family and community was as much a part of him as breathing.

She turned to her sister to make her understand she wasn't choosing Sean over her. "I'll call you later, okay? Staying with Sean will only be for tonight."

"Sure." Mia hugged Charlie, the bones in her arms sharp. "You look after her, you hear? I can't lose her."

"I will. I promise." Sean's voice was low, and he and Mia exchanged a look Charlie couldn't read.

"I don't need you to look after me." It had been a long time since Charlie had let anyone look out for her, a man most of all.

"You may not need it," he said, "but I want to."

Charlie opened her mouth and then closed it. Even though she shouldn't, she wanted it too. Wanted the comfort and care she'd once found with him. Which they'd once found together.

After giving Charlie one last hug, Mia walked back to the car. She walked with a sexy little wiggle of the hips that Charlie used to envy and had never mastered. Now, though, her sister didn't look sexy. Even from behind, she looked tired and forlorn. Her shoulders were hunched, and her body was rigid.

Charlie stumbled forward and stopped. "I'll call you later."

Mia gave a jerky wave and got into the car, leaving Charlie alone with Sean, the ruined cottage, and a leaden weight the size of a basketball lodged in the pit of her stomach.

Sean parked the MG in the space behind his house and cut the engine. "Here we are."

Charlie huddled in the passenger seat. She'd wrapped a blanket around her like a cape, and her chin was tucked into her chest. She opened her eyes and blinked at him, like a sleepy owl.

Protectiveness rolled over him. "My house. We're here." He tried to see his place through her eyes. The soft gray clapboard with a big stone chimney to one side, the wrap-around porch, and the bay windows upstairs and down; a new house nevertheless part of the Vermont landscape, solid and rooted in place.

Sean rubbed his palms across his temples as the reality of the day and what he could have lost hit him afresh. He steadied his breathing. Charlie was stubborn and hard-headed, but she was also so damn sexy that every time he got close to her he was like a horny teenager again.

"Oh." She struggled to sit up straight. "I'll be fine once I shower and change. I texted Linnie and asked her to loan me some clothes." Her bright smile didn't fool him for a second.

He got out of the car and came around to Charlie's side to open her door and grab her stuff from behind the seat. Only he wasn't a teenager, and something had changed between them today, something he wasn't sure he was ready for. He slung Charlie's backpack over his shoulder and took her arm to help her out of the car.

"I can manage." Charlie stepped forward and bumped into Ty's skateboard, propped outside the back door.

"Humor me. I promised your sister I'd look after you." Sean righted the skateboard and bit back a grin at the shocked expression on Charlie's face. Mia was looking out for Charlie to protect her in a way he hadn't expected, a way he respected, since it was rooted in love.

"What will your mom say when she finds out I'm staying here?" Charlie's expression became wary.

"It's none of her business." Although his mom had made it clear she didn't want him having anything to do with Charlie because she was a Gibbs. When he'd asked why, she'd snapped her mouth shut like one of the turtles in the mudflats along the river outside town and refused to answer.

He handed Charlie the dry-cleaning bag, then opened the door and led her through the garage, past his work truck, and into the mudroom, where Shadow greeted them with a frenzy of barks and tail wagging.

He leaned against the kitchen door. The bravado on her face, mixed with vulnerability, twisted his heart. As if sensing that he was trying to figure out what she was thinking, she dropped to her knees beside Shadow.

"Hey, girl." She rubbed under Shadow's chin. "How did you get in here?"

"Once the fire was out, Trevor needed to get her out from underfoot. He brought her up to the house."

"Oh." Charlie rested her face against the dog's head, and Sean's stomach somersaulted. "I bet you were real scared today. It's okay," she whispered. "All okay, precious." She stifled a yawn. Her eyes were purple-shadowed. Her shoulders slumped as if her head was too heavy for her body, and she rested her weight on her right side like she did when she was tired, when her leg hurt and she didn't want anybody to guess.

Sean let out a breath he hadn't realized he held. "I'll show you around and let you get settled."

She stood and followed him into the kitchen, Shadow ambling beside her. "Nice." Her eyes widened as she scanned the bright, airy room with state-of-the-art appliances. She ran a hand across a granite work surface and checked out the maple wine rack he'd built himself.

"You hungry? I can barbecue steaks." Even though there was at least a foot of space between them, Sean sensed the warm softness of her skin. Her wariness and shallow breathing told him she was as affected by him as he was by her.

"I don't eat meat anymore." She turned away from the patio door leading to the wide deck and gave him a dry smile. "You go ahead. I'm not hungry anyway."

"Oh." He was a meat, potatoes, and gravy kind of guy. "If you change your mind, there's salad fixings in the fridge and tomatoes from Linnie's garden. I got bread at the bakery in town earlier."

He moved out of the kitchen into the living room, which ran along the western side of the house and overlooked the lake. The setting sun reflected off prisms in the light fixture he'd hung from the cathedral ceiling and bathed the simple wooden couches topped with plump green cushions in a rosy glow.

"You like it?" He didn't analyze why it was important she like his place. Only somehow it was.

Her head swung around, and her eyes were a warm brown with no guile. "It's like a cottage." The corners of her lips turned up. "A very special cottage."

"That's the idea." He'd wanted a house that fit into the north woods like it had grown out of them, so he'd found an architect to design it.

"Did you and Sarah live here together?" She walked toward the big fieldstone fireplace that anchored one end of the room.

"No. We had a house in town. Sarah never liked it out by the lake."

"Sarah was with you today after the fire?" Charlie studied the wooden duck decoys on the mantelpiece.

"She was." Sean came close beside her. "Did that bother you?"

"Of course not." Charlie shrugged and stuck her chin out.

"She'll always be Ty's mom, but Sarah and I were over a long time ago." He cupped her chin in his hands. "What you and I had, I never found with anyone else."

"Me neither," she whispered.

"But I'm still a small-town guy and you're..." He shut his mouth fast.

"We're both who we are. Not who we were." She touched his hand before she moved away, swaying.

"Come on. You're asleep on your feet." Logic won over his heart, and he led her up the wide stairs to the landing. "Ty's room." He pointed to a closed door. "I'm on the other side at the front." He showed her the main bathroom, another room he used as an office, and the guest room. "You think you'll be comfortable?"

"It's great." She poked her head into the guest room decorated in blue and white, a brass bed tucked into one corner. "I can even see the lake." She pointed to a rectangle of blue through the window before putting the dry-cleaning bag over his grandmother's rocking chair. He followed and set her backpack in the middle of the carpet.

"There's a bathroom in here." He opened a smaller door tucked into the eaves. "Towels and toiletries are in the cabinet under the sink. A robe's behind the door."

"You have a beautiful home." She turned away from the window to face him.

"It's a lot of space for Ty and me, but we usually have Christmas here, so there's a houseful." He tried to smile. Those big family Christmases with Ty shuttling between his place and Sarah's were yet another reminder his family was fractured, of how he'd failed. "People sleep on couches, over in the old cottage even."

Charlie raised an eyebrow. "You didn't tear it down?"

"Why would I? My grandfather built it to last." Like her grandfather built the Gibbs cottage. "Ty and his friends like staying there. My nieces do too."

"I—"

"No." He stopped her. Afraid whatever she said would destroy the fragile connection between them, destroy what he'd begun to feel for her again. Not only the ever-present sexual desire, but something deeper, more profound. "It's been a rough day. You need to get cleaned up. I do too. Then you need to sleep and rest your leg."

"Is my leg that obvious?" She let out a shaky breath.

"Only to me."

"Oh." She dug a bare toe into the carpet. Somewhere along the way she'd lost Naomi's shoes. "About today..." She paused. "You were there for me and I appreciate it. You even found my necklace." She pulled it out of her pocket.

"I'll take it to the jeweler in town for you. She'll fix the chain as good as new."

"Mom gave it to me after the miscarriage. She said it was because the baby would always be in my heart." Charlie's voice was muffled.

"Since you told me, the baby will always be in *my* heart." Sean's throat burned as he took the necklace from her, his fingers closing around the tiny heart. He couldn't forgive Charlie for not telling him, but he couldn't doubt the loss of their child had hit her hard and she'd grieved. A part of her still did, judging by the pain in her eyes. "You were there for me too. You had my back. That's what you said, out on the lake."

Those words had shaken him to the core because up until the last she'd always been there for him, looked out for him. Maybe even when she left him and made a decision he wouldn't. Or couldn't.

"That's what friends are for." Her smile was forced.

"I better let you have your shower." He cleared his throat, his voice gruff. He motioned to the bathroom. "Take as long as you want. There's plenty of hot water."

And the water would sluice across her body, and he'd join her, bury himself in her softness. "I need to head to the workshop and make sure everything's okay there." If he thought about Carmichael's, he wouldn't think about her. "Make yourself at home."

"Thanks." She pushed a strand of silky hair away from her face, hair his fingers itched to touch.

"Shadow, no." Sean called for the dog. What was he doing? The woman had been through hell today and was practically falling over from exhaustion, and all he could think about was getting her naked.

"She looks comfy."

Stretched across the foot of the bed, on top of Linnie's log cabin quilt, Shadow thumped her tail. "You know you're not allowed on beds." Sean grabbed the dog's collar. "Ty lets her sleep with him sometimes, but you're a guest, and she wants to see what she can get away with."

"It's okay." Charlie stopped him. "Shadow wants to keep me company. Don't you, precious?" Her small fingers stroked Shadow's ears.

Shadow's tail hit the quilt again and the dog cracked a smile.

"We can have a girls' night in. Would you like that, Miss Shadow?"

Shadow rolled over to give Charlie access to her tummy. Her paws twitched and her eyes drifted closed.

"I bet I can find dog treats for you." Charlie's laugh rippled out, warm and rich, and Sean ached for her, for the woman she was, not the girl she'd been. "Go take your shower and get to work. I'll be fine. You know I love dogs."

He took a last look at Shadow, nose-to-nose with Charlie, and gritted his teeth. He was jealous. And what kind of guy was jealous of a dog?

Chapter Twelve

Charlie lurched upright, the bedsheet twisted around her hips. Her breathing was labored; sweat drenched her body. Moonlight slanted through a gap in the curtains and illuminated the strange room.

She fumbled for her phone and squinted at the time. Two in the morning. Her throat was tinder-dry, and vestiges of the nightmare pressed in on her as she wrestled the sheet away. She reached for the bedside table light and switched it on.

She was in Sean's guest room, with Shadow asleep at the foot of the bed. She reached for the dog and brushed her warm fur. Shadow's back rose and fell in a steady rhythm.

She eased out of bed and straightened the unfamiliar clothes. Linnie's clothes. A tight purple T-shirt and too-short purple-and-white pajama bottoms. "Shush, precious," she whispered when Shadow opened one eye. "I'll be right back after I get a snack."

Charlie padded to the bedroom door, pushed it open, and moved into the hall, where a night-light cast a soft glow. She rested her hand on the polished wood banister and tiptoed down the broad stairs. For a guy who'd grown up on the mill side of town, in a pocket-sized bungalow full of kids and dogs and noise, Sean had come a long way.

In the kitchen, moonlight showing her the way, she opened the freezer compartment of the fridge. He might not have any. She rummaged among several foil-wrapped parcels labeled PICKEREL. He did. Her mouth watered as she reached for the tub of ice cream. Strawberry Swirl, Simard Creamery's gold-medal winner, year after year.

Not bothering with a bowl, she found a spoon, sat on the floor by the patio door, peeled the lid off the tub, and dug in.

"Charlie?"

She dropped the spoon. It bounced across the floor, coming to rest by Sean's bare feet. Her face heated.

"Strawberry Swirl, huh?" Voice amused, he slid the patio door open and cool night air wafted in through the screen.

She scrambled to retrieve the spoon and brushed his leg. The fine blond hair set her nerve ends on fire. "Remember when your dad said he wished he could buy shares in Simard Creamery because we ate so much of this stuff?"

"I sure do." Sean's deep laugh rumbled. He grabbed two bowls from a kitchen cabinet and two more spoons from a drawer. "Were you really going to eat the whole tub?" He sat beside her, long legs bare beneath a pair of gray shorts. Heat radiated off him, and Charlie shivered.

"Yesterday was a bad day." She bent her head and used a clean spoon to scoop ice cream into a bowl, trying not to look at his naked chest. It was more muscular, powerful. A man's body, not a boy's.

He laughed again, his abs rippling. "You can take the girl out of Firefly Lake, but you can't pry the ice cream out of her grasp." He leaned in close and Charlie's heart skipped a beat. "Remember what we used to call it?"

"No." The lie tripped off her tongue.

"These lies are getting to be a habit with you, Pinocchio." He tweaked her nose and grinned before spooning ice cream into his bowl to empty the tub. "Sex on a spoon."

"That was a long time ago." She stared at his lips, mesmerized.

His tongue darted out to wet his bottom lip. "Not so long I don't remember how you liked it when I licked it off your—"

"Don't." Her nipples pebbled at the memory.

"We had some good times." His voice was raw, and desire crackled between them.

She couldn't let herself think about those times. "Shouldn't you put more clothes on?"

"You used to like it when I went without a shirt." His eyes darkened, so blue they were almost black. "I heard a noise." He gave her a slow smile. "But I pulled on shorts in case you got modest."

Her breathing quickened and hair rose on her arms. She pulled at the hem of Linnie's pajama bottoms to hide the scar. But when she raised her head, he wasn't looking at her legs. He was looking at her chest, how the points of her nipples pushed at the thin cotton top.

"What are you doing up?" His voice was a sexy caress.

"I had a nightmare." Charlie stared into the night, where the dark outline of the trees behind the house gave way to the space where the woodlot had been. The jagged shapes were eerie in the moonlight, and the smell of smoke lingered.

"About the fire?" His voice changed, comforting instead of sensual. He moved closer, and sandalwood soap replaced the smoky scent.

"Not exactly." Although the fire had likely triggered the nightmare she'd had since the accident, the one that made her remember what she wanted to forget, and made her worry about going back to work too. And then she worried more because she couldn't tell anyone what was happening without looking like she couldn't cope.

Sean snaked one arm around her shoulders. "Give yourself a break. What you went through yesterday is enough to give anybody nightmares."

Charlie rested her head on Sean's chest, and the reassuring thump of his heart reverberated against her ear. "I keep seeing the cottage," she whispered, "the flames shooting from the roof. Those old trees." She squeezed her eyes shut.

"The trees will grow back." He stroked her hair, his fingers gentle.

She moved her head and stilled his hand. "It won't be the same, at least not in our lifetime." Until she'd been out in the middle of the lake and seen the inferno on shore, she hadn't realized how much she'd counted on the cottage always being the same. A link with her mom and her childhood no matter where she was in the world.

Sean let out a heavy breath. "If you sell to Tat Chee, it won't be the same anyway. They'll bulldoze the lot. Thanks to the fire, they've got a head start."

He moved away and Charlie's skin cooled.

"After I talked to Mia, I called one of my contacts in Boston last night," she said. "Jason covers environmental stories, community stories, some travel pieces, all across New England. He agreed to do some research."

"Thank you." Sean rested his elbows on his knees.

"The right media coverage might help us find another buyer." Or it might not. It might make things worse. Charlie pushed that thought away because she had to do something. Mia had been honest with her about why she wanted to sell, and she'd been honest with her sister about her doubts, even though she needed the money too. But they both wanted to be true to their mom's memory.

"Trevor told me a group in town wants to raise money to buy your place." Sean held her gaze, his eyes intent. "The historical society thinks there was an Abenaki hunting camp where the woodlot is. It could be an important cultural site."

"I see." Charlie stared out the window at the bare tree branches framed by dark hills. Mia was her only family. She wouldn't go behind her sister's back.

"It's still only talk." Sean's voice was strained. "Besides, that group would need to raise a lot of money to match what Tat Chee's bound to offer you. At least if what they offered me is any indication."

"Did you talk to another lawyer?" She avoided his gaze, afraid of what she might see.

"I did, but if you won't break up the lot, there's not much I can do. I don't have that much spare cash right now. Not after buying the marina in town." He let out a harsh breath. "Ty's got college soon. My mom's older and she'll need help."

So he'd support her. Charlie filled in the words Sean

didn't say. He was still a good guy. Responsible and honorable, the kind of man a woman could count on for the long haul.

If she was thinking about the long haul, which she wasn't, Charlie reminded herself. If only she had the money to help Mia and secure her own future. But she didn't.

Sean's expression turned grim. "My dad devoted his life to Carmichael's. My grandfather did too. They were the best men I ever knew. I promised them I'd keep the business going to look after Mom and the rest of the family."

"You've kept your promise and more." Charlie laid a hand on his arm, the muscles tight under her touch. "Nobody could fault you."

"Mom depends on me." Sean pulled his arm away. "Trevor does too, even my sisters and their families. Jess works in the office, Megan does the books, and Jill manages our courses." He stood, his back to Charlie, shoulders rigid. "Crystal helps out at the marina to add to her college fund. All of us have a stake in Carmichael's."

"Who do you depend on?"

Sean turned, and she drew a sharp breath at the small sun tattoo on his right biceps. A tattoo she figured he'd have had removed long ago. "I don't know what you mean."

"You keep talking about your family and how they depend on you. What about you?" She got to her feet and stood beside him. "You're so busy looking after everybody else. Maybe you haven't noticed they've got their lives."

"I don't depend on anybody. I don't need to." Sean slammed the patio door shut. "I kept Carmichael's going because I wanted to make a success of it for me too."

She forced the words out through numb lips. "Linnie said Trevor did fine yesterday. Maybe you need to let go.

Trust Trevor more and trust yourself." Part of Charlie's mind registered the irony. She was asking Sean to do things she couldn't.

"I can't." A muscle worked in his tight jaw. "If I lose Carmichael's..."

Charlie dug her nails into her palms. "This isn't about Carmichael's. When it comes down to it, Carmichael's is a piece of real estate. Land, buildings, and good water frontage are what Tat Chee sees."

"That's not what I see." His voice throbbed with anger.

"You're more than Carmichael's." There was a sour taste in her mouth. "When you stayed to help me, fight the fire with me, you could have lost Carmichael's anyway."

"I didn't." His eyes were hard. "I depended on you more than anyone. But I stopped depending on people when you broke my trust. You lied to me then. How can I be sure you're not lying now?"

She stared at him for a long moment. Then without a word she turned and left the room, her footsteps making a dull *thud* on the carpeted stairs.

He'd hurt her. Sean looked around the kitchen, quiet apart from the low hum of the appliances. With the words that had come out of his mouth before he'd stopped to think, he'd put a look in Charlie's eyes that would haunt him for a long time, maybe forever. He picked up the empty ice cream tub and tossed it in the trash.

Although what he'd said was true, he didn't need to tell her, not when she was already hurting, not when it was too late to make any difference in how things had turned out.

He left the kitchen and went upstairs. On the landing, he stopped in front of her closed door.

A man like his dad would knock on that door and apologize. If he was half the man his dad had been, he wouldn't hesitate. The door swung open before he could raise his hand.

Charlie's face was red and blotchy like she'd been crying. Except Charlie wasn't a crier.

"Charlie." His voice rasped. "I want to—"

"No." Her voice was thick. "I shouldn't have judged you. I need to take a hard look at myself first. Even if I don't like what I see."

"I shouldn't have said what I did either." Sean let out a slow breath and his anger eased. "That was all a long time ago. It doesn't matter now."

"Doesn't it?" Charlie rubbed the back of a hand across her face, and her T-shirt strained across her breasts.

"Even if it does matter, it's over. I need to let it go." And he had to stop blaming her and blaming himself. He reached out and tucked a piece of hair behind her ear. The feelings he kept trying to bury roared to life as the thick strands slid through his fingers.

"Can you? Let it go?" Her face was inches from his, and her warm breath brushed his nape.

"Yes." The truth shocked him. He didn't want to spend the rest of his life tied in knots because of one woman. A woman who'd be gone again in another few weeks and he'd probably never see again.

All along he'd wanted Carmichael's for himself. Wanted to make it a success. Except he was kidding himself. He also wanted something else. Maybe even more than he wanted Carmichael's.

"Peaches," he murmured.

"What?" Her expression was puzzled.

"You smell like peaches." He leaned closer. Why did he torture himself? Why did he let himself still want her?

"It's Linnie's body lotion."

"No, it's you." His fingers grazed her cheek, and the softness of her skin made his breath tight.

Charlie moved back into the bedroom. She stopped and shifted her weight from one foot to the other. In the glow of the light from the bedside lamp, her face scrubbed clean, she looked young and innocent, like the girl he remembered.

He pulled his gaze away from her. It landed on the bed behind, covers tangled, pillows bunched. Shadow sprawled on the floor and watched them.

"I'll say good night." He cleared his throat.

"Good night." She hugged herself tight.

He grabbed the door handle, his legs all of a sudden unsteady. "What is it?"

"I'm scared." The words came out like she'd wrenched them from a hidden place deep inside. "Scared if I go to sleep, the nightmare will come back. Scared if I stay awake, I'll think about the fire and the cottage and Mia and Mom and the baby...oh, everything."

The anguish in her voice moved something deep inside him too. "What do you want from me?" His voice was as raw as hers, the pain as sharp.

"Stay with me?" She looked at him, a heartbreaking mixture of desirable woman and frightened girl. "Not for sex." Like he'd had any doubt about what she might be offering. Her face reddened. "I don't want to be alone."

His heart pounded because of what it had cost her to admit there was something she couldn't handle. He went to the bed and straightened the covers. "Get in."

She moved to the far side and tucked her feet underneath her. The pajama legs slid up to her knees. He took a ragged breath at the network of scar tissue that encircled her left calf.

She yanked the pajamas down and covered herself with the quilt to her chin. "Sorry."

"What do you have to be sorry about?" He sat on the edge of the bed.

"My leg is ugly." Her voice was muffled. "So ugly I can barely look at it. So ugly I can't wear shorts or skirts or swim."

"Can't or won't?"

"What's the difference?" She turned her head on the pillow, away from him. "Everybody would stare at me and wonder and whisper and ask questions."

"So what if people notice? What makes it their business?" He touched her shoulder. "For anybody who knows you, who cares about you, that scar won't make any difference. Why would you think it would?"

"I'm not me. I'm not the person I used to be." Her words came out in an anguished cry. She twisted, and the hurt in her milk-chocolate eyes hit him harder than the scar on her leg had.

He slid into bed beside her, and the mattress gave under his weight. "You can still write your stories. Come winter, if you want, I bet you'll be back on your snowboard."

Her eyes widened. "How do you know I snowboard?"

"That picture you've got on your Facebook page is a good clue."

"You found me on Facebook?" Her smile was amused and reminded Sean how easy it used to be between them.

"Ty did. Remember those articles you wrote last year

about African farmers? That *think globally, act locally* idea is right up his street." He leaned on one elbow and faced her. "You have a scar on your leg. What happened to you must have hurt like hell, but that scar's on the outside. Sure, it changed how you look, but who you are on the inside is up to you."

"You really mean that, don't you?" Doubt flickered across her face.

"I do." Tiredness slammed into him. He reached over and flipped off the light, plunging the bedroom into darkness.

"Maybe I'm not sure who I am on the inside." She tugged on the quilt. "Not anymore."

Typical Charlie: Once she got hold of an idea, she was like Shadow chewing on a bone. Sean grabbed his half of the quilt. "Do me a favor. Wait to figure out the big questions of life until daylight." He pulled harder on the bedclothes. "Don't hog the blankets either."

"I only—"

"You need to learn to switch off." He anchored the quilt under his shoulder.

She burrowed into the covers, and her breasts brushed his arm. "Said the pot to the kettle."

He rolled on his side so she wouldn't nudge the telltale bulge in his shorts. "I can switch off."

"Prove it." She moved closer. The peach scent was intoxicating. He wanted to taste her skin. Every inch of it.

He clenched his jaw and willed himself not to roll back over, cover her body with his, take what he wanted and give her what she used to want too. "Let's spend the day together tomorrow. Go bike riding, swim, have a picnic, and get takeout for dinner."

"I...uh...swimming, I can't." Her voice got small.

"You said you want to figure out who you are. The girl I remember could swim halfway across the lake without breaking a sweat." He tugged on his shorts in a vain attempt to ease the pressure in his groin. "I've seen your leg."

"Mia called the insurance company, and they're sending a guy out to the cottage in the morning to start the claim process. I should be there when she talks to him." Charlie sounded so earnest Sean almost believed her.

"What do you want?" He gripped the pillow to keep himself from turning to touch her.

She hesitated for several endless seconds. "I want to spend time with you. As friends, like we used to."

"Then that's what we'll do." He could do this friend thing. How hard could it be?

A cold nose bumped his arm and two paws slid on the edge of the bed next to his face. "Don't even think about it, Shadow." He leaned over and eyeballed the dog. "Charlie may have let you sleep with her, but you're not getting on this bed while I'm in it." He edged the dog's paws away. Shadow turned around three times and flopped onto the floor.

Out of the darkness Charlie's laughter warmed him.

"What?" He glanced over his shoulder.

"We never slept together, did we? Shared a bed like this?"

"No, I don't think we ever did." He leaned over and kissed her forehead. The kiss was not about lust or the passion always there between them but rather about healing. And maybe even about hope. "Try and get some sleep, Sunshine." He settled back onto his side of the bed.

"You too." She spooned into his back, soft and warm, everything he'd ever wanted and needed.

But even as he curled against her and drifted toward sleep, he reminded himself that he already had what he wanted and needed. And he'd stopped thinking about forever a long time ago.

One day with Charlie wouldn't change that.

Chapter Thirteen

Trevor wedged a stack of file folders into the only clear space on Sean's desk. "Charlie still asleep?" His blue eyes had a teasing glint.

"She was when I left." Sean picked up the top file without seeing it. Instead, Charlie's luscious body sprawled across his guest room bed came to mind. The little mewling noise she made when he eased away from her. How he'd forced himself to not run a hand along her bare arm, to not nuzzle the soft skin at her neck. "She was pretty tired after yesterday."

"I guess Linnie won't be setting you up on more dates anytime soon." Trevor's voice shook with suppressed laughter.

Sean shoved the files aside. It would take weeks to get the office organized again, but Trevor had saved their grandmother's painting, their grandfather's plans, and more. He'd done everything Sean would have if he'd been there. "You saw the damage to that cottage. Charlie needed a place to stay."

"Sure she did." Trevor grinned. "And wasn't it convenient you were there to help her out? Always the gentleman." He snorted.

"You watch too many chick flicks with those girls of yours. Fried your brain." The files toppled to the floor, and Sean swore.

"Whatever you've got going on with Charlie's your business." Trevor sobered. "As long as you remember she'll leave in a few weeks."

Like Sean could forget. Or forget that her first loyalty was to Mia. "You also spend too much time around women. Analyze everything women do."

Trevor picked up the scattered files and sorted them in alphabetical order, methodical as always. "I love Linnie. With her and our girls in my life, sometimes I wonder how I got this lucky."

Whereas despite Ty, despite Carmichael's, and despite the family and friends who kept him busy and needed, Sean wondered about the aching hole in his life. A hole that had been there since Charlie left, although he'd only just recognized it. A hole he couldn't fill with work or another woman, no matter how hard he tried. "Linnie's one in a million."

Like Charlie was one in a million. The woman he could fit with, body and soul. But could he trust her not to break his heart again? And if he gave her his trust but she betrayed him again, that hole would get so big it'd suck the biggest part of him clear away.

Trevor set the folders aside. "I found something yesterday when I grabbed stuff out of those files of Dad's we haven't gone through yet. Something I think you should see." He reached into his back pocket and pulled out a slip of paper.

Sean's heart squeezed. More than his dad's clothes and bowling trophies, more than his chipped coffee mug, the essence of his dad was in those tattered manila folders. By unspoken agreement, he and Trevor had avoided them. Until now. He scanned the familiar writing. "What the hell is this?"

Trevor raised an eyebrow. "I got the looks. You're supposed to have the brains."

Sean grabbed his glasses and read the paper a second time, then a third. Shock and disbelief churned through him. He hadn't had much sleep, but he wasn't so out of it he'd imagine this.

"An IOU, for twenty thousand plus interest." He swallowed and tried to work moisture into his dry mouth. "It's issued on behalf of the business with Mom and Dad's house as security."

"Made out to Dr. James Elliot Gibbs." Trevor's voice was gruff.

Charlie's dad. A man who disapproved of him and judged him and his family. "Back then, twenty thousand was a fortune, at least for a guy like Dad."

"The deal was witnessed." Trevor pointed to the signatures. "Philip Richards and Kenneth Green. Remember them from the golf club? Dr. Gibbs's attorney buddies."

"Sure do." He'd caddied for both men a few times and they'd been mean tippers. "The house...Do you think Mom knew?"

"'Course she did, dumbass. You think Dad would have borrowed money from Dr. Gibbs, and at that kind of interest rate, without telling her? Or risked their home to keep Carmichael's going?"

Black spots danced behind Sean's eyes. All these years he'd held his dad up as a hero, the man who'd saved Carmichael's when it was on the brink. Never once had he questioned how his dad had done it. "Have you talked to Mom?"

"No, and I don't plan to. That hornet's nest doesn't need stirring. Mom and her high blood pressure. To dig all this up again would send it sky-high."

Trevor was right. If his mom were younger, if his dad were still alive, he and his brother could talk to them together. But not when they couldn't change what was done. "I won't say anything either."

"Dr. Gibbs didn't have a generous bone in his body. He was always out for himself." Trevor's face went red. "Carmichael's was going under. No bank would touch us. You can bet Dr. Gibbs knew it. He shamed Dad by charging him three times as much interest as a bank would. Remember how he talked to us? Like we were scum under his feet. He wanted to keep our family down, and maybe even keep you away from Charlie. If he'd really wanted to help us, he'd have been fair."

"Dad must have been desperate." Sean rubbed his fist against his chest.

"Dr. Gibbs was a big-shot doctor, but the guy was a snake." Trevor's nostrils flared. "You always tried to protect Charlie, but apart from her and maybe Mia, everybody around here knew what he was like, what he got up to with his running around. And Mrs. Gibbs pretended not to notice."

Sean shivered. "How did Dad pay all that money back?

There's no repayment schedule. If Dad had defaulted, the house would have been worth more than the original loan."

"Look on the other side." Trevor flipped the paper over.

Sean scanned the columns of figures, pencil marks smudged but still recognizable as his dad's handwriting. "One month at a time for more than ten years, the original loan and the interest." He blinked away the sudden moisture behind his eyes.

"You remember when Dad did all those odd jobs? Milking cows, cleaning over at the high school, and farm labor?" Trevor's voice was husky. "Mom took in sewing. I thought it was for the business, like we worked nights at the creamery. It was for the business but not like I thought. It must have been to pay back Dr. Gibbs."

Sean rubbed his arms. "Dad did what he thought he had to."

And as a result of that decision, Sean had also done what he thought he'd had to. He'd taken on Carmichael's and blamed Charlie for everything that had gone wrong between them, but he hadn't been there for her either.

Sunshine filtered through the half-open window blind. The rays slashed across Trevor's face to add lines and grooves. For an instant, it was like their dad stood in his twin's place, asking Sean not to judge. Asking him to understand, to forgive. "What I don't get is why Dad didn't tell us."

"How could he? The terms of that loan meant Dad had to work himself to death. A man like Dad wouldn't have wanted his kids to know he couldn't provide for his family." Trevor gave him a look. "It must be why Mom and Mrs. Gibbs weren't friends anymore. Why Mom turned against Charlie even before Charlie broke up with you."

"No man would want his kids to know." Sean looked at his hands. What would he have done in his dad's place? He couldn't know. A dead man couldn't defend himself either.

And now he risked losing Carmichael's again.

"You think Charlie knew about the loan?" There was a sharp edge to Trevor's voice.

"I don't know." But he'd find out. His stomach contracted. Had she lied to him about this too?

Trevor moved away from the desk and opened a filing cabinet with a *clang*. "Maybe Mom's right. Maybe you can't trust any Gibbs."

Sean tensed. His brother could take the easy way out. Only, for him, it wasn't that simple.

Naomi's phone vibrated and she dug in the pocket of her shorts. Hidden by the stiff white tablecloth, she angled the screen toward her to read Ty's text.

"What did you say?" She looked at her mom on the other side of the table in the breakfast room at the Inn on the Lake.

"I asked you to look after Emma while I meet Nick McGuire and somebody from the insurance agency at the cottage." Her mom twirled a spoon in her empty coffee cup. Although she wore the same clothes as yesterday, she still looked fresh and crisp.

"Sure." Naomi hit REPLY and started to type.

"What are you doing?" Her mom's voice was anxious and not even her usual perfect makeup disguised the shadows beneath her eyes.

"Nothing." Naomi gave her a big smile and tapped SEND. "You want to go for a swim, Emma? We can buy suits here."

"No." Her little sister continued building a castle with the remains of her pancakes, drizzling maple syrup to make a moat. "I don't like this hotel. I want to see Auntie Charlotte."

"I want to see your auntie Charlotte too, but she's not answering her phone." Her mom signaled for the waiter and pasted on a smile. The kind of fake smile parents used when they didn't want you to worry about stuff. "She probably slept in."

"What about Dad? Did you get ahold of him?" Naomi finished her orange juice and glanced out the window at the formal gardens and manicured lawn that sloped down to the lake, bright blue in the morning sun. The boat dock sat square in the middle, INN ON THE LAKE spelled out in white stones along the shore. Ty's text said he'd be at that boat dock in less than ten minutes. Somehow she had to lose Emma long enough to see him.

"I talked to him, but your father's closing on a couple of big deals." Her mom scrawled their room number on the bill. "He's still in Dubai." She flashed what Naomi guessed was supposed to be another reassuring smile. "Everything's fine, honey. I can handle things and Nick's helping. We'll be home before you know it."

Which was definitely not fine. Going home meant not seeing Ty again. Naomi pushed her chair away from the table and tried to smooth the creases in her shorts. She wore the same clothes she'd worn yesterday, but she didn't look anywhere near as fresh as her mom. "I better go and—"

"Naomi?" Her mom folded her napkin into a tidy square. "You said you'd watch Emma. I hope I'll be able to get clothes from the cottage today, but if not, we'll have to shop."

"Crystal Carmichael says Kincaid's got bigger stores than here." Naomi's phone vibrated again. She curved her hand around it and edged closer to the window.

"We'd only need a few basics to tide us over." Her mom's sneakers squeaked on the polished floor as she joined Naomi at the window. "You stay here with Emma. I'll see to the cottage and track down your aunt." She dropped a kiss on Naomi's head, then Emma's. "Why don't you two play croquet?"

"I don't want—" Emma began.

"Croquet will be fun." Croquet sounded about as exciting as math problems. A motorboat nudged the end of the dock. Naomi caught a flash of blond hair. "You go on. Emma and I'll be fine."

"I don't want to play croquet." Emma's voice rose in a whine as Naomi pulled her toward the door that led to the veranda. "I don't want Mom to go, and I want Auntie Charlotte." Her sister's blue eyes filled with tears. "I want to go home."

"Don't cry." Naomi crouched beside her. "We'll have fun here. Mom will be back soon and maybe she'll bring Auntie Charlotte with her."

"Really?" Suspicion clouded Emma's heart-shaped face.

"Fingers crossed." Naomi spotted Ty on the dock. "I need you to help me."

"How?" Emma tucked her hand, sticky with maple syrup, into Naomi's.

Naomi squeezed Emma's hand. "We're going to play a special game at the boat dock. Race you there?"

Emma broke into a run. Naomi waved to Ty and followed. Out of breath, she skidded to a stop at the edge of the dock.

"Ty," Emma squealed.

"Hey, short stuff." Ty picked Emma up and spun her around in a circle. "Naomi." His voice lowered and he looked at her over Emma's head. The light in his blue eyes made Naomi's legs wobble.

"Naomi said we can play a special game," Emma said as Ty set her on the grass.

Ty quirked an eyebrow.

"Hide-and-seek," Naomi improvised. "Emma, you stand over there by that big tree. Cover your eyes and count to a hundred. While you count, Ty and I'll hide."

"I'm not very good at counting." Emma looked between them.

Naomi knelt at Emma's level. "You want to be a big girl, right?"

"Yes." Emma stuck her thumb in her mouth.

"Then you can do it. Count out loud." Naomi got to her feet and patted her sister's back. "Off you go. Ty and I will hide where we can hear you. And see you."

"Okay." Emma trotted off.

"In here." Ty gripped Naomi's hand and tugged her into a white gazebo by the shore beyond the dock. A patio table surrounded by chairs sat on the side facing the lake. "I've only got a few minutes. My dad doesn't know I'm here."

"Where does he think you are?"

Ty didn't let go of her hand. "He sent me to the fishing lodge, half a mile in the other direction." He bent his head, and the scent of citrus soap captivated her. "But I wanted to see you. Yesterday, the fire, I was real worried you were caught in it."

"You were?"

His lips played against his white teeth. The sun behind him dazzled her, and she blinked.

"I was." He dipped his head. Then his lips grazed her jawline and inched toward her mouth. "When I found out you were safe, I wished everybody would disappear. All I wanted to do was this." His mouth captured hers in the kind of kiss she'd dreamed of. A kiss that turned her insides to mush and set off a blaze of fireworks behind her eyes.

"Ty." She breathed against his mouth and tasted minty toothpaste. When she opened her mouth, he slipped his tongue inside to touch hers.

Naomi swallowed a gasp and stumbled against him. Was she doing this right? Were her braces in the way? Could he tell she'd never been kissed before? At least not kissed like this. She rested her hands on his forearms and tried to follow his lead.

He drew back. "Relax," he whispered.

She licked her lips. "Emma's right over there, and if she sees us, she might tell my mom and..." She put her hands to her face to stop her babbling.

Ty ran a finger across her lips, slow and oh-so-gentle. "I have to stay in Kincaid for the next week. My mom's taking my sisters and me back-to-school shopping, and we're going to visit her family in Montpelier." He made an apologetic face. "But we're all going to Blueberry Jam a week from Friday. You think your mom would be okay with you meeting me there?"

"I'll see." Naomi's voice wobbled like she was Emma's age. "I'll text you." This time her voice came out loud, too loud.

"Crystal said if you need clothes, she can drop some by. You're smaller than her, but some of her stuff might fit."

Smaller, like two cup sizes smaller. Naomi crossed her arms in front of her chest. "Thanks. Either Mom's getting our clothes from the cottage today or we'll go shopping."

"Eighty-five, seventy-eight, eighty," Emma's voice rang out.

"I better get back," Ty said. "My dad and Uncle Trevor should be done arguing. I think that's why Dad sent me over to the lodge. Lucky for me he did." Ty's smile made Naomi's stomach lurch like she was at the top of a roller coaster, hurtling down.

"What were they arguing about?"

"I didn't hear much," Ty said. "They were in the office and those walls are pretty soundproof. They were talking about that developer buying your cottage and Uncle Trevor said Dad was making a mistake."

"You didn't happen to see my aunt this morning, did you?" Naomi picked at the nail polish on her thumb and chipped it.

"No." Ty moved away. "Isn't she at the inn with you?"

Naomi shrugged and her heart pounded. "Quick, before Emma turns around." She stared at Ty's lips, then took a deep breath and pulled him close.

"Naomi?" His eyes darkened as his arms went around her shoulders.

Her chest was light and excitement bubbled inside her. She stood on tiptoe and kissed him like girls did in movies. Girls with bouncy breasts who didn't have braces.

Ty kissed her back, hot and urgent, before he pulled away, looked deep into her eyes for several endless seconds, then headed for the dock at a jog.

"One hundred. Ready or not, here I come," Emma yelled.

Naomi sank onto one of the patio chairs. Ty had kissed

her, really kissed her. Her first honest-to-goodness grown-up kiss. The kind of kiss his dad had given Auntie Charlotte. And she'd kissed Ty back, and she must have done okay because he hadn't laughed or looked disgusted or said anything about her braces.

"Found you." Emma ran in and hopped onto the chair beside Naomi. "But Ty left and you didn't hide. What kind of game was that?"

"Ty's at work. He couldn't stay long." Naomi gathered Emma's hair and began to braid it. "Tell you what. I'll play any game you want."

"Barbie's wedding?" Emma tipped her head back. "There's a computer in the guest lounge."

"Absolutely." Naomi had played the game with Emma hundreds of times. "What do you think about going to the fair next week?"

"Would there be ice cream?" Emma handed Naomi the pink hair tie wrapped around her wrist.

"You bet. Cotton candy and farm animals too."

Emma's eyes sparkled. "Ponies?"

"Country fairs always have ponies." Naomi hoped she was right. "Maybe you could even ride one." She wound the tie around the end of Emma's braid. "I bet if you ask her, Mom would take us."

"You think?" Emma twisted her head around.

Naomi smoothed a stray strand of hair away from her sister's face. She wasn't doing anything wrong. Not anything Alyssa or her other friends back home wouldn't do. Besides, her mom was stressed about the cottage and whatever was happening with her dad. Naomi couldn't talk to her about Ty. She was actually doing her a favor by not telling her.

"When Mom gets back, you ask her. Tell her how much you want to see the cute animals."

Charlie shielded her eyes against the midday sun and followed the rutted path from Sean's house to the workshop, Shadow at her side. The fire had come close here. Too close. Fifteen feet away, the blackened trunk of a maple tree, its branches stripped and lifeless, listed toward the ground.

Although the nearby soil was churned up, roots exposed, with brush littering the path, the square log-and-stone workshop with big windows overlooking the lake was unscathed. The screen door was propped open, and inside, the whine of a saw rose above the rhythmic beat of a song about a small town.

She stopped and inhaled the scent of wood and varnish. By the time she'd woken, Sean was gone, like he'd never been in bed beside her, a scrawled note telling her he'd be in the workshop.

She cringed as she remembered how she'd asked him to stay with her, pretty much thrown herself at him. She glanced at her leg and the scar beneath Linnie's denim capris. What did it matter? He'd seen her leg. She'd seen his face when he caught sight of it and heard his sharp intake of breath before his expression went blank, his features a polite mask.

"Charlie?" Sean came out the door. "You could have come in. You didn't have to wait for me out here." He pushed the door shut behind him, but not before she glimpsed Trevor, his blue eyes cold, his face unsmiling. "Were you chilling out with Blake?"

"Who?" Charlie looked around and tugged on Linnie's green tank top to ease it away from her breasts.

"Blake Shelton, the guy singing 'Small Town Big Time' a minute ago." He handed Charlie a bag with the Firefly Lake Market logo, then bent to pat Shadow. "You've never heard of him?"

She shook her head. "Country music doesn't get much airplay where I come from. What's this?" She swung the bag in one hand and kept it away from Shadow's curious nose.

"Linnie sent you a swimsuit."

"You called her?"

In navy board shorts and a MONTREAL CANADIENS T-shirt, his blond hair glinting in the sunlight, Sean didn't look like he'd been up half the night.

"I sure did. Trevor brought it for you when he came to work."

"We don't have to go out today, if you have to work." Charlie tightened her grip on the bag. Sean and Trevor had always been close. As twins they shared a bond she envied. It was the kind of bond she didn't have with Mia.

"I'm my own boss. I can take time off." Sean looked over his shoulder at the closed door. "Trevor can handle things this afternoon."

He turned toward the house. "How's your leg? Are you up to bike riding?"

"Biking's fine. My leg's a lot better today."

It was her heart that was the problem. Waking up in Sean's house, it was all too easy to imagine this could be her life. If she didn't have the job she did, if she didn't need the money from the cottage sale, if Mia didn't need her. And most of all, if she could let herself trust again.

Guilt wormed its way into her stomach and curled up her chest. The worry in Mia's voice when she'd talked to her earlier echoed. She should be over at the cottage with her sister and Nick, not here. But she wanted to be with Sean, to snatch this little bit of time to savor when she was far away again, separated from Firefly Lake by much more than geography.

"Crystal keeps her bike in my garage. You can borrow it. There's a place along the trail we can eat. Or we can get lunch in town first."

"The trail is fine." She wasn't ready to face anyone in town and field questions about what she and Mia planned to do with the cottage. Or pretend to ignore the looks at her and Sean together.

Sean smiled. "You were sound asleep when I left. I figured you needed it. Besides, I left you in good hands. Or paws. Shadow wasn't going anywhere without you."

"She's a great dog."

At the sound of her name, Shadow darted in loopy circles between them.

"Yeah, she is. The animal rescue in town found her by the side of the highway, likely dumped by somebody who couldn't be bothered with her anymore." Sean whistled and Shadow came to heel. "She's wary with a lot of folks, but she's really taken to you."

"She's lucky to have you and Ty, and I'll miss her when I leave." And the clock was ticking on that departure, as Max kept reminding her. Her first day back at work was just over two weeks away. A story was waiting for her. She couldn't let herself get too attached to a dog. Or to a place. Or, most of all, to a man.

"Yeah." Sean's voice was flat. "She'll miss you too."

He rounded the corner by the house and pulled open a door to the garage. "Crystal's bike is the red one." He flipped on a light and pointed to the far wall, beside a white pickup with Carmichael's logo on the door. "There's a water bottle and a backpack if you want them." He wheeled out his bike, sleek, black, and top-of-the-line, designed for a serious rider.

Charlie put her camera and the swimsuit bag into the backpack he indicated. Somehow she had to explain about her humiliating outburst in the middle of the night. Her stomach churned. Not even in a war zone did she ever lose control. But around him, she had, not once but twice in the last twenty-four hours. She hadn't cried, though, so at least she'd held on to some shreds of dignity. But what if she lost control at work the first time there was a loud noise or worse?

She also had to tell Sean about the email she'd gotten from her contact in Boston. Which had her churned up in a different way.

She grabbed Crystal's bike and followed Sean to the driveway, wiggling her toes inside Linnie's running shoes. Like every other part of her, Linnie's feet were smaller than Charlie's.

"No, Shadow, you can't come with us." Sean nudged the dog toward the house and into the mudroom. "She'll be fine." He answered Charlie's unspoken question. "Trevor will take her to the workshop after we leave. She'll find a sunny patch by a window and watch squirrels."

He swung a leg over his bike. "You want to spend time with my dog or me?"

"What a question." She manufactured a smile, her skin tight across her cheekbones. "Um...about last night, or rather, this morning, I'm sorry. I don't know what came over me, getting all emotional." Her voice was tinny, a stranger's voice. She pulled the backpack onto her shoulders.

"Forget it." His voice was neutral, and he slid on sunglasses that hid the expression in his eyes. "You had a rough day with the storm, the fire, and all. You're allowed."

"Allowed what?" She wheeled Crystal's bike next to his.

"Allowed to be human, allowed to be scared." He pulled on his bike helmet and adjusted the strap under his chin. "You're allowed to need someone."

"Yes, well." Charlie cleared her throat. "Cool under fire, that's me." Despite what the doctors said, maybe she didn't have PTSD. She was anxious about going back to work, that was all. She smiled until her jaw muscles hurt with the effort. "Max, my editor, is British, and he says I'm as tough as old boots."

"Old boots, huh?" Sean's voice was amused. "Max knows you well, does he?"

"We've worked together for more than ten years." Charlie caught the helmet Sean tossed her. "He gave me a chance at the big stories because he said he knew I could do it. And I did." She wedged the helmet onto her head.

"Working with someone doesn't mean you know them." He reached between the bikes, linked her hand with his, and traced the outline of her fingers. "The woman wrapped around me in bed last night didn't feel anything like an old boot." He grinned and took his hand away. "Come on, Gibbs, let's hit the trail and see who the tough one is."

Despite herself, Charlie laughed. "On that bike, you can rip up the trail. Not a fair competition."

"We'll take it nice and easy." He pedaled down the driveway and Charlie followed. "Okay with you if we take the trail away from town and head toward the far end of the lake?"

"Sounds good, but first I need to find somewhere else to stay."

"I checked again this morning. Every place is full through next weekend with the golf tournament and then Blueberry Jam." The breeze ruffled the hair at his temples. "It looks like you're stuck with me."

"What about Ty?"

"He's with Sarah and Matt until a week from Sunday. Every year Sarah takes him to see her family around this time." Sean raised an eyebrow, and his smile held a hint of a challenge. "Besides, even if Ty was around, you'd be in the guest room, wouldn't you?"

She yanked the helmet over her forehead. "If your guest room is free, I'll take you up on your offer."

"Sunshine, the room's free, but I didn't say what I offered." His smile slid from teasing to wicked before he turned away and steered the bike along the path, which forked left, deeper into the forest.

The trail was rough and too narrow for them to ride side by side, so Charlie tried to focus on the scenery. The tall pine trees, the sliver of blue lake as they rounded a curve, the pattern of the sun and shade on the forest floor, and the distant cries of birds. She tried to focus on anything but Sean in front of her. How his blond hair waved above his shirt collar, how his long legs moved the bike forward, muscles rippling.

The path flattened out and widened. The big tree the locals called Queen of the Pines came into view at the head of the lake. She pedaled harder and sped up until she was beside him. "Sean?"

"Did I tire you out already?" He gave her a cheeky grin.

"Of course not." She grinned back and matched his pace, caught up in the joy of riding a bike like she used to. The joy of being in this place again. Then she remembered the email. "I need to talk to you for a minute."

He slowed and she bumped to a stop beside him. "What's up?"

"I had an email from Jason, my contact in Boston." She leaned on the bike's handlebars and stared at the trees, where dragonflies swooped and darted among the leaves. "It looks like Tat Chee invests in real estate to get green cards for their kids. It's legal under a federal government program."

Charlie turned back to Sean, who eyed her in disbelief. "There are rumors, though, that Tat Chee hasn't been transparent in some of its dealings. It sounds like they've brought in their people and not hired locals, like they're supposed to. Jason also has a hunch they have a history of questionable environmental practices, and some of their projects aren't in good shape. If he's right, he'll do a story."

"Really?" Sean touched her hand, and her heart squeezed.

"All he needs is for you to put him in touch with people in town who've signed the petition, and members of the historical society and the Abenaki Tribe for the cultural angle." Charlie studied his profile, his strong jaw and full, sensual lips. The nose with the bump that to her teenage eyes made him look rugged, sexy, and even a bit dangerous.

"Of course. You went out on a limb for me and Firefly Lake."

Charlie eased her hand away from Sean's and tightened

the strap on her helmet. "I keep thinking about what Mom would want. Firefly Lake was a big part of her life, as well as mine. Maybe I went out on that limb for me too."

"What about Mia?" His blue gaze was steady and honest. "Family loyalty goes bone-deep for me. I wouldn't expect any less of you."

That loyalty was tearing her apart. "I talked to Mia earlier. She loves Mom as much as me. Deep down she knows Tat Chee isn't the right buyer. Involving Jason is a risk, but it's one we both agreed to take because the cottage and Firefly Lake were so special to Mom."

Charlie's heart gave a sickening thump. Although she'd convinced her sister Jason might be able to help them find another buyer, what if she was wrong? What if neither she nor Mia got the money they needed?

Except Sean was special too, and sometime in the last twenty-four hours she'd let herself want him again. Maybe even want him enough to risk her heart.

Chapter Fourteen

Sean might be headed for trouble but damn if it didn't feel good. Today the lake was tinged silver-blue, and a fringe of pine trees cupped the half-moon-shaped beach only the locals knew about.

"Are you okay?" Charlie quirked a dark eyebrow.

"Fine." He gave her a slow, sideways smile. "Enjoying a beautiful day and time with a beautiful woman."

She blushed and busied herself with the lunch they'd picked up at the snack bar at the head of the lake. "I didn't think you were listening to me."

"Sure I was." Sean snuck one of Charlie's potato chips, and she batted his hand away. "I want to know what happened to the camel."

"It disappeared in a cloud of dust." Charlie gave him a saucy wink that matched the cheekiness in her voice. "Like how I won the race you challenged me to." She dug in the paper lunch bag for apples and Twix bars, and the movement made her breasts strain against her tight shirt.

"I went easy on you." He caught the apple she tossed him and let his gaze linger on her chest. "Which you took shameless advantage of."

She flashed him an impish grin. "You might have slowed down. A bit."

Sean's laugh erupted at the mischief in her eyes. "You made up that story about the camel, didn't you?"

"I rode a camel when I covered a riot in the Middle East." She juggled an apple. "The camel might have ambled off rather than ran. Makes a good story, though."

"You should write fiction." Charlie was the only person he'd ever sparred with like this. Teased and been so comfortable with. They'd talked about her travels, his work at Carmichael's, and movies they both liked. Everything except what really mattered.

She tipped the last chip out of the bag. "I'm a journalist. I report the facts." She sent him a mock-stern look before digging into a Twix bar.

"Really?" He bit into the apple. "Those facts, you never put your spin on them? I've read your stuff online."

"There are lots of ways of reporting a story. It's my journalistic voice." Her skin was the color of those ripe peaches he smelled whenever he got near her. Sean's breath caught.

"I think it's you. Always was, always will be." He reached for her hand and curled her fingers around his. "Tell me more about your life in London. What do you do for fun?"

"I walk dogs at a shelter. I go to photography exhibitions. I run in a park near my apartment. I'm in a book club with friends." She made a wry face. "Which is less about reading books and more about meeting for drinks and protesting things."

Sean chuckled. "Remember when you protested in front of the Firefly Lake Market, fair prices for Vermont dairy farmers?"

"Of course. There was a picture of me in the newspaper." Her gaze met his and held. Desire curled in the pit of his stomach. "My parents were so mad and Mia didn't speak to me for three days."

"I didn't protest, but my dad was sure mad too." Sean stroked Charlie's thumb, her skin soft beneath his. "I helped you with the poster and brought you lemonade. That was enough for him to say you were a bad influence. Bad for business."

Her tongue darted out to wet her bottom lip. "I was only eleven."

"It didn't put me off you." His voice got husky and his fingers tingled.

"It didn't?" Her breath hitched and her pupils dilated as he caressed the soft curve of her arm.

"Nope." With an effort, he took his hand away. Before things went any further between them, he had to tell her about the loan and find out if she'd known. If she'd kept it from him, like the baby. And if she had, why? If he couldn't trust her, everything he'd begun to feel for her again would be meaningless.

"Sean?" Her expression was guarded.

"You stood up for what you believed in. You didn't back down. You did what you believed was right." So why had she changed? The Charlie he thought he'd known had been honest and true.

"Don't make me out to be some kind of heroine." She stared at the water lapping against the rocks. "It was a long time ago. I was more idealistic then."

"You don't believe you can change the world? You don't believe in doing what's right?" He usually trusted his gut, but when it came to Charlie, he didn't know what to trust.

"It's not the same thing." She looked at her leg where scar tissue bisected her flesh.

"That girl's still part of you." He steeled himself to face the truth, no matter what it might cost. "I found out something this morning." He shot her a narrow-eyed glance.

She returned his gaze, unflinching.

"About my dad, your dad too."

Her face went white and then red, but still she held his gaze. In her eyes he saw sadness. And the truth.

"Why did you lie, Charlie? Not only did you lie to me about our baby, but you lied to me about the loan." Dark anger surged through him and he drew in a shaky breath. "Why?"

"I didn't lie about the loan." Her mouth tightened. "I promised I wouldn't tell because...your parents didn't want anybody else to know. That's different."

"Different how?" His body was rigid and he tightened his hands into fists. "You still didn't tell me the truth."

She looked beyond him toward the lake. A heron flew up from the reeds near the shore and arced into the blue sky. "I was ashamed. My dad boasted about how he'd gotten the better of your family. For your dad to have to borrow money from mine was bad enough, but then..." Her dark eyes were despairing.

Despair that almost got to him, but not quite. The hurt had gone too deep. "You kept that secret all these years?"

"Mom, Mia, and me." She dropped her head to her knees. "How did you find out?"

"Trevor came across a note about the loan in files of

Dad's we hadn't looked at. With the fire so close, he pulled everything out of an old cabinet." His pulse raced. "My dad made a deal with a guy he never liked, and who never liked him. It must have given both my parents a lot of worry and you didn't tell me." She jerked her head up, and he pinned her gaze with his.

Charlie gulped. "I know you're mad, but you have to believe me. I didn't mean to lie, and my mom never got over losing your mom's friendship." Her expression was pleading. "Right before she died, she talked about your mom, like they were girls together again. Mia thought it was the morphine, but it wasn't. Mom wanted to go back to the time she was happiest."

"My mom talks about your mom, but she's a stubborn woman and her pride must have been hurt."

Sean's thoughts spun. Could he forgive Charlie? At least for not telling him about the loan? It *was* different from the baby. Maybe she'd wanted to protect his dad. With how things were between them back then, how would he have reacted if she'd told him? Given how much his dad hated Dr. Gibbs, Sean might not have believed her.

"Your mom told me to stay away from you and to keep Naomi and Ty away from each other so no more lives would be destroyed." Charlie's voice cracked.

His mom had said as much to him, which at the time hadn't made any sense. "What's going on between Ty and Naomi is a crush. Ty's a good kid. Sarah and I talked to him. I trust him to not do anything stupid." He trusted his son more than he trusted himself.

"Naomi's a good kid too." She scrubbed a hand across her face. "Which leaves us."

Her words echoed. He hadn't been an *us* in more years

than he wanted to count. "What are you doing here with me?"

"I tried. I really did, but I couldn't stay away from you." She moved closer, and her hair brushed his arm.

He couldn't stay away from her either. "I don't have any answers." Although he wished he did. "All I know is neither of us can change what happened back then. Or change how my mom feels."

"I think she's sorry." Charlie's voice was small. "At least sorry about what happened between her and Mom."

Sorry didn't change the past or the present. "My dad paid your dad back, all the money he borrowed and that obscene interest."

Charlie's face was wan. "It cost your dad more than money. That's what your mom can't forgive."

"It cost all of us." His voice was bitter. Maybe him and Charlie most of all.

He stood and shucked off his shirt. A tangled mix of anger and desire knotted his stomach. He didn't trust himself to be this close to her and not touch her. But he was afraid he'd ask her where they went from here. Or if things were so broken, could the two of them go anywhere.

Charlie's eyes widened. "What are you doing?"

"Going for a swim." His head battled with his heart and his heart won. At least for now. This whole thing sucked but, unlike his dad, Sean had a choice. He couldn't fix the trust, but he could stop some of the hurt and anger.

He stripped off his shorts and adjusted the swim trunks he'd worn underneath before he dug in his backpack and tossed her a towel. "Want to join me?"

"We just ate lunch." Her gaze darted around the deserted beach. "There's nowhere to change either."

"Neither of those things ever stopped you before." He

dropped his sunglasses on top of his towel. "Do you honestly believe we'll get cramps and drown after a couple of sandwiches?"

"No, but..." She touched her leg.

"Change behind a tree. I'll keep my back turned." He walked toward the lake and waded in.

"Promise?"

"Scout's honor." He turned to face her again, warmth spreading through his body.

"You were never a Boy Scout." Still fully dressed, Charlie stood with her hands on her curvy hips. Much as he wanted to, he couldn't stay mad at her.

"No, but I was a lifeguard. I can rescue you if that Twix bar gives you problems." And he'd cover her lush mouth with his and taste her sweetness.

"I was a lifeguard too, remember?" The corners of her mouth twitched. Then she grabbed her pack and flounced into the woods with a little swivel of her hips that made him think about things he shouldn't think about.

He moved into the water, and his body cooled. He lifted his face to the August sky, where puffy white clouds drifted across the blue as in those endless childhood summers. Back when he thought life was simple and his parents had all the answers.

Sean closed his eyes and floated on his back, lulled by the gentle motion of the water and the silence broken only by the rustle of the wind in the trees.

There was a splash and he opened his eyes. Charlie bobbed in the water next to him. The breath whooshed out of his lungs.

"What?" Arms above her head, she slicked back her wet hair.

"I...uh..." His tongue got stuck to the roof of his mouth, as awkward as the boy he'd once been.

"Put your eyes back in your head. You've seen me in a swimsuit before." She crossed her arms in front of her chest.

But not like this one. He'd never seen Linnie in this suit and didn't want to imagine it on his brother's wife. The green one-piece plunged deep between Charlie's breasts and hugged every one of her delicious curves. The swimsuits she'd worn as a teenager were functional, black or blue, designed for speed in the water. This one was designed to drive a man wild. He moved closer and brushed a drop of water off her cheek. "You take my breath away."

As much as he'd wanted the girl, despite everything, he wanted the woman more.

Her eyes darkened. "Sean?"

"You want this as much as I do." He cupped her breasts in his hands and caressed her taut nipples with the pad of his thumbs. She groaned low in her throat.

"We can't." But even as she said the words, she rocked her hips into his.

"Can you stop this?" He slid one strap of the swimsuit down to expose a rosy nipple. "I want you, Charlie." His body throbbed. "I want to touch you and feel your hands touching me." And he wanted to be so deep inside her, he could forget all the reasons he should stay away from her. "But we spent too much time in my truck, in the woods, in the boathouse, on a blanket on this beach even, always in a rush, afraid we'd get caught. This time I want it to be different."

"Different?" Her eyes were hazy and unfocused.

He slid the swimsuit strap back up her delicious body

and lingered on her breasts, barely contained by the suit's tiny cups. "Slow, for a start, and in my bed, where we won't be interrupted."

"Slow?" Her voice was thick.

"To savor." He smoothed her wet hair, sleek like a dark cap against her head, before his hand drifted to her waist, spreading ripples of water.

"Yes," she whispered. "I want you too. Even though I know it can't—"

He raised a finger to her lips. He didn't want her to say anything to stop what felt so good, so right. "I know the rules, remember?"

She knew the rules too.

Charlie smoothed her dress. The emerald fabric hugged her breasts and skimmed over her thighs before it flared out again to her feet. Reflected in the mirror in the bathroom off Sean's bedroom, her face was flushed and her eyes bright. She wanted this. Even if this one night was all she had, she wouldn't look back with regrets.

She took a deep breath as she pulled open the bathroom door and stepped into the bedroom. It was decorated in navy and cream and dominated by a king-sized bed piled high with pillows. Sean leaned against the headboard, the top buttons of his white dress shirt undone. His hair glowed in the soft light cast by the pillar candle on the nightstand. The raw desire in his eyes made her breath hitch and her chest get tight. "Hey."

"Hey, yourself." His voice was low and sensual.

The curtains swayed in the cool breeze blowing through the screen. Water lapped against the beach, and frogs called.

Sean rolled off the bed and got to his feet, closing the distance between them. "Ever since you came back, I've fantasized about being with you here."

"You have?" Charlie's heartbeat quickened.

"Yes." His touch against the curve of her cheek sent flames licking through her. "But I never imagined you'd look like an incredibly sexy mermaid." His hand slipped lower and grazed her neck and the line of her bare shoulders. "That's a whole other fantasy."

Charlie trembled as his hand drifted across her collarbone and found the pulse point on her neck. His hand drifted lower still to trace the curve of her waist. "It's a pretty fancy dress for eating takeout, but I wanted to wear it for you."

She'd imagined seeing the same heat in his eyes she saw now. Imagined how his pupils would dilate with arousal.

"I'm honored." His voice was rough, and he bent his head to suck the sensitive spot on her neck.

The ache between her legs intensified. "You said you wanted to take it slow."

"Yeah, I did." Sean's chuckle was quiet.

She lifted her hair away from her face and ran her fingers through the strands. Then she stepped back and wet her lips with her tongue, remembering how the gesture used to turn him on.

"You always were a tease." He reached for her, but she slipped out of his grasp, drawing courage from the dress, and the heels that added four inches to her height.

"I thought you'd have forgotten." She ran a hand across her breasts.

His eyes glittered. "I didn't forget anything about you, especially not that." His breath stuttered.

Her face heated and she moved to the window seat. She knew he watched her. How her hips swayed in the figure-hugging dress. "I didn't forget anything either." Teasing gone, she turned to look at him and her heart caught. "All these years, I've remembered what it was like between us. Tonight, will you show me again?"

He crossed the floor in two strides and caught her in his arms. "Oh, Charlie." His voice roughened as his mouth sought the curve of her neck again.

She swayed and held on to his shoulders. "There," she whispered as she tilted her head toward his warm lips. She writhed in his arms, clawed at his shirt, found a button and undid it.

"God." He covered her mouth in a hot and hungry kiss that told her how much he wanted her.

She pulled his shirt out of his black dress pants and ran her hand across his bare skin, his back muscles corded tight. "Take your shirt off," she murmured against his mouth.

"My pleasure." He guided her fingers to the buttons and helped her work them through the holes. He slid the shirt off his shoulders as he edged her toward the bed.

She gave him a tentative smile, all of a sudden shy. "We never..." She stopped and rested her palms flat against his chest.

He cupped her face in his hands, his expression serious. "I did." Moving away, he slid open the nightstand drawer and pulled out a box of condoms.

A new box. Meaning he hadn't used them with anyone else. Meaning he'd thought about this, and planned it. Even more than she had. Her heart thudded as she took the box and peeled off the plastic wrapper. There was no doubt she was the only woman in his life right now. She was special to him, almost like she belonged. "Thanks for taking care of it."

"I'll keep you safe this time, I promise." He reached for the box again, and opened it. "I bought these in Kincaid." He gave her a sexy grin as he shook several foil packets out. "No point giving folks in Firefly Lake something else to talk about."

"Smart man." She grinned back, shyness gone, then trailed her hands down his chest to follow the fine line of blond hair to his navel, leaning in to taste his skin.

"Charlie." His voice got tight.

"What?" She slid to her knees and undid his belt buckle. When the buckle was free, she unbuttoned his pants and eased the zipper down, brushing her fingers against his erection. At his sharp intake of breath, she touched him again, harder this time.

"Don't stop." His body jerked against her hand.

"I won't." She slid his pants off his legs one-handed and cupped the arch of one bare foot. She looked at him, naked apart from a pair of white boxers, his skin golden in the candlelight. She breathed in the scent of vanilla from the candle mixed with the crisp sandalwood of his soap.

He eased her to her feet. "My turn."

Her stomach somersaulted at the look on his face and the sexual excitement in his eyes. He kissed her, thrusting his tongue deep into her mouth, before turning her to face the window. He pulled her back into his body. His fingers tugged on the zipper of her dress, and cooler air hit her hot skin.

"Sean." She rubbed against him and he groaned, even as he held her firm.

"Slow, remember?" His voice was strained, the urgency barely contained. He lifted her hair and kissed the back of her neck as his skilled fingers inched the zipper lower. "You aren't wearing a bra." He traced the bare line of her spine.

"This dress has a built-in..." She let out a hoarse cry as the sequined top came away from her body and his hands cupped her breasts, found the hard points of her nipples and stroked.

"What a dress." He slid it over and off her hips in one quick motion, and the fabric pooled around their feet. He lifted her and set her on the bed.

"My shoes." She started to stand, but he pushed her back, gentle but firm, and rolled onto the bed beside her.

"Leave them on." He dipped his head and sucked one of her swollen breasts into the wet heat of his mouth, his tongue rough on her skin.

She fisted her hands in his hair as erotic sensation spiraled through her. She clenched her legs together and twisted her hips, and her lacy white thong rubbed against the quilt.

He lifted his head, hair tousled and face flushed. "You're so beautiful." He traced the curve of her face, his touch tender and achingly sweet. "Even more beautiful than you were all those years ago."

"It's the dress." She caught his hand in hers, his palm calloused.

"You're not wearing the dress." His smile was both suggestive and sweet. "Which must mean..." He slid his big hand across her breasts and over her stomach to the top of her thong panty. "It's you."

He eased her legs apart and ran a finger under the edge

of her underwear. She whimpered and arched against him. He dipped his head and kissed the path his fingers had made before continuing lower to trace a path to her knees.

Charlie tensed. "No." She pulled away and sat up, the heel of one shoe tangling in the quilt.

"What is it?" He stopped and moved up the bed to gather her into his arms.

She tried to squirm out of his grasp, but he held her tight. "Don't touch my leg."

He stroked her back in a tender caress. "It hurts?"

She shook her head and buried her face in his shoulder.

"Why can't I touch it?" His fingers continued to soothe her.

"Why would you want to touch it?" His skin was smooth and hot against her cheek.

"I want to touch your leg because it's part of you, and I want to touch and taste all of you." Sean's voice was gentle, and he put one hand between her legs again and slid up and down, finding the most sensitive spot. "Will you let me?"

Charlie raised her head, and his hand stilled. Waiting for her to trust him enough, believe in him enough.

"Yes." She locked her eyes on his.

Not breaking eye contact, Sean edged her knees apart and moved between them, resting one hand at the top of her calf. She forced herself to relax as his fingers massaged the back of her leg and traced the outside edge of the scar tissue, his touch feather-light. "Is this okay?"

"Yes." Her throat clogged. For the first time since the accident, someone was touching her leg in a way that wasn't clinical, as a woman instead of a patient. A sexy, desirable woman.

"What about this?" Sean's breath warmed the inside of her calves as his thumb followed the biggest part of the scar, the jagged tear that reached almost to her ankle.

"That's okay." She groaned as his other hand returned to her waist and he slid a finger under the waistband of her thong.

"Only okay?" He chuckled. "I must be losing my touch." His finger probed. "Lift your hips, Sunshine." He slid the scrap of lace down her legs and off, over her shoes. "I never thought shoes could be such a turn-on, but these are so sexy."

"This is too." Her hands sought the bulge in his boxer shorts.

"No you don't." Sean groaned and his body pulsed against her hand. "I won't last ten seconds."

"And that would be bad?" She squeezed harder and his whole body shook.

"Very bad." He eased her hand away and pinned it to the quilt, then ran his other hand between her legs again and slid his fingers into her wetness.

"I might not last ten seconds either if you start that." Charlie arched her hips against the mounting pressure and whimpered as he stroked harder, faster, and slipped first one finger inside, then two, using the pad of his thumb where she needed it most.

"You always had a fast recovery time." His breathing was labored.

She tightened her inner muscles around his fingers, and he growled.

"So did you." She gasped and teetered on the edge as he let go of her hand and flicked one of her tight nipples with his thumb.

"Come for me, Sunshine," he murmured as he added a third finger and thrust hard.

She tumbled, panting, trembling as tears stung the backs of her eyes, holding on to him while the world swung around in a kaleidoscope of color. She hummed with pleasure as he held her tight, a fine sheen of sweat coating his skin against hers together with a faint musky smell.

She stared into his face to memorize his features. It was the face of the man she'd loved for almost her whole life. He had full lips, blue eyes, and the blond fairness that contrasted with her dark hair and eyes. The man a part of her still loved and always would.

And the man who'd given her much more than an orgasm. In accepting the scars on her body, Sean had also brought healing to the scars on her heart.

Need roared through him as Sean watched Charlie, her cheeks rosy, eyes half closed, lips parted. Her body still trembled as the aftershocks of the orgasm rocked through her. In the muted light, her skin was almost translucent, and her lush breasts rose and fell in time with her rapid breaths.

He kissed the side of her mouth, and her eyes flipped open. "Checking to make sure you're still awake."

Her satisfied sigh filled him with pride. He'd given her that pleasure. She stretched and her breasts lifted. "Sorry." She chuckled, soft and warm. "I left you behind."

"Make it up to me." He thumbed her nipple, liking the little squeak she didn't suppress.

She rolled to face him and traced the sun tattoo on his biceps. "I'm surprised you kept this." She gave the tattoo a gentle kiss before her tongue trailed across his arm and over to his chest.

"It never meant anything to anybody but you and me." He quivered as she nipped his chest.

She tugged at his boxers and, when they were off, cupped his erection and stroked him, like she was learning the shape and size of him all over again.

He groaned as she picked up the pace, thoughts of keeping it slow forgotten.

She kissed him, hot and intense.

"Wait," he murmured against her mouth, even though she was killing him with what she was doing to him with her mouth and hands. But he'd waited to be with her again like this for a long time. "I want you so much." He searched her face and read the truth in her eyes but needed to hear her say it.

"I want you too, so let's stop talking and get on with it." A cheeky grin flashed across her face. "I came first, so it's Gibbs one and Carmichael zero. I'm ready for round two."

He'd forgotten this part of sex with Charlie. The teasing and how she'd been as competitive in bed as out of it. He pushed her back against the pillows, kissed her breasts again, and stroked her. "Round two, huh?"

"You bet." She grabbed a condom from the nightstand, handed it to him, and watched as he tore the package open and rolled the latex over his shaft.

"Tell me what works. I don't want to hurt your leg." He stroked her arm and fought for control.

"You won't." Her breath came in little puffs as she pulled him on top of her and spread her legs wide. "This works for me."

"It works for me, Sunshine." Taking it slow, he slid into her. Her body adjusted and welcomed him again.

"Don't hold back." She lifted her hips to take him

deeper before wrapping her legs around his waist like she used to. "Don't treat me any different."

"I won't, I . . ." He cried out as she rocked against him.

"Faster," she urged.

Lust pounded through him, pushed him toward release, pushed her to another release too.

When it was over, when he'd come deep inside her and collapsed on top of her, murmuring into her hair, Sean knew what they'd done had changed things.

It was no longer casual and no longer about what had been between them before either. It was something new, something he'd never felt before.

It scared the hell out of him because he didn't know if he could trust her with his heart again. And it was already the first week of August. She'd be back at work soon. Could he count on her to stick around for longer than a summer fling?

Chapter Fifteen

Charlie turned her head on the pillow as her eyes adjusted to the velvety darkness. Even in sleep, Sean had an arm around her to hold her close, and her legs were pinned by one of his. She hadn't had a nightmare, but for the first time in years, she'd dreamed of the baby, seen its blue eyes like Sean's and his smile on its tiny face. She eased out of Sean's grasp and held her breath as the bed frame creaked.

She slipped out of bed, stepped over her dress, found Sean's shirt, tucked her arms into the sleeves, and buttoned it. The tails brushed her thighs. Giving up on finding her underwear, she tiptoed to the bedroom door, inched it open, and crept down the stairs into the living room.

Moonlight pooled across the wooden floor and taupe rug. In shades of green and brown, the room echoed the forest outside. Watercolors of Firefly Lake hung on the walls, and wooden duck and loon decoys were arranged along the mantelpiece.

"Hey, Shadow," she whispered as the dog sat up in her bed beneath a window.

Shadow wagged her tail and made a noise between a bark and a whine.

"No, sweetie." Charlie patted one of the couches on either side of the stone fireplace. "You have to be quiet, but you can sit by me while I watch TV." She curled up on the couch and found the remote control on a pine blanket box. Shadow nestled beside her and Charlie scrolled through channels until she found a twenty-four-hour news station.

Shadow nudged Charlie's bare leg with her cold nose.

Charlie scratched the dog's ears, then grabbed a throw from the back of the couch to cover her legs. She stared at the flickering images on the screen without seeing them.

She didn't regret making love with Sean. Three times, each a mix of urgency, tenderness, and sweet rediscovery. Each time oh-so-right. She burrowed into his shirt and inhaled his familiar, reassuring scent, warm and spicy. But great sex didn't mean there could be a future for them. She'd lost her chance at that future even before she'd miscarried their baby.

Before coming back to Firefly Lake, she'd kept the memories of the baby under control. She'd only let them in on the anniversary of her due date. On the anniversary of the day she miscarried. And whenever she saw a child the same age her child would have been or looked like it might have looked. But especially after tonight, those memories, and the ghost of the child that might have been, were everywhere.

With an effort, Charlie straightened and increased the sound on the TV.

"We join Lauren Moore, live." The male anchor's perfect teeth gleamed at Charlie before the shot changed to Lauren on a hotel balcony, a cloud of smoke billowing skyward, the staccato of gunfire in the distance. Her slim figure was hidden by a flak jacket, strawberry-blond hair covered by a helmet.

"She a friend of yours?" Sean moved into the room wearing only his boxers.

Shadow raised her head and thumped her tail.

Charlie stilled and muted the sound. "Yes." Her body thrummed at Sean's nearness.

"Shadow knows she's not allowed on the furniture, but she also knows you're a soft touch." Sean inclined his head toward Lauren. "Do you two work together?"

"Not now, but we met when we were both rookies. Women reporters on the front line stick together. Even though I work in print and digital and she's in television." And Lauren's world was Charlie's world, the one she was going back to in nineteen days.

"You didn't want to work in TV?" Sean sat and looped an arm around her. His hard body warmed her inside and out.

"No. Lauren gets a lot of attention for how her hair looks, what she wears, and her makeup." And Charlie never wanted to be the center of attention.

"People were firing shots right behind her." Sean was disbelieving. "It's real, not a movie. Why should what she looks like matter?"

"You'd be surprised. Whereas me, I file my stories and nobody sees me." Although it didn't stop the hate mail and threats from the people who disagreed with what she wrote.

"You miss it, don't you?" A cloud slid across the moon to darken the room and shadow Sean's face.

"It's the only life I know." And she'd always loved her job. In the last few days, though, she'd glimpsed a different life. One where she didn't live on the edge, always on a deadline, pumped up on coffee and adrenaline, chasing stories, the truth of those stories more important than the truth of her heart.

"I'm trying to understand your life, but this is the only life I know." Sean's voice echoed in the quiet. "When I woke up and you weren't beside me, I thought you might have left."

Charlie shook her head. After making love with Sean again, leaving him would be like ripping out a chunk of her heart. "I started thinking about the baby and who we were back then."

Sean covered her hand with his and hit the OFF button on the remote. "I've thought about that a lot too. Maybe we weren't ready to be parents, but you'd still have been a good mom. Never doubt that." His gaze was tender, and Charlie melted a bit.

"Well, you'd have been a good dad. You're a good dad to Ty." And when she saw Sean and Ty together, her heart squeezed tight. What if all those years ago she'd given up the only man she'd ever truly love to chase a dream that, when she hadn't paid attention, had turned to dust?

"Ty and I have our problems, but I keep trying to figure things out. Linnie says it's the best you can do." Sean tucked Charlie's body into his.

"Linnie's a smart woman." With the kind of smarts Charlie didn't think she had. The kind you couldn't learn from books.

"You're smart too." Sean's voice was gruff. "I bet our baby would have been smart and as pretty as you if we'd had a girl."

Charlie's chest ached and her eyes stung. "Or a boy who looked like you." A boy who'd have been tall and strong and good.

"Boy or girl, with our genes they'd have gotten into a heap of trouble like we did." Sean's laugh was forced. "It's a wonder we didn't drown ourselves in that lake with some of the stunts we pulled. Lucky for me, Ty's more sensible."

Charlie cleared her throat to will back the tears. "I'm not exactly the maternal type. I spend most of my time in a flak jacket. Not a lot of women who do what I do have kids." And after Sean, she'd convinced herself a husband and family were complications she didn't need.

"You always followed your own path. If you wanted kids, you'd make it work." Sean let out a long breath.

"Women like Mia and Linnie are cut out for motherhood. Not me. I never even played with dolls when I was little." Except her heart ached when she saw her sister with her nieces because Mia had the life Charlie had missed. And so until this summer, she'd made her rare visits brief.

"Being a mom isn't a one-size-fits-all job description." Sean gave her a heart-melting smile.

"Can you see me with a baby?" She forced a laugh, trying not to let him glimpse the hurt, the sense of loss still so profound it rocked her to the core.

"Sure." He turned on a low light. His expression gentle and so caring she wanted to hold on to him and never let go.

She glanced at her phone, beside her on the couch where she'd left it the night before. The screen was dark but still accusing. When she switched it on, there'd be another message from Max asking why she hadn't finished the research he wanted. Charlotte Gibbs might officially be on medical leave, but she still never missed a deadline.

But she didn't have to be Charlotte yet. Charlie nestled into Sean and gave herself permission not to think about Max or work. She knew better than to let herself trust anyone, to let herself believe in Sean or this life, but she could take the comfort he offered, hold it close and store it for the lonely days and nights ahead.

"Aw, hell." His warm breath feathered her hair as he wrapped her close. "What are we going to do?"

"I don't know," she murmured. The future was something she didn't want to think about. She traced the fine hairs on his leg, and he groaned.

Sean was growing on her and maybe she was growing on him, but she wasn't ready for him, for them, or where all this might lead.

Eight days later Sean stopped outside his kitchen door as the words he'd intended to say died on his lips. An ABBA song Charlie's mom had liked blasted from the iPod docked on the counter, and Charlie and Shadow danced along. Charlie held on to the dog's front paws as Shadow glided across the floor on her hind legs. Charlie laughed and threw her head back, a dark cloud of hair framing her face.

"You want a treat?" She let go of Shadow's paws and reached into a low cabinet, giving Sean a heart-stopping view of her butt and her bare legs beneath his baseball shirt.

Each day he got more comfortable having Charlie around to borrow his clothes and fill his bathroom with her stuff. But almost without him noticing it, she'd filled an empty place in his heart. Waking and sharing breakfast with her. Stopping work at midday to share lunch with her too. After work, walking Shadow, having a meal and spending time together talking, watching movies, and making love. All those things had shaped his life into a new pattern.

Although neither of them had used the word, what they shared wasn't about sex. It was about love. Not what they'd once shared either. The easiness and bone-deep comfort he'd always found with Charlie were still there, but they'd deepened into more.

Shadow barked and Charlie turned. "Hey." She muted the music.

In the sudden silence, the truth Sean had been avoiding hit him with the force of a freight train. He didn't want to lose Charlie again, but he didn't see how he could keep her either. This was temporary; in another week she'd walk out that door to go back to work like she'd always planned. And Ty would come back from Kincaid on Sunday afternoon, and he'd have to talk to his son about Charlie before that happened.

"What have you been doing since breakfast?" He moved into the kitchen, homey in a way it had never been before, with Charlie's laptop on the table, a stack of newspapers on a chair, and a teapot he'd forgotten he owned on the counter beside a mug of tea.

"Shadow and I have been very busy." She snapped her fingers, and the dog sat with a look of adoration.

"Busy how?" He pulled Charlie close and dropped a kiss into her hair.

"When you came in, we stopped to play, but she helped

me." Charlie's voice turned serious. "Do you remember asking if I'd written about the accident?"

"Yes." He tensed and held her tighter.

"This morning I did." She tilted her face to his. "I'm going back to work soon and I have to get ready. Not just physically, but intellectually, emotionally. Shadow lay across my feet, like she knew I needed her, and when I started typing, the words came out." Pain flickered in the depths of her eyes, but it was a softer, more muted pain than before.

"Was it okay? At least as okay as it could be?" He held his breath.

She tucked her head into the curve of his shoulder. "It's not writing I'll ever send to Max, but you were right. It was something I needed to do."

"Good for you." Sean spoke around the sudden lump of emotion in his throat. The days of having her close like this were numbered.

"I owe you." Her voice was husky.

"I didn't do much."

"Yes, you did, more than you know." She patted his shoulder. "I've been thinking, before I leave, why don't we go away for a few days? I've heard about this great hotel in the White Mountains in New Hampshire. You can even bring dogs. Linnie said Ty can stay with them. My treat, to say thank you."

"I...I..." The words stuck in his throat. "That's great of you, but we're real busy. It's summer. I can't just take off."

"Oh, of course." Her smile slipped away.

"Maybe some other time?" His belly knotted as his jaw locked tight.

"Sure, whatever." She pushed the newspapers off the

chair, sat and stared at the screensaver on her laptop, travel images in a swirl of color, which made his vision blur.

"I'm sorry, I—"

"No worries." She glanced at the brown envelope he held. "What have you got there?"

"I found some old photos in Dad's files." Sean moved toward the table. "I thought you might want them."

Charlie took the envelope and slid open the flap. "Want a cookie?" She pointed to a bag of Oreos on the counter beside the tea.

"No thanks." He brushed cookie crumbs from her cheek. He must have imagined the look when he said he couldn't go to that hotel with her. Maybe it hadn't been important after all. "I'm not complaining, but you don't look like you're dressed to go Blueberry Jam." He pulled out another kitchen chair and they sat side by side.

"I can get ready in five minutes." Charlie bumped her chair closer to his.

That was one of the things Sean liked most about her. She always looked good but didn't spend hours preening. "I can help you get out of that shirt real fast." Getting her naked and moaning in his arms was one of his most favorite things.

"Priorities, Carmichael. I want to look at these pictures first." Shadow moved to sit beside her, resting her chin on Charlie's knee. "Later, Shadow and I have a surprise for you." She put a finger to her lips. "No, you can't tell Sean. It's a surprise."

"You know she can't talk, right?" Charlie had taken over his dog, which should have been weird but instead was so sweet he got a funny feeling in his chest whenever he saw Charlie and Shadow together.

"She may not talk like we do, but she's still an excellent communicator." Charlie tipped the photos out of the envelope. Shots of the Gibbs cottage and his mom and hers as young girls, out on the lake in one of Carmichael's canoes and in front of the old workshop with fishing rods.

Sean pointed to a black-and-white photo of a young woman with dark hair in an old-fashioned summer dress, who stood on the pebbled strip of beach at the end of the point. "This must be your great-grandmother, Elizabeth McKellar. Mom said she grew up here and met your great-grandfather, Hugh McKellar, over at the inn one summer. Elizabeth and Dad's great-aunts worked as maids at the inn. Hugh came from Montreal on a fishing trip and swept Elizabeth off her feet. The story is she came back to visit decked out in diamonds and a fur coat. Riled a lot folks with her nose in the air. Some of her old friends never spoke to her again."

"Ouch." But Charlie's voice was soft, and her eyes glistened. "Mia looks like her."

"Your family has deep roots in this place. Like mine. Elizabeth McKellar might have gotten uppity, but she was still Old Vermont."

Charlie cradled the photo between gentle fingers, and an unfamiliar expression flitted across her face. Tender, sweet, vulnerable, and sad. All those things she never showed to the world or even much to him.

"Mom never told Mia and me much about her family." Her voice was wistful. "I have this whole history I know nothing about and now that Mom's gone I can't ask her."

"Maybe my mom..."

Charlie's head jerked. "No." Her voice was fierce.

"Mom loved your mom and someday..." He stopped.

Someday couldn't happen without trust and time and all the other things they didn't have.

"Have you talked to Mia today?" Sean leaned back in his chair and blew out a breath.

"Of course. I talk to her every day." Charlie's face went tight and she set the photo aside. "Tat Chee made us a new offer, but I said I wasn't ready to accept it. I need to give Jason more time. I have to believe there's another option for the cottage, but Mia, she's... We don't have a lot of time." She put a hand to her face.

Sean swallowed. What she said, as much as what she didn't say, showed him how her love for the cottage and her love for her sister were tearing her apart.

"Since both of us have to agree to sell the place, we've hired a company from town to shore up what's left of the porch and make the cottage safe. Nick's helping because Jay's working on some big deals. Or so he says. I wanted to help, but Mia won't hear of it."

He touched the curve of her cheek and, for a moment, let himself imagine the cottage wasn't between them. That whatever was going on with Mia and her husband wasn't happening, and Charlie wasn't going back to her real life. And most of all, that he could trust her to tell him the truth. "Mia won't let you help because you're staying with me?"

"No." Charlie hesitated, and the pain in her brown eyes ripped him apart. "It's me. Mia thinks if I don't see the cottage, it'll be easier for me to let it go."

"Will it?" There was a rasp in his voice he hated.

"Maybe... I don't know." Charlie pulled away from his touch and fisted a hand to her mouth.

"You and Mia are a lot alike." This time he made sure to keep his tone neutral.

"We're not." Charlie moved her chair. It scraped along the floor, making Shadow yelp.

"You are." He studied the little flecks of gold in her eyes. She was so beautiful she made his heart ache. "I think Mia's shy and vulnerable even though she hides who she really is, what she really feels, behind those fancy clothes and makeup. Like you hide by pretending you're as tough as old boots."

"You think so, Dr. Carmichael?" Charlie gave a tinny laugh.

"Beyond what's on the surface, underneath, the two of you are cut from the same cloth. Both of you are set on doing things your way, by yourself."

She stuck her chin out. "You don't know anything about it."

"When did you last ask anyone for help?" He gave her a level look.

Shadow edged between them, and Charlie fiddled with the dog's tags. "I don't remember. Mia and I have gotten closer this summer than we've been in years, but..."

"All I'm saying is, don't shut people out." Especially not him. The words he wanted to say but couldn't bring himself to.

Charlie shuffled through the photos and gave him a sunny smile. "Here's one of us." She changed the subject like she always did when anyone got too close or tried to make her talk about things she didn't want to talk about. "How old were we? Thirteen?"

Sean found his glasses in the pocket of his black Carmichael's polo shirt and slid them on for a closer look. "You were still twelve. I was thirteen."

The picture brought the day back to him with perfect

clarity. It was a Saturday in June and he hadn't seen Charlie since the previous September. When she turned up at the marina to surprise him, he'd been blindsided by a girl who'd begun to sprout breasts and curvy hips. A Charlie who was and wasn't the girl he'd always treated a bit like one of the guys.

"I remember." Her voice got low and husky. "You were my friend who'd turned into a cute guy. Your mom took this picture to mark how much we'd grown, like we were two of her tomato plants."

"And you were my friend who'd turned into a pretty girl. I didn't know how to act around you or how to talk to you even." The moment he'd set eyes on her, his body had stirred in that new way; his jeans had gotten tight, and he was afraid she'd notice. "You were what my grandpa called citified."

"Maybe on the outside, but I never was on the inside." Her eyes sharpened as understanding dawned. "After we moved from Montreal, you never came to Boston to visit me. My dad, your family—"

"Not only because of them." He shrugged like it didn't matter when it mattered a hell of a lot. "I never fit in cities. Not even when I was grown up. Sarah and I and Ty lived in New York City for two years."

"Really? Why?" She eased Shadow away and moved to sit on his lap. His baseball shirt rode up to give him a glimpse of silky peach panties the same color as her skin, and his body hardened like it had when he was thirteen.

He wrapped her fingers around his. "I wanted to make something of myself. I did the first two years of my business degree part-time at night school, but it took so long, I went full-time the last two years. Nobody in my family had ever gone to college, but everyone pitched in to help with Carmichael's so I could."

"I always knew you were smart. Those glasses make you look pretty smart too. And hot." Charlie wiggled on his thighs, and his body jumped. The tease knew exactly what she was doing to him.

He arched into her. "Sarah loved the city. She wanted to stay there and for me to work for a bank or some big company. A suit-and-tie job, big-house-in-the-suburbs, fancy-parties kind of job."

"What happened?" Charlie stilled.

"That life wasn't for me. Sarah never forgave me for not doing what she wanted, for not being the man she wanted."

She flinched. "But if you loved each other, you had Ty and—"

"We didn't love each other enough." He slid a hand under her shirt and ran it along her spine.

"You and I didn't love each other enough either." Her breath came in little puffs.

"Maybe not back then." He slid his hand out from under the shirt to cup her face.

"Sean—"

"No, I let you down and I was too stubborn to come after you when I should have. Then I got involved with Sarah because you didn't want me and she did." His breathing sped up. "I thought if I tried hard enough I could forget you. I wronged her, but you and me, we have another chance and—"

"Don't say it."

The hoarseness in her voice almost undid him, but if he didn't tell her the truth now, maybe he never would. And he'd always regret it. "I have to. I love you. I did back then, I still do, and I always will."

"I love you too." The words burst out of her on a strangled cry. She trailed kisses across his cheek, hot and desperate, like she wanted to memorize the taste and feel of him. "I've always loved you, way back from when I was a little girl."

But was that love enough? As Sean kissed Charlie back, pliant and responsive in his arms, he pushed the doubts away.

Chapter Sixteen

Charlie tucked her hand into Sean's, and happiness fizzed inside her like soda pop. When they stopped by one of the white tents that ringed the town fairground, she inhaled the smells of popcorn and candy floss, cooking oil and fries.

Of course he couldn't take a trip with her. She should have remembered summer was Carmichael's busiest time. Maybe he could come to England to see her this winter. With more frequent flier miles than she knew what to do with, they could travel anywhere they wanted from London. Or meet in Texas or Florida at New Year's, after she visited Mia and the girls for Christmas.

"Are you ready for your surprise?" she asked, excitement tempered by the memory of Mia's face when she'd seen her earlier. The lines of strain around her sister's mouth, how she'd avoided talking about Jay, why he was at work instead of here when his wife and family needed him. And what that meant for all of them.

"You already gave me a surprise today." Half hidden by the tent flap, Sean's fingers grazed the underside of her breasts. "Lots of surprises."

"Not that kind of surprise." Charlie bounced on her toes and evaded his sinful fingers. She wouldn't think about Mia and Jay. Or worry about things that might never happen. "I meant the surprise from Shadow and me."

"How did my dog fix a surprise?" He held her hand again, safe and all hers.

"You'll see." She drew him into the crowded tent, past a white-draped table with vases of pink and white hollyhocks, yellow daisies, and orange daylilies. Past another table with shiny carrots lined up in regimented rows.

Following the directions Linnie had texted, Charlie spotted the photography section near the back. She scanned the display until she found pets. She squeezed through the crush of people and tugged Sean after her.

"How did you get that picture?" His expression shifted from puzzled to surprised, and then pleased, as he looked at the framed black-and-white photo of Shadow with the first-place red ribbon beside it. "She never poses for me." The dog sat in one of Carmichael's canoes, ears cocked and a look of lively intelligence in her dark eyes.

"Dog treats." Charlie tucked her arm through his. "Not the store-bought kind. Linnie found this recipe made with peanut butter, which Shadow loved. It took a lot of tries and a lot of treats to get her to stay still, but we managed in the end."

"It looks like a picture you'd see in an art gallery." Sean still studied the picture. "The craft gallery on Main Street has photos like this."

"I took the picture in color and used photo editing soft-

ware. It's easy. I can show you if you want." Charlie let go
of Sean's arm. The words had come out before she thought.
Words that made it sound like she was a real part of his life,
like she planned to stick around.

"You won a red ribbon at Blueberry Jam. Will you post
that on Twitter and Facebook?" The love in his voice and
intimacy in his smile warmed all the lonely places in her
heart.

"I might." Or she might not. The ribbon was special in a
way she didn't want to share with the world.

"Thanks, Charlie. You and Shadow gave me a fantastic
surprise. Linnie too." Sean hugged her and grazed her
cheek with the pad of his thumb. She breathed in his clean,
masculine scent. "I'm going to hang this picture somewhere I'll see every day. I'll tell everyone you took it."

"Not in your bedroom, then?" Charlie joked.

"No." His smile was pure sex. "I could take a picture of
you for my bedroom." He winked. "One of you in those
shoes and—"

"Stop it." Charlie pushed at his arm. "We're in public."

"I can fix that if you want." His blue eyes twinkled with
provocative intent. "All you have to do is say the word,
Sunshine."

"Even I need some recovery time." She loved that she
could tease him, and loved how comfortable they were
with each other. "Want to look around the fair some more?
Find Mia and the girls and get something to eat before
checking out the haunted house?"

"The haunted house, huh?" Sean traced the outline of
her mouth. "I still haven't forgotten what you did to me the
last time you wanted us to check out the haunted house."

"All you have to do is say the word, Carmichael."

Charlie laughed and looped an arm around his waist. "We missed lunch. That popcorn smell reminds me I'm hungry."

"Hungry for what?" He pulled her into him.

"Food, of course." She held back a laugh.

"Whose fault is that, my insatiable investigative reporter?" He tickled her ribs. "But what the lady wants, the lady gets. What do you say we get some food for you to nibble off me?"

"I'd say you...oh..." Charlie's laugh died in her throat and she jerked away as the scent of hot buttered popcorn was overlaid with a floral perfume.

"Sean?" Ellen Carmichael stood in front of a photo of an Irish setter with a ball, Linnie and Trevor on either side of her. "Charlie?" Sean's mother looked between them.

"Mom." Sean bent to kiss Ellen's cheek.

"Hello, Ellen." Charlie forced a smile, her jaw tight. "Linnie, Trevor."

Sean's twin inclined his head and looked at the picture of Shadow.

Linnie hugged Charlie. "Charlie took that photo. Isn't it great?"

"Good job." Trevor's voice was gruff, but he glanced at Sean and managed what passed for a smile.

Ellen's sharp blue eyes studied Charlie. "Beatrice always said Charlie had a special gift for taking pictures."

"She did?" Charlie's heart skipped a beat.

"Your mother was real proud of you." Ellen's eyes softened. "Up there in heaven, I reckon she's still proud of you, looking down and smiling."

"Thank you." Emotion clogged Charlie's throat.

Ellen smoothed her blue skirt with an unsteady hand.

"Although some bygones are better off staying bygones. Your mother's in her grave and she suffered."

"Mom—" Sean began, but Ellen silenced him with a laser-like look Charlie remembered from old.

"Beatrice would be proud of her girl taking such a nice picture and winning a prize. Like I'm proud of our Linnie here. She won eight red ribbons today." Ellen beamed and counted with her fingers. "Apple pie, drop cookies, homemade jelly, yeast breads, pieced quilts, embroidered samplers, knitted dolls, and homemade pickles. She's set to win the best-in-fair trophy for the third year in a row too."

"Congratulations." Charlie still reeled from Ellen's words. The grudging respect in the older woman's face and the brief acceptance she'd glimpsed in her eyes.

"Thanks." Linnie beamed. "You need to congratulate Sean too. Between him and Trevor, the two of them pretty much cleaned up in the wood-carving classes."

Charlie swiveled toward Sean. "You didn't tell me."

"We got here late, so I didn't know." He raised his eyebrows and her face heated. "I was kind of busy earlier."

Charlie focused on a point above Linnie's head to avoid her friend's knowing look. She'd been busy too. A getting naked on a chair, on the floor, and then in the shower kind of busy. With Sean.

"You'll be leaving us soon, won't you, Charlie?" Ellen's gaze narrowed. "Back roaming the world?"

Sean took Charlie's hand and tightened his fingers around hers. "Charlie is a respected journalist. I wouldn't call what she does roaming the world."

"I don't deny Charlie's done well for herself, but I'm thankful my family stayed where they belonged." Ellen gave a satisfied smile. "I couldn't sleep at night if my kids were scattered everywhere. Or maybe you might stick around for a while?" Her voice sharpened. "Not sell the cottage? Put down some roots?"

"Mom." Sean exchanged a look with Trevor.

Charlie's insides quivered. Ellen's acceptance would come at a price. A price maybe too high for Charlie to pay. Mia's worried face swam before her eyes again and she heard the desperation in her sister's voice, felt her rib bones when they'd hugged last. Mia had always been slender but not skin and bones. Then she pictured her last bank statement and the amount she still owed on her mortgage. The medical bills. The state of her retirement funds. She needed money almost as much as Mia did.

Ellen's shoulders slumped. "I would never interfere, but as you and Charlie are such good friends again, you can't blame me for wondering what she'll do about that job of hers. Or the Gibbs cottage. You can't deny she's got a whole other life somewhere else. Mia and those girls of hers do too."

Charlie's vision blurred and the tent spun. The raucous fairground noise made her head ache. No matter how much she loved Sean, she didn't belong here or with his family. Maybe with Mia she'd finally found a way to fit, but to be with Sean she'd have to change her whole life, and she couldn't trust enough to take that risk.

"Mom, you're interfering." Sean's voice was strong, firm. "I won't have it."

"Sean's right." Trevor moved to stand shoulder to shoulder with his brother. When the chips were down, the Carmichael twins always stuck together.

Like her and Mia. Charlie's stomach heaved, and she swayed as pain shot through her leg.

Then Sean's hand was on Charlie's arm to steady her. He murmured something to Trevor before he steered her out of the tent. Past the lines for the Ferris wheel, the swing ride, the kiddie train, the games of chance, and the petting zoo. Not stopping until they reached the other side of the fairgrounds by the lake.

"I'm sorry." He captured both her hands in his. "I won't excuse what my mom said. Her family's her whole world, and she's never been farther away from home than Niagara Falls, so she can't understand your life. Besides, you know she always has to stick her oar in. She cares about me and wants me to be happy, but she needs to let me be the judge of that."

"I know." Charlie dug a toe into the yellowed grass, which had been trampled by many feet.

She cared about Sean too. Cared about him so much she didn't want to come between him and that family. Ellen's words stung because they were true. Even if her loyalty to Mia wasn't an issue, how could she make anything but a superficial life here when she was on the road for months at a time?

"As for Trevor, he's got a good heart, even if he can't always show it." Sean grimaced. "With the bad blood between our families, he's caught in the middle, but you heard him. He's coming around. It'll take some time."

Time Charlie didn't have. "My life *is* different. I don't bake pies or make quilts." Her voice came out as uncertain as it used to back when she'd thought she never measured up to Mia.

"Have I ever said I want you to?" Sean nudged her chin to force her to look at him. "I can buy all the pies I want from the diner. As for quilts, between Linnie and my mom, they've made enough to cover every bed in my house and then some. What I can't buy is how you make me feel."

She couldn't doubt the love in Sean's eyes or the sincerity in his voice.

He moved even closer and touched her hair, so tender Charlie's legs almost went out from under her. "It's hot and noisy out here. Why don't we get Shadow and have a late lunch and ice cream? We can celebrate that first-place ribbon of yours with Strawberry Swirl." His smile turned wicked.

"Okay." She tucked one arm into his as desire spiked and threaded through her.

"I need to pick up a leaky gas can at the marina here in town, but after that I'm all yours." The wind off the lake ruffled his hair above the collar of his Carmichael's polo shirt. A white one, as the black one he'd worn earlier had ended up on the kitchen floor. With the rest of their clothes.

Charlie's heart lurched. "Don't you want to see those ribbons you won?"

"Later." He hugged her, his solid body a bulwark against the world. He pulled her beside him along the wide, sandy path next to the lake.

She looked at him under her lashes, as flirty as Mia. "I know summer's busy for you, but what about this winter? Want to come visit me for a few weeks? I could take you around London, be your personal tour guide. Paris is really close too." And she'd always wanted to visit the city of love with someone she loved.

He bent his head and nipped her earlobe. "I'd like to see where you live, but with Ty still in high school, I can't take off for a few weeks. We've also got some big jobs booked this winter." His voice was laced with regret.

She wrapped an arm around Sean's waist and forced the doubts away. Of course he had Ty. And he ran his own business. He couldn't be a free spirit like her. "A weekend in Montreal would be fun. Or New York if we flew from Burlington on Friday and came back Sunday night. What do you think?"

"That sounds great, Sunshine. I want to make you happy." His voice deepened to a low, sexy rumble and Charlie's heart beat faster, desire together with a love so strong her breath caught in her throat.

What she wanted was for Sean to always look at her like he had over the past few days. Like she mattered to him more than Carmichael's. Mattered more than anything and anyone apart from his son.

Most of all, she wanted to be able to believe in him enough to change part of her life for him. And for him to be willing to change part of his life for her.

As they left the fairgrounds and rounded the lake where it deepened into a small harbor, Charlie's mouth dropped open. "Wow." Proof of Sean's success was in front of her.

"You like it?"

"I sure do." The spacious white marina building, tucked into a grove of trees next to Old Harbor Park, was the center of a much bigger operation than she remembered. More profitable too, judging by the tall sailboats, smaller motorboats, and big cabin cruisers berthed in neat lines. "Your dad would be proud."

"Thanks." Sean's pride of ownership was evident. "This will only take a second." He led her to a berth where a white cruiser bobbed on the water, the name NORTHERN SPIRIT in black lettering.

"Yours?" The dock bobbed under Charlie's feet.

"Yeah." Sean gave her his arm to help her across the gangway. "Watch your step." He swung down the ladder into the cabin and waited for her to follow.

"Remember when we—"

"What the hell is going on?" Sean's voice cut across Charlie's. He stopped so fast she bumped into him.

"Dad? What are you doing here?"

Over Sean's shoulder, Charlie glimpsed Ty sprawled against the headboard of the double berth, a blue-and-white patchwork quilt rumpled behind him—face flushed, blond hair tousled—and Naomi buried against his bare chest.

Charlie put a hand to her mouth. She pushed past Sean and stumbled toward her niece.

"It doesn't matter why I'm here. I asked you a question." Sean pulled Ty away from Naomi. "I want an answer." His voice was as hard and unyielding as Vermont granite.

"Honey?" Charlie's stomach heaved as she grabbed the quilt and pulled it around Naomi's bare shoulders. "What are you doing?"

Stupid question. It was obvious what the teens were doing.

"I didn't…we didn't…" Naomi's voice broke. "Ty, he didn't…"

Sean's eyes pinned Charlie's over Naomi's head. Was he remembering the things she was remembering—when they'd been Ty and Naomi's age and swept up in a passion bigger than either one of them?

Evidently not. His face was set in a blank mask, only the glitter in his eyes betraying the anger beneath the surface. Anger rooted in love for his son.

"I didn't hurt her. I'd never hurt her." Ty reached for Naomi again, but Sean held him back.

"I know you wouldn't," Charlie said.

Naomi still had her bra on. And her shorts. Charlie breathed a silent prayer of thanks.

"Let's get you dressed, sweetie." She found Naomi's T-shirt and maneuvered her into it.

"Please don't tell my mom." Naomi's voice wobbled and tears spilled out, rolling down her face. She wound her arms around Charlie like she'd done as a little girl, when her biggest worry was whether Santa got her Christmas letter.

"I have to." Even if she wanted to, which she didn't, there was no way she could keep this from her sister. She should have seen this coming, maybe could have stopped it if she hadn't been so wrapped up in herself, in Sean, and in what was happening between them.

Sean let go of Ty and balled his fists. "The two of you are fifteen. What were you thinking? Oh, who am I kidding...? You weren't thinking."

"Like you weren't thinking the same thing when you were our age." Ty flung the words at Sean, then grabbed in the bedding for his shirt and pulled it over his head.

A muscle twitched in Sean's jaw. "That's beside the point." His voice vibrated with barely controlled anger.

"We were...like...messing around." Naomi's face went from white to red and her body shook with suppressed sobs. "Please don't tell my mom. I'll do anything if you don't tell her."

"It's not Naomi's fault." Ty's voice cracked. "We love each other and you can't split us up."

"You don't know what love is," Sean said.

"If I don't, whose fault is that?" Ty made an insolent face.

Charlie's hands shook as she smoothed Naomi's hair away from her wet face. "Where does your mom think you are?"

"I told her I was getting ice cream." Naomi's voice was muffled against Charlie's shoulder. "Emma wanted a pony ride and Mom was on the phone to Dad again. They were arguing. Polite arguing, but still arguing." A fresh wave of sobs broke. "Alyssa...all my friends, they think I'm a baby because I haven't...and I wanted to..."

"Hush," Charlie soothed. "You made a mistake—"

"I didn't. Ty and I aren't a mistake." Naomi's voice rose.

But Mia would think so when she found out about this. Mia, who was scared of her daughter getting pregnant like Charlie had and hurt like Charlie had been hurt. Mia, who didn't need this worry added to all her other worries.

Charlie took a deep breath. She wasn't Mia, but she had to handle this situation like a mom might. "I understand, honey. You got out of your depth." Had Charlie gotten out of her depth with Sean? No, she'd known exactly what she was doing and where it might lead, but she'd gone ahead anyway because she loved him. Nothing else mattered.

"Out of her depth?" Sean spat the words out. "I'd say it's a lot more." He turned to Ty. "What about your mom? What did you tell her?"

"I said I was meeting friends." His voice was sulky. "I'm not a little kid. I don't have to tell her where I am every second."

"You and Naomi snuck off, behind her mom's back, and you brought her here, to my boat, to..." Sean stopped and fought for control, the warm, loving man Charlie had teased moments earlier replaced by a stranger. "Your mother and I raised you better."

"Sean." Charlie raised her hand. "We all need to calm down."

"My son and your niece, who are both, in case you've forgotten, underage, were about to have sex here and you want me to calm down?" Charlie hugged Naomi closer. Sean was her lover, but he was a parent first. "What about protection? Did either of you think about that?"

"We weren't..." Ty cleared his throat.

"We weren't going to have sex," Naomi whispered. "Ty wasn't pressuring me or anything. I wanted to do what we did. I love him like he loves me." She clenched Ty's hand.

"Pumpkin, we'll work this out." Charlie's heart caught. "I'll talk to your mom if you want."

"Mom says we aren't coming back here. Ever." Naomi's breath came in short gasps. "But I have to see Ty again. I absolutely have to."

"Don't worry." Ty's expression was serious and he looked older, as if in the past few minutes he'd changed from a boy to a man. "I'm not going to break up with you." He glowered at Sean. "Unlike some people, I stick to my commitments."

"We'll talk about this later. In private." Sean's voice rasped as he yanked out his keys from the pocket of his shorts. "I have to find Sarah. I'll get a boat back. You take my car, Charlie. I'll see you at the house." His face was a tight mask, but his eyes pleaded with her.

"Why would she see you at our house?" Ty looked between them. "You said it was over between you and her years ago. But it's not, is it? You lied to me."

"Ty, son." Sean stepped forward. "Charlie's staying at our place because of the fire. The cottage isn't safe and there wasn't a room anywhere else with the fair, the golf tournament—"

"I'm not stupid." Ty's gaze narrowed. "All that may be true, but it's not the whole truth, is it?" The words came out in a hiss, and Charlie flinched.

"I..." Sean's face crumpled, and his eyes darkened in pain. "I'm sorry. I should have told you sooner but I didn't. I was wrong. I didn't mean for you to find out like this."

"You mean not after you already had sex with her in our house?" Ty's mouth curled into a sneer.

"I admit I was wrong, but you will not speak that way in front of Charlie. Apologize."

"Sorry," Ty muttered, his face red. "No disrespect." He stared Sean down, his eyes cold. "I get you have a life, but you've never brought anybody home before. Why now, without even telling me you were seeing her?"

"What's between Charlie and me is new and we're still figuring things out." A sheen of sweat dampened Sean's forehead.

"I told you Naomi was important to me. And all the time you were going after her aunt." Ty's Adam's apple worked. "Which, at your age, is totally disgusting and this whole thing is like you'd see on one of those dumb TV reality shows."

"You have to believe me. I didn't plan to hide anything from you. But you were with your mom this week." Sean's face was gray.

"I'll stay at the inn." Charlie helped Naomi to her feet. She'd almost had it this time, but the dream she'd begun to let herself believe in was disappearing like the early-morning mist on the lake. "Or I'll get a room at the motel."

Once she delivered Naomi to Mia, maybe she could even catch an earlier flight out.

"Wait." Sean touched her shoulder. "Don't run out on me."

"You and Ty need to talk. Sarah too." She forced the words out between quivering lips. "And I need to find Mia."

He held out one hand, and the keys dangled from his fingers. "Take my car. Please?"

The pain in his voice mirrored the pain in his eyes, the same pain as all those years ago. A solid lump of fear and regret lodged in Charlie's stomach.

He waited.

She waited.

Then Charlie reached out with a shaky hand for the keys and closed her icy fingers around the unyielding metal, still warm from his hand.

Chapter Seventeen

Charlie wasn't back, and she hadn't answered her phone either. The curtains at the house were still closed against the heat of the day and the windows were shut. Shadow barked from inside the workshop.

Sean secured the motorboat to a wooden post and walked across the narrow strip of beach and around the side of the workshop. He'd give Charlie ten minutes before he took the truck and went to look for her. He found the spare key in its place under the flat stone next to a maple tree and unlocked the door. "Hey, Shadow."

The dog barked again in greeting and wagged her tail as she wound herself around his legs.

"You're out of luck. Charlie's not here."

At Charlie's name, Shadow whined and sat in the doorway, her ears cocked to listen as she watched the empty path where the fire-blackened trees cast long silhouettes.

He hadn't intended to fall in love with Charlie again. But while he'd been busy falling in love, he'd taken his eye off the ball with Ty. His son had turned into a kid who snuck off with girls, a kid who was old enough to challenge him about his sex life. Which had resulted in one hell of a mess he had no idea how to fix, or if he even could fix.

"Ty's growing up." Sarah's voice echoed in his head. She'd stood in the dusty parking lot at the fairgrounds, Ty hunched in the passenger seat of her Taurus parked ten feet away, her two girls, Emily and Olivia, strapped into car seats in the back, their blue eyes as round as saucers. "He's making independent choices. You might not like those choices, but your way isn't the only way. Maybe you should think about that before I bring him back tomorrow."

Then she'd walked away, calm and unruffled as always. Her jeans and pink T-shirt hugged her trim figure, and her blond hair brushed her shoulders the same as when he'd met her.

Sean moved into the workshop and ran his hand along the benches to sweep wood shavings into a neat pile. He picked up a hammer and set it down again. Of course Ty had to make his own choices, mistakes as well. But why did one of those mistakes have to be with Charlie's niece?

He looked around the workshop, at the skeleton of the racing canoe he and Trevor were working on. The scattered tools fit into his hands like they belonged there. They were the tools he'd used since childhood, watching his grandfather's hands, his father's too, learning the skills he'd passed on to Ty.

"Carmichael's will be yours, son." His father's voice was as clear as if he were in the room with him. "I trust you and Trevor to keep the business going. Promise me?"

Sean sat on a three-legged stool, found his favorite carving knife, and angled the blade into a piece of scrap pine.

He'd kept his promise because he'd always wanted Carmichael's, but maybe the business wasn't enough. Ty would be off to college in a few years and then what?

Shadow gave three short, sharp barks and Sean looked up.

Trevor came through the open door. "You'll lose a finger carving in the dark like that." He flipped on a light. "You're letting all the bugs in too." He closed the screen and gave Sean an assessing look.

"Who made you the health and safety police?" Sean dropped the knife with a clatter. "I have to find Charlie and—"

"If she's gone, she's gone. Another few minutes won't make any difference." Trevor pulled up another stool and sat. His twin wore his usual jeans and a blue T-shirt Sean recognized as one Trevor had borrowed from him and never returned.

"What are you doing here?" Sean tossed the scrap wood after the knife.

"I heard what happened with Ty and Naomi." Trevor's expression was careful.

"How?" Shadow leaned against Sean, and he rubbed her ears.

"One of the guys at the marina saw you come off the boat." Trevor gave Sean a wry smile. "Heard you yell at Ty too."

Great. His family business was public knowledge. "Who?"

"Kyle, but I doubt he'll say anything else. You sign his paycheck. He won't want to piss you off."

Which was some comfort. "Linnie hear anything from Charlie?"

Trevor shook his head. "What's with those Gibbs girls? A lot of the guys here had a thing for Mia too. Nick McGuire for one."

"You never had a thing for anyone but Linnie." Like he'd never had a thing for anyone but Charlie, even though he'd tricked himself into thinking he could make himself love Sarah the way she deserved.

"True." Trevor's smile was one of a man happy with his life. "You'll fix things with Ty."

"I screwed up bad." Although he wouldn't admit it to anyone but Trevor, today had shown Sean how much had gone wrong between him and his son. The kind of wrong it wouldn't be easy to make right.

"So? It's not the first time." Trevor's voice was amused. "Take it from a man who lives in a house with five women. Boys are a hell of a lot easier to figure out. You were a boy. Put yourself in Ty's shoes."

"That's what I'm afraid of." Sean grinned at his brother, then sobered. "How's Mom?"

"I told her to stay out of your business, but she's scared." Trevor's eyes narrowed. "You and Charlie can't keep your hands off each other, but we all remember what happened last time. Although Mom doesn't know we know, that loan business must have hurt her bad."

"It's not the same thing."

Trevor snorted. "Charlie hasn't loaned us money, sure, but she's still leaving, isn't she? And she and Mia still plan to sell the cottage to that Tat Chee outfit?"

Sean let out a breath. Charlie and Carmichael's. The two things he'd always wanted most in life, now pitted against each other in a way they'd never been before. It was a situation that was a recipe for sleepless nights, and could not only hurt him but hurt people he cared about. Like Ty. His stomach lurched. His first responsibility was to his son.

Trevor sent him a long look. "Whatever you've got going on with Charlie's your business, but thanks to her and Mia, we've got bigger problems. When you were at the house this morning, Brent Michaud, the Realtor, was over at the Gibbs cottage with three Asian guys in flashy suits. Younger ones, not the two who were here before. Suits. Except for Nick, nobody wears suits around here."

"Charlie told me Tat Chee made them a new offer, but she and Mia didn't accept it."

Trevor stood and shoved the stool away. "Maybe Charlie's telling you the truth and maybe she isn't, but with the woodlot burned out, you can see their place real clear. Those guys took pictures, measured the frontage, and came right to our property line and took pictures of this place too. Even took a boat out. A big one they trailered in."

Had Charlie lied to him again? She'd lied to him about the baby and why she'd broken up with him. And she hadn't told him about the loan either.

Shadow barked and darted to the door. Sean's MG rumbled into the driveway, and the light over the garage came on to illuminate the dusk. The tightness in Sean's chest eased.

"I'm on your side, bro, but are you sure you can trust Charlie?"

"I want to." Except in his heart of hearts, Sean wasn't sure he could. Charlie had broken his trust too often, and Trevor knew him too well.

Trevor searched Sean's face. "As long as you don't get more involved than you should. Before you know it, she'll be out of here like before. You're not that stupid, right?"

"Drop it, little brother." Sean raised a hand and then let

it fall. He hadn't taken a swing at his twin since they were
eleven and argued over a hockey trading card.

Trevor's brow furrowed. "I don't have a head for busi-
ness like you, but I'm going to the garden center tomorrow.
We need to get some trees planted. The fast-growing kind.
We also better think about hiring marketing help. Tat
Chee's bound to have one slick marketing machine."

"Shadow?" Charlie's sweet voice floated across the still
evening air. "Where are you?"

The dog erupted in a frenzy of barks and nosed at the
door as her tail spun like a windmill.

"Don't forget we need to get ready for the class." Trevor
opened the door for Shadow, who bounded through it and
raced up the path to the house.

The canoe-building workshop they ran the second week
of September was so popular it sold out as soon as they ad-
vertised it. "I'm on it." Sean wasn't, but they'd taught the
course so many times he could do it in his sleep.

"I trust you. You're full of shit sometimes, but you always do the right thing." Trevor's smile was their dad's,
and Sean's stomach contracted.

Sean left his brother behind and walked along the dark
track to the house. A light shone from the kitchen window
and Charlie was silhouetted in the open patio door, the lush
swell of her breasts in profile as she bent over Shadow.

His heart pounded. The last thing on his mind was doing
the right thing.

Charlie poured fresh water into Shadow's bowl. So much
for letting go of the past. Instead, she'd gotten herself
caught in it until past and present were so tangled she
couldn't tell where one ended and the other began. "Here

you go, precious." She set the bowl in front of the dog. She could count on one hand the times she'd do that simple task before she left.

"Charlie?" Sean stepped into the kitchen. "I'm glad you came back. I wasn't sure you would." His shoulders slumped, and his arms hung slack at his sides.

Guilt punched her chest. After she'd left a still-sobbing Naomi with Mia, she'd thought about coming back to Sean's place only to grab her suitcase. She could've left his car at the marina in town and caught a bus at the gas station. "I had your car and keys."

"An arrest for car theft wouldn't look good in those newspaper headlines." Sean opened the fridge and stared at the contents like he didn't see them. "Are you hungry?"

"No." Mixed with the guilt was sadness. She hadn't run, but he'd expected her to. And she'd wanted to. "I came back . . ." She swallowed as the words stuck in her throat.

He shut the fridge without taking anything out.

"You asked me to come back." She shifted from one foot to the other. "Seeing Naomi and Ty together was a shock, and I didn't . . . handle things as well as I should have. From what I've seen, Ty's a good, hardworking boy, but Mia doesn't want Naomi dating anybody. Would you tell him for me?"

Sean took her arm. "I didn't handle things very well either." He led her into the living room and shut the connecting door on Shadow. "But you can tell Ty yourself."

"I wouldn't know where to start. I'm not good with kids." She sat on the nearest couch.

"You do fine with your nieces." He flipped on a table lamp, then sat beside her.

"I sure messed up with Naomi." And after what happened today, opening up to Sean's son would cross a line she was too scared to venture over. It would make her vulnerable and a part of both their lives in a way she couldn't handle.

"You don't think I've messed up with Ty?" Sean raised his eyebrows. "I didn't tell him what was happening in my life, and I should have."

"You'll try to get it right." Charlie hugged a throw pillow to her chest. "Look at the example you had. Your mom and dad, your whole family was pretty near perfect."

"There's no such thing as a perfect family, only families doing the best they can." Sean's voice roughened. "After the way my mom's carried a grudge all these years, how can you think she's perfect?"

"She loves her family."

"You ever think that kind of love can suffocate a person?" Sean's face was etched with weariness.

"Your mom needs to let go, but you'll try to get it right with her." That was the kind of man Sean was. A man a woman could count on. Maybe even trust.

"I want to try to get it right with you too." Sean moved closer.

"What's to get right?" Charlie pasted a smile on. She couldn't let herself trust, maybe not ever. "We both went into this knowing the rules. The past week has been fun, but you need to figure things out with Ty."

"Fun?" Sean's voice hardened. "It's been more than fun and you know it. We need to talk about where we go from here. I want you to tell me more about your life. Let me be part of it."

"Okay. Once you talk to Ty, we'll talk." She forced herself to smile again until her jaw hurt. "I still need to figure things out with the cottage. That's the reason I'm here, remember? Besides, I had an update from Jason this afternoon."

"Your journalist friend?"

"Yes. He's got enough for a story." Charlie's stomach rolled. She'd gambled and lost. Like she'd gambled and lost with her investment portfolio. "Although there's not enough evidence yet to prove the woodlot was an Abenaki hunting camp, Jason's uncovered some environmental legislation that means this lake's not big enough for the boats Tat Chee wants to bring in."

"What about the casino?" Sean's eyes widened. "Trevor said some guys took pictures over at your place earlier."

"I don't know what that was about, but there's such a big public protest, the planning decision for the casino should be a no-brainer."

"You mean Carmichael's is safe?" Sean leaned forward.

"It looks like it." Charlie clutched the pillow tighter, and her heart pinched.

"That's great news." Sean punched his fist in the air. "But what does it mean for you and Mia and finding another buyer? Wasn't that the point of getting Jason involved?"

"Tat Chee's offer is the only one on the table. The group from town hasn't raised enough money." Her voice hitched. "There isn't another buyer yet. I really tried. Jason too."

"Maybe with the publicity..." Sean stopped.

"It's a long shot. The article should bring more tourists to Firefly Lake, and you might get more orders and requests for courses." She'd been wrong, and she had to face Mia and fix the mess she'd created.

Sean's eyes shone as he covered her hands with his. "I

never wanted Carmichael's or Firefly Lake to change, but some changes could be good ones."

Charlie blinked away the unexpected moisture behind her eyes. She was all about change, but Sean was as rooted here as the old pines that grew along the shore, broken and blackened by the fire but still clinging to the earth.

He frowned. "Where does this leave you and Mia?"

"We'll figure something out." One day was all she had to let herself be here with him. The last time she could take the safety and comfort he offered. "If Tat Chee counters, we'll have to sell, but I bet the state environmental agencies will keep an eye on them."

Sean's eyes locked with hers. "You'll still let Tat Chee bulldoze your memories?"

"I might not have any other option." After she'd spent time here and fallen in love with both the place and the man again, if there'd been another way out, she'd have taken it. "When does Ty get back?"

"Sunday afternoon. Sarah will drop him off before supper." Sean's voice was flat.

"I booked a room at the inn so I can be out of here by then." She studied her hands. "The golf tournament is over and Blueberry Jam ends on Sunday. There's lots of space."

"You didn't have to do that." Sean took her hands away from the pillow and caught them in his.

"You and Ty need your space." She squeezed his dear, familiar hands, then touched his fingers one by one to memorize their size and shape. "We still have tonight and tomorrow." While good-bye sex wouldn't solve anything, it might dull the pain, at least for a while.

"Charlie…" Sean hesitated. "You ever think someday you'll have to stop running?"

"I get bored in one place." The lie burned her tongue, but she couldn't let him guess the truth. She had to run because it was the only way to keep her heart safe and protect herself from a soul-wrenching hurt. A worse one this time because she loved him even more than she had all those years ago.

"Maybe you've never had a good enough reason to put down roots." Sean's eyes narrowed.

Charlie flinched, then manufactured a smile. She'd given up on roots when she learned they hurt too much. "I'm like Mary Poppins. I leave when the wind changes." She pretended bravado she didn't feel, and her stomach knotted.

"It's always been all or nothing with us, hasn't it?"

"I'm an all-or-nothing kind of girl."

He looked deep into her eyes for several heartbreaking seconds. "I don't believe you. I love you, Charlie, and I think you love me too. More than you're willing to admit."

She did, but sometimes, no matter how much she wanted it to be, love wasn't enough.

His house still had a scent of peaches. Charlie's scent. Sean wandered into the kitchen. Shadow's tail drooped as she followed at his heels. "Charlie's only at the inn. She's coming back after I talk to Ty."

A car door slammed and Sean slid the patio door open. He waved to Sarah, forced himself to smile and grab Ty's duffel bag—and to face his son.

"You got any pizza?" Ty opened the fridge, his back to Sean.

"No." Sean leaned against the counter. "We need to talk." The breeze that came through the patio screen held the first hint of fall. "I think I understand what you're going through."

Ty slammed the fridge door. "How could you?" He popped the tab on a can of soda and moved into the center of the room. His faded Levi's rested low on his hips, and he wore a FIREFLY LAKE FALCONS baseball shirt. The team Sean had coached three years in a row to be more a part of Ty's life. "You don't have any idea what I'm going through."

"Okay, maybe I don't, but I'm trying. Help me understand." And he had to get it right this time.

"Whatever." Ty pushed past him. "Are we done?"

"No, we're not." Sean exhaled. Ten years ago he'd have sent Ty for a time-out, but his son was too big for them now.

"Whatever you say won't break Naomi and me up." Ty swallowed some soda and hooked one long leg over a kitchen chair. "As soon as I'm eighteen, I can do what I want. It won't be anything to do with you."

"I don't want you to make a mistake." Sean grabbed another chair and eyed Ty across the table. "I've made mistakes and I see a lot of myself in you."

"So?" Ty crossed his arms and stared Sean down. A teen who was pissed off because he was hurt.

"Some of those mistakes have shaped my life." And Sean would do anything to help Ty not make the same ones.

"Like having me?" Ty looked beyond Sean, out the patio door to the blackened forest. "Was I one of those mistakes?"

"Of course not." Sean leaned closer. "Your mom and I wanted you. Every day, for almost sixteen years, my life has been better because you're in it."

"Even if I don't do what you want?" In Ty's eyes, Sean saw anger, hurt, and vulnerability.

"With Naomi, you mean?" Sean steadied his breathing. "I overreacted on Friday, but the two of you together, it..." He stopped. Who was he to judge? At Ty and Naomi's age, he and Charlie were making out. They'd just never been caught.

"You're growing up. That means you have to take responsibility for yourself and for keeping Naomi safe." Which he hadn't done with Charlie, even though he'd been three years older than Ty at the time.

Guilt pricked Sean. What if he told Ty what had happened between him and Charlie back then? It would shock his son, sure, but it would also show him where Sean was coming from. The words trembled on the tip of his tongue and then he stopped. He couldn't tell Ty. It wasn't only about him. It was about Charlie. Telling his son could hurt her even more. He couldn't take that risk.

"Mom already gave me the safe-sex lecture." Ty flushed and drank more soda. "It's not only about Naomi. It's Carmichael's too."

"What about the business?" Sean tensed. This was the issue he'd avoided all summer. The one he and Ty had circled around. And Sean hadn't pushed his son on it because he'd been caught up in Charlie and blinded by his own stubbornness and stupidity—in what he'd wanted rather than what his son did.

"I don't want to spend my life building boats. I don't want to study business at college." Ty snapped his sports wristband. "Maybe you see yourself in me, but I don't want to be like you."

Sean's stomach clenched. "I always wanted Carmichael's,

but you don't, and you didn't think you could talk to me, did you?"

"Nope." Ty drained the can of soda and set it on the table with a *thump*. "Naomi understands. I can talk to her and she listens."

Like Ty couldn't talk to him. Like he didn't listen. Sean scrubbed a hand across his face, his throat tight. "When did you decide you wanted a different future?" He pictured Ty working beside him after school and on weekends from the time he could hold a hammer. Had he not wanted to be there?

"Last winter maybe. This summer definitely." Ty's face was pinched. "It's not that I don't like working with you and Uncle Trevor. I do. When I was little, I wanted to be exactly like you. But now...I don't want to build boats or run a business about them for the rest of my life."

"Son, I..." He'd failed, but he had to try to make things right, to not make new mistakes. "What do you want to do?"

"You'll think it's dumb." Ty's expression was guarded.

"No, I won't." Sean took a deep breath. "I'm listening. Tell me."

"Sports medicine. I want to be a doctor."

"A doctor? Wow. We've never had a doctor in the family." Only the summer kids and the kids who grew up in the big Victorian houses on the other side of town became doctors.

"I knew you'd think it was dumb." Ty hit the table with the palm of his hand.

"No, I don't think it's dumb. It's a surprise." And Sean wasn't good with surprises. "You've always done well in science and math and you like sports." He stopped as the seconds ticked by, life as he'd always known it changing and forming into a new pattern. "A doctor, huh?"

"In sports medicine, I could help people who race canoes and kayaks if they get hurt. I could help them heal. Help other athletes too." The hope in Ty's blue eyes winded Sean. "You get it?"

"Yeah, I get it." Sean reached for Ty and slapped his shoulder. He got that he'd been a fool. "If sports medicine's what you want, I'll help you get there."

"You will?" Ty's eyes widened.

"Of course. You're my son. All I want is for you to be happy." He forced himself to smile, even though the taste of regret was sour in his mouth. "You deserve a chance to go after your dream."

"Thanks, Dad." Ty gave Sean a high five.

"Medical school will cost a lot of money. I still expect you to work for me in the summers to help pay that tuition." Sean hesitated and tried to find the right words. "As for Naomi—"

"Dad." Ty's face reddened to the tips of his ears. "Give it a rest, okay?"

"Okay, but can you stick to taking a girl bowling? At least for a few more years." He and Charlie had gone bowling, but they'd done lots of other things. Sean shuddered as he remembered his teenage self.

Ty sighed and rolled his eyes. "I get it, all right." He pushed his chair away from the table. "Dad?" The red color crept along his neck. "About Charlotte Gibbs..."

"What about her?" Sean made himself meet Ty's gaze.

"I don't mind you seeing her." Ty's voice cracked. "But you didn't tell me and it's kind of weird since she's Naomi's aunt. Mom's got another family, but in this house, it's always been you and me."

"I didn't set out to hide anything from you, but I can see

how it might have looked that way. I don't know what's going to happen with Charlie, but it doesn't take anything away from you and me."

Ty shrugged and didn't look at Sean. "What I said about you and her was because I was pissed."

"Charlie's never been one to hold a grudge. She thinks you're a good kid. None of us are happy with what you and Naomi did, but it's not you specifically Mia objects to. I trust you, son. When the time's right, any girl will be lucky to have you look out for her."

"We're okay, then?" Ty gave Sean an awkward smile.

"Yeah." Sean's chest tightened. If he couldn't trust Charlie, how could he let her into Ty's life? He couldn't let her hurt his son too. Or let his relationship with her disrupt the new and fragile bond he was building with Ty.

"You want to order pizza?" Ty pushed his chair away from the table and stood.

"Sure. What about Mario's Deluxe Hawaiian?" Maybe it was time to try something new.

"You mean it?" A grin split Ty's face in two. "I love Hawaiian, but you always order a Vermonter."

"Why not?" Sean reached for his phone and scrolled to Mario's number.

"Dad?" Ty's voice deepened, and Sean was reminded his son was closer to being a man than a boy. "You ever think Crystal might want to take on Carmichael's someday?"

"Crystal?" Sean stopped, his fingers poised over the keypad.

"She's always around the workshop to help out. She's a better wood-carver than me. Haven't you noticed how she watches what we're doing and asks questions?" Ty was earnest. "She runs the marina here a lot of the time."

"Of course I've noticed her." If Sean was honest, he depended on her more than Ty. "But your uncle Trevor says she wants to be a vet assistant."

"That's what she wanted years ago. You guys need to get with the program." Ty's smile was open and honest.

"We sure do." Hope flared in Sean's heart. "You really think she wants to learn the business and take it on someday?"

"She's never come right out and said so because Carmichael's was supposed to be for me. It's not only the boatbuilding side; she's got some great ideas about our website and social media."

Ty's teasing expression reminded Sean how long it had been since he'd had this sense of ease with his son. "Hey, we've got a Facebook page."

"Which you posted something to once." He rolled his eyes. "Come on, Dad."

"I'll talk to Crystal. See if she wants to give us a chance." And he'd talk to Trevor and Linnie too, although his sister-in-law would likely have already guessed about Crystal's dream.

Ty grabbed Sean's phone and hit Mario's number. "She'll give you a chance all right. She loves Carmichael's like you and Uncle Trevor do. Like Grandpa did. She'll make you proud."

"I'm already proud. I'm proud of you, son." Sean took a deep breath. "I always will be."

Chapter Eighteen

Mia stood in the open cottage door. The ruined porch was in front of her, and scorch marks blackened the white clapboard. She held a rolled newspaper in one hand.

Charlie's heart pounded. "Let me explain—"

"No need." Mia dropped the paper, and sheets drifted to the ground like snow. The twilight tinged her skin with a gray cast and her dark eyes were bleak. "Tat Chee's halved their offer. Unless we accept it in seventy-two hours, it'll be off the table completely."

"I thought I was doing the right thing for Mom." Charlie choked out the words. "I thought we'd find another buyer. You know I'd buy your share if I could."

"I wanted to do the right thing for Mom too." Mia's chest heaved beneath her simple white T-shirt, and she fisted her hands on her hips. "It's not your fault. I said it was okay for you to talk to Sean and Jason and help Jason with the story. That environmental legislation would have come to light before the sale closed anyway. Then there's the public protest. Tat Chee mentioned it as part of the new offer."

"Let's talk to the Realtor. Surely there's somebody who wants a cottage here, and if we drop the price a bit, I could find the money to pay you the difference. Take out a second mortgage or get a loan." Charlie's thoughts whirled and she fought for breath. "I'll talk to my bank as soon as I get back to London and—"

"It's too late." Mia tugged on their dad's chair and dragged it across the charred porch. The thumping noise echoed in Charlie's head.

Charlie picked her way among the fire debris and stood where the porch steps had been. Her sister's body radiated tension, and her mouth trembled. "This is about more than selling the cottage, isn't it?"

"Remember how Dad used to sit in this chair and tell us what to do?" Mia heaved the chair off the porch, and it bounced to a stop beside the rutted driveway. "Meanwhile, he cheated on Mom, over and over again." Her voice shook.

Charlie tasted bile. "I never knew." But she had. She hadn't wanted to admit it because Mia had been their mom's confidante. Whispered conversations half over-heard, her mom's tears in the bathroom late at night, the arguments and cold silences.

Mia jumped off the porch and landed with exquisite grace at odds with the ravaged expression on her face. "It was bad enough in Boston with his nurses and Mom's friends at the club, but even here, he couldn't keep his pants zipped." She picked up an ax one of the workers had left and swung it at the chair. "You asked if I remembered coming here, if it meant anything."

"Yes, but I—"

"Dad chasing waitresses at the inn is what I remember about coming here. Everyone in town gossiped about it, but I never wanted you to know. I couldn't protect Mom, but you were my little sister. I could protect you." Mia swung the ax again and the arm of the chair splintered. Sweat beaded on her upper lip.

"Why tell me now?" Charlie's chest constricted. She'd distanced herself from her family because she never felt she belonged, but that family was a mess of cheating and lies she'd never have fit into anyway. And it had scarred her and Mia both, just in different ways.

"Jay's the same as Dad, but I never wanted to believe it, which makes me like Mom." Mia dropped the ax and wiped her hands on the front of her jeans. "I thought if we could find another buyer, somehow I could make things up to Mom, but I failed again."

"Of course you didn't fail. We tried. Mom would understand." Charlie reached for Mia, touched her sister's shoulder and then pulled her close.

"Jay's having an affair with a twenty-two-year-old marketing intern. Tiffany. I met her at the company Christmas party. Big blue eyes and body like a *Sports Illustrated* swimsuit model. Stupid me, I was nice to her because I thought she looked lonely." Mia wheezed. "I guess she was lonely all right. She's pregnant and Jay's left me and the girls. He's too big a coward to tell them together, so I have to do it."

Charlie bit back a sob and, since she couldn't find any words to help, held Mia tighter. Her sister's body shook, and her skin was clammy.

"I put the top divorce attorney in Dallas on retainer this

afternoon, which will cost a bundle." There was a strength and determination in Mia's voice that was new. "Before Jay gets hit for child support, the girls and I will need money to live on. Even though I've already cleaned out the joint accounts."

"How did you know to do that?" Charlie let go of Mia and wrapped her arms around her middle. She'd tried to convince herself she wouldn't have to let the cottage go, but her sister didn't have a choice, so she didn't either.

"When you spend as much time around a country club as I have, you learn things." Her mouth tilted into a half smile and held a hint of the sparkle Charlie remembered.

"You should talk to Nick too." If there was anything else Mia needed to do to protect herself and the girls, Nick could help.

"I already did." Mia's smile broadened. "I used a computer in his office to access the bank accounts. Maybe I'm paranoid, but I didn't want to use my tablet or involve you in case Jay traced stuff back."

Charlie studied her sister's face. "Not paranoid, smart."

Mia's beautiful eyes hardened. "I'm thirty-eight. It's long past the time I stood on my own two feet."

"What will you do?" Charlie cocked her head, looking beyond Mia's striking bone structure, the air of fragility she'd always worn like a cloak, to the strong woman beneath.

"I don't know yet." Mia considered her tennis shoes. "Somehow I'll figure it out."

"You know I'll help you." Charlie took a ragged breath. Mia and Naomi and Emma had never needed her more.

"I love you, Charlie." Mia leaned against her, warm and confiding. "One good thing this summer is you and me are real sisters again."

"I love you too, Mimi." And now that she'd found it again, Charlie would never take that love for granted. For the first time since early childhood, she belonged with family and knew her sister, imperfections and all.

"This thing with you and Sean is only sex, right? A fling?" Mia rocked against Charlie. "If there's more between the two of you, you'd tell me. Wouldn't you?"

"There's nothing to tell." She couldn't let herself take that next step. Take a chance on a love that might get her hurt again.

"Truly?" Mia stopped rocking.

"I'll sell the cottage like we planned." Charlie ignored Mia's question and the searching look in her sister's eyes. "Let's get Nick to talk to Tat Chee. Ask him to renegotiate the offer. Even if Tat Chee can't go ahead with a marina or a casino, they can still build a small hotel, and we've got a lot of lakeshore. Tat Chee's playing hardball, but Jason's article doesn't make them look good. We must have some room to negotiate."

"Thank you." Mia reached for Charlie's hand. "If you want anything from here, I'll arrange—"

"No." Charlie's voice came out louder than she intended. She'd never let herself be tied down by things. "You take what you want." All she needed were the memories she'd keep in her heart and the photos Sean had given her.

She turned away from Mia, toward the lake, misty purple in the twilight. The dark outline of Carmichael's workshop loomed behind the burned-out woodlot, and yellow light spilled from the windows. She drew in a breath of clean lake- and pine-scented air. Soon she'd be far away from this place and these people. And the past would be back where it belonged, like she'd intended all along.

Mia stood too, her T-shirt riding up, exposing her bare midriff, enviably flat for a woman who'd birthed two babies. "You want to get the girls with me? They're with Linnie."

Charlie shook her head. "I have to say good-bye to Sean." And Shadow. Her stomach lurched.

"I'll pick you up on my way back from town." Mia's eyes softened. "You're doing the right thing. Like I've said all along, there's nothing for you in Firefly Lake anymore. Nothing for either of us."

Nothing but maybe the only man she'd ever love, the only place she'd ever been truly happy. "When are you telling the girls about Jay?"

"Tonight, after we get back to the inn. I can't wait. Jay's already moved his stuff out of the house. He had it all planned, right down to the last golf club."

Charlie winced at the pain in Mia's face and the bitter note in her voice.

"I don't know if he even went to Dubai, or if the trip was another one of his lies. I was so naive and stupid."

"We've all done stupid things." Charlie's involvement with Sean again wasn't smart either. "Jay's the stupidest of all. You and the girls will be better off without him."

"You think?" Mia gave her a hesitant smile.

"Any man who'd cheat on his family—and a gorgeous woman like you—isn't worth anything at all." Charlie linked her arm with Mia's.

"You're not bad yourself." Mia's smile blossomed. "Inside and out."

"Let's check out of the inn early. Tomorrow morning if

we can." Charlie was warmed by Mia's smile and words. "The girls will be upset. We all need a distraction. Let's spend our last few days in Montreal. You're already driving me there to catch my flight."

"Well…" Mia bit her bottom lip.

"It would be fun to take Naomi shopping, and I've heard the Biodome is fabulous for kids. I bet Emma would love the animals. Let's stay at a nice hotel. Call it an early Christmas present from me."

"I'd like that." Mia tugged on her T-shirt. "I don't even know who I am. It's like my closets full of designer clothes belong to somebody else."

"You'll figure it out." Charlie hugged her sister, the gesture comfortable and familiar. "But if you ever want to get rid of some of your shoes, I'd be happy to take them off your hands."

"In your dreams." Mia's voice was playful. "My feet are bigger than yours anyway."

Charlie laughed before she turned serious again. "What do you want to do with Dad's chair?" She motioned to the scattered wood, where nails glinted sharp in the moonlight.

"Sean can use it for firewood. It'll be winter soon. He has a fireplace, doesn't he?" The bitter note was back in Mia's voice.

Charlie pictured the fireplace in Sean's house on a cold winter night. Logs would crackle as orange flames danced in the grate and the sweet scent of wood smoke curled up the chimney. Sean would be stretched out on the couch with Shadow at his feet, snow drifting outside and the lake thick with ice. "I'll wait for you at the end of his driveway when I'm done." Done doing what she had to do for Mia and for herself. The only choice to keep her safe.

As a Luke Bryan song blared out of Ty's iPod, Sean shut down his laptop, flipped off the lights in the office, and moved into the main workshop. He straightened scattered tools and tapped his booted feet in time to Luke's voice as he remembered the excitement on Crystal's face and in her voice when he'd talked to her earlier. And such a flood of ideas, he'd need to rein her in. But not yet, not when he'd opened the door to make a dream come true. A dream he hadn't realized she had but one that warmed his heart maybe even more than hers.

Shadow barked and darted to the door.

Sean sensed Charlie's presence and smelled her peach scent. Then the screen door squeaked and she was there. Her curvy body was poured into tight white jeans. A coral T-shirt with a scoop neck outlined her luscious breasts.

"Hey, Sunshine." Emotion made his voice husky. "You get my voice mail? The whole town's talking about Jason's article. My phone hasn't stopped ringing."

"That's good." Her voice was low and tight.

Sean moved toward her, but she sidestepped him and ducked behind a workbench. "You wrote it, didn't you?"

"Not exactly." Her gaze was fixed on a point above his head.

"The byline might say Jason Rossi, but I'd recognize your writing anywhere. Besides, you took the picture of Shadow and me he used." The back of Sean's neck prickled. Something wasn't right, starting with that look in Charlie's eyes. A look he didn't trust.

"I helped Jason a lot, but you can't tell anyone. Nobody

but Mia knows. I thought it would help us, but..." She finally met his gaze, but her eyes were still blank.

"Of course I won't. What you did for me and Firefly Lake is amazing." But why had she done it?

"Where's Ty?" She fiddled with Shadow's collar.

"At the house. A baseball game just started on TV." Sean tried to smile. "We won't be interrupted. If you can stay awhile I'll take you back to the inn."

"I can't. We leave early tomorrow. This is good-bye." Her voice was devoid of emotion.

Charlie was on the run again. The look in her eyes told him she was scared, like a deer he'd found in the woods once with its leg caught in a trap. His body went cold, and sweat trickled between his shoulder blades. "It doesn't have to be good-bye. We need to talk this out. Before we never talked and—"

"It's best this way." Her voice hitched.

"Best for who?" He tried to look her in the eye, but she avoided his gaze and, as he reached for her, she slid toward the door. "Not best for me and not best for you either."

"Don't. Please don't touch me. If you touch me, I..." Her chest heaved, and she wrung her hands.

"I want to be with you. These past few weeks, you've shown me what's missing in my life." Like fun and laughter and the ease of being with someone who knew him better than he sometimes knew himself. "It's not too late to try again."

"It's too late for me." The words were as distant as her voice.

Luke moved on to a love song, slow and sweet, and Sean shut the music off. His heart pounded so hard he had to remind himself to keep breathing. "Why?" Eighteen years ago, he'd made the mistake of letting her run out of his life, and he'd paid for it ever since.

"It just is." Her Charlotte voice was back. That clipped stranger, but her eyes were no longer blank but filled with so much pain Sean's stomach dropped. "I'm fit for international assignments, so I'm going back to work like I planned. I'll sign the papers for the cottage sale as soon as Nick and the Realtor work out a new deal with Tat Chee."

Sean's vision blurred. "I thought you loved me."

"I do." Her voice shook. "But I can't let myself...I just can't." She sucked in several breaths. "Please believe me when I say any offer we accept for the cottage will be for something that won't hurt Carmichael's or Firefly Lake."

Something shifted inside Sean. His breath hitched, his body tensed, and his throat grew tight, painful. "Forget about the cottage. I'm talking about you and me. I let you into my life, but you...you're lying to me again, aren't you? You're using the cottage and your job as an excuse to run out without dealing with the real issue here."

"No." Her voice was an anguished moan. "My job is all I have. All I can count on." Her eyes glistened.

"This time you can count on me. I want to be there for you." His voice was raw. "I know you're scared. I'm scared too. I never said you had to give up your job. If you really want to, we can work it out. Commute, whatever. I'm proud of you for what you've achieved, but do you really think you should go back into the field?"

"It's the only work I know. I'm good at it." She stuck her chin out.

"Of course you're good at it. You'd be good at anything you tackled." He had to make her understand it wasn't a choice between her job and him. It was about whether they

could trust each other enough to figure out a future together. "All I want is for you to let me love you, to build a
life here with you. Won't you even try?"

"I can't." Her voice cracked and she knelt, wrapped her
arms around Shadow, and buried her face in the dog's fur.

"You can." He pushed out the words. "Trust me—"

"Dad cheated on Mom, over and over again. Mia told
me tonight. And now Jay's left Mia. He ran off with a
woman almost half his age. That's why Mia needs the
money from the cottage sale." A guttural moan escaped
from her throat. "My family was so messed up, I can't
make good choices. I'd only hurt you."

"You need to trust yourself to make good choices. I'm
not your dad, and I'm not Jay either." Sean let out a shud-
dery breath. Thanks to small-town gossip, everyone knew
what Dr. Gibbs had gotten up to. But he'd always tried to
shield Charlie from the truth. Until this summer, he'd never
suspected Mia had done the same.

"I could hurt Ty too."

Sean's heart pinched. His son would soon be a man,
but he still needed a family. A stable family and a dad he
could count on. He couldn't let Ty get hurt, and Charlie
knew it.

She let go of Shadow and stood to face him. "You love
your son. Like you'd have loved our baby." Her voice
broke and Sean's heart broke along with it. "I can't let you
say things you don't mean."

"Why do you think I don't mean them?"

"Maybe you do now, but what about a year from now?
Five years?" She put a hand to her heart. "You'd be here,
always waiting for me to come back from an assignment.
Or what if something happened and I didn't come back?"

The magnitude of the risks she faced hit him afresh. He couldn't keep her safe. Couldn't protect her like he wanted to. "Did you ever think it doesn't have to be your life?"

"I fought hard for my job. I can't let it go. I can't let myself..." Her shoulders shook. "You deserve a lot more than I can give you. I can't take a chance on loving you, and it all going wrong. I can't trust myself, so how can I trust you or us?"

Shadow whimpered. Charlie linked her hands together and backed away from the dog.

"You haven't tried. You haven't let me try either." Sean watched her for endless seconds as her expression hardened, the barriers slid back, and the Charlie he loved turned into the unknown Charlotte. "This is it? Good-bye?"

"It has to be." Her voice was steady. She kissed his cheek, her lips icy.

"You ever think you're telling other people's stories because you can't face your own?" Sean touched his face and traced the imprint of her mouth. She'd dumped him. Again. His body went cold, anger mixed with bone-deep hurt. She'd walk out that door and he'd never see her again. And she wouldn't let him fight for her, for them.

She flushed. "You ever think you're doing what your grandfather wanted, what your dad wanted, because you can't bear to disappoint your family?" She stared him down. "What were you ever willing to give up for me or risk for me?"

"You know I wanted Carmichael's. It's not the same..." Sean stopped as his stomach churned. "It isn't."

"Why not?" She straightened her shoulders. "You expect me to change, but you can't change either. You say all the right things, sure, but you still can't come visit me. You can't even go away for a few days with me."

"I have responsibilities and—"

"That's my point. You've got Ty and Carmichael's and this town and everything that goes along with them. You always have and always will."

Sean's lips moved, but Charlie couldn't hear his words above the roar in her ears. The agony on his face, though, slammed into her heart. She eased Shadow away from her legs. "No, precious, you can't come with me. Not this time." She choked back a sob.

With a last, heartrending look at Sean, she opened the door and stumbled into the night, her legs like jelly. She wouldn't cry. Not even back at the inn with Mia and the girls. She had to keep herself together until she was alone.

In the darkness of the driveway beyond the house, she grabbed a tree trunk. The bark cut into her palm. What had she done? She swayed as she fought nausea and willed herself not to throw up.

She'd saved herself a lot of heartache. Sean might think he wanted her, but Mia was right. It was a fling. They'd both gone into it aware of the rules. Even though she might have tricked herself into thinking they had, those rules hadn't changed. She didn't have it in her to give Sean what he needed.

And Sean couldn't give her what she needed either. Although he'd never cheat on her, she'd hoped he'd be able to change for her, reach out and take a chance for her, for them. If he loved her enough.

She took her hand away from the tree and set one foot

in front of the other, her sneakers crunching on the gravel. She'd put herself back together before and she'd do it again.

The wind picked up and brought with it the scent of a campfire, of dead leaves, of fall. Rubbing her bare arms, she walked to the end of the driveway and stood by the mailbox, which gleamed white in the starlight. Sean wouldn't mean to hurt her, but he would in the end because he couldn't change for her.

If she was right about what she'd read in his face, he hadn't thought about the need to change for her. And she couldn't change enough for the two of them.

Headlights swept around the curve of the road, and Mia's rental car slowed and pulled to a stop beside her. Charlie wrenched open the passenger door. "Hey, girls." She plastered a smile on her face.

"Charlie?" Mia peered at her from behind the wheel. Her eyes were puffy and red behind the glasses she never wore.

She clicked her seat belt into place. "I'm fine." Or she would be as soon as she left Firefly Lake and made herself forget about loving Sean.

"Linnie gave me ice cream," Emma said from the backseat. "Chocolate and strawberry. Two whole scoops." She giggled. "Way bigger scoops than Mom ever gives me."

"That's exciting." Charlie turned to look at her niece. Her heart ached for Mia and Naomi and Emma too. She glanced at Naomi, who stared out the side window. "Did you have ice cream?"

Naomi shook her head. "I wasn't hungry." She fingered the silver wishbone on her necklace, unsmiling. In her expression, Charlie read the truth. Somehow, she already knew what was coming. Knew her family was shattering around her.

Charlie reached for Naomi's hand between the seats. "It'll be okay, I promise."

Except she didn't know if she wanted to reassure Naomi or herself.

Chapter Nineteen

Naomi scanned the lake again. Her mom could drag her away from the inn and Firefly Lake with no notice, but she had to say good-bye to Ty. After today, she'd probably never see him again.

She sat on one of the suitcases and tapped a sandaled foot against the veranda floor. Ty's text had said he'd be here by eight thirty. Where was he?

"We're leaving in ten minutes, honey." Auntie Charlotte propped her backpack against the suitcases.

"I can't. Ty said he'd come say good-bye. I have to wait." Naomi rubbed a hand across her eyes.

"I know." Auntie Charlotte wrapped an arm around Naomi's shoulders. "But he might not come, and you have to accept that. You'll be back at school soon, with your friends and your regular routine, and Ty—"

"He'll come. I know he will." Naomi turned back to the lake, where white-tipped waves tumbled onto the sandy beach. "See?" She pointed to the motorboat at the dock. "I knew Ty wouldn't let me down."

Auntie Charlotte sighed. She wore a pair of old jeans and a wrinkled pink T-shirt, and there were dark circles under her eyes. "You go on. I'll talk to your mom. Stay where I can see you."

"We won't...you know." Naomi's cheeks were hot. "I mean..."

"I know what you mean, but I also remember what it's like to be fifteen. Even from the little I've seen, Ty's a lot like his dad." She gave Naomi a tiny smile. "Scoot, before I change my mind."

"You're the best." Naomi half ran, half slid down the hill behind the inn to the lake, the dew on the grass cold between her toes.

Ty met her halfway. "Sorry I'm late. My dad was pretty bent out of shape this morning, but when I told him I was coming to see you he didn't stop me."

"You really told him?" Naomi looked up at him, blond and gorgeous, and something inside her melted.

"Of course. I'm done sneaking around." Ty's grin showed a dimple in his right cheek she hadn't noticed before.

"On the boat, you and me, I never meant...It was only, I..." Naomi looked at her feet. "I'm sorry."

"Hey." Ty pulled her against his shoulder. "It's okay. I went too fast for you. I'm the one who needs to apologize."

Naomi swallowed, unsure.

Ty cleared his throat. "I forgot you're almost a year younger than me." His face colored. "My mom and dad gave me hell for what happened, and I haven't...I've never, with any other girl, I..."

Naomi dug her sandal into the grass. "Me neither. My mom was mad too. But now my parents are..." Her voice caught. This was big, bigger than she could handle alone, but telling Ty made it real and made it part of her. Forever.

"Your parents are what?" Ty's voice was kind.

"They're splitting up, and I don't know what will happen." There, she'd said it, and hearing the words wasn't as bad as she'd thought.

Ty took one of her hands in his. "That's bad. But you never know. It might be okay in the end."

"How?" Naomi sniffed to keep back the tears. Nothing her mom had said the night before sounded like anything could be okay ever again. Especially since her dad was going off to make a whole new family with somebody else.

"I don't know, but if you still love me, maybe I can help." He squeezed her hand. "I'm like a poster kid for divorce."

"Of course I still love you. But I live far away and my mom, after what happened...I'm lucky she said I can even be friends with you." Naomi stopped. It wasn't only her mom. It was Ty's dad and whatever was between him and Auntie Charlotte, which nobody talked about but was still there, as large as life. She shivered.

"You're cold. Take my sweatshirt." Ty let go of her hand to pull the shirt over his head and loop it around her shoulders. "You can keep it."

"Thanks." Even though she wasn't cold, the shirt smelled of him and was warm and comforting like him.

Ty gave her an easy grin. "As far as our folks have to know, we're friends, but that won't change how I feel about you."

"Me neither. How I feel about you." With her world

turned upside down, she needed all the friends she could get, but what she felt for Ty was more than friendship. It was also new and scary, though.

"You might come back to Firefly Lake."

"Mom says we won't." And when her mom made up her mind, she never changed it. Although last night Naomi had sensed something different. Maybe her mom wasn't the person she'd always thought she was.

"Your auntie Charlotte might come back." Ty glanced toward the inn. "I think she and my dad could be good together. Unless it's to do with his business, though, Dad never sees what's right in front of him."

"You think he and Auntie Charlotte might...like, you know?" When she'd passed Auntie Charlotte's bedroom door last night, she'd heard muffled sobs.

"Don't know." Ty shook his head. "I told Dad about the sports medicine thing, and he was more okay with it than I thought." His blue eyes softened into a look so tender Naomi caught her breath. "I'd never have been able to tell him if I hadn't talked to you. You helped me see I shouldn't give up on my dream."

"I did?" Most of the time she had no idea who she was and what she wanted, let alone helping anyone else figure that stuff out.

"You did." Ty moved in close. "I'll see you again someday. I'm sure of it. But until then..." He dipped his head and kissed her. His lips were firm and warm, and his body was big and solid against hers.

Naomi wrapped her arms around him and kissed him back to memorize the feel of him.

All too soon, he stepped away. "We're supposed to be friends, remember? Besides, your aunt's watching."

Naomi gave him a shaky smile. "FaceTime you?"

"As soon as you get to Montreal. Text me before then okay?"

"Okay." Her voice wobbled, and Ty touched her lips, gentle and all too brief.

"See you." He waved at Auntie Charlotte before turning toward the boat.

"See you," she whispered. She touched a finger to her lips and walked backward to keep him in sight.

"Naomi?"

She swiveled at her mom's voice, and tripped over a croquet wicket. Had Ty seen her stumble around like a little kid? No. He was already on the boat, slipping away from the dock.

She jogged up the hill and stopped at the top to look at the lake one last time. Ty raised his hand and she waved back until the boat disappeared around the end of the point.

"The car's packed and we're ready to leave." Her mom didn't sound mad and she had a smile Naomi hadn't seen in years. A smile that made her look younger, less uptight, and, for a mom, more fun. "You okay, sweetie?" Her mom pulled her into a hug.

"Not really." She forced the words out.

"Me neither." Her mom held Naomi tighter.

"We'll be okay." Auntie Charlotte appeared on her mom's other side, holding Emma's hand. "All of us."

"Me too?" Emma looked at Naomi with worried blue eyes. Her little sister had spent most of the night in Naomi's bed. The two of them had held each other, comforted each other.

"Absolutely you too," Auntie Charlotte said. "You have your Barbie dolls?"

Emma swung the bag.

"From what I remember about Barbie, she was the ultimate okay girl. Look at all those careers she's had." Auntie Charlotte's voice was loving. "Nothing ever stops her."

"I guess." Emma's voice wobbled.

"Come on," Naomi said. "We'll make up the best adventure for Barbie she's ever had."

"You'll play with me all the way to Montreal?" Emma's eyes got big. "And teach me how to play Crazy Eights and some other card games? I might be getting too old for Barbie."

"Sure, but you're not too old for Barbie." Although Emma had always been a pest and nothing like her idea of what a sister should be, maybe she'd been wrong. Maybe her little sister needed her. And maybe she needed Emma.

"You better not compare me to Barbie," her mom said to Auntie Charlotte.

Auntie Charlotte leaned in and whispered something in her mom's ear Naomi couldn't hear. It must have been funny because her mom laughed and whispered back, elbowing Auntie Charlotte in the ribs like she was teasing.

"You drive." Her mom tossed the car keys to Auntie Charlotte and opened the passenger door. "Hop in the back, girls."

Naomi slid in beside Emma and buckled her into her booster seat. "Auntie Charlotte, on our way out of town could we..." She stopped. Auntie Charlotte still stood beside the car and stared at the lake and encircling green hills.

"What did you say?" Auntie Charlotte turned and, before she fixed her face into a smile, Naomi saw something in her eyes she'd never noticed before. Sadness, and maybe even a glint of tears.

"It's not important." Naomi arranged Emma's dolls and the deck of cards on the seat between them.

Auntie Charlotte started the car and turned up the volume on the radio. "You girls ready to hit the road?"

Taylor Swift's voice singing "Fifteen" filled the car.

Naomi hugged Ty's sweatshirt and turned to look through the rear window until the inn disappeared, then Firefly Lake, all like a mirage she'd imagined.

Apart from Ty. She buried her face in his shirt, which smelled of lemon laundry detergent and him. Ty was real, and she'd had a real summer romance. Maybe she wasn't ready for more right now, at least not with the stuff going on with her mom and dad. But this time next summer, she'd be sixteen and he'd be almost seventeen. Sixteen was a whole lot older than fifteen, and somehow she'd find a way to see him again.

Her mom's head was bent toward Auntie Charlotte, whispering again. Maybe by this time next summer she could make her mom understand about Ty too.

As far back as Sean could remember, his mom's late-summer barbecue hadn't changed. The whole family took the Friday afternoon off work. His mom and sisters fixed salads and desserts in the kitchen while his nieces arranged chairs on the patio, giggling about whatever girls giggled about. Ty, Crystal, and his brothers-in-law played road hockey in the driveway. And each year, the kids got bigger and he got older.

"Charlie and Mia still in Montreal?" Trevor flipped a burger on the grill. A black apron with DON'T MESS WITH THE CHEF in white letters covered his shorts and Carmichael's polo shirt.

"How would I know?" Sean popped the tab on a can of beer and looked out over his mom's backyard. The corn grew high in her vegetable garden, and red and white hollyhocks bordered the path to the garage.

"Mia and the girls are flying to Dallas from Burlington this afternoon." Linnie set a stack of empty plates on the picnic table. "They left Charlie in Montreal. She flies out from there tonight."

"Did she call you?" Sean turned to his sister-in-law.

"I called her this morning." Linnie wore a blue sundress and a big smile. "I wanted her to be the first to know. Apart from Trevor." Her smile broadened.

"You're not . . . ?" It was none of his business if Linnie and Trevor were having another kid. He swallowed some beer, the taste sour in his mouth.

"Of course I'm not pregnant." Linnie's grin was cheeky. "We already have four girls. There's no way we're trying for a boy." She sent Trevor the kind of intimate look that made Sean feel both excluded and alone.

"What I wanted to tell Charlie is I've got a new job. Meet the trainee resident assistant at the nursing home on Lake Road." Her expression was a mixture of pride and unexpected shyness. "I've also registered for a licensed nursing assistant course." She spun in a circle and her dress floated out around her. "Trevor and the girls are pitching in to give me time to study."

"That's great." Sean grabbed her for a hug.

"Charlie encouraged me, and she helped me with the applications. I'd never have been able to do it without her. She's really something." Linnie stood on tiptoes to hug him back.

Charlie was something all right. She'd made him

laugh. She'd made him happier than he'd been in years, and she'd made him fall in love with her all over again. And then she'd run out and made him miss her all over again.

"What are you going to do?" Trevor took a plate from Linnie and slid a cooked burger onto it.

Linnie exchanged a look with her husband Sean couldn't read. "You guys need more plates." She patted Sean's arm and disappeared into the house.

"Do about what?" Sean pointed to the stack of empty plates. "What's Linnie talking about? We don't need more plates and—"

"Not Linnie. I meant Charlie."

"I'm not doing anything about Charlie. Why should I? The two of us were never right for each other." Sean had to put the past few weeks out of his mind and get on with his real life again.

"Did Charlie tell you that?" Trevor dropped more meat on the grill with a sizzle.

"No, but that's all you told me after she left last time. Mom too, and Dad before he died." Sean looked at his brother in astonishment.

"That was back when you were still pissed off. Of course I'd take your side. As for Mom and Dad, think about it. Because of the loan, any talk of Charlie was bound to push their buttons. These past few weeks, when Charlie was around, you were happier. Had a real look of satisfaction about you too." Trevor smirked.

"She left again." Sean picked up his beer. And he'd had an ache in his chest from the moment the workshop door had shut behind her.

"You ever think she pushed you away because you were

pushing her away?" Trevor's blue gaze was steady. "You can be a pain in the ass sometimes."

"Like you aren't." Sean gritted his teeth.

"Yeah, but I've got a beautiful wife and I'm getting laid regularly. I'm allowed." Trevor gave a self-deprecating smile. "Whereas because you fucked it up, all you've got is a big house and an empty bed."

And a life that no longer fit.

"I never said I didn't like Charlie." Trevor continued to study Sean. "When she came back here, I didn't want you hurt again. But from what I see, you're hurt anyway. Maybe she is too, because both of you got in real deep, real fast. Or maybe you never let go in the first place."

"Charlie and I were going in different directions. I couldn't leave here. I'd never have let Dad down, and he couldn't manage the business without me. We're still going in different directions." Which was why he was here and she'd soon be on a plane to London.

"Don't tell me it was all about Dad. You get a rush from running Carmichael's. You always have. But maybe you got so caught up in that rush, you let yourself down." Trevor's expression turned smug like he'd just found a cure for cancer and brokered world peace.

Sean stared at his brother "I...you..." His muscles tightened. Then the truth hit him like a sucker punch. His twin had seen what he hadn't.

All around him, the people he loved were changing. Ty, Linnie, Crystal, and even Trevor. Meanwhile, he'd stayed stuck, trapped in his comfort zone and caught in a net of obligations, mostly of his own making.

Charlie was right. It had all been on his terms. Sure he'd wanted Carmichael's, but he hadn't ever thought about another path. He'd let Charlie down even worse than he'd let down Ty because although he'd had a second chance with her, he'd blown that too.

When he'd finally figured out what *he* wanted, what he needed more than anything, he'd still been blinded by what he thought was his duty, his responsibilities. He hadn't considered what he might have to give up to get it. He hadn't even been able to go away with Charlie when she'd asked.

What have I done? His body shook, and there was a sick feeling in the pit of his stomach. "I have to go."

Trevor pulled the apron off. "I'll drive you." He signaled to Crystal to take over at the grill.

Halfway across the deck, Sean stopped. "Even if it means…?" He was done being stuck, done living his life for everybody else. Life was short, and whatever time he had, he'd be damned if he'd spend it watching life pass him by.

"We can't keep you here if you don't want to stay." Trevor grinned and held out a hand.

Sean tossed his brother the keys to the MG. "I need to talk to Ty. He—"

"Can stay with us for a while if he needs to. Shadow too. You've always looked out for everybody else. Isn't it time you looked out for you?"

Sean hit the backyard at a run and met Ty in the driveway.

"Where's the fire?" Ty tossed Sean a basketball. "Want to shoot some hoops?"

"Ty, I…" Sean let the ball bounce. Hesitated to find the words to tell his son what he was thinking and feeling. Without sounding like a girl.

Ty wrinkled his forehead like he used to when he was little and scared of the dark. "Mom's okay?"

"Your mom's fine, but I need to go to Montreal. I could be gone a few days." If he couldn't catch Charlie before her flight left, he'd be on the next one after her.

A slow smile spread across his face. "It's Charlotte Gibbs, isn't it? You've got it bad for her."

"I guess I do." Which scared the hell out of him, especially when he thought about how Charlie was so much a part of him he ached for her to his bones, but he'd still let her walk out of his life.

Sean raised his arm and dropped it. His boy was too big to want a hug from his dad. "I need to make sure you're okay, we're okay."

"Go for it, Dad." Ty scooped up the basketball. "You're okay with me going after what I want. I need to let you go after what you want." His face went pink. "Besides, Charlotte Gibbs is pretty awesome."

"How did you get to be such a great kid?" Sean looped an arm around Ty's shoulders.

"You raised me, didn't you?" Ty cracked a smile and then moved in and hugged Sean like he used to before he'd gotten too grown-up for hugs.

From the end of the driveway, Trevor hit the horn on Sean's MG, two shrill beeps.

"You better get a move on," Ty said.

Sean swallowed the sudden lump in his throat. "I'm coming back. Even if I fix things with Charlie, until you're through high school, I won't—"

"We'll figure it out." Ty pushed him toward the car. "Whatever happens, we'll still be a family."

Sean slid into the passenger seat and found his sunglasses on the visor.

"Ready to roll?" Trevor spoke above the roar of the engine.

His mom came out the kitchen door with a tea towel tucked into the waistband of her slacks. "Boys?" Her mouth shaped the word, other words too, which he couldn't make out.

"I'll talk to her." Trevor put the car in gear and the MG shot out of the driveway. "Mom's a stubborn woman, but even she can't hold a grudge forever. Before the loan business, Mom liked Charlie fine. I bet she will again. The only person you need to think about is Charlie."

Like he could think of anyone else. But was Charlie thinking of him? Sean checked the clock on the dash for the third time in as many seconds. At least in a way that meant they could have a future together? Or would he be too late?

Chapter Twenty

Charlie rested her feet on her backpack. She was grounded. The one time she wanted to be anywhere else, she was still stuck in Montreal, still stuck in the airport. She folded the newspaper she hadn't read and stared out the window of the boarding gate. The white bulk of the Airbus rose out of the darkness, and the runway lights gleamed yellow in the rain slapping against the tarmac.

She'd said good-bye to Mia and the girls at the hotel early that morning and promised to visit at Thanksgiving. And she'd given her sister one last hug, her life intertwined with Mia's in a way it hadn't been since they were children.

"You think we'll be delayed much longer?" The voice that came from Charlie's right belonged to a woman with short gray hair. Her hazel eyes were anxious behind a pair of gold-framed glasses.

"I don't know." Charlie unfolded her newspaper again. Usually she liked talking to people, but not tonight. Not when all she could think about was the crater-sized hole in her heart. The betrayal stamped on Sean's face when she walked away. And how she had to build a life again without him.

"I've only flown once and never by myself." The woman waved a pair of knitting needles at Charlie, and blue wool trailed across her lap. "You think they can fix whatever's wrong?" Even though she didn't look like Charlie's mom, she was somebody's mom. She had a mom look to her. Comfortable, cozy, and safe.

"I'm sure everything will be fine. Those mechanics know what they're doing." Charlie tried to make her expression reassuring. "I fly all the time. It's safer than driving in a car any day."

Dimples dented the woman's apple cheeks. "I'm silly, aren't I? This trip was supposed to be with my husband for our fiftieth wedding anniversary. Then Jean-Claude got sick. Before he passed, he said he wanted me to go anyway. 'You do it, Joanie,' he said. We never had the money to travel far, and he knew how I longed to see a real English castle."

"Fifty years is a long time." Giving up on the newspaper, Charlie hugged her purse. Apart from Sean, she'd never dated anyone longer than a few months. "You must miss him."

"Every day." She continued knitting. "He was the only one who called me Joanie. I miss that too."

"I'm sorry." Charlie clasped her purse tighter.

"Don't be. Jean-Claude and I had a good life. Sure, I wanted more time, but I was still lucky to have him for fifty years." Her voice was wistful.

"Didn't you ever, in all those years...?" Charlie paused. She'd never see Joanie again. She was in an airport sur-

rounded by hundreds of people she'd never see again either, the din of hundreds of anonymous conversations. "If
you don't mind me asking, how did you make it work?"

Joanie chuckled. "It wasn't all sunshine and roses. We
had our ups and downs, but we stuck it out."

"How?" All of a sudden, Charlie didn't only want to
know; she needed to know. Needed to know more than
she'd ever needed to know anything before.

"I was only nineteen when we got married, so I had to
learn to compromise. Jean-Claude did too. The two of us
learned to give and take, change together. He was French
and Roman Catholic, and my family was English and Baptist. Mama Leblanc sure had plenty to say about her only
son marrying a girl like me, but she came around. Even
though Jean-Claude and I fought sometimes, there was
plenty of loving." She chuckled again, warm and intimate.
"In bed at night, with Jean-Claude beside me, there wasn't
anywhere else I wanted to be."

Charlie stared at Joanie's round face as the pieces of a
puzzle fell into place. In bed next to Sean, there wasn't
anywhere else she wanted to be either. Changing together,
compromising together. What had Sean said? It was all or
nothing with them.

She'd agreed with him. She'd left him again because she
was too scared to listen to the truth of her heart and believe
her life could be different. Too scared to trust him. And too
scared to trust herself.

"I . . . .Thank you," she stuttered.

"You got man trouble?" Joanie bundled her knitting into
a floral-patterned bag.

"There's a man, yes, but it's more."

All her life she'd vowed not to be like her mom. Her

mom had stayed with her dad, too scared to leave. But was she really any different? She'd always been too scared to stay. She'd convinced herself she didn't belong anywhere except in her job, and so old choices and outgrown feelings still shaped her present and determined her future.

Joanie pushed her glasses up her nose, and her sharp eyes assessed Charlie. "You look like a smart woman. You'll figure things out."

Charlie's breath hitched. "You think so?"

"There's a way around every problem if you look hard enough." Joanie's expression softened. "A problem shared is a problem halved. A good man has broad shoulders, and there's no shame in leaning on those shoulders when you need to."

Charlie's mouth fell open. She'd been blind. Not only in fooling herself about how much she loved and needed Sean, but about how she felt about going back into the field for her job. She was about to sign the cottage away too, because she'd never let herself imagine there might be another answer. A simple answer. She grinned and stuck out her hand. "I'm Charlie. Not many people call me that either."

"Nice to meet you, Charlie." Joanie patted her hand.

Charlie scooped her backpack from the floor and slung it over one shoulder. The flight was already delayed by two hours. Maybe it wouldn't go tonight, but even if it did, she wouldn't be on it. "Enjoy those castles and don't worry about the flight."

"You're leaving?" Joanie raised her eyebrows. Her expression was wise, far seeing.

"No. This time I'm staying."

She got to her feet and held her purse by its strap.

She'd spent most of her life wanting something more. New places, new people, always on the move. She'd lost sight of what she really wanted.

Someone to visit those new places with. Someone who'd always called her Charlie. And with that someone, a place she could truly belong.

She scanned the boarding lounge. Max would bluster but, underneath, her editor was a softie. If he cared about her like she thought he did, he'd want her to be happy. And he'd want her to heal. Besides, being around Mia this summer had taught Charlie a few things about sweet-talking.

She waved good-bye to Joanie and broke into a jog, dodging people and luggage to zigzag her way back toward security.

She was done running away. Done telling other people's stories instead of finding and living her own.

This time she was running toward someone. Someone with broad shoulders just right to lean on. A good man who was also a forever kind of man.

Sean hadn't counted on the traffic at the Canadian border and on the way to Montreal. Or the time it had taken to find his passport and throw a few clothes into an overnight bag. Charlie's flight would be long gone.

The airport doors whooshed open and let out stale air and elevator music. He brushed raindrops off his sleeve as he walked through the deserted terminal, following signs for the ticket counter. Although he could have asked Trevor to stay with him, this was something he needed to do by himself.

He'd book the next available flight and find a hotel near the airport. Then he'd text Charlie. Who, by the time he got to London, might already be off somewhere else. If he had to, he'd follow her there too. His phone rang and he pulled it out of his pocket, squinted at the screen.

"Charlie?" His heart hammered.

"Hey." Her voice, not Charlotte's but Charlie's. Warm, loving, and so close she might have been in the same room.

"Where are you?" Sean's fingers tightened around the phone.

"Behind you."

He spun around. Charlie walked toward him across the terminal, her backpack hanging from a shoulder, her purse tucked under her arm. She wore jeans and a green hoodie and looked scared and so beautiful he caught his breath, unable to believe it was really her.

He broke into a run and she did too. They met beside an abandoned luggage cart.

"You didn't leave." Sean's hand shook as he stuck his phone back in his pocket.

"No." She dipped her head and tucked her phone into her purse. "You came after me even though..." Her voice cracked. "I'm sorry," she whispered.

He dropped his bag, grabbed her, and held on tight. This time he wouldn't let her go. "I'm sorry too. So, so sorry." He buried his face in her hair, the scent of peaches strong and part of her fragrance. "I was an idiot eighteen years ago and an even bigger one a few days ago."

"I was an idiot too." She sniffed, wiped a hand across her face, and stumbled against him.

"Your leg. You should sit." He grabbed his bag but kept his other hand in hers to guide her to a row of empty seats and sit beside her.

"Sean, I—"

"Me first." Fate had given him yet another chance, and this time he had to get it right. "I love you so much. I was a pigheaded fool, but I want to be with you. Everything else is details."

She squeezed his hand so hard her nails dug in. "I love you too. And I want to be with you, but..."

"Forget about everything—the loan, the cottage. None of it matters. I thought Carmichael's fulfilled me, but without you, it's nothing. This is only about you and me, and if you trust me enough to give me another chance, I'll spend the rest of my life making it up to you." This woman had brought him to his knees, and he'd stay there as long as it took to keep her in his life.

Charlie stilled. "I broke up with you because my dad told me I had to choose."

"And you were right. We wanted different things back then, and I never thought about compromising or that I'd have to change. I did the same thing last week when I said I couldn't go to that hotel in New Hampshire you picked out, couldn't come see you in London." Sean traced the sweet curve of her jaw. "Both times you took the only way out you knew."

Charlie's mouth got tight, and she turned away from his touch. "For us to be together, there can't be any more secrets between us." Her skin was ashen under the harsh fluorescent light. "I know I lied to you and I'll always regret it, but I couldn't tell you the truth then. Apart from taking away my college money, my dad also said if I didn't break up with you and if I told you about the baby, he'd take back the loan."

Sean struggled for breath as the realization of what she'd done for him and for his family hit him. "You..."

He blinked, and the words stuck in his throat. "For me, my dad, you..." He pulled her into his arms.

Charlie, who never cried, had fat tears rolling down her cheeks. "No. It was for me. I convinced myself I'd protect you by saving Carmichael's. But by not telling you, by not giving you a choice, I protected me too. I was scared you'd choose the business instead of me, and then I really would have had nothing."

Sean stroked her hair, and heat suffused his body. "I'd never have chosen Carmichael's ahead of our baby, but I was also stubborn, blinded by pride, and stupid. And we were kids headed along different paths. What matters is what I choose now. That's you, Charlie, if you'll have me."

He brushed the tears off her beloved face. The face he wanted to see first thing every morning and last thing every night for the rest of his life.

"If I have to move to London to be with you, I will, at least once Ty finishes high school. I've got some customers in Europe who might be able to help me find a job. In the meantime, we'll work things out, travel back and forth and talk every day."

Emotions flitted across her face. Love, fear, acceptance, and then, finally, a glimmer of trust. Fragile, precious, and a gift he'd never again take for granted.

Charlie nestled into his shoulder. "Give up Carmichael's for me? You couldn't."

"I could if I had to. A business can't grow old with me, can't love me. All this time I thought Firefly Lake was home. But the home that really matters is with you, wherever you are." His tongue was thick in his mouth. "You complete me, when you don't scare me."

"Me scare you?" The sweetness of Charlie's smile

warmed the dark places inside him. It chased away any doubts he might have had, and any last fears about whether he could trust her, whether he could let her into his life and Ty's for keeps.

"All the time." How much he loved her, the life he wanted to build for them together.

"You scare me too. This scares me. I'm not good at relationships or thinking about someone else, whereas you..." She bit her bottom lip. "I convinced myself I didn't belong anywhere except at work because it hurt too much to lose people and places I cared about. My family, you, and Firefly Lake. Even at work, I've never stayed in one place too long."

"Aw, Charlie." His heart thudded so loud she must hear it. "We'll help each other. That's what this is about."

"Compromise," she whispered, "changing together."

"Exactly."

She took a deep breath and then another. "Carmichael's is part of you like being a journalist is part of me, but you're not the only one who needs to make changes in their life." She hesitated and her mouth worked. "I have PTSD. I tried to tell myself I didn't, that the doctors were wrong, but they weren't. I need more help so I can really get better. And I don't want to go back into the field like I did. The accident made me lose a part of myself, and I can't be the journalist I was before." She gulped. "I don't want to be either."

"Sunshine." Sean got light-headed. He'd suspected she had PTSD, but now that she'd admitted it, the pieces of a puzzle slotted into place. "I'll help you get that help. Whatever you need, I'll be there for you. But you're a great journalist. What...? How...?"

"I'll ask to be reassigned to the Boston or New York bureau, and work remotely from Vermont as much as possible." She sounded as determined as ever, but there was a vulnerability in her voice that was new. "I want to cover different stories and hang up my flak jacket for good."

"I never wanted you to give up your job, but knowing you were going back into war zones..." Sean brushed a hand across his face. "The thought tears me apart. All I want is to keep you safe, and on those assignments, I can't."

"Being in a war zone's an adrenaline high. I got hooked on it. Max once told me you know when your luck's running out. The accident was a sign, even though I didn't want to admit it at first." She sniffled, but a ghost of a smile played about her mouth. "I don't want to tell those stories anymore. They're not me, but there are lots of other stories to tell that *are* me. I don't want my job to be my life either."

Sean kissed her mouth and lingered to taste before he pulled away. "Maybe building boats isn't me. Not like it is for Trevor, anyway. I'd already thought about hiring someone to help him so I could focus more on growing the business. It's what I like best, and I could do that almost anywhere. Or I could do something else."

"We'll work it out." Charlie laced her fingers with his. "As for the cottage, Mia and I still need the money, but I don't want to let it go. I'll sell my place in London. Property prices have skyrocketed since I bought it. I should be able to pay off my mortgage, buy Mia out, and still have some money left over."

Sean traced the kissable outline of her lips with a gentle finger. "Whether you protected yourself or me, I still owe you. My family owes you. If anybody buys Mia out, it should be Carmichael's." He took her hand, pulled her to her feet, and kissed her again, sweet but all too brief.

"No." She looked at him through those thick lashes, his Charlie, still feisty but with a gentleness and a light in her eyes that told him how much she loved him. "No more owing each other. We'll buy her out together. So we start off right, a team."

He liked the sound of that. "No more all or nothing?"

"Not unless it's you and me together."

Sean liked the sound of that too, but he needed to be sure. "And Ty, when he's not with Sarah and Matt?"

"Of course Ty." Like there'd never been any doubt he and his son were a package deal. "Shadow too."

"As if you'd let me forget her." Sean laughed.

Charlie's lips curved into a teasing grin. "Living with two guys, I'll need another girl around." She pointed to an overhead monitor. "See there? My flight's delayed until morning." She tucked a hand into his. "I get a hotel room. You interested, Carmichael?"

"What do you think, Gibbs?" He grinned back.

Then he wrapped his arms around her and dipped his head for a long, slow kiss, showing her what was in his heart. Now and forever.

Epilogue

February, almost six months later

Sean waved, and a smile almost split his face in two. He stood a head taller than everyone else in the international arrivals area at Boston's Logan Airport, and his arms were outstretched, waiting for her. Charlie's anchor, no matter where she was in the world. "Hey, Sunshine." He drew close.

"Hey, you." She slid into his embrace and wrapped her arms around his back. She'd been gone only a week, but it seemed like forever.

"I missed you." He returned her hug. It was the kind of hug that meant she was home, right where she was meant to be.

"I sure missed you too." She fingered her engagement and wedding rings. It was three months since the gold wedding band had joined Sean's grandmother's engagement ring, an emerald flanked by diamonds in a vintage setting.

A ring Charlie had cherished from the moment he'd asked if she'd do him the honor of wearing it. The happiest three months she'd ever known.

Sean kept one arm around her and took her suitcase and laptop bag. "How was Brussels?"

"Fine." Although she loved her new job, she'd had something more important on her mind so she'd hardly noticed Brussels or the environmental summit she was there to report on. "I brought Ty some Belgian chocolates."

"He'll love those." Sean kissed the top of her head. "He missed you."

Warmth crept around Charlie's heart. "You and Sarah have the tough job. I get to be more of a friend."

"You all set for the ski trip?" He tugged on his tie and undid the top button of the white dress shirt beneath his suit jacket, the clothes he wore to make the deals that kept Trevor and Crystal so busy they'd hired extra staff to help over the winter.

Charlie swallowed. The ski trip to Lake Placid, New York. Ty, Sean, and her on vacation together for the first time. "Are you sure you can take time off work?"

"Of course." Sean looked at her in astonishment. "We're busy, but the new guys are doing fine, and Crystal works after school and on Saturdays."

"That's good, then." Charlie swallowed again.

"Ty's really excited about this trip." Sean grinned. "Since he's never snowboarded, he wants you to give him some tips and make him look like a pro."

"Snowboarding tips, huh." Charlie twirled her rings.

"You should have heard him telling Naomi last week. He had his tablet in the kitchen so I couldn't help overhearing."

Charlie raised an eyebrow. "Despite all those calls, Mia still says Naomi and Ty are friends."

"That's what Ty says too, but if they want to be more than friends, we'll have to accept it." Sean dug in his pocket for the parking stub. "We can stay here tonight and pick Ty up at Sarah and Matt's tomorrow. I left Shadow at the condo. Even though you talked to her every day, that dog moped the whole time you were gone."

"She couldn't figure out where I was." Charlie smothered a yawn. They'd bought a condo in Boston, where Sean stayed with her when she couldn't work from Firefly Lake or only had a few days between assignments. Except those assignments had changed. No more front-line conflict. Not as many long trips either. Instead, she told stories about people fighting for peaceful causes. Ordinary people doing extraordinary things.

"Mia called earlier." Sean shepherded Charlie through the throng of arriving passengers and toward the parking pay station. "She wants to talk to you about your mom's foundation."

"My sister has a lot of executive ability. Nick's helping, but I never imagined the foundation would get off the ground so quickly." She yawned again. "She's got a purpose. For the first time in her life, she's making her way in the world and she likes it."

"The Beatrice McKellar Gibbs Foundation has given my mom a purpose too. You'll always be Charlotte Gibbs for work, but in Firefly Lake you're a Carmichael, and Mom stands behind family." Sean's voice was amused.

"Since it's for my mom, your mom's got all of Firefly Lake behind our first project. The summer camp will be amazing. All those kids who've never seen a lake before, never gone out in a canoe or sat around a campfire. It's a perfect use for the cottage property."

He reached into his jacket pocket and pulled out a plastic container. "My mom sent your favorite cookies for the drive home." He pried off the lid. "She says you don't eat right in what she calls those 'foreign' places."

Charlie began to laugh, but the floor seemed to shift beneath her feet, and her vision blurred. She swayed and reached for Sean.

He grabbed her elbow. "I don't like to admit it, but Mom might be right. You get so caught up in work you forget to eat. Here, have a cookie." He pushed the container toward her.

She waved him away and covered her nose and mouth. Her stomach heaved at the smell of peanut butter and chocolate.

"What is it?" Concern shadowed his eyes. "You don't look good. Didn't you sleep on the plane?"

"I slept." All she wanted to do was sleep.

"Then what...? Charlie?" Sean caught her as she tilted toward him. "What's wrong?" His voice was sharp, urgent. He propelled her to a seat, eased her into it, and pulled her coat off her shoulders.

"I'm okay." She looked at her black pants, which all of a sudden were tight at the waist. "I'll tell you when we get home." She didn't want all the big moments in her life to happen in airports.

"No. Tell me now." Sean sat beside her and patted her arm. "I know something's up."

Charlie hugged herself, unsure. What if he was upset? He'd put a good face on it, but she'd know if he wasn't as happy as she was, as excited as she was. As scared as she was too. She crossed her fingers. "I'm pregnant. I know we didn't plan it, but—"

"You're what?" Sean's face went white. "Pregnant? For real?"

"It's real all right." She touched the gold heart necklace her mom had given her, blinking back hot tears. Sean already had a child, an almost-adult child. Maybe he didn't want to start over again with the sleepless nights, diapers, and teething.

He took her hands and, together with amazement, his face radiated joy. "A baby." He pulled her in to his chest, and she let the tears fall against his jacket. "When?"

"Early September. I've never been clockwork regular, so I didn't guess. I thought I'd eaten something bad on the flight over because I got sick the first morning. When I wasn't better the next day, I saw a doctor, and she did a test. Linnie said being sick is normal, maybe even a good sign."

Sean's eyes crinkled at the corners. "What does Linnie have to do with this?"

"I told her I was asking for a friend. When I called her. Two days ago." Charlie's face and voice were solemn. "I didn't tell her it was me. I wouldn't tell anyone before I told you."

"A friend? Linnie would never believe that, but she didn't say a word." Sean's laugh rumbled.

"Even though I won't ski, maybe our trip's not such a good idea." She'd spend the next seven months covering Firefly Lake news for the *Kincaid Examiner*, not budging more than twenty miles from home, if that was what she had to do to keep this baby safe.

"We'll get you checked here, but the trip should be fine." His mouth quirked into the teasing smile she loved.

"Maybe for the first time in your life you'll put your feet up and relax. I'll be with you every step of the way."

"I still can't believe it's a baby. It was only once we..." Her face heated.

"Once is all it takes, Sunshine. I didn't complain, did I?"

"No, but I'm scared." She already loved this baby with a fierce protectiveness and wanted it to the very core of her being.

"Scared of another miscarriage?" Sean's voice softened.

She gave a jerky nod. "Even though the doctor said everything looks fine." She rummaged in her purse for a precious white envelope. "I was so worried she did a scan." She drew out a piece of paper and showed him. "See?"

"Our baby." Sean's voice caught and he traced the edge of the image.

"You're okay with this? Really and truly?"

"I couldn't be more okay. Trust me, the two of us having a family is great." His eyes went misty blue.

A family. Charlie tasted the words on her tongue. Her family. And because she did trust him, she knew, beyond a doubt, he was right.

She took his hand and put it over hers to cradle where their baby grew. "Let's go home."

Sean's hand trembled as he traced the soft curve of her stomach. He cupped her face with his other hand and looked deep into her eyes. Then he pulled Charlie into his arms and his voice was soft and low. "Let's take our family home."

Please see the next page
for a preview of

Summer on Firefly Lake

Chapter One

"You want to hire me?" Mia Connell laced her fingers together, and the pad of her thumb lingered on the bare space where her wedding and engagement rings had once nestled.

"Why not? Friends help each other out." Nick McGuire's smile had a sexy edge, and Mia's breathing quickened. "In this part of Vermont we all depend on one another."

That sense of community was one of the reasons she'd moved to Firefly Lake last month. "I appreciate the offer, but I've already got a job. Two jobs. When school starts, I'll have substitute teaching and some private music students. Besides, you've helped me out so much already."

And Mia had a plan. To be independent and stand on her own two feet. To take control of the life that had gotten stuck on hold when she'd married young and given everything to her family.

Nick's smile broadened. "Why can't my hiring you to

help my mother be part of your new start? It'd only be for a few weeks."

The new start, part of the new life she was determined to build out of the rubble of the old one. Mia glanced around the gracious hall that led to a country-style kitchen where July sunlight flooded through French doors at the back of the house. "I'm surprised your mom wants to sell Harbor House."

"This place is way too big for her." Nick scrubbed a hand across his face. "We've made an offer on a new bungalow in the development by the lake. She's thrilled. She won't have to go up and down two flights of stairs every day, and the house has a small yard, so it'll be easy to maintain."

"She's lived here so long." Mia held his mom's dry cleaning over one arm and backed toward the kitchen.

"Too long." Nick took the dry-cleaning bag, hung it on a hook behind the kitchen door, and followed Mia.

He nudged six-four and with his dark hair wind-ruffled, a white shirt open at the neck, and a tie hung loose, Nick was a lifetime away from the badass kid Mia remembered, the one who'd hung around the edges of her life during those endless vacations she'd spent at her family's summer cottage on Firefly Lake outside town. He was the kid who'd become a man who never lost control and who, in the last year, had also become her friend, cheerleader, and steady compass in a world that had spun off its axis.

"I'm not a professional organizer." She tried to ignore the flutter in her chest that was new. It had nothing to do with friendship and everything to do with the way Nick's shoulders filled out his shirt.

"Mom doesn't want a stranger in her house. She wants

someone she already knows and trusts. With all the moves you've had, you'd be a natural."

"Surely your sisters want to be involved. They're her family."

"They'd help if I asked them to, but..." A pulse ticked in Nick's jaw. "Cat's teaching summer school in Boston. As for Georgia, she couldn't organize herself or anyone else. Besides, she's at that yoga center in India until Christmas."

"My daughters..." Mia's chest tightened and her throat got raw.

"Are with their dad in Dallas for the next month." Nick closed the distance between them.

As if she needed a reminder of the custody and visitation agreement with her ex-husband. Sending her two girls thousands of miles away to stay with him and another woman had torn Mia apart. "My sister needs me to help get ready for the baby. Charlie's an older mom and I'm the only family she has."

"Her husband and his whole family hover over Charlie twenty-four/seven."

Mia sucked in air as Nick moved even closer.

"Besides, if Charlie needs you so much, why did I find her barricaded behind her laptop yesterday in the back booth of the diner? And why did she make me promise not to tell anybody, you included, where she was?"

"She's almost eight months' pregnant. Pregnant women are hormonal."

A shadow flitted across Nick's face and was gone almost before Mia registered it. "Charlie didn't look hormonal. If you ask me, she looked pissed off."

"See, she's hormonal."

Mia looked out the French doors at the terraced gardens surrounding the stately Victorian perched high above Firefly Lake. The small town was spread out below, and the spire of the Episcopal church rose out of the trees near the town green. A patchwork of rooftops sloped toward the gentle scoop in the lake from which Harbor House took its name. The whole scene was encircled by the rolling Vermont hills that made her feel safe and protected in this little corner of the Northeast Kingdom.

"Please?" Nick's breath warmed her cheek, and the scent of his aftershave enveloped her, cedarwood and amber topped with something crisp, confident, and suave. "While your girls are in Dallas, you could stay here. Mom could sure use the company."

His mellow baritone tugged at an almost-forgotten place inside her, and Mia smoothed a wayward strand of brown hair. She was being ridiculous. Why shouldn't she help Gabrielle? The money Nick offered was more than generous, and it was money she needed as more security for the girls. Besides, staying in Harbor House would be perfect. She wouldn't have to live in a construction zone while the new kitchen was installed at her place.

It was time to stop the excuses. It was also time to stop the self-doubt, which had made her defer to others and ignore what she wanted and needed.

"I'd have to have a contract." She tried to sound competent and professional. "To get this house ready for sale is a bigger job than you might think."

"Of course." Nick gave her an easy smile, all business. His eyes were dark blue with a hint of steel. "We can work on one together."

"I couldn't work set hours." She smiled in return. The kind of smile she'd perfected as the doctor's daughter, the executive's wife, and the queen of more beauty pageants than she could count.

"Completely flexible. You'd be doing me a big favor." Nick pulled at his tie, took it off, and stuffed it in the pocket of his suit jacket.

"I can start today if you want." Mia's stomach churned.

"Mom will be thrilled. I knew we could count on you."

Everyone had always counted on her. First her parents, then her husband and daughters and all the organizations where she'd volunteered in each new city her husband's job had taken them. She was helpful Mia and dependable Mia. But she was also a thirty-nine-year-old woman, and it was more than time she learned to count on herself. Depend on herself.

"There's one more thing." She plumped a stray cushion and slid it back onto a chair in the breakfast nook, a sunny alcove that overlooked a pond thick with water lilies.

"Anything." Nick gave her the smile again that almost made her forget he was her friend—the only male friend she'd ever had who didn't want something she couldn't give.

She nudged a dog basket aside with one shoe, and the red kitten heels gave her a confidence she didn't feel. "I agree your mom needs help. She hasn't gotten her strength back after being sick. You work all the time and your sisters aren't around much, so she's here alone."

"I gave her Pixie."

At the sound of her name a tiny whirlwind barreled past them with its tail up. It had fluffy white fur and short legs. It also had a bark at odds with the dog's small size.

A laugh bubbled inside Mia and rippled out before she could stop it. "Your mom needs more in her life than a dog."

The Maltese gave her a bright-eyed stare.

"But—"

Mia lifted a hand as she glimpsed a flash of orange under the weeping willow by the pond. Nick's mom in her garden smock. "You think your mom needs to move, but I'm not so sure. This house has been in her family for generations. She's rooted here."

And she had the kind of roots Mia longed for.

"It's not like she has to leave Firefly Lake. She'll still have friends nearby and all her clubs." Nick avoided Mia's gaze.

"Harbor House is her home. To leave it, even if she's as excited about the new bungalow as you say, is bound to be a wrench." Mia stepped around Pixie and gestured toward the window. "Look at those beautiful gardens. Those plants mean the world to her."

It wasn't only the plants. It was the memories of children who'd toddled on chubby legs around the garden paths, and the pencil scratches on the kitchen door to mark how they'd grown. The memories of Christmases and Thanksgivings and birthdays that, when put together, made the fabric of a life and a house a home.

Mia swallowed. This wasn't her house or her garden. She had to focus on her daughters. To provide for them and be a mother they could be proud of.

"I'm looking out for Mom." Nick's expression hardened. "That's my job."

"Of course it is." One of Mia's heels snagged Pixie's basket and she grabbed a kitchen chair to keep her balance.

"But if I help your mom like you want, looking out for her becomes my job too. It means more than dropping off her dry cleaning and popping in every few days with cookies or a casserole." She took a deep breath and straightened to her full height, which even in the shoes only brought her to Nick's collar, stiff, white, and unyielding.

"That's what I'd pay you for."

Mia channeled the woman she wanted to be instead of the one everyone expected. "If your mom changes her mind about selling Harbor House, will you accept her decision and not stand in her way?"

"Why would she change her mind?" Nick picked up the dog, who eyed Mia unblinking. "I want you to help Mom, but I don't want—"

"You can't have it both ways. I'll help your mom and live here with her for the next few weeks, but I won't let you push her into anything."

Or let him push her into anything, either.

"I'm only doing what's best for Mom." Nick's features were a careful blank.

"Best for her or best for you?"

Nick opened his mouth, closed it, and fiddled with his watch strap.

Before she lost her nerve, Mia turned and walked out of the kitchen, her heels a comforting staccato on the tiled floor.

Nick set a wiggling Pixie in her basket and pressed his fingers to his temples in a vain effort to erase the image of the little sway to Mia's hips as she walked away from him in those sexy red shoes. How her hair, fastened away from her face with a clip, was like a sleek, dark pelt, except for one rogue curl that had escaped to brush the perfect curve of her cheek.

He fisted his hands and looked out the window. On the upper terrace, a breeze off Firefly Lake stirred the patio umbrella, and his mom walked up the gravel path to the old summer kitchen. His breath caught as she wrestled the light screen door open. She didn't welcome his help, but illness had made her vulnerable.

Mia was vulnerable, too. It was in the tight set of her jaw and the stiff way she held herself. It was in the tension that radiated off her and the pain that lurked in the depths of her beautiful brown eyes.

Pain that caught him unaware and sparked feelings as unwelcome as they were unexpected. Mia was his friend and a single mother. Two good reasons, if he'd needed any, why he couldn't let those feelings go anywhere.

He shrugged out of his suit jacket and draped it over a kitchen chair. His mother had to move. That was the plan. Then he could go back to New York City, leave the apartment over the law office on Main Street behind, start his life over, and claw back the self-respect his ex-wife had yanked away.

Nick moved into the hall. The formal dining room was to his right. The massive oak table where he'd eaten Christmas dinner for thirty of his thirty-nine years was piled high with art supplies, and an easel stood in front of the bay window. Sunbeams bounced off the crystal in the glass-fronted cabinets and gleamed on his great-grandmother's silver tea service.

"Mia?"

Pixie bumped his leg and yipped, the click of her nails muffled by the thick carpet.

He shook his head at the dog and crossed the hall again toward the living room at the front of the house. Pale sunlight filtered between heavy-patterned drapes. Decorated in faded gold and cream, it was an obstacle course of side tables, spindly chairs, two Victorian horsehair sofas, and a baby grand piano nobody ever played.

"You don't know what your help will mean to me, honey." His mom's voice came from the alcove off the living room. Connected to the summer kitchen by a short passage, the small room had once been his dad's office.

"I can stay here while my daughters are with their father."

Mia's gentle voice comforted him like the liquid amber of single-malt Scotch whiskey. Except those days were long gone. He'd turned his life around. In all the ways that counted, he wasn't the guy he'd once been.

"Nick's right. This house is too big for an old woman to rattle around in alone." His mom's trademark silver bracelets jingled.

"You're only sixty-two," Mia said. "That's not old."

"The cancer was a wake-up call." His mom's voice was low. "I thought I had all the time in the world, but it turns out I'm as mortal as anybody else. Besides, this house needs a family."

Nick's body was heavy. It should have been his family here. Before he'd found out he couldn't give his wife the children they both wanted and he'd never be a family man.

"I'm happy to help you, Gabrielle." Mia said his mom's name with the musical French intonation that was a legacy of her Montreal childhood. "Whatever you need, all you have to do is ask."

"Oh, honey." His mom's voice had a wobble Nick hated because it reminded him how close he'd come to losing her.

He cleared his throat and stuck his head into the room. "Hey, Mom. Mia."

Perched on a low, blue love seat, his mom wore an orange smock that lit the room like a beacon and was in stark contrast with her cropped silver hair. She gave an elegant shrug and glanced at Mia beside her. Cool, confident, and still as out of reach as the glamorous girl who'd spent her summers in Firefly Lake and all the guys had wanted to date.

Nick moved into the alcove. His dad's law books were long gone, as was the big desk and the black chair Nick and his younger sisters used to spin around in until they got dizzy. They'd been loaded into the moving van with the clothes, the football trophies, the golf clubs, and the NUMBER 1 DAD mug Nick had given him for Father's Day. As if his dad had never existed.

"I told your mom I can help with whatever she needs to get ready for the move." Mia's voice was brisk and efficient, and that loose curl of hair still mocked Nick and made him want to yank out the clip and run his hands through the thick, dark strands.

"I'll miss my flowers." His mom's tone was wistful as she glanced out the half-open window, where white roses tumbled over a wooden trellis.

"Think how much fun you'll have this winter planning the garden at your new place," Nick said. "Besides, you can take cuttings from here."

"I suppose so." His mom sighed and set her sketchbook and watercolor pencils on a side table. "Some of those

plants are irreplaceable, though. Like the trees I planted when you and your sisters were born, and when my parents died. To leave those behind, well…"

Mia covered one of his mom's hands with hers. Her chest rose and fell under her clingy top. From the top of her glossy, dark head to the tips of her designer shoes, Mia was a walking, talking reminder of the world he'd left behind. The woman who'd left him behind.

"Do you ever think this house and everything in it holds you back?" Didn't his mom realize he wanted to protect her? That it had been his job since he was eleven?

Mia looked up and something sizzled between them. Then she flashed him a smile that made her look younger and a lot more available. "Leave the psychology to the professionals. You need to relax."

"I am relaxed," he lied. Lately, just when he'd gotten his life stable again, being around her had him wound up tight and wanting something, someone, he couldn't let himself have.

"No, you're not. You should try yoga. I got Charlie into yoga and she's a new person."

Nick's laugh spilled out, rusty. "Your sister's a new person because she's blissed out with Sean." And his friend was blissed out, too, and settled into married life like he'd never known anything else. A cozy domesticity as strange as it was unsettling. "Next thing you'll tell me I need a cat."

Mia shrugged, and a dimple dented her right cheek. "Even though I've never had one, I like cats. They're low-maintenance and independent."

Cool and aloof, too, a lot like her. Yet another reason the two of them weren't suited. If he had time, he'd have a dog. Open and uncomplicated, dogs wagged their tails when they were happy to see you, unlike cats who strolled along with their noses in the air and a twitch in their tails.

"Like I told you, I want what's best for my mom."

"I do too." Mia's smile didn't reach her eyes.

"I'm glad we agree." Nick jammed his hands into his pants pockets.

Pixie clambered onto the love seat and gave him a fixed stare.

"See, Nick, you got what you wanted. You go back to work and Mia and I'll get started." His mom waved a hand to dismiss him. "I'm sure you have lots of important things to do."

He did, but as he looked at Mia and his mom, with Pixie sandwiched between them, maybe what was most important of all, what he really wanted, was right here.

Chapter Two

Four days later, Gabrielle shut her sketchbook and abandoned the half-finished outline of a rose, budded tight. She tugged at her wide-brimmed straw hat and stared at the lake.

She'd told Nick and Mia she'd miss her flowers, these terraced gardens her French Canadian mother had carved out of the rocky northern soil when she'd come here as a bride, but she'd miss this view of Firefly Lake even more.

The lake, her lake, was still and ice-locked in winter, snug in a blanket of silver-blue snow. It came alive in spring as the sun-warmed ice cracked and the boom echoed off the cliffs below Harbor House, where dark water foamed onto the beach. In summer, it was a gentle blue, dotted with green islands and white sails. And come fall, it was framed by a panorama of red and yellow leaves with splashes of orange, a paint box of colors she looked forward to all year.

Yet as the seasons rushed past, day by day and year by year, so did her life. And it had slipped through her fingers.

"I'm a foolish, sentimental woman, Pixie."

At the foot of the sun lounger, Pixie opened one sleepy eye, her expression quizzical.

"And you're a very wise dog." Gabrielle drained her glass of ice water. "Nick's right. I can't stay in this house. Neither he nor the girls want it. But that bungalow? Promise me you won't tell him how much I hate the idea."

Pixie whimpered and moved to lick Gabrielle's face.

"I know you promise." Gabrielle sighed, long and heavy. "Maybe you can tell me where I went so wrong with my children. Cat and Georgia only come home when they have to. As for Nick, even though he'd never say so, he can't wait to leave."

"You ever think your kids might share some of the blame?"

Gabrielle jumped and her sketchbook hit the terrace with a *thud*. She swung her legs off the chair, grabbed Pixie's collar with one hand, and smoothed her light sweater with the other. "Who's there?" she called as Pixie barked.

"I'm sorry." A man near her age stood at the top of the stone steps from the lake. "I didn't mean to frighten you." He wore jeans and a blue shirt with the sleeves rolled to his elbows. A backpack was slung over one shoulder, and a camera dangled from a strap around his neck.

Pixie barked louder. Gabrielle scooped the dog into her arms and got to her feet. Although Firefly Lake wasn't a hotbed of crime and the man didn't look threatening, a woman on her own couldn't be too careful. "This is private property."

"I realized that as soon as I spotted you." When he smiled, deep grooves between his nose and mouth creased his face. A shock of gray hair stuck out beneath a battered red ball cap. "By then, though, it was too late to go back the way I came." His warm blue eyes searched hers. "Your dog had already seen me."

"What are you doing here?" Gabrielle stroked Pixie's ears. "Hush."

He whistled, soft and musical. Pixie stopped barking and cocked one ear.

"I was taking pictures by the lake. When I saw steps through the trees, I had to see where they went." He moved closer and stuck out a hand. "Ward Aldrich."

"Gabrielle Brassard." She slipped her hand into his, the handshake cool, firm, and decisive. Pulling her hand away, she patted Pixie, her fingers still tingling from Ward's brief touch.

"You've got a beautiful place here." His eyes were deep blue, almost violet, the color of the irises she'd planted in the border by the house the year Nick was born.

"Thank you."

Pixie squirmed and she set her on the flagstones. The dog scampered over to Ward and sniffed his shoes.

"Pixie, no." Gabrielle stepped forward, but Ward laughed.

"She's okay."

She was more than okay. What was he? Some kind of dog whisperer? Pixie was wary of strangers, and apart from Nick she didn't like men. "Are you here on vacation?"

"A working one." Ward touched the camera. "I'm a filmmaker, nature documentaries for the most part, but also the people who live in those places." He grinned, all of a sudden boyish. "When I was a kid, I wanted to be an explorer. It's pretty much what I grew up to be."

Gabrielle's breath hitched. He was an attractive man, but she was a woman with a whole lot of life behind her, not the impressionable teenager who'd papered her bedroom walls with peace signs and David Cassidy posters. Not the girl who'd fallen into lust and mistaken it for love. "I should let you get back to work."

"No rush." He gestured to her sketchbook. "Are you an artist?"

"An amateur one. I taught art at the high school in town." Before she got sick and her body betrayed her. When life was still rich with possibilities.

"May I take a look?"

She picked up the book and handed it to him. Gabrielle's little hobby, Brian called it, her ex-husband's smile patronizing like she was one of the children. "They're nothing special."

"I disagree. The detail and the way you've captured the light are extraordinary." He squinted as he flipped through pages. "You have a keen eye."

Warmth stole through her at his words of praise. "I always liked drawing, but—"

Pixie barked and shot back to Gabrielle's side.

"I didn't realize you had company." Mia moved onto the terrace, her ballet flats soundless on the flagstones. She held out a tray. "I brought you a snack, but there's more than enough for two. I'll get an extra cup and—"

"No, wait." Gabrielle inhaled the heavy scent of the roses. The buzz of a bee half drunk on nectar punctuated the sudden stillness. "Ward, this is my friend Mia."

Ward exchanged a greeting with Mia, then took the tray

from her and set it on a low table with the sketchbook before he looked back at Gabrielle. "I don't mean to intrude, but if it's not an inconvenience, would you show me your garden sometime?"

Her gaze locked with his and shut out Mia, shut out everything. "Of course." She gave garden tours all the time. Or at least she had. There was no reason for the little quiver in her chest.

"What about tomorrow morning? Around ten?"

"Fine." His eyes were so blue she could swim in them. Gabrielle tried to work moisture into her dry mouth.

"Nice to meet you, Mia. You too, Gabrielle." He paused, his gaze still intent, like he could see into her soul. Then, with another smile, he moved to the steps and disappeared into the trees, like a mirage she'd imagined.

Mia knelt by the table and poured a cup of tea from Gabrielle's favorite chintz-patterned pot. "That's what my daughter Naomi would call one hot guy."

"He's a filmmaker. He's interested in plants." Gabrielle's face heated as she sat back on the sun lounger.

"He's interested in more than plants." Mia gave her a pointed look before she straightened and her expression sobered, the lovely face hiding a hurt Gabrielle could imagine too well. "About Nick, I don't want you to think I'm—"

"Forcing me to move?" Gabrielle reached for the teacup Mia held out.

"He cares about you, but if leaving Harbor House isn't what you want, you have to tell him." Mia shook a linen napkin over Gabrielle's lap.

Gabrielle sipped some tea, and the hot liquid eased the tightness in her throat. "Nick's my son, but he can be..."—

judgmental and controlling but passionate, too. And so wounded Gabrielle's heart ached. "He thinks I need looking after. He has ever since his dad left us. But maybe he's right about this house. For once in my life, I have to be practical." Gabrielle set her cup aside and covered Mia's hand.

The younger woman gave her a too-bright smile. "I don't want to come between you and Nick, but I'm on your side, whatever you want."

Gabrielle bit back a sigh. Mia was another wounded soul. "Thank you, honey. This past little while, you've been more of a daughter to me than my girls." Although Cat and Georgia cared about her as much as Nick did, they darted in and out of her life like dragonflies, never still, always looking ahead and never back.

Mia squeezed Gabrielle's hand before she untangled her fingers. "Your daughters are busy and Firefly Lake's a small town. You know the sign out on Lake Road that says population twenty-five hundred? Nick jokes that since the girls and I moved here, the town should change it to twenty-five oh three because of how slow the population grows." She gave Gabrielle a wry smile. "See, I made you melon balls with the fresh strawberries I got at the farm stand."

Gabrielle took the bowl of fruit Mia had prepared and picked up the silver fork. Its monogram was worn with age but shone with fresh polish. Maybe Ward was right and what had gone wrong between her and her kids wasn't all her fault. Maybe she had a chance to fix it, starting with Nick.

And even to help Mia.

Gabrielle eyed Mia from beneath the brim of her hat.

Mia needed a good man in her life, one who'd treat her and those beautiful daughters with the care and respect they deserved. Her son was a good man who needed a good woman. And Harbor House needed a family. Her family.

Gabrielle bounced and the sun lounger wobbled. It was so simple. And so perfect she should have thought of it before.

"Can I get you anything else?" Mia bent beside Gabrielle's chair.

"Not a thing. Just keep me company for a bit. You're already doing a lot more than Nick hired you to."

"It's a pleasure." Mia patted Gabrielle's knee. "I don't want you to overdo things."

Gabrielle popped a strawberry into her mouth and savored the sweetness of the fruit, like sunshine. She gave Mia her most innocent expression. "I won't."

At least not overdo in the way Mia meant. But was it wrong for her to look out for two people she loved? She glanced at Pixie, who spun in circles after a butterfly. No, it wasn't. Her dear mother always said the Lord helped those who helped themselves.

Gabrielle spooned a perfect melon ball as Mia sat on the chair across from her. All she'd do was give Mia and Nick a nudge in the right direction, so subtle they'd never even notice.

And she'd help Pixie, too. The little dog nosed Mia's slender ankles. Pixie would hate being cooped up in a bungalow even more than Gabrielle.

Fall in Love with Forever Romance

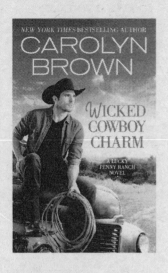

WICKED COWBOY CHARM
By Carolyn Brown

The newest novel in Carolyn Brown's *USA Today* bestselling Lucky Penny Ranch series! Josie Dawson is new in town, but it doesn't take long to know that Deke Sullivan has charmed just about every woman in Dry Creek, Texas. Just as Deke is wondering how to convince Josie he only has eyes for her, they get stranded in a tiny cabin during a blizzard. If Deke can melt her heart before they dig out of the snow, he'll be the luckiest cowboy in Texas...

THE COTTAGE AT FIREFLY LAKE
By Jen Gilroy

In the tradition of Susan Wiggs and RaeAnne Thayne comes the first in a new series by debut author Jen Gilroy. Eighteen years ago, Charlotte Gibbs left Firefly Lake—and Sean Carmichael—behind to become a globetrotting journalist. But now she's back. Will the two have a second chance at first love? Or will the secret Charlie's hiding be their undoing?

Fall in Love with Forever Romance

TOO WILD TO TAME
By Tessa Bailey

Aaron knows that if he wants to work for the country's most powerful senator, he'll have to keep his eye on the prize. That's easier said than done when he meets the senator's daughter, who's wild, gorgeous, and 100 percent trouble. The second book in *New York Times* bestselling author Tessa Bailey's Romancing the Clarksons series!

THE BACHELOR AUCTION
By Rachel Van Dyken

The first book in a brand-new series from #1 *New York Times* bestselling author Rachel Van Dyken! Brock Wellington isn't anyone's dream guy. So now as he waits to be auctioned off in marriage to the highest bidder, he figures it's karmic retribution that he's tempted by a sexy, sassy woman he can't have ...

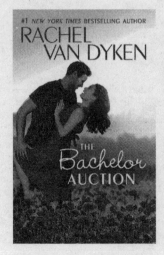

Fall in Love with Forever Romance

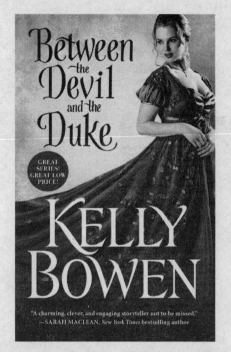

BETWEEN THE DEVIL AND THE DUKE
By Kelly Bowen

The third novel in Kelly Bowen's A Season for Scandal series—perfect for fans of Sarah MacLean, Elizabeth Boyle, and Tessa Dare! When club owner Alexander Lavoie catches a mysterious blonde counting cards at his vingt-et-un table, he's more intrigued than angry. Instead of throwing her out, Alexander offers her a deal: come work for him. For Angelique Archer, refusing him means facing starvation, but with a man so sinfully handsome and fiercely protective, keeping things professional might prove impossible…